HART OF DARKNESS 1

ACE OF HART

WITH

BIRTH OF THE DARKNESS

A NOVELLA

HART OF DARKNESS 1

ACE OF HART

WITH

BIRTH OF THE DARKNESS

A NOVELLA

VIOLETA M. BAGIA

PRESS

VULPINE

PRESS

Published by Vulpine Press in the United Kingdom in 2024

ISBN: 978-1-83919-669-0

www.vulpine-press.com

To twenty-five-year-old me, who doubted. We did it!

BIRTH OF THE DARKNESS

CHAPTER ONE

ACE

The meeting was boring. Endlessly, unsurprisingly dull. I suppressed a yawn and hid my face behind my palm. Unbeknownst to General Simmons, I was falling asleep.

These meetings had been the same since word reached us about the potential shift in the Iraqi cells we were infiltrating. That information was important, but after about four weeks and no new developments, I wasn't even sure the info was legitimate.

"Sergeant."

My eyes shot up. "Sir."

"What is your take on this?"

"My take?"

"Yes. Your take, Sergeant Hart."

Was now a good time to tell him I hadn't heard a word he said? Yet somehow, I knew what the conversation was about. Something inside me drew my attention to the small scale-drawing of the surrounding desert. It was a replica of the entire insurgent camp and the surrounding built-up areas, most of which American forces had inhabited.

"I think it's premature."

"How so?"

"Well," I began, clearing my throat. I leaned over the table and poked the small roll of tape representing our post. "We're here, and

1

the cell we're watching is there; it's too far, too much could go wrong. And, if I'm not mistaken, wasn't there a convoy a year ago that went MIA there?"

"Go on."

"If we're to believe the intel, wouldn't the insurgents have made a move by now? Especially considering they've been successful in the past."

"They could be biding their time."

"For?"

"For the right convoy to come."

Searching his face, I stopped for a moment; there was something he wasn't telling me.

"They could." I leaned back. "But they're not."

"How can you be sure?"

"I don't know how to say it without sounding like—"

"Like what, Sergeant?"

"Like I'm telling you, it's a gut feeling."

"I see." He leaned back and narrowed his eyes. "A *gut* feeling."

The two lieutenants in the room averted their gazes, but I felt something I didn't understand. It went deep like it was in the pit of my soul; I *felt* their understanding. But Corporal Westen looked at me intently. He didn't just understand, he agreed, and he was on my side; he always was. I forced my eyes away from his striking ones and looked back at the map.

Hesitating for a moment, I cleared my throat and kicked myself mentally. This was no time to be a little bitch. He asked for my input, and that's what I was giving him.

"You asked me what I think. This is what I think."

"What would your plan of attack be?"

"If I were to rewrite the mission?"

Simmons nodded.

I looked across at the lieutenants and the corporal, taking strength from their support. I'd been leading them for over six months and working with Westen for nearly eight years. I'd always gotten us out, I'd always made the right decision, and they trusted me. And out here, trust was the only thing we held on to.

"Sergeant?"

"I would forget the intel," I blurted out. "At this stage, we're sitting where we were months ago. Nothing they've given us has been useful. We already knew where the original convoy was taken, we already knew they killed everyone and searching for them came up empty. We've been out here for more than eight months now, and we know these people, how they work, how they think. We can follow them, infiltrate like the original unit was planning to."

"All of this is going off the basis that everyone in that unit died."

Sifting through the layers of doubt, I stood my ground and nodded.

"If someone did survive, then we have even more reason to do this, to bring them home." My eyes flicked to Westen's, something akin to sympathy met me before he tore his gaze away.

"Considering the last operation tasked to search for survivors was unsuccessful. What makes you think yours will have luck?" The general drew my attention back to him.

"Maybe we're the right convoy."

"There are a lot of maybes here, Sergeant."

"I know." I nodded. "I understand, but this is what I believe to be the best course of action."

"How would you engage?" He motioned for me to continue.

"I'd task two teams, one taking the south and the other east. One team with me and the other from the north. You said two others are ready to join us from the base. Then we use them too. Surround them, get them when they're not expecting us."

"And how would we know they're not expecting us? They could very well be making the same plan they did last time."

"I don't think so, sir."

"Your gut feeling?"

Ignoring the jab, I nodded. "Yes. Because right now, they think we're cowering; they hit us when we weren't ready, and we're still regrouping after that loss. We have to take action now."

"And your taking action is hitting them head-on?"

"Exactly. Four angles, and strictly speaking, they won't see us until we're on top of them, sir. And then, it's game over. We do what the first group couldn't."

"Game over."

"Yes, sir."

He gave me a pointed look before turning his attention to my men. "Give us a minute."

They got up and unanimously nodded, leaving us but not before Corporal Westen gave me a quick nod of encouragement.

"Ace," Simmons said.

Turning back to him, I looked down at the map. He searched my face before he ran a hand over his tired jaw.

The years had taken a toll on him; short spikes of greying hair peeked out from the regulation cap matching the light speckling of silver facial hair dusting his tanned skin. Beneath all that, his face was angular, and the lines told of a life well lived.

"I know I'm not giving you much to go on, sir."

"Your father was as gifted as you regarding mission planning."

"I'm sorry?"

He smiled, showing perfect white teeth that made him the handsome George Clooney type.

"Your father and I trained together many years ago now," he explained. "He didn't stay with us, but his time in the army was immeasurable. He was never wrong, even as a young private." He smiled like he was remembering a faraway time. "I'm not surprised you inherited your father's *gut feeling.*"

A flutter in the pit of my stomach sparked to life. I couldn't process it. My father was in the army? It didn't make sense, I couldn't picture it; he was a businessman, for as long as I could remember, for as long as my parents told me.

"Write up your operation brief, work with Jacob; he'll make sure everything is communicated to the teams."

"Thank you, sir."

"Thank you." He nodded, squeezing my shoulder gently. "Make sure you get some rest too."

Chapter Two

I closed the file and pressed my forehead to the table letting out a long and tired breath. God, that was a pain in the ass. Jacob was great at his job, but he was super pedantic, and he questioned every move I wrote down. I got it, it was his responsibility to make sure we were all safe but damn, I couldn't get a word in.

Finally, seven hours, eight cups of coffee, and fifteen rewrites later—we both had a plan we were happy with. He got up and left me with a smile and a spring in his step while I could barely peel myself from the seat.

Groaning, I collected everything and got up.

"Ace?"

I turned on my spot, smiling when Alex rounded the corner.

"Corporal." I nodded, rearranging the last few things I needed to take, a journal from the last unit and several files filled with aerial photographs.

"Need a hand?"

"No, I've got it, thanks." I chuckled, somehow managing to stash everything together.

When I turned around, he'd plopped himself down on the end seat and looked up at me with a smile, the same smile that always made me turn red.

He was hot. Extremely hot. I couldn't hide the way my body lit up when he was around. His eyes were as green as a forest after the rains had come through and his smile the widest and most genuine.

His short sandy hair was arranged neatly but there was always a messy, tousled look about him that stole my breath.

Both of us had been eyeing each other since I can remember yet nothing aside from a few casual glances or touches had ever transpired, and that made me ache in more ways than one.

He raised his brow with a grin and nodded to the paperwork I was holding.

"What's that?"

"Operation plan."

"Yours?"

"Yes. Well, more or less."

He cocked his brow.

"Jacob checked over it a thousand times but yes, mostly mine."

"I can't tell you how glad I am to hear that."

Grinning, I chanced a look across at him and when both our gazes locked again, a slow and steady burn started in my chest. I darted my eyes away and tightened my hold on the files.

"Thought you might say that." I forced my voice to remain even. "I've got you and Ricky on my team, I tasked the other three teams with Jacob's help."

"How'd that go?" he laughed, taking a piece of fruit from the bowl at the end of the table.

"As good as you can imagine."

"He's a bit…intense."

"Just a bit." I nodded to the door. I wasn't planning on spending my entire afternoon here.

"Have you had time to rest?" He followed me, finishing the apple and tossing it in the trash.

"Not yet. This took a lot longer than I thought."

"What'd Simmons say?"

We continued through the doors, walking past two privates who curtly nodded and quickly looked away as I passed.

Alex smirked.

"What are you grinning at?"

"Nothing." He shielded his laugh with his hand.

"You're not good at this poker face thing."

"It's nothing. It just makes me laugh every time I see their reactions."

"Why? Because I'm a girl?"

"No. Because they're scared shitless of you."

"They're not scared of me."

"You're kidding, right?"

Turning my face back toward them slightly, I stumbled when they quickly turned their gazes away like they were *scared* that I caught them looking.

"See?"

"They're not scared of me."

"They always look at you like…"

"Like what?"

"They don't know what you're about. They know you're smart and all that, a stellar fighter, but they don't know you."

"No one knows me."

He stopped me beside a tall pillar and turned me slightly.

"I know you."

"No, you don't."

"You'd like to think that." He winked.

I smirked and shook my head. He knew how to push every button, and I always let him.

"Come on." I chuckled. "I do plan on getting some rest."

"Okay, sergeant." He smiled, giving me an exaggerated salute. "I'll see you in the morning."

8

"Yes, you will. Get some sleep, corporal."

"Love when you get all commanding."

I slapped him across his head with my free hand and laughed. "Shut up and go to sleep."

"Yes, ma'am." He saluted and grinned again.

CHAPTER THREE

I *was running. I knew that I was in danger, the real kind that meant* *the end of my life, sort of danger. But I didn't know why. I didn't know where I was or who I was with.*

All I could comprehend was the fear. My eyes darted frantically, taking in my surroundings. Desert. As far as the eye could see.

But I wasn't alone.

Someone was coming toward me, someone I knew I didn't need to be afraid of. As the day bled out, spilling into the oncoming blackness, a dense, fluid fog quickly filled the horizon, and I felt my legs give way.

My eyes shot open. I let out a long and staggered breath, pulled my sweatshirt off, and tossed it aside. Another weird dream. They'd been getting stranger and stranger as the months went on here. I didn't dare tell anyone about it, not even Alex. They'd probably think I'd finally cracked, all the sleepless nights, dangerous tasks, endless death.

I ran a shaky hand through my hair and looked up at the ceiling. The fan spun slowly. Everything was just as before I went to sleep, yet somehow it all felt so different. Like today would be different.

Grinding my teeth until my jaw hurt, I forced myself to get up; I was making something out of nothing.

They were just dreams.

They didn't mean anything.

As much as I was relieved that the morning came swiftly the accompanying headache did too. This was becoming a regular occurrence. I had no idea why I always woke up with migraines.

Actually, that was a lie; I didn't always wake up with migraines, I woke up with them after I had one of those weird ass dreams, and since they were happening more frequently, it might as well have been every day.

Running my hand over my face, I dropped my head with a sigh. This was more than the migraine; deep under the tightly knotted tension in my neck and shoulders, there was a sick, gut-wrenching feeling that something would go wrong today.

Every operation, every time we went out there, every calculated risk was going to be scary, that was normal, but this was different. I couldn't work out why my head was all over the place.

Regardless of what my *gut feeling* was saying, I couldn't let that influence me right now. We had a job to do, outlined in a large manila folder full of names, squads, and objectives.

We couldn't fail.

A slight tap at the door drew my eyes up.

"Can I come in?"

Alex's voice was muffled through the door, but I could tell he had a grin on his face; his mood was light and maybe it would do me some good.

"Give me a minute," I called out, quickly throwing my fatigues on, cringing that I'd slept in and missed my shower.

"Get enough beauty sleep?" He laughed through the door.

"Shut up or you're on dish duty again." I smirked when he remained silent.

"Corporals don't get dish duty."

"They do if I say so."

"Ouch," he replied with a chuckle, making me laugh to myself.

11

Once I'd fastened my hair with enough pins, I opened the door and stepped back.

"Sergeant." He nodded.

"Corporal."

He closed the door with a quiet thud and leaned back against it. That same gorgeous smile made my cheeks flush.

"Feeling good about today?"

I cleared my throat. Alex was someone I'd learned to trust, almost immediately, someone I told all my secrets to and cared about a lot, despite the strict rules against fraternization.

The rules could suck it; when I looked at him and saw how he looked at me, I knew he thought the same.

So, as I contemplated shrugging it off, I mentally kicked myself. There was no reason to lie to him. If I told him he could make me realize how ridiculous I was being, or he could tell me I was right to worry. Either way, I began to flush with nerves.

His brows knotted, and a frown tugged on his full lips.

"What's wrong, Ace?"

Unease rolled through me, and I sat on the edge of my cot, shaking my head with a sigh.

He stayed by the door, forcing my heart to speed up and then slow down. I had to get myself under control. This was not the time or place to let my emotions run wild.

Tipping my chin up, I met his eyes. From across the room, he exuded confidence, leadership, and faith—everything I was lacking right now.

"I have a bad feeling," I said quietly.

"About the operation?"

I nodded.

"It's okay to have a bad feeling; this is a big operation. A lot could go wrong."

"That's the thing, though. I feel like I *know* that something will go wrong."

"That's not unheard of. The odds are always bouncing around, it could go either way."

"You're not listening. It's not could or may. I *know*."

"Ace." He said my name in such a way that made everything in my head stop.

He flicked the lock on the door and silently moved over to me, kneeling at my feet. Something about the gesture conveyed so much. My eyes found his, and some deeper understanding passed between us.

"What do you want to do?"

"We should abort."

Sighing, he dropped his gaze. "Did you get any rest?"

"I'm not tired, Alex."

"Hey." He tipped my chin up. "I'm not insinuating anything."

I'm sorry." I swallowed a sigh. "Had bad dreams most of the night, so no, not really."

Alex got up and gently seated himself beside me. A few moments of hesitation passed before he wrapped an arm around my shoulder and pulled me closer.

"Have you spoken to Simmons?"

"Not yet."

"What are you going to say?"

"God. I don't know. I'm sure he already thinks I'm a loon."

"I highly doubt that; you're one of the highest-ranking officers here and the youngest. You did that on your own. You don't give yourself enough credit."

"He knew my dad," I said suddenly.

"No shit?"

"Yeah. Apparently, he served with him years back. When they just started."

"I didn't know your dad was military."

"Neither did I."

"Strange that he wouldn't tell you."

"Strange that I ended up with General Simmons. Same guy my dad knew."

"What are you saying?"

"What if nothing I've done or achieved was because of me, because of my skills—"

"I'm going to stop you right there." He turned me toward him, letting both hands rest on my shoulders. "You've achieved everything here on your own. I trained with you, from the beginning. We've known each other for more than eight years." He paused, searching my eyes. "And I've seen what you can do, what you have done. This is all you."

"What if it isn't?" The crippling self-doubt came hard.

Before I knew it, I was questioning everything. Every moment, every decision. Every time I succeeded and was pushed ahead, somehow excelling quicker than most.

"You're really taking this seriously?"

"Of course I am. I don't know anything; for all I know, he could have paid them off to have me here, I mean *here*, in this position."

"You know that's just your hard-ass judgment of yourself talking. Right?"

"Maybe it isn't."

"It is." He smiled. "Trust me."

"I should go, I have to speak to Simmons."

"It can wait."

"It really can't."

"Just stay. Please."

Not risking a stupid move, a move I knew could get us both kicked out, I got up and moved away from him.

As I reached the door, his hand shot out and stopped me from unlocking it.

"If this bad feeling of yours is right and everything goes to hell today, then I don't want this to be the last time you and I miss a damn opportunity."

"Alex..."

"Let me say this. Please." He shook his head, "I'm so sick of hiding. I'm so sick of pretending I don't want to kiss you..."

His hands fell to my hips, and he gently turned me so we were toe to toe.

"You and me, we're one of a kind, we see the danger, and we embrace it, but here"—he waved around the space surrounding us—"when it's just you and me. We run, and I'm sick of running."

"We can't."

"Why? Because some ridiculous book says so?"

"It's the rule book, Alex. *The* rule book. We could both get kicked out."

"I've had a hell of a run, serving with you, saving the world. I'm ready to leave."

"You can't leave."

"I would for you. I'd leave, and then that rule book wouldn't mean shit."

"You'd be giving this up."

He laughed softly before he swept his hand over my cheek, brushing a loose strand of hair behind my ear.

"Yeah, all the barracks, the awesome food, wake-up calls at five am. Yeah, I'd miss all that."

"I'm serious," I said, unable to hide the small blush spreading over my cheeks.

"So am I."

"You'd be giving everything up."

"But I'd be getting you."

My heart somersaulted.

"After this operation, I'm handing this in."

My gaze followed his.

"I wrote it last night."

"What is this?"

He reached into his pocket and handed me the folded paper and watched as I opened it up. I skimmed the first few lines and stopped when I read *immediate resignation*.

My eyes shot up to his. The smile on his face matched the brightness in his eyes.

"You're serious?"

"Only if you're with me, Ace."

I smiled, looking back at the letter, as much as I wanted nothing more than what he was offering, guilt gnawed at me.

"I can't ask you to do this."

"You're not." He smiled. "I'm doing this. I've thought about it for a while, but I know it's the right thing to do. I've known for a long time."

Wetting my lips, I gathered my thoughts. Could we do this? Really make it work if he left? Would I eventually leave too? My heart said *yes*, because I didn't want to do this here, without his support. He was always in my corner, which meant much more than I could ever tell him.

"I know this job means a lot to you, what we do here, hell it's your calling. You were born for this. I get that and never want to take that from you."

"God, this is, I don't know what to say."

"Say you're with me."

"Alex…"

"Say you're with me." He laughed, sweeping his hands over my arms.

"Yes!" I smiled, wrapping my arms around his neck. "I'm with you!"

"Good." He laughed, pulling back and cupping my cheek. "After tonight, we're free to do whatever the hell we want, all things we've been fighting."

My cheeks heated up as his intense gaze found me.

"That sounds good."

"Of course it does, because it's going to be great."

As he stood in my room, towering over me, watching me with his brilliant emerald eyes, I did something I knew was wrong, making me enjoy it even more.

I stepped forward, closing the small gap between us, heart racing and pounding against my ribs, and when his hand swept over my cheek it was as though he pushed every breath out of my lungs in one long and agonizing move.

Slowing my pace, I leaned into his touch and exhaled sharply when his hands swept over my hips and behind, wrapping around my waist. I reached up, cupping my hand over his cheek and slowly, eagerly, brought his lips to mine.

A quiet gasp was lost as he held onto me and gently tightened his hold. He deepened the kiss, the kiss we'd waited so long for. And it was sweet. It was perfect, filled with all the hope and anticipation of what tomorrow would bring, but as his hands trailed across my skin and his lips set mine on fire, the nagging feeling of dread, deep in the pit of my stomach, intensified.

Tonight was going to fail. And he was right, this would be the last night we spent together.

CHAPTER FOUR

If someone told me a decorated, fierce-as-hell general could lose his shit the way Simmons was right now, I wouldn't have believed it. But, as I stood with my arms folded neatly behind my back, I braced myself for the onslaught.

He was beyond furious.

"You want to withdraw everything?"

"Yes, sir."

"Let me get this straight. You're recanting?"

"Yes, sir."

His voice grew louder with each syllable, and I was sure he'd eventually scream the roof down. But I stood tall, staring at a spot on the wall behind his head.

"I don't understand," he muttered.

"It's the same thing."

"Your gut feeling?"

"Yes, sir."

"Sergeant. You know I'm willing to consider anything you say, but this? This is too far!"

Flinching, I remained firm in my stance.

"Do you have any idea how many strings I had to pull to get your operation signed off?"

"I do, sir."

"Then you know that the Pentagon will not approve another change."

"We have to make them. Sir, I know this is a lot to ask for."

"No. Sergeant, this is not up for discussion. You'll proceed with the operation, get your squad ready and move out."

"Sir—" My eyes snapped to him; he couldn't be serious after everything I'd just told him.

"Now. Get out of my office."

Gritting my teeth, I gave him a curt nod and promptly left, closing the door a lot harder than I probably should have.

Sighing, I let out a groan. If I were alone, I probably would have screamed. God knew I wanted to. I was so angry, and tears rapidly filled the back of my eyes, but on the surface, I composed myself.

How ridiculous would it look if I just burst into hysterics? The Sergeant of a sixteen-strong squad, the leader of one of the best forces in the country right now, a woman who was entrusted with some of the Pentagon's most trusted intel.

Instead, I inhaled deeply and then got my shit together and moved.

I smoothed my jacket and walked down the hall, stopping at the door. Taking a deep breath, I pushed it open and nodded to the privates. They got up, standing to attention. And just when I thought my shitty mood couldn't get any worse, another corporal, transferred from another squad, looked across the room at me with what I could only describe as contempt. *Why the hell was he here?*

"At ease," I said, averting my eyes.

Everyone sat back down and looked up, eagerly awaiting my next words. In the corner, in *my* corner, Alex dropped his gaze. I was pretty sure that in my absence, he'd informed them of the potential change in plans, maybe that's why Corporal Higgins was brought in, to make sure I didn't go off the rails. He was a hardass, and he wasn't afraid to be disliked.

"The operation will go as planned."

There was a pregnant pause and I took a moment to compose myself before handing out a folder to each private and the two corporals.

This group of men and women were the brightest, most promising recruits. Having them on my team gave me a great sense of pride and confidence, if this squad and the three others like it couldn't complete this operation, I wasn't sure anyone could.

And in the far right, Higgins looked over my file and dropped it with a smirk.

"Something on your mind, Corporal?"

Alex's eyes shot across the room and landed on Higgins.

"No, ma'am."

"Something in that file bother you?"

"Who authorized this operation?" His eyes narrowed, looking right through me.

"You're out of line, corporal," Alex shot, immediately drawing the attention of the other privates.

"It's fine, Corporal Westen." I looked at Alex and then back at Higgins. "It seems like we've got some issues here. I'd rather have them aired now than come back to bite us in the ass when we're knee deep in dead insurgents."

Higgins smirked again.

"Well?" I offered.

"It seems a little anal. Sending out this many squads."

"That may be the case in normal circumstances, but I assure you, corporal, these are anything but."

He was unappeased.

"We move out in two hours; Humvees will be waiting at the post. Godspeed," I said without letting him open his mouth again.

Everything inside me screamed to tell him to get his attitude in check, but allowing the squad to see how he'd rattled me, was a bad idea.

Each private nodded their acknowledgment, took the file I'd handed them, and left. Everyone but Higgins. He clutched his file and walked over to where Alex and I were standing.

"I heard there was a lapdog here, but I didn't know it was you, Westen."

My brows shot up into my hairline.

"You need to back the hell off," Alex spat.

"All I'm saying is that it takes one hell of pretty...dossier to climb the ranks around here." His eyes traveled over my body and swept back up to my face.

Alex moved toward him so quickly I had no idea how to react, and when my brain finally caught up Alex had already pinned him to the wall. Higgins grinned.

My heart sped up, thundering with rage. How dare he insinuate-

"Wanna ease up, soldier?" Higgins laughed.

"Want to keep talking?"

He looked over Alex's shoulder and looked me up and down again. "Just calling it how I see it."

"And if you keep calling it, it'll be the last thing you do with your mouth for a while," Alex snapped back, releasing him.

"I'm just fucking with you."

Alex smirked, but I didn't see the humor reach his eyes.

"Insubordination is a dismissible offense," I offered.

"So is fraternization."

My jaw locked, and I was just about ready to slam my fist through his face. Luckily, Alex had a lot more self-control. He clapped him on the back, letting out a sarcastic laugh.

"Keep your conversation with the sergeant respectable and we won't have any problems."

"You got it." He nodded, with a smirk, straightening out his jacket.

"You're dismissed, corporal," I said sternly and turned as soon as he left.

When Alex and I were alone, I slumped back in my chair and looked up as Alex walked over and stopped beside me.

"You can sit down."

He nodded, taking a seat.

"Don't let that asshole get to you."

"I'm fine."

He gave me a pointed look.

"I'm fine," I repeated when his eyes narrowed, searching mine.

"You're not fine; they may be fooled. I'm not."

"It's fine; he's just a dick."

And I realized, without meaning to, that I'd sighed really loudly and probably made a grimace.

"Hey," he said softly, squeezing my hand. "You know he's just a jerk."

"What if that's what everyone thinks?"

"What?"

"That I slept my way up the ranks."

A line worked in his jaw. "No, Ace."

"Maybe they do."

"Higgins said what he did because he's a jealous asshole. He's been trying to get to your position at General Morten's camp for years. He's just not good enough."

What he was saying made sense; I'd heard about Morten's camp; he was tough but just. If someone didn't make the ranks, it was purely about skill. But it still hurt.

"Believe me, Ace. No one thinks that about you."

22

"You can't know that. Maybe they're all thinking it, and he just had the balls to say it."

"No one thinks that, trust me."

"How can you know that?"

"I just do." He held his hand when I opened my mouth. "And before you ask me how, take my word for it. No one thinks you slept your way up the ranks."

I bowed my head and shook it.

"I mean, people probably think I did that, to get to your side."

Slapping his arm, I snorted, choking on a laugh. "You're a dick."

"In all seriousness, though, I should have knocked him on his ass."

"I appreciate what you did, but I don't want them to get the wrong impression. That I can't fight my own battles."

"You know that's not what that was about."

"I know."

"He was speaking down to a ranking officer; that's not on, regardless of who that officer may be."

"I know, I'm sorry."

"It's all good," he said softly. "Just know I've got your back, on the field and off."

I smiled and turned my eyes down to the paperwork.

"You're worried and not just about what he said."

I looked across at him and forced a smile.

"I'm just anxious."

"How'd the talk go?"

"With Simmons?"

He nodded, and I responded with a long breath.

"That good?"

"He's annoyed, I can't blame him. I pushed for this plan and now I'm recanting."

"You never recant. He knows this is different."

"Yeah, well. He's pissed," I muttered, collecting the last operation guidelines and tucking them under my arm. "He was practically screaming at me."

"Simmons?"

"Yeah. He can yell. Who'd have thought?"

He let out a chuckle. "Well, don't worry. Just because we have to go through with this doesn't have to be all bad. You get to ride with me."

"Yeah, and Higgins."

Alex scowled. "Leave him to me."

"You don't have to do anything."

"I'll keep him in check. That's my job; yours is to lead."

As much as his light mood helped to lighten mine, I couldn't help the heavy feeling settling and embedding itself into my heart.

My weapons were already holstered, and the nerves began to rise like they always did, but unlike other times, I was starting to feel increasingly unwell.

"I'll keep you safe," he said quietly. "I promise."

"Thanks." I laughed. "See you in the Humvee."

"Yes, you will."

♥

I waited by the doors, making sure everyone was in before I climbed in after them. I readjusted my holstered weapons and slung my bag underneath my seat, Alex chose the seat beside me and smiled as he buckled himself in. He'd said something that made Higgins ride in another Humvee.

"We're ready to go, ma'am," the driver spoke over his shoulder.

24

Ricky was a good friend, he and Alex went way back and found it great that Alex and I had a thing, without making it a thing. He was big on taking chances and doing anything for love.

He married his girlfriend in secret; she was an enlisted officer too, which made it really risky. Sometimes his attitude was infectious, and I questioned why I hadn't done the same.

Alex looked over at me with a smile, probably trying to get me to relax.

"Sergeant?" Ricky called over when I remained quiet.

"Let's roll."

As soon as we were settled in, four Humvees took off, moving toward the designated meeting point where the others would meet us and continue the convoy—thirty-two soldiers. I sincerely hoped that'd be enough.

Alex kept his eyes on me; the concerned expression grew increasingly worried as the miles went on. It probably didn't help that I probably looked like I was about to be sick.

"Everything all right, ma'am?"

Forcing a smile, I turned my eyes to the woman beside me and nodded. "How far?"

She looked down at her watch. "Twenty minutes."

"Got a good speech for us, Sergeant?"

I laughed when the private sitting in front of Alex spoke.

"Yeah, some words of encouragement?"

Rolling my eyes at Alex, I nodded. "Fine."

"This'll be good." He chuckled, encouraging me with a cheeky grin. "I can't wait."

The cheery mood in the vehicle was suffocating. As much as I tried to force a calm over myself, it did no good. I was terrified and freaking out. I couldn't tell where the feeling was coming from or why it was so intense.

As the comms clicked on and all channels were connected, I looked at Alex and took strength from the warmth in his smile.

"The men and women in this unit are the finest soldiers I've ever fought with. I'm so honored to have worked with you; I'm so humbled that you've allowed me to be your leader, to guide you out there, and bring you home. Thank you for giving me the privilege. Let's keep this streak up and do what we came to do."

Unanimous cheers came through the comms but the dread stayed inside me, as did the grim expression on Alex's face when he met mine.

I opened my mouth to reassure him but immediately closed it when a feeling I couldn't place suddenly overwhelmed me. Darkness was building inside me, like dread and fear all rolled into one, but the anticipation seared me, almost like I was waiting for something to happen.

As I leaned across to look out the window, a sudden jolt sent the Humvee careering backward, smashing into the one directly behind us. The Humvee landed with a loud crash, settling on its roof. Without wasting a moment to recover, I jerked my head up as the sound of rockets whistling toward us sent me into combat mode. I ignored the jarring pain in my neck and quickly looked at the three others in the vehicle with me.

"Everyone down!"

The rocket made contact with something outside, sending loud, deafening roars of flames toward us. I shielded my eyes and kicked the door open, dragging myself out, rifle up and ready.

Alex moved quickly behind me, helping Ricky who was pinned by the blown-in door. I moved to the private who was sitting in front of Alex; she groaned as I dragged her out, she was hurt but alive. Blood stained her khaki pants where the shrapnel hit her—it would hurt, but she would live.

We just had to get out quickly, stay hidden and work together.

The sound of shooting reverberated through the steel chassis, and the ringing in my ears was disorientating. I shook my head, desperately trying to get my bearings back.

"Where the hell is the shooting coming from?" I yelled.

Alex's eyes darted around like mine; his weapon trained ahead.

Flashes off to my right gave away a location so I started firing off in that general direction and when the clip emptied, I tossed the rifle and dragged my duffle out of the car, pulling out my crossbow.

"Find the shooters!" Alex called over the noise.

"Bravo team, do you copy?" I called over the channel, taking cover behind the blown-out vehicle.

"Copy Bravo team," Higgins yelled back.

My throat constricted. "Charlie and Delta teams?"

"Delta team copy."

I held my breath, looking up at Alex. His face was covered in sand, and a large gash under his eye was rapidly spilling blood.

"Charlie team, do you copy?"

Gripping the bow, I sucked in a deep breath.

"Does anyone have a visual on Charlie team?"

"Delta team, we see Charlie team taking cover from fire; comms must be down!" Higgins replied. The echo of gunfire from his end sounded in my ear.

"Copy that!"

I repositioned myself and gripped the edge of the door. The firing continued making that pit of anger inside me flare.

"We need to find the shooters. Now!"

"Copy that!" Alex shouted, unholstering his rifle, quickly assembling it. "I'll go high!"

He was the best sniper I'd ever known and the way his hands worked the weapon was something to behold, I was pretty good at what I did, but he was something else. I'd always admired his skill and he'd always grinned when he caught me looking. But this time was different. When his eyes met mine, they weren't filled with the same spark I'd always seen, there was only fear.

He ground his jaw.

"Don't say it. Just go," I said, hating that I didn't stand my ground and call this off.

"Cover me."

"Go!" I shouted, loading my bow.

He took off, heading behind the upturned Humvee, expertly shooting the two enemy insurgents that got in his way while his rifle remained safely strapped over his shoulder. I watched in awe as he took on another two in brutal hand-to-hand combat he wrapped his arm around another and broke his neck while the next one lunged at him with a knife which Alex kicked out of his hand before shooting him in the head.

I returned to the fight before me as Alex reached the peak and took cover behind a blown-out post.

"What do you see?"

"Two snipers to your six, another two to your nine, I can take them out, but you've got a whole other problem."

"What problem?" I spat back, shooting an arrow at one of the Iraqis who got around the team in front of me and came at me with a grenade. As he went down, my heart stopped. He'd pulled the pin.

"Take cover!" I shouted to whoever could hear me, throwing myself over the embankment and down into the sandy pit. I buried my head in my hands as the explosion rocked the vicinity around me, sending up a plethora of sand.

"Ace!"

"I'm good!" I shouted and shook the sand off. "Cover me!"

Two, well-placed shots killed two men who were running at me.

"Thanks," I hissed out, getting up and quickly taking cover. "So, what was that problem again?"

When I reached the shell of a car reclaimed by the desert, I ducked behind it and looked around, checking on the positions of each of my squad.

Before Alex responded, I saw it. The problem was massive; we were hopelessly outnumbered. And that feeling of fear was quickly replaced with anger. This operation was doomed from the start, we never should have been here, and I should have fought harder; I should have made him change the plans. But it was too late.

As the convoy of dozens of Iraqis moved in on us, I clutched onto my bow like a lifeline. We would take them out or we'd go down fighting. Either way, we weren't about to make this an easy fight.

"Does everyone read me?"

Unanimous answers came through the comms.

"We have to make our numbers count. They're coming hard and fast."

"Copy that!"

Gritting my teeth, I got up, staying low and out of sight. It was time to shine.

CHAPTER FIVE

Alex took out another two insurgents as the firing continued to rage on. My ears were still ringing, and with each explosion it got worse. I ignored the deafening roaring in my head and fired as I ran. I was an expert marksman; I always had been but now, when the lives of my team were at risk, my determination to be the best I could be, outshone even my expectations.

"Delta team, I need you to cover; I'm going for the tanks!"

"Take cover by the post!" Higgins called. "I'll cover you!"

"Copy that, just don't leave me hanging!" I ran and threw myself behind the post, which was just as well, two Iraqis rounded the corner where I'd just been standing, and before I could blink, they were taken out.

"Move!" Alex called over the comms and I did.

Running over the hood of another sand-covered, burnt-out car, I landed and quickly ran on. Alex and the Delta team soldiers were firing behind me, giving me a clear path which I took advantage of and ran faster.

With my bow trained dead ahead, I shot another man who came at me, yelling. As he went down, he dropped the grenade he'd been holding and I dove for the ground again, covering my face as the explosion sent sand into the air.

Taking a second to recover, I shook off the sand and got up, but that second cost me. When my body finally moved, I was surrounded. There were at least a dozen Iraqi insurgents with their weapons trained on me; my eyes frantically darted around; we were surrounded. Alex was up ahead, on his knees, with his arms folded behind his head with two insurgents holding guns on him.

"Stay on your knees," one of the Iraqis shouted.

Up ahead, where the rest of the unit was being surrounded, I saw Higgins trying to fight one off, which earned him a bullet—a cry caught on my lips. Swallowing back the bile, I looked back at the man holding his gun at me.

"Collect their weapons," he spoke.

My brain went into overload. His voice wasn't laced with a heavy accent, at least not one that hailed from these regions. He was American. My eyes fell on his uniform; it was American, standard issue.

What the hell?

"You seem surprised."

"Who the hell are you?" I hissed.

"I'm assuming you're the sergeant."

"I am," I said and then repeated, "who the hell are you?"

"There'll be time for an introduction later."

He gave me a half smile that said a lot of bad was coming my way. I swallowed the lump and looked around, squinting against the sun high on the horizon. I became hyperaware of the burning on my skin and the heat beneath my knees dug deeply in the desert sand.

My squad looked to me. Anger burned through me. This should never have happened. I momentarily squeezed my eyes shut, willing more than anything to tell them how sorry I was, that I had failed, that I had cost them their lives. I released a slow breath and looked back up at the soldier.

The American knelt before me, his face mere inches from mine as he searched my eyes, and at that moment, I felt something I couldn't quite explain; first, it was a sensation deep inside, followed by tingles spreading through my fingers and then, like an electric shock, it jolted through my head causing me to fall to my hands and scream out in pain.

Darkness enveloped me, dense and heavy; no matter how much I screamed or thrashed, I couldn't see past the suffocating blackness and there, throughout it all, there was something, a light…a tiny pinprick like a tiki-torch ignited in a sea of dark. My eyes refused to adjust, but just as I was getting pulled back, I saw a silhouette of a tall man with broad shoulders and hair tied back.

He was running through the darkness, and now, as I looked harder, fragments of his surroundings started to form, he was running through the desert…running toward me only it wasn't now, it was in the future.

I jerked back, jolting in the sand.

A sharp cry left my lips as I looked up at the American through watery eyes.

"Ace!" I heard Alex shout, but I was focused on the man in front of me.

He had answers. He knew more than he let on.

"What the hell was that!"

"You don't get to ask the questions here."

"Fuck you," I stammered.

He smirked, giving the man behind me a quick nod and as soon as the gesture registered, a painful blow to the back of my head threw me to the ground.

"Bring the Alpha and Bravo teams; kill the rest."

"No!" I shouted, ignoring the man behind me who'd picked me up and dragged me to my feet like I weighed no more than a small child.

Gunfire erupted, and my heart stopped. I saw their faces as they all looked at me, knowing what was coming.

I went wild. I kicked out, managing to land a blow on someone. I got up. I didn't think as I ran forward. I spotted Alex in my peripheral; he'd broken free too.

But it was too late. Before I even crossed a few feet of sand. They were eliminated.

They'd looked to me, their leader, their friend—for hope, for some way to stop what was about to happen but I couldn't. I couldn't do a damned thing, and this was my fault. Their deaths were on me. I choked on a scream as their limp bodies were tossed aside like trash. Anger bubbled inside me and the well of tears I'd been holding at bay came flooding with no end in sight.

Alex's panicked gaze caught mine as they dragged me through the sand, but I couldn't react. I was frozen, completely unable to process what just happened.

Before I could take in our location, a thick sack was thrown over my head and I was thrown into a vehicle which quickly sped off, and then the panic set in. I was out of my depth, I was terrified, I didn't know why we were kept alive, I didn't know what they wanted, I didn't know anything.

The noises outside were loud; there were voices, music, and banging like someone working with wood. Inside the vehicle were three others, no one from my squad, I didn't even know if they were still alive.

The American had said to bring them, but he could have changed his mind, he could have been lying. A fresh coating of tears wet my eyes, making my throat tighten.

"When we reach the base, I want her in the room, keep the others below," the American spoke, making me flinch.

How did this guy become their leader? Insurgents didn't take shit and they certainly didn't take orders from soldiers, let alone

Americans. What had he promised them, or worse yet, what had he done to get them behind him?

As the drive continued and the pain in the back of my head continued pounding, my eyes started to get heavy. I'd been hit a few too many times that I wasn't ignorant to the onset of a concussion.

The American's words started to fade out, just like everything else except the warmth of sleep coming over me.

♥

A groan quietly left my lips, making every muscle ache and spark to life. The tightness around my wrists quickly told me I was bound, and the angle at which they were tethered told me I was suspended from the ceiling.

"And she's up."

Another groan.

"Hanging in there?" He laughed.

God. If my head wasn't pounding I would have rolled my eyes.

"You'll be happy to know that your team is still alive. For now."

Why were we kept here alive? Who was he?

"You're alive because I need you. As for who I am, you'll learn in time."

My eyes snapped open, barely managing to stay focused. The headache was splitting my brain in two, and the floodlight's brightness directly pointed at me was blinding. I tried to squint through the light, but it was pointless. From what I could tell from my limited sight, there was only one other person aside from the American.

"Bit uncomfortable?" he asked.

"What do you want?"

"Not much for chatting?"

"Screw you."

He laughed.

"Now, let's get the introductions out of the way, shall we? I know who you are." He smiled. "As for me, I'm Sergeant Luke Grimes."

"Am I meant to know you?"

The man behind me yanked the chain as if on cue, forcing my body up and a scream to get caught on my lips. I refused to let him have the satisfaction.

The blinding light was suddenly switched off, plunging me into darkness. My eyes adjusted for a few moments before I could finally look at him properly.

Grimes was tall and broadly built, his eyes were a rich shade of blue, and his light-colored hair was cut short. His face was tanned from being out here for so long, and a light dusting of facial hair covered his jaw, hiding a large, violent scar from his left ear right down across his cheek. Aside from the fact that we were here, and I was chained up, I never would have picked him for an insurgent.

But more than just the grin on his face and the shitty situation I was in made me uneasy. Something more was going on here, something I had no control over, and that scared the shit out of me.

He moved closer, taking his time with each slow step.

Keeping my eyes on his, I put up a brave front. There was no way I was going to cower in front of him. Whatever this was, I could face it.

He smirked as though he'd just heard what I thought. That was ridiculous. I shook that thought and forced my eyes back to his.

"You're here for one reason," he said.

"And what's that?"

"You still haven't learned."

The guy behind me yanked the chain again, forcing my arms up tighter above my head.

"Do we understand each other?"

35

A series of creative responses were on my lips, but each one died as the searing pain in my shoulders reminded me that I was in no position to be a smartass.

"Good. You learn quickly."

I kept my mouth shut and my fear at bay.

He looked over my head to the guy holding the chain and nodded. "You can release her now."

As soon as he loosened the chain, I slumped, falling to my knees against the concrete. With whatever strength I managed, I stayed upright.

He moved toward me and knelt, stabbing a syringe into my neck, forcing a hiss from my lips. He pulled the syringe out and placed it on the floor beside us.

"I want to explain a few things to you," he said quietly. "Okay?"

I jerked my head back, breaking free from his grip, but the motion made me queasy; whatever he'd injected me with was fast acting.

He grabbed my face squeezing my cheeks and forcing my eyes to his.

"Understand?"

Gritting my teeth, I nodded.

"Good."

His eyes swept across me and then returned to my face.

"I don't have any problems killing you or your team. I don't have the time or patience to be played around with, and having said that, soldier, I don't have any problems hurting you to get what I want."

Well that was a good start. At least he was talking; he was divulging. I could work with that, what I couldn't work with, was the unknown. But what I couldn't get my head around was why he was here.

He stalked around me and laughed. "And I bet you're also wondering why I'm here with these guys, am I right?"

My eyes snapped up to his; nothing made sense about this.

"I'm here because our good ol' Uncle Sam and all that, let me the fuck down."

"They're monsters."

"Oh, come on, they're not that bad." He chuckled. "Sure, they're a little rough around the edges, but they're good fun."

I couldn't believe what I was hearing.

His eyes were dangerously bright, he was psychotic, and he was so far from being someone you could reason with. He had the look of a wild animal caught between a hunter's crosshairs and a predator's teeth, ready to snap, kill and do whatever else he needed to, and I was in his way.

"Now, I'm going to ask you some questions, and don't make the mistake of thinking that I'm bluffing."

The shaky breath caught on my lips came out before I could stop it.

He smirked and got up.

"Now, let's begin."

CHAPTER SIX

Grimes walked behind me, unhooking the chain from around my wrists; if I could move out of his grasp quickly enough, I could...his hands tensed around my wrists, and then he was standing right in front of me with a smirk.

"Don't even think about trying to fight me."

My eyes snapped up to him, and my heart stopped.

His only response was another smirk. "Are you going to behave?"

Forcing a nod, I held my breath. *What the hell just happened?*

Moving back around, he unwrapped the chain from my wrists; as soon as they were free, I fell forward, throwing my hands in front of me, barely breaking my fall. My eyes were struggling to stay open.

"Get up."

Struggling to get my strength up, I slowly moved, getting up to one knee and then the other; as soon as I could manage it, I got to my feet and stood in the room, in front of this asshole, trembling from the concussion, whatever he'd shot me with and probably fear.

He walked away for a moment, brought over two wooden chairs, and set one in front of me.

I sat. He nodded his appreciation and sat in the other one.

"You've fought me more than most." He nodded, musing. "I'm impressed."

Fought? I barely breathed unless he'd told me to. And that was something else that needed some serious explaining. What was happening to me?

"That's not what we're here to talk about. What I want from you is some answers."

A sound outside the door caught my attention and I immediately recognized it; they were bringing water, troughs of it.

General Simmons always spoke about being prepared to expect the worst. Expect pain, torture, insurgents with no regard for you or who you are, especially being on the team I was in, especially being a woman. We weren't just soldiers; we were the highest trained and most experienced in one way or another, which meant that we were gold to them and always a target.

And I was prepared or, so I thought. Knowing what was coming as soon as that door was opened brought a fresh torrent of fear, but it was mainly because this was unexpected.

I'd been prepared for the insurgents; I'd been prepared to die to protect our secrets. But this American was...well, he was unexpected. He was cool, calm, and eerily perceptive, almost like he was reading my mind, and I was at a loss.

"I'm going to ask you once, and then, we get creative."

Disregarding his earlier warning, I looked up. "How did you get them to follow you?"

He chuckled and folded his leg over his knee.

"They gave me something my country couldn't."

"Your country? You're a traitor."

"And you're so narrowminded, just like the rest."

"What happened to you?"

"You know what?" he said with a severe expression. "I'm going to tell you. I think you've earned it."

I grit my teeth and kept my mouth shut.

The sloshing water in the next room stopped and the sound of a metal chair being set down made my throat tighten and something told me that no matter what I told him now, I wouldn't be spared the horrors behind those doors.

"You know about the operation like yours; you know it went wrong. All we had to do was get in, infiltrate and eliminate the target, only there was an ambush, much like the one you had the unfortunate pleasure of experiencing." He explained, pausing for a moment. "My team was killed, I was spared because I was the sergeant, and they thought I had information."

My heart began thundering and I let out a long breath. There *were* survivors; there was him.

"Which brings me to you." He nodded at me. "Sergeant Hart."

My breath came out in a staggered gasp. They never found him; they didn't look hard enough—they'd left him here to die.

And then, another realization hit me.

Whatever was coursing through my veins right now was making me weak, and I was starting to feel every nerve in my body, like I was hyperaware of every bone and every cell. This was not good. My head was heavy, and I felt like holding myself up was beginning to be a challenge.

"Like you, I was the best they had, almost unlike anyone else they'd ever trained, like I was better somehow, and like you, I knew how important I was to my general. So, I knew all I had to do was hold out, keep my mouth shut and deal with what they threw at me because someone was coming for me."

My head lolled forward, and my body started shaking.

"I endured three months of torture," he explained, tipping my chin up. "I was electrocuted, beaten, drowned, all for one question, one question I failed to answer because I was a good soldier, a loyal sergeant, that and the fact that I had no fucking idea what they were asking me."

"What…what was…the question?" My words slurred.

"Ah. *The question.*"

My eyes fell closed and I forced them back open, breathing through the rapidly building nausea.

"The question they asked me over and over again was simple," he began, looking at me intently. "Where is Ace Hart?"

CHAPTER SEVEN

He grinned. Like the bombshell he just dropped on me was nothing more than a casual chat between friends.

"Of course, I had no idea who Ace Hart was; I had no idea why he was asking; I was just another American fighting for our freedom and all that. But you"—he pointed at me with a shake—"you were the reason I was tortured and left behind. I couldn't tell them what I didn't know, so the torture continued, and no one came. I guess it was insurance; make sure I was dead so no one else could talk."

My heart stalled.

"So, imagine my surprise when I heard that an operation was tasked to find me, not because I was a POW, but because I was a risk, because I may talk."

"We didn't even know there were survivors."

"No, you didn't." He nodded. "I believe you, but dear old Simmons knew."

My eyes slowly traveled up to his.

"Why do you think he insisted on approving the operation and nearly had a conniption when you wanted to withdraw?"

None of this made any sense. My brain was jumping from scenario to scenario. How did he know? Was someone on my team working for him?

"You tried to back out at the last minute, no?"

"You can't know that."

He grinned. "Sadly, I know more than they think. Just not when they were asking and not when it mattered to save my own ass."

"But you didn't know anything," I whispered.

"No, I didn't. But the good general didn't think so. He thought someone had spilled the beans about you and your gifts."

"What are you talking about?"

"You don't know?"

"Know what?"

"Oh man!" He slapped his knee, laughing harshly. "And I thought they couldn't get any more convoluted."

"What are you talking about?"

"Well, sergeant. You don't have the clearance for that information." He laughed again. "How's that for fuckery?"

A thousand and one questions raced through my head.

"It's one hell of a thing you've got; I have to say I'm a little envious. Shame you'll never get to experience your true potential."

"You're crazy."

He chuckled, standing and folding his arms behind his back. "Now that I've shared some of my stories with you, I'm going to ask you one question and look, I know you said you're in the dark about it all, but I know that the Pentagon has entrusted you with a ton of juicy information. So my answer lies somewhere in that pretty little head of yours."

"What the hell are you talking about?"

A wide, toothy grin came in response, and I froze. Nausea in the pit of my stomach grew, causing my insides to lurch.

"What did they want you for?"

"I don't know what you're talking about."

"I told you I'd give you one chance." Before I could register what he meant, he nodded and the door to the adjoining room was opened—the room with the slushing water.

"Get her up; she can't walk."

What? Why couldn't I walk? My eyes darted around, landing on each of the men that came through the door.

One of them moved behind me and yanked me up, dragging me across the floor, my legs were limp, and nothing moved. What the hell did he shoot me with?

He walked behind us, and as my eyes fell on the occupants of the room, my heart sank. No. God no. Alex was bound to one of the metal chairs I'd heard being dragged around before, his face was bloodied, and the source of the blood was a split lip and eye socket.

His angry expression quickly changed when his eyes fell on me.

"Let her go, you fucking animal!"

"Oh, this is going to be sweet." Grimes laughed and turned his back on Alex.

He didn't care about him; Alex was here as leverage. Leverage to make me talk because God knew I would do anything to keep him safe.

"Sit her down there," he ordered.

The Iraqi holding me obeyed and dropped me into the chair; another proceeded to tie my hands behind my back and fasten them to the metal frame.

"Ace!" Alex's voice faded in and out of my head. Consciousness was quickly leaving me.

"What did you do to her?" he shouted, earning a punch to the stomach.

He grunted, but his fury didn't die down.

"What the fuck did you do to her?"

My head dropped.

Grimes stood beside me and yanked my head back by my ponytail.

"Gave her a little cocktail I've been perfecting. You should know all about the Serum, right, Westen? You've had to use it once or twice, no?"

Alex's eyes snapped back to me as Grimes' eyes searched mine.

As soon as he released me, my head lolled forward, and a sickening mixture of bile and blood filled the back of my throat. Reactive tears instantly spilled over.

"It's a mixture of sodium pentothal and Rohypnol and something else I've been toying with. You could say it's a new variant, stronger, more efficient."

Oh God. I blinked back the coating of tears filling my eyes: date rape drugs and truth serum as they were known on the street.

"How does it feel?"

I took in a deep breath and looked up.

"I asked you a question."

I slowly brought my eyes to Alex, he was shaking with rage, but the insatiable urge to do as Grimes said took over every other bit of higher reasoning I had.

"I…I'm tired."

Grimes laughed.

With a click of his fingers, the Iraqi behind me pulled my head back and the other threw a thick rag over my face and poured water over it.

As the water spilled into my mouth, I was too late to catch my breath; the cold liquid invaded my lungs and choked me.

Just as the pain grew intolerable, the rag was pulled free, and I sucked up a greedy lungful of air, coughing and heaving as I did.

The water spluttered around my mouth, and the shouting from Alex intensified.

"We're just getting started, Sergeant. I hope you've got some fight in you."

♥

The fight in me kept me going for about ten rounds and then darkness. I felt my eyes close first and then my hands went limp and then came the silence, except for Alex's screams. His voice kept me awake through it all, but toward the end, even he started to quieten. I was falling into the murky depths of the icy water.

"What did they want you for?"

"I don't know what you're talking about," I managed through the body controlling shivering.

Again, Grimes shook his head, and the Iraqi behind me moved. This time there was no wet rag, no yanking of my hair. He untied my arms, and another Iraqi pulled me out of the chair and dragged me across the room past Alex, who looked like he'd been beaten since the last time I'd seen him. My heart broke.

"Stop!" he shouted as Grimes walked ahead and stopped beside the trough of water, I'd heard yesterday…or the day before…I couldn't remember.

Everything was blurred and the only thing that stood out was the confusion. Every time he asked me the same one question, I saw the desperation in his eyes, the desperation to get the answer he probably thought was somehow related to why he was left behind…to why they kept asking him about *me*.

Alex kept yelling and swearing, and the one maintaining guard beside him kept throwing punches, and each time he yelled out, my heart broke a little more.

This wasn't how this was meant to go. He was going to resign, and we were going to have a life together. I was going to tell him I loved him, that I have for years, and I'd been too afraid to say anything. I was going to tell him that he was the only person I'd ever trusted, cared about…

Tears stung my eyes as they forced me to the ground and Grimes knelt beside me wrapping his hand around my ponytail before slamming my head into the cold, murky water. At that point, several things happened.

The fear that coursed through my veins suddenly turned to anger, the nausea that kept my throat constricted turned into fuel and the foggy hold over me suddenly vanished; I wasn't scared anymore.

I grit my teeth as the hand around my hair tightened and the air from my lungs disappeared. As soon as he pulled my head free, I moved. I threw my head back, hitting his face causing him to yell out in surprise and stammer backward.

Daring a quick look at Alex and the horror on his face made my stomach drop. It took two seconds flat for Grimes to retaliate. He lunged at me and slammed his fist into my face, breaking my nose, I didn't let the pain stop me. I hit back with a right hook, followed by a body shot, and cracked his ribs. He moved quickly and kicked me in the stomach, forcing me to my knees.

The seedy cocktail he'd shot me with was wearing off and I could fight. This was more like it. I grinned through the blood pouring from my nose and caught his foot as he tried to kick me in the face. I threw him backward; he stammered for a moment before I jumped back up and lunged at him. The men he had in the room moved toward me, but he called them off. The sick bastard was having fun.

He reached into his back pocket and retrieved a switchblade. Oh great.

"I'm impressed. The cocktail wore off quicker than I thought."

What the hell was this guy on? He was making no sense.

"I knew it wouldn't last long on you, but this is impressive."

I squared against him, keeping my eyes on the blade and how he held onto it. Some of us were expert marksmen, some at hand-to-hand combat, but Grimes was all about the knives. I'd seen enough in my time to be able to spot someone's skills.

He came at me again, lunging with the knife, nicking my arm, slicing through the fabric of the jacket.

When he came at me the second time, I wasn't prepared, he landed a kick square in my middle, pushing me backwards. In the second it took for me to catch my breath, he shot forward, his hand closed around my throat, quickly flipping me around. He wrapped his arm around my neck and forced me down to my knees in a chokehold.

Alex shouted over the commotion and I closed my eyes tightly. I'd blown it.

The American slowly brought the blade to my cheek.

He looked at Alex dead on, and Alex lost it.

Every threat under the sun left his lips, but all I heard was the blood rushing in my head. Grimes wasn't going to kill me. That's all that kept me sane. That was the only thought I kept repeating to myself. He needed me. He wouldn't kill me.

"Reckon she'd still be a babe with one eye?" he spoke to Alex.

"Fucking touch her, and I will rip your throat out."

Sweat broke out across my forehead.

Grimes brought the blade down to my hand that was desperately clawing at his forearm pressed against my throat. "What about a few missing fingers?"

Another breath caught in my throat. Alex continued yelling threats, but I couldn't hear any of it over the blood rushing in my head.

Grimes brought the blade back to my face.

The cold blade felt like ice against my hot cheek and my heart raged a million miles an hour. He traced it across my face applying pressure but not breaking the skin.

I kept my eyes focused on Alex's, the silence from his end scared me. He'd stopped yelling; he'd stopped thrashing. There were no threats, just silence. He was terrified.

"What did they want you for?" Grimes whispered in my ear, letting his lips linger far too close to my face.

"I don't know."

"Why are you lying to me?" He traced the blade over my cheek again.

"I don't have the answer."

He made a small, disapproving sound and then he moved the blade and swiped it across my cheek with a quick, precise flick, so fast I barely felt it. The pain that came after was nothing compared to the fear when Alex screamed.

I was pulled up to my feet and dragged back to the chair. I didn't need to look down to see the blood splattering on the floor to know how bad it was. The whole left side of my face felt like it was on fire, burning and wet.

"Now, if you've had enough fun."

He strapped me back to the chair and left me sitting in my drenched clothes and bleeding face.

"Don't go too far, we'll be back in a jiffy."

They all left.

Alex and I were alone, and I couldn't even look up at him. I couldn't face him.

"Oh God, look at me, Ace."

My eyes were glued to the spot on the floor, rapidly turning red. At least it was going numb. I let out a long and even breath. It could have been worse, that's what I had to keep reminding myself. Still had all my fingers and both eyes.

"Ace. Look at me, please."

Slowly, I dragged my eyes up to his and bit back the sob on the verge of escaping.

His eyes were so full of pain that it nearly broke me in two.

"You're going to survive this," he whispered.

Those few words broke down the walls I'd been holding up.

"You're hurt," I murmured back.

He shook his head, keeping his eyes on me. "I need you to keep fighting; I need you to hold on, okay?"

"He's insane," I stammered.

"I know."

"He keeps asking what they want me for."

His face hardened; he was concerned, almost like I told him something he already knew, and the way he turned his head away told me I was right.

"What do you know?" I pleaded. "They kept asking him about me; that's why he was left here. But you already knew that."

"He was special ops."

He found my eyes but remained still.

"If you know something that can help me, you have to tell me."

Sadness filled his eyes, and he turned away from me again.

"Alex," I urged. "If you know something…"

"He—"

The door opened before I could question him, and the American returned with two men and a large box.

My eyes didn't leave the case, not even when he set it down and looked at me.

"I have all day, don't know about you."

I quickly looked over at Alex, and the way he was shaking in his seat set me on edge. He was on the verge of a breakdown. His eyes were wide, full of fear, and his fists were clenched over the ends of the chair he was strapped to.

"Did you know that electroshock therapy was one of the most widely practiced methods of shocking sanity into people?"

My heart thundered.

"The 1930s were a wonderful time; that's when most psychiatrists started to really experiment with electroshock."

When my eyes remained transfixed on what he was unpacking, he laughed softly and paused. "But it wasn't until later that we started to get creative."

Behind me, two Iraqis moved, and no matter how much I thrashed against them or how much Alex screamed and threatened them, they remained focused on what they were doing. My boots and socks were pulled off and placed beside me while the other shoved a rubber tube in my mouth and fixed it into place.

Alex's shouting sounded like it was miles away, I could barely hear him, and even if I did, I didn't think I'd be able to make sense of what he was saying between the cursing and the insults.

But Grimes' voice was loud and clear. He stopped and looked down at me, ensuring I was paying attention.

"You've heard of the *Parrilla* method, haven't you?"

Alex's shouting doubled, and my heart raced so fast I thought I would die.

My silence answered his question since I couldn't really talk anyway.

"You know they loved the use of that method, especially on female soldiers, tore down all their walls and defenses; what better way to destroy a woman than to destroy her like that? The ultimate rape of body and mind."

Tears caught in my eyes, causing everything in my line of sight to double and bleed into one horrifying image of chaos.

"I'm not barbaric, Sergeant; I wouldn't do that to you," he said sternly. "Quite frankly, I couldn't think of doing something so degrading to another human being. That's not what I'm about. But…the rest of your team might not be so lucky; I can't say what my men will do."

A breath caught in my lungs.

There wasn't a hint of sarcasm in his voice. He was all business.

"What I am about is the truth. I want to know why they kept asking me for you."

Again, I stared at him.

"I want to know why I was tortured and held down here; I want to know why you're so important."

When he unpacked everything, he stopped and turned to the Iraqi closest to me. "Get her jacket off," he ordered, keeping his striking eyes on me the entire time.

I gritted my teeth and flinched when my sleeves were pulled down as far as they'd go with my arms tied behind my back.

The cold air sent a chill over my exposed skin, which the sand-colored T-shirt didn't cover.

He knelt, rolled up the cuffs of my pants, and looked up at me for a moment. My heart was racing, and I had no idea if I could face what was coming.

A pointed look found me before he got up and returned to the box.

"One over her heart, the other on her back," he said, turning his back.

Alex thrashed against his restraints again, only this time when he shouted; the Iraqi closest to him slammed the butt of his rifle into Alex's head. The shocked grunt was cut short, and then he was silent.

I wanted to scream, but all that came out through the gag was a gargled cry.

My eyes were glued to Alex. His body was slumped forward, and a fresh cut above his eye was steadily bleeding.

Forcing my attention back to Grimes, he nodded to the Iraqis. One pulled the collar of my T-shirt down and stuck an electrode and fixed it into place with a thick strip of grey tape, the other did the same on my back and handed the two sets of wires to my captor.

He walked over to the large box, and only now, I saw that it was a car battery, cleverly disguised. Jesus Christ, I was about to become *Tony Stark*. He hooked up the first set of wires attached to my chest and held up the other end turning to me.

"What did they want you for?"

I hoped he'd see the answer in my eyes, so I screamed against the gag. I had no idea what they wanted me for. I'd never heard of them; I'd never heard of him.

Unsatisfied with my answer, he lowered the wire and as the copper made contact with the terminal, a jolt of electricity shot through me so quick and so powerful it sent my head back and blocked off a scream from the depths of my soul.

My jaw clenched shut and fierce, reactive tears spilled from my eyes as my muscles tensed and tightened, coiling and squeezing, threatening to snap from the tension. And then the wire was released, and I slumped forward, wheezing, greedily sucking in air.

"What did they want you for?"

Shaking my head and ignoring the aftershocks, I gave him another pleading, desperate look, hoping he'd see I had no idea.

He didn't. He lowered the wire, and this time, as it connected to the terminal and my head snapped back, a dark and ominous presence began to fill my heart and quickly, as the electricity coursed through me and my muscles locked up, I felt the welcome blanket of pain coming hard and fast but not before something inside my heart cracked, whatever *it* was, was fierce and it was fighting with me.

CHAPTER EIGHT

First, my eyes opened, and then I felt my fingers and toes slowly moving. My muscles ached like I'd been running a damn marathon for days. Only it hadn't been a marathon, and it hadn't been days. I'd passed out after minutes. That's all it took, and I'd folded.

Groaning, I looked down; I was again suspended from the ceiling by my wrists. This time, Alex was silent. His wide eyes were focused on me and only me. He was so still I thought he might have cracked or gone completely catatonic. But the way he'd look at my face and then down over my chest and back up to my face told me otherwise.

Slow, broken breaths left his lips, and I suddenly felt increasingly concerned.

There were certain things that General Simmons had told us about preparing for resisting torture, some were related to having faith, finding strength in the fact that you're fighting for a cause, for a higher purpose, and then there were the things most of us were there for. To make the world a safer place, because of that, we couldn't succumb to torture. But holding out, that was a different story altogether. He'd told us about trying to push yourself somewhere far away, somewhere where your mind was free, locked away from the pain. A few men had managed to master it, and when they were brought home, they were never the same.

When the shocks started, and I felt the burning of my skin and the pain inside my heart, well I didn't have faith in myself.

Looking at the way Alex sat stunned, staring at me, probably at the hideous mess I'd become, made me want to curl up and call it quits. But I wasn't a coward, I'd never run, not when I could still protect my squad, the men and women who trusted me to do so even if there were only a handful left. Tears spilled over my cheeks and I bit back an angry sob.

A tremble ran down my left arm into my heart, making me gasp—Alex's eyes snapped back to mine.

Feeling conscious of the cut on my face, I cast my eyes down and tried to assess my situation.

Whatever I did made the pain in my shoulders worse. The jarring ache of the strain was enough to make spots explode across my vision and double the previously mild case of nausea.

A shaky breath from Alex made my eyes flick across to his. He was suffering; he'd been beaten, drowned and beaten again. No doubt trying to get me to talk. But he didn't; he endured, and I also had to.

The bruising on his face had almost made his right eye swell shut, my heart broke, and I felt like a fucking coward.

"I'm so sorry," I whispered to him, barely making the words form.

My mouth was dry like I'd eaten a bag of cotton wool.

"Don't," he said just as quietly. "This isn't on you."

"The hell it isn't."

The sadness in his eyes hurt.

"Ace," he said so quietly that I barely heard him.

I sobbed when I found it in me to look back at him. His eyes were filled with tears.

"They're all dead."

What? No. No. I, I refused to believe it. I couldn't...he forced a weak smile and nodded.

"You have to be strong. You must survive this, Ace; you're all that matters."

My breath caught in my throat and the tightness in my chest drew another broken sob from me.

"Promise me you will fight. No matter what happens to me, no matter what happens here and what you learn."

Tears built and the pain inside me grew but this pain was worse than the jarring in my shoulders or the cut across my cheek, this pain was real—consuming me from within, building and coursing through my veins. The feeling was surreal, like an entity controlling me, trying to take over, threatening to explode.

"Alex…"

"Promise me, Ace. Promise you will fight and you will live. Long after you get out of this shit hole."

"Stop talking, we're both getting out. All of us are."

"They're all dead."

"You're sure?" my tongue was too heavy.

"They're all dead, Ace. There's no one left. You need to survive this. Promise me you'll live."

Tremors raced through my body and fear set in.

"We're meant to get out of here together…"

"Not this time, baby. This is all you now, Ace."

"No…"

"Promise me you won't shut yourself off, please."

"Alex—"

"You'll find someone to love. You'll have a sickly-sweet life. You'll see."

"Stop," I whispered, hating how much I was crying.

If they were all really dead, Alex would be next.

Moments after that sickening thought formed, the door opened, and Grimes followed by two Iraqis came in—the same two men from before. They were his confidants, that was important. If I could get them to understand, to let me down maybe I stood a chance.

Grimes looked over at me as he set down a duffle bag.

"You're not going anywhere. Just hang tight," he said to me, before turning to Alex. "How are you holding up man? You look like you've seen stuff."

"Fuck you," Alex said firmly and spat, narrowly missing Grimes' shoes.

He laughed and turned his back to Alex and focused on me again. "Now. We've wasted enough time. I want my answers, sergeant, and I think I know how we will get them."

"I've told you before; I have no idea what you're talking about!"

"I think you do. I think you've known all along."

"You're crazy! I don't know what you want!"

He laughed again.

"We'll see." He turned to Alex and nodded. "And I think you know more than you've led me to believe."

"What are you doing?" I yelled back, ignoring the tightening in my chest.

Something bad was coming, something that made the panic inside me rise tenfold, something I couldn't explain, fear and anticipation, pain, and agony. I felt the tears building before I could stop them.

Alex thrashed against the restraints they put him in, tying his arms above his head, hoisting him up just like I was.

"Leave him alone!" I screamed as one of them punched him in the stomach, when Alex retaliated.

Grimes shook his head at the spectacle and turned to me.

"I will tell them to stop just as soon as you give me what I want. I don't care who tells me, I just want the answer."

"We don't know!" I shouted for the hundredth time.

Panic rose when he turned from me and unzipped the duffle bag. He pulled out two long whips and unfurled one, turning to Alex.

Without warning, he cracked the whip through the air and sliced it across Alex's back.

His low grunt was muffled by my scream and the tearing of his shirt and flesh.

Alex focused his eyes on me, and Grimes cracked the whip again. Over and over, each time, Alex flinched but kept his eyes on me, and which each broken breath he released, I felt my resolve failing. Tears fell but I couldn't make them stop. I didn't know what they wanted, I didn't have the answer.

"What did they want her for?" he asked calmly, and again when Alex couldn't answer, he cracked the whip, bringing Alex to the point of finally yelling out.

That's when he turned it up. He dropped the whip on the table and launched his fist into Alex, cracking his ribs with the force.

Whatever composure I'd tried to hold onto, disappeared. I lost it.

"Stop!"

But he didn't; he hit him over and over until, eventually, Alex stopped grunting and all he did was cough out the blood that was pooling in his mouth. His eyes found mine and the pain in them scolded me.

"I thought you'd be willing to suffer, sergeant, but I really didn't think you'd let someone else suffer for you."

"Screw you."

"What did they want you for?"

"Kiss my ass."

"What did they want you for?"

"To make my killer risotto."

"What did they want you for?"

He rounded the table, picking up the whip. *I could do this.*

"What did they want you for?"

"Fuck you."

That's when he lost his patience. Up until this point, he'd been calm and collected. The rage fueling him started to show through the cracks of the *crazy* he'd tried to hide.

He stepped behind me and I took a deep breath when I heard the whistle skimming the surface of the leather as it raced toward me. The crack was deafening as it snapped against my back and ripped through the fabric of my shirt and my skin, catching a cry on my lips.

"What did they want you for?"

"Fuck you!"

I braced myself. *I could do this.*

The whip broke through the air, tearing my skin as it ripped through the thin fabric of my shirt again.

"What did they want you for?"

"I can do this all day."

He laughed, seeing right through my bluff.

The whip raced through the air again, and again as it made contact, I suppressed the scream on my lips. *I could do this.*

"All of this can end; all you have to do is answer my question."

"Go to hell."

And so it went, again and again, over and over, until I was on the verge of passing out, and he was on the brink of losing all of his composure.

As he dropped the whip for the last time and my whimper escaped, he released the chain holding me up and I fell to the floor, curling up as soon as he left.

The Iraqi behind me pulled the chain still connected to my wrists and hooked it up to the wall, ensuring I couldn't go further than a few feet.

Through tired eyes I looked up at Alex, the Iraqi had let him down and propped him up against the wall hooking his chain to the old radiator that probably hadn't worked for decades. The steel pipe beneath it looked to be the only solid part of its structure.

The heaviness in my eyes crept up on me and against my better judgment, I curled up, letting sleep claim me.

CHAPTER NINE

Several hours later, my eyes flickered open when a shudder of pain rippled through me when I realized I'd turned on my back and the blood had dried my shirt and skin to the concrete beneath me. Expelling a low hiss, I gently dragged myself up and looked around.

"Alex," I whispered, hoping he'd hear me though I didn't dare let anyone else hear.

Nothing. He was still.

"Alex!" I hissed, louder this time, getting to my knees and moving as close as the chain would allow.

Still nothing.

His head lolled to the side, and I fully saw the damage they'd done to him. His right eye was completely swollen shut, and his lower lip was split. I couldn't see his back, but I saw how his sand-colored shirt was drenched with sweat and stained red all over.

Anger quickly filled my veins.

"Alex!"

This time he stirred, slowly turning his head toward me.

"Open your eyes, corporal," I encouraged, desperately hoping that he had enough strength.

When he let out a low breath, I noticed the way he winced, his ribs were broken. I'd seen and *felt* enough of those injuries to know that he wasn't breathing properly and the little gasps he could take in were painful.

"Keep your eyes on me, okay?" I whispered, wincing as the movement stretched the broken skin on my back.

He smiled a very small smile and focused his good eye on me. The striking, vibrant color was dulled to a scary shade. He was so weak, and I couldn't do a damned thing to help.

Why did they want me? Why did they kill so many people to get to me and why did they think he knew?

Endless thoughts tormented me and the one constant that kept circling back and winding me was the realization that all those people were dead, because of me.

A painful sob ripped through me and I dropped my gaze from Alex. This was my fault. I should have fought Simmons harder to abort this operation.

"Hey…" he whispered, startling me. "Ace."

Trying to hold my tears back, I glanced at him and smiled.

"How are you holding up?" he asked softly.

"I'm okay…"

Silence fell between us.

"None of this is on you."

How did everyone know what I was thinking? Before I could ask, Alex smiled and nodded.

"There's so much you don't know about who you are, about how brilliant you'll be. About our world."

"What are you talking about?"

"When the time is right, someone will find you and they'll tell you everything. And, Ace…I never wanted things to end this way, but I always knew the possibility was there."

"What do you know?"

"Remember what I told you before we left?"

The words refused to form around my heavy tongue. Instead, I swallowed and blinked back the tears.

"I know who you are, and I love every part of you; I always have."
He smiled. "I mean it."

"I don't understand."

"You will."

"Alex…"

"You're Divine, Ace. You will know everything when it's time. That's all I can say to keep you safe, I'm sorry, so sorry."

The door swung open, cutting off my chain of thought.

Grimes walked in, two Iraqis at his heel, and stopped before me.

"Get up."

Sticking my middle finger at him, I remained glued to the floor.

"You still refuse to cooperate."

"I refuse to talk to terrorists!"

"You disappoint me."

"You're an idiot."

"Get up," he said firmly, ignoring the rest. "I'm not going to ask you again."

"Then I guess you're going to be pretty pissed."

"I think not," he said quietly and looked at Alex.

Without warning, he retrieved his gun so fast my brain didn't have time to link what I saw before he fired.

A scream filled the air, silencing my scream, as Alex was hit.

I heard him cursing, he was alive, oh God.

"You're fucking crazy!" I screamed.

"Get up."

Forcing my hands to the floor, I pushed up and stood. My legs trembled under the pressure but my eyes were focused on Alex.

Grimes shot toward me and grabbed my face, squeezing my cheeks. "I've told you before that I don't have a problem with doing whatever it takes to get my answers."

I jerked my face back and stumbled slightly.

"I already told you, you fucking psycho. I don't know anything and neither does he!"

The Iraqi closest to me set down the metal chair and pushed me down into it. The other tied my arms to arm rests and my legs to either side.

Grimes set down the box from yesterday, pulled down the collar of my shirt, and attached an electrode to my chest and another to my back, only this time, he repeated the gesture and added two more. My heart raced so fast that I thought it'd break through my chest.

"Still refuse to speak?"

"Fuck you."

He smirked and nodded.

My eyes fell to Alex, he was losing too much blood and his skin had taken on a deathly pallor.

Forcing myself to take long and even breaths, I tried to prepare myself for the pain, but nothing prepared me for the explosion of electricity that ripped through my veins this time.

My jaw clenched shut and my muscles locked up, seizing with the current running through my body. Involuntary spasms traveled over me and sweat broke out across my skin and then a long, agonizing moment later, the current stopped.

A broken breath left my lips and a trickle of blood followed—I'd broken my teeth from the violent force, and worse than that, as my head dropped, I'd noticed the wetness seeping through my pants. I'd pissed myself.

"Those are quite normal reactions," he said as an afterthought. Though, it didn't stop him from looking down at me in disgust.

"I'm going to kill you," I shot.

"I'm sure you'd love to try."

"Why don't you untie me and see how you'd go."

"While that does sound interesting, I don't have time for that."

"You should make time."

"You should really start talking; this will only get worse."

"Bring it."

And he did. He connected the wires to the car battery, and yet again, the force of the current running through me forced my jaw shut and I ignored everything else that came after that because the excruciating, never-ending torrent of pain drowned everything else out.

My muscles spasmed and the bones in my arms and legs felt so tightly wired, I was afraid they'd break if I moved.

Finally, he released the wires and the electricity stopped but the pain didn't. I let out a broken scream and forced my eyes up to his.

"Just answer my question. I don't want to keep doing this to either of you."

"I can't answer what I don't know," I stammered through the aftershocks, twitching in the chair.

"I don't believe that."

"I can't help you."

"That is a shame."

He looked at me, intently, like he was wondering what to do, and then, in a moment that seemed to last an eternity, he looked over at Alex whose eyes were solely focused on me, and, in that eternity, several lifetimes passed; lifetimes Alex and I would never share.

My heart slowed, and my tears slipped out onto my cheeks. *No.*

"Ace…"

His eyes were wide, full of pain and understanding.

Grimes cocked his pistol and fired. The scream that came from me faded until it became a long chain of broken cries.

Alex didn't groan, he didn't do anything. He was gone. There was only silence.

"What did they want you for?" Grimes asked quietly.

And I didn't do a damned thing. I sat still, letting my tears fall, letting the electricity fire through me, letting it break me, feeling the pain, embracing it. It was over. I was done.

CHAPTER TEN

Pain.

Pain was what woke me.

Consuming every fiber of my being, slicing through every nerve ending in my body and setting me on fire.

Forcing my eyes open, I shuddered in the cold; my body was wet; why was I wet?

Glancing around, I choked on a sob when my gaze landed on Alex, they hadn't even bothered to move him—not like they buried the enemy here anyway; maybe it was for the best.

His good eye was still open, but it was vacant. Sometimes the dead could be mistaken for sleeping, but not him. He was so pale and so bruised and swollen, there was no way you could mistake that for anything else.

The color of his usually vibrant green eyes, eyes I'd loved so much were so dull, they were almost grey.

Forcing my eyes away, I looked around the room. I was alone and freezing. Why the hell was I wet? Like a punch to the gut, I remembered passing out, then being woken with buckets of water being thrown on me, all while I was on the floor.

My arm was still shackled to the wall.

Crawling to my knees, I moved toward Alex; with each movement, my heart thundered louder and louder and my eyes blurred from the constant flow of tears.

He couldn't be gone, not like this, not because of me.

I held out my trembling hand and pressed it gently over his face, and the sob I'd been holding in, erupted and I crumbled.

Doubling over, I cried into his blood-soaked t-shirt and gripped his arm tight, but no matter what I did now, nothing would ever settle the pain in my heart.

Letting the sobs consume me, I ignored everything else; I ignored the nagging feeling telling me to move, to get up and fight when the doors opened.

Before I could kiss his forehead, a rough pair of hands circled my torso and pulled me back.

That was when I decided I would fight—I was finished being this asshat's toy, I was finished crying, but mostly, I was finished letting him win.

As the Iraqi moved toward me again, I kicked my leg out with as much force as I could, and when he stammered backward letting me go, I used the moment to put some space between us. The other one came at me a lot faster than I'd anticipated, and as he raised his rifle, I wrapped the chain around my wrist, using it to steady myself and launched my foot at the butt, kicking it out of his hands.

When the first one jumped me again, I grabbed my chain, holding it tight, and executed a perfect cartwheel kick, breaking his jaw. He dropped to the ground, yelling for help but the other came at me again throwing his weight around my waist, and tackling me to the ground. As he pinned me down, forcing my hand to pull the chain, I screamed out in pain but used it to fuel me, I had to wait, I needed the perfect moment.

Blow after blow landed on my face, each hit harder than the one before and when I saw my opportunity as he raised his arm again, I knocked it out of the way, threw my hand under his underarm, pulled him down, and flipped him over. With one precise jab, I hit him in the throat, momentarily stunning him, then I threw him down, wrapping the chain around his throat, pulling until I saw him start to go lax, and then I yanked it tighter, snapping his neck.

Through all the commotion, Grimes must have heard his man's cry for help because he came through the door in less time than it took me to discard the body.

He looked over me and then at the scene around me.

He folded his arms over his chest.

"Your reputation precedes you."

I heaved, sucking in deep breaths ignoring the blood pooling in the back of my throat. I'd taken a few good blows and was sure my eye socket was broken along with a bunch of broken or missing teeth. How I was standing and fighting was beyond me. I'd heard of adrenaline kicking in and experienced it myself, but this felt like much more was driving me.

I released the chain and faltered for a moment before steadying myself.

"I am going to kill you," I said.

He didn't flinch.

"So why don't you come closer? Because right now, I've got nothing to lose."

"Everyone thinks that until they realize there's much more than life to lose."

"I've had enough of this bullshit."

Apparently, he had too. I managed to dart out of the way and miss the fist coming at me.

When he recovered his position, he rushed me again only this time I couldn't evade him and he ducked low, swiping his leg out at my feet effectively forcing me to lose my balance.

I fell backwards, hitting the ground hard on my hip. He rushed me again this time launching his boot at my chest. I slapped his foot away, but my exhaustion and his speed made this a losing battle for me.

This was now a dirty fight. I was scrambling to get to my knees and crawl away when he caught hold of my foot and yanked me back. The ground disappeared from under me and Grimes flipped me over onto my back.

In the second it took for me to catch my breath, he'd gotten up, wrapped his fist around my throat and dragged me to my feet.

I tried to slap his hands away, but he was too strong and I was too injured. Panic raced through me, making my blood rush fast and furious.

He pushed me back, pinning me against the wall and when he pointed his gun at me, *the weapon* that killed Alex, something inside me flared.

It was quick, my eyes focused like I saw the scene unfolding before me in slow motion, like it was all clearer, somehow louder.

Rage rushed through my veins, and in the second it took for him to fire and the men to storm into the room, time froze—I closed my eyes for a moment, and when I opened them, I knew what was about to happen. I was going to be shot, there was nothing I could do about it but I could survive it if I moved at the right moment.

The shot echoed, I threw myself to the left and the bullet hit me in the shoulder.

As everything I'd seen and felt came flooding into every pore, consuming everything building inside me a scream formed and I released it from the pit of my soul from a place I didn't recognize, and it went on for an eternity, everything I held onto, everything that made me who I was, was breaking.

I sprung to my feet, dodging another attempt at my life, all while my body and mind were fragmenting. It was as though the cells inside me were splitting, ripping apart, and fusing back together.

Grimes rushed me; this time, though, I wasn't in control as my mind spiraled, and something raw, almost detached from within, took over. I threw my hands out and screamed as a rush of something I couldn't comprehend erupted. The sound came from a dark, untouched part inside me. And as the sadness broke me down, I let it unravel everything I'd been holding back, all the fear I was afraid to feel, all the pain, everything that I had lived through in this godforsaken place. And when I couldn't scream anymore, I dropped, falling to my knees, letting all the pain flow free, crying through the breathless gasps. And that's when I felt *it.*

It was still, deathly silent, and the atmosphere was dense like a thick fog had descended. Grimes and all his men were dead and their eyes were staring up at the ceiling; the shock was etched onto their faces like they were killed mid-thought, stopped dead in their tracks.

A breath stuck in my throat.

A chill crawled over my skin, and I looked around. Whatever happened here wasn't natural. I looked down at my hands. They looked normal. They were shaky, covered in my own blood but nothing more, nothing to show me what I'd just done.

It didn't matter right now. Right now, I needed to get out. I started searching for something I could use, I looked for anything I could break the shackle with. Lucking out, I groaned and tried pulling it free from the wall.

When that didn't budge, I moved closer and checked the metal loop holding it there. It was a much weaker link; this was my out.

Pulling off my T-shirt, I twisted it into a tight, firm strip of fabric and wrapped it around the link and twisted.

As I twisted the fabric harder, I grit my teeth and forced it as far as my strength would allow and a painful minute later, I heard the link give way and snap off the wall, but I couldn't do anything about the shackle attached to me.

Wasting no time, I pulled my shirt back on and wrapped the chain around my wrist. Quickly rushing over to Alex, I pressed a kiss to his forehead and took the letter he'd written from his pocket, stuffing it into mine.

Knowing that I'd have company soon, I kissed his forehead one more time, wiped the tears from my eyes, and got up. I picked up a discarded rifle, slung it over my shoulder, and moved quickly to the door. I waited a few moments to ensure no one was coming and as soon as I was clear, I slipped out quickly and moved through the corridors.

Sounds outside echoed through the mason walls making me stop every few feet or so, when I was clear, I continued navigating the unfamiliar building.

As I rounded the corner leading out to another bunker, I stayed quiet but the moment I turned I came face to face with two Iraqis. They reacted quickly, reaching for their weapons but I was quicker. I fired taking one out before the other one lunged at me, knocking me down. We grappled on the floor before I got the upper hand and flipped him onto his back, using my weight to hold him down and wrap my arm around his throat.

He struggled for a few moments until he went limp.

Getting up, I ran, I couldn't afford any more surprises, my shoulder was on fire and I was losing a lot of blood. Something told me the haze coating my eyes wasn't just from the tears.

Taking a rocky staircase up, I found myself in what I assumed was the living quarters. There were plates and cups, jackets slung over chairs, and discarded packets of cigarettes lying on the table. I snatched a jacket and carefully pulled it on. There was a baseball cap hanging off the edge of the chair and I pulled that on too.

I kept moving, staying out of sight, and when I reached the door, I stopped and assessed my next move. A lot could go wrong; a lot probably would go wrong. I was alone and frankly terrified out of my mind, and to top it off, I was losing blood, struggling against a concussion, and hopelessly outnumbered.

Taking a deep breath, I leaned against the door and looked around. I could do this. I had to.

This was it. I gripped the handle tightly and slowly pulled it open. There were people everywhere, men and women working, children running in the streets and further down, I saw the source of the music I'd heard when they brought me in.

A few young boys were playing instruments to a small crowd that had gathered and as I moved through the tapestry hanging in the doorway, I suddenly remembered that I probably looked like hell.

Wiping my face with my sleeve I walked past them with my head held high and the rifle tightly gripped in my hand.

Passersby looked at me but didn't pay any more attention than that—I walked through with little more than a curious look and the insurgent jacket and Grimes" hat, got me by with little trouble.

But that wasn't the only thing I had to worry about; the pain in my shoulder was getting worse, and the blood loss was reaching critical levels.

Remembering my training, I followed my orders and started heading back to the location where our convoy had been ambushed.

All I could think about now was my mom; God, I wanted to hug her, have a big cry and eat some cake.

Maybe I'd even go on that ridiculous hike dad always spoke about, the hike no sane person would ever attempt.

I laughed out loud. This hike through the desert would have made him proud. I'd walked miles with a hole in my shoulder, a few busted ribs, and a cracked face. Yeah, he'd have something to say about that.

Hours must have passed because the sun had stopped beating down on my body and instead cool, desert air sent chills over my drenched skin.

Bringing my attention back to where I was walking, I pushed myself until I couldn't breathe. Staggering through the harsh terrain, stumbling over my own feet. I felt the energy leaving me, and through hooded eyes I saw a silhouette in the distance, running toward me, moving quickly.

I stopped. How could I fight? Did I have anything left in me?

Then the realization hit me, and I laughed. I couldn't. I dropped to my knees and as the silhouette approached, I closed my eyes. If this was the end, it would be on my terms.

Falling backwards, I braced for the impact of rough desert sand, but it never came.

CHAPTER ELEVEN

A strong metallic taste in the back of my throat forced me awake. I had a momentary panic attack before I realized where I was, and when I moved, a stinging and burning sensation stopped me. The previous fear and everything else that consumed me was chased away as I looked around.

I was in what looked to be makeshift medical quarters, a combat medic sitting by my side, reading my chart intently.

When I stirred, his eyes quickly found mine. "Sergeant. How are you feeling?"

How was I feeling?

Violated, betrayed, angry…?

"You're very lucky to be alive."

"Lucky?" I croaked.

Lucky was the fact that I found clothing I could escape in and disguise myself; lucky was whatever killed those men. Lucky was that no one happened to be patrolling the forgotten convoy when I got there.

I was not lucky. The things that took place there, they would never leave me.

"Your bones are going to heal fine, the bullet wound was infected but we've given you some blood and antibiotics. The burns on your back and chest will go down over time, but the cut on your face…" He gave me a sympathetic look. "I had to stitch it up the old school way; we don't have the cosmetic stuff here. I'm sorry."

"My teeth."

"Your second and third molars on the top were shattered. I've removed them but you will need to see an oral surgeon when you get back home, maybe a cosmetic one too."

Home...

Everything was a blur, and it hurt as he continued through the laundry list of injuries he'd patched up. It was the kind of hurt that was all over you, inside you, filling every crack and void. I was vain, I was scared, and I could admit it.

The medic took a deep breath and looked at me.

"I'm sorry for what happened."

"Did they go back for my squad?"

He nodded, folding his hands together.

"They tracked your convoy, that's how they found you, but we were too late."

"They're getting burials. Right?"

"Of course."

That's all I needed to know. Everything else was irrelevant at this point. "And Corporal Westen, I want to see him."

When he looked down, I felt a frown tug at my lips.

"What is it?"

"Ma'am, we weren't able to recover Corporal Westen's body."

"What do you mean?"

"We searched every house, shack, and makeshift shelter in that place. They couldn't find him."

"I don't understand."

"I'm sorry, Ma'am."

Useless tears burned my eyes as my throat closed. I took a deep breath and looked up at the ceiling. *What had they done to him?*

"Do you want to sit up?"

I swung my eyes back to the medic and nodded.

"Can I get you anything?"

"I'm fine."

"The general wants to see you when you're ready."

"For a debrief, I'm sure."

"He was worried about you."

Yeah. Like he was worried about Grimes.

"I'm ready now," I muttered. The sooner I could get this over with, the better. "Where's my stuff?"

"Your clothes are there but I don't think you want to put them on, there's a fresh set of fatigues on the chair."

I would never put that uniform on again or the fatigues, but I needed what was inside, I rummaged through my pants until I found Alex's letter, stuffing it into the track pants I'd been dressed in; I ignored the medic's disapproving expression and left.

Dropping the blood and piss stained pants over the edge of the cot, I limped across the room and found my way down the hall—I was no stranger to these rooms, unfortunately.

General Simmons' door came into view and I made a beeline for it.

Several privates looked over at me as I walked past them. Some stared in shock, others in awe. And the common denominator here, was me. I didn't look like someone who'd been doing this for almost a decade, nor did I look like one of the best out there, and if this is how I came back, what hope did they have?

I grit my teeth and pushed the door open.

Simmons was about to protest but immediately shut his mouth when his eyes landed on me.

Expelling a shaky breath, I stood at the edge of his desk and gripped on to it to steady myself.

"Who was he?"

His eyes narrowed in confusion,

"The American, the soldier you left behind," I clarified.

His fingers steepled under his chin.

"You left him behind to get tortured, only to really entice him to come after us, after *me.*"

When he remained quiet, I pressed my hands to the desk and leaned heavily against it.

"But you knew that already; that's why you refused to abort the operation, right? You wanted us to go in, you knew he'd retaliate, and we'd have to kill him because he was a high-value target. Cover your asses and all that."

Simmons bowed his head.

"But you didn't anticipate that he'd be waiting for us."

"Sergeant Luke Grimes was a decorated soldier, but he lost his way."

"Bullshit," I snapped. "He didn't lose his way, he was thrown under the Goddamn bus, he was left to rot. Why?"

His eyes flared, but he didn't say a word. How could he? Luke Grimes was messed up, but he had been betrayed. I knew it, he knew it.

"What did he want?" he asked when he'd finally found his voice.

"Funny," I said without a hint of humor. "You should know; you sent me in there."

"He was crazy, sergeant."

"No, I don't think he was."

"Someone who's been through as much as he has—"

"Don't lie to me!" I slammed my palm on the table, rocking his kinetic sticks into motion before sucking in a long breath. "Don't fucking lie to me."

Simmons' eyes widened but he didn't say anything about my conduct.

"He was asking about you, wasn't he?"

"He was asking why I was important."

Simmons looked away for a moment, steepling his fingers.

"What was he talking about, sir?"

"You don't have the clearance for that."

"You're shitting me."

"Sergeant."

"You led me into his territory; you knew he was still out there, biding his time, mulling over me, and guess what, Sergeant Hart was coming right to him."

Simmons looked down at his hands.

"What did they want with me. What the hell was all this about?"

"I understand that you're angry, sergeant. But rules still apply to me and you and you do not have clearance for this information."

"But Corporal Westen did, right?" My heart broke, Alex knew something, and he died because of it.

"Corporal Westen knew the risks."

"They all died!" I yelled again, slamming my fist into the table. "For what?"

"They all knew the dangers of working on this task force with you." He raised his voice this time. "Every last one of them."

My brows shot into my hairline. "Working with me?"

"Yes, sergeant. They knew working with you would bring dangers and they were prepared."

My tongue grew heavy in my mouth.

"With their clearance levels, they were informed; I'm sorry, Ace. But there was no other way."

"Is that what you called me in here for? To tell me good job, soldier? Great work getting out, sorry about your team."

"No. Unfortunately, I called this meeting to discuss some personal matters."

Anger coiled inside me. "After everything that happened, I'm not going to listen to—"

"It's about your family, Ace," he said softly, his voice taking on an edge I'd never heard before, and then he rose, a stoic expression formed on his hardened face.

As soon as he looked at me, my heart sank. I knew, somehow, before he even said a word. I dropped into the wooden chair and folded my hands in my lap.

"When you were with Grimes, there was an accident, your parents were killed."

Words fell short. Nothing I could say could articulate the pain that suddenly burned through me. I'd lost everything. I'd lost someone I cared about deeply, I'd lost my faith, and now, I was alone. I'd lost the people who were my constants, the only people I trusted and loved unconditionally.

A stray tear slipped down my cheek—I was so numb it was a wonder I'd felt anything.

"We called them when you went missing, we didn't know if you were alive; they were on their way to the airport."

When I remained silent, he let out a breath, and I licked my lips, hoping that the gesture would somehow alleviate my discomfort. It didn't.

"How?"

"They lost control of their car and hit a light pole."

Tears wet my cheeks.

"We searched for you, *I* searched for you, Ace."

A shudder rolled through me, if I hadn't made it out, by whatever miracle killed those men, Simmons would have found me like they'd found the others.

"Your family loved you very much, Ace."

A sob broke free.

There had to be some mistake. I was going to go home and talk to dad about his time in the army, go hiking. I was going to hug my mom and tell her about Alex, I was going to go home.

"I'm so sorry."

Before he said another word, I got up. I placed Alex's letter on the table and held my emotions at bay.

"I'm done," I whispered, finding my voice. "So was Alex."

It made sense, like nothing else had so far. Like somehow everything had been leading to this moment. Guiding me and me driving me toward a decision I knew in my bones was right.

"Please, Ace, reconsider."

"He's dead now. I killed Grimes. It's over. I'm done. I'm going home."

Those were the words I never thought I'd speak, the words that made me realize just how much had changed, just how much I'd been through and how much I'd grown.

Alex was right, someday, maybe soon I'd be brilliant, I wouldn't be afraid like I was for so long and maybe I'd even stop running. But for now, I just wanted to go home. I wanted to say goodbye, I wanted to go somewhere no one knew me, maybe I'd even get a regular job in a store or something, work like everyone else, live a normal life.

Simmons got up but nothing he said would change my mind. Maybe he knew. Or maybe, maybe he thought it was best to let me go. After all, a soldier who'd been through the things Luke and I had gone through, was never really the same again.

"Where will you go?"

"New York," I murmured, stopping at the door. "I'm going to New York."

♥

ILLARION

The urgency of the situation didn't allow for wasting time, time *she* didn't have time.

I focused my attention on Michael and slammed my fist against the table when he spoke over me. He was heading this operation for as long as I'd been on it, he'd been facilitating the infiltrations, the surveillance and the recruitment so now, when the situation was critical, all I was getting were responses which didn't answer any of my questions.

"Agent Lazarev, take it down a notch."

"You're going to get her killed."

"General Simmons is doing everything in his power to find her."

"He's not doing enough."

"Agent Lazarev," he said sternly, folding his arms over his chest. "This isn't your operation."

"The hell it isn't."

His eyes narrowed, shooting me a warning look. "Agent Westen is in place."

"And we both know how powerful Grimes is; he won't hesitate to kill them both."

"Grimes will not kill Sergeant Hart—he needs her."

"That's even more reason to go in after her. He'll torture her for information she doesn't even know she has."

Michael rubbed his temple, letting out an exasperated sigh. "Operation Lullaby is active, Westen is active. Stay out of this and let him do his damn job."

"We have a duty to keep her safe."

"And your duty lies within the New York division," he explained. "The Agency does not have jurisdiction out there; we cannot break protocol. Westen can handle it."

"He hasn't checked in, has he?"

Michael's eyes narrowed and he found a spot on his desk suddenly interesting.

"He could be hurt or dead, leaving Sergeant Hart on her own."

"Or perhaps he hasn't been able to check in without being compromised. Perhaps his comms are down from the ambush."

"Or you're afraid of stepping on Simmons' toes."

"Enough, Illarion," Michael said firmly. "You're out of line."

I pushed away from the desk and faced him square on. "You're making a mistake."

"Just let Westen work his operation; when he checks in, we'll know more."

"Fine," I bit, taking a quick look at the surveillance photos and map strewn across the table. "If he doesn't check in, I want to know."

Michael gave me another pointed look. "You'll know. Now let Westen do his job."

Gritting my teeth, I nodded. "Copy that, sir."

Memorizing the locations on the map, I gave Michael a quick look and left.

♥

The sun blared down and the knot in my stomach doubled. If she was out here, in this heat, injured and without proper equipment, she wouldn't make it very far.

I'd followed her progress for ten years, I saw her first day at the barracks and her first day fighting the insurgents as a sergeant. She was fierce and she was brave, I'd seen the way she fought and the way she led, but the fear inside me now wasn't because of her inability to survive this, but because I knew Grimes and I knew what he was capable of.

He was malicious, he didn't feel remorse or pain; he didn't feel anything. He was tainted and fueled by rage, and I had experienced it firsthand during one of my tours, years before Ace was deployed.

I looked up at the sun, wincing at the strength of the rays. I had to move, time was running out.

The convoy was a few miles up the sandy banks; they'd been following the path that Grimes' team were on when they were ambushed. Gritting my teeth, I repositioned the satchel on my back and hurried.

I stopped twice to check the compass. Once I made sure I was heading in the right direction, I hurried my pace. Up ahead against the backdrop of a setting sun I spotted the bunkers on the horizon. I stuffed everything back in my pockets and ran.

Relieved that the sand dunes were high, I used them to blend into the background and remain hidden, the sand-colored khakis served their purpose well because I rushed past a post with two stationed Iraqis, without being seen.

I ramped up my shield that all Sensitives were born with, moved through the desert, and snuck inside the bunker.

My heart sped up as I felt the presence in the building. There were insurgents, the space pulsed with negative energy, but there was no fear—no one alive.

Swallowing back the nausea, I moved through the hallways; she'd been here not long ago but I couldn't tell whether it was before or after she was brought down.

Taking the final hall at the end, I pushed the door open and looked around, stopping abruptly when I spotted Grimes and his men. Their eyes were open, wide and unseeing. They were dead like they were cut down in their tracks and when I felt the energy radiating through the room, I took in a deep breath. She was powerful, stronger than we'd first thought.

This wasn't good. That much power was bound to go astray if not properly harnessed. I had to find her.

Looking around, I stopped when my eyes fell on Alex Westen. My heart sunk. I knelt, pressing my hand to Alex's cheek. "I'm sorry."

He and I had trained in America together, we were friends, and I would never forgive myself for listening to Michael and not coming sooner.

"So sorry," I whispered, pressing my hand to his shoulder, hanging my head.

He was a good agent, dedicated and passionate and he deserved better than a bullet to the chest chained up to a wall.

I yanked my hand around the chain and pulled, using all the strength inside me to pull it free from the wall.

"I will bring you home," I said, laying him down and folding his arms across his chest. "That, I swear to you."

First, I had to make sure Ace was alive. Forcing myself to my feet, I focused on her essence. Time was running out.

When I made it back outside, I kept myself flush against the walls until I was back in the desert. Protocol dictated that she'd head back to the Humvees, that's where they'd look for her, but the way the general had conducted his searches so far didn't instill much faith in me.

Keeping my speed steady, I continued through the sandy dunes, ignoring the fatigue and muscle strain. I had to get to her. That was the only thing that mattered now. Keeping her safe, getting her back.

When I climbed up the final dune, breathing in sharply through the heat I faltered when I saw her. It was unmistakable, a lone figure on the horizon silhouetting against the burnt, orange sky, stumbling, barely walking.

Ignoring everything else, I ran.

She was disoriented, she was swaying on her feet and when she saw me, she stopped, a moment of panic was chased away by fatigue. We were only yards apart now, I didn't want to scare her, so I slowed my pace to a steady jog, watching her eyes scan the horizon and stop on me, but she wasn't really seeing me at all. In a matter of moments, I'd all but closed the space between us.

I knew that look on her face. She wasn't here, her mind was in a far-off place, somewhere where she was safe, away from all of the pain that had found her in Grimes' basement. She was completely exhausted and running off pure adrenaline. With little more than a breathless shudder, she dropped to her knees and without a second thought, I threw myself to her side, catching her in my arms.

My heart stopped when I saw the pain in her eyes slowly fade away, she smiled, the warmest, most welcoming smile I'd ever seen.

It was relief that I felt at first, then gratitude.

"You're okay," I whispered, gently sweeping the blood-soaked strands of hair behind her ears, delicately avoiding the cut on her cheek.

I wanted nothing more than to help her, to give her my strength but I couldn't. There were protocols we had to obey and lines that couldn't be crossed.

Bowing my head in anger, I reined in my emotions about the bureaucracy that plagued us. She deserved better than this, but more importantly, she deserved a normal life, a life without the Agency, without people like Grimes on her heel, a life without me.

"Everything is going to be okay," I said quietly, knowing in my heart that this was wrong.

There was something about being here, holding her, seeing her in person that fired every nerve inside me, lit up every sense, made everything feel alive, like I'd been sleeping all these years.

Whatever I wanted, whatever I felt was irrelevant. She had to be safe and I had to make sure she wouldn't remember this when she woke.

"You can let go," I murmured, closing my hand over her forehead. "When you wake up, you're going to forget all of this and you'll forget me."

Her gaze found mine and she nodded, closing her eyes.

"Let go."

"Thank you," she whispered before falling limp in my arms.

ACE OF HART

Chapter One

New York

Ace

Fifteen minutes. That's all it took, and my perfectly good night was ruined.

I stuck my glittery black purse under my arm, freeing up my hands, and yanked the elastic from my hair allowing the dark strands to tumble around my shoulders.

Why did trouble always seem to find me?

All I wanted to do was go out, get drunk, and dance. Instead, I was tossed out on my ass, banned from a not-so-fine drinking establishment, and threatened with jail time. All of this because of one moron who couldn't keep his hands to himself.

Apparently smashing someone over the head with a glass when they grabbed your butt was frowned upon. Whatever. This world had a funny way of protecting women.

I zipped up my jacket, hoping the leather would shield me from the cool night air. The chill that settled over me was unnatural.

I slowed and looked around. I'd done this walk through Central Park a dozen times, even at night, but tonight something felt off.

I looked around slowing my pace and scanned the tree line stopping briefly on the glistening surface of the lake in the moonlight. Nothing but the soft ripples of the water moved. Everything was so still. A chill washed over me, and I had the sudden urge to flee.

Before I could act, I was gripped by strong hands and yanked back. Cold fingers wrapped around my wrist as I struggled, throwing me off balance. I stumbled trying to remain upright.

Muggings happened all the time, I could deal with this.

Steadying myself, I dropped my purse and squared off with the mugger. Half of his face was hidden from me by a bandana, but I could tell he was Caucasian and blond. He was taller than me by almost a foot, but he moved clumsily. Where some martial artists would draw their arms gracefully, his movements were jarred and awkward.

He reached behind him, his lips quirking into a grin and for a moment, my heart stuttered. I stepped back, unsure of my next move. I should have run. I should have done what any normal person would do.

As his hand moved from behind his back and revealed a small, shiny knife, relief flooded me, it wasn't a gun.

Without hesitation, he lunged, throwing his armed hand toward my chest. I grabbed his wrist, twisting and forcing him back. He kicked out his foot, connecting with my shin. As I moved backward, recovering, I sidestepped and he lunged at me again. This time, I wasn't as quick, and he nicked me with the blade. A small, precise gash appeared across my thigh, quickly dampening with blood.

Damn it. I was rusty.

He came at me again and as I moved, readying myself for a roundhouse kick, an almost undetectable warmth spread through me stopping every thought previously occupying my mind.

That moment of distraction earned me a kick to the stomach, and I was knocked down.

I rolled and narrowly missed the knife aimed at my chest. He took another stab but, before the blade connected with my skin, the mugger was gone, flung to the side, and knocked out.

I looked up and saw a man in the shadows. It was only for a moment, but the moment lasted a lifetime. Before I could run after him, he disappeared.

CHAPTER TWO

ACE

The breath I'd been holding escaped in a shaky whimper. Who the hell just saved me? A concerned citizen? A vigilante crime fighter? Dusting myself off, I got to my feet. Central Park was creepy as hell at night.

My eyes roamed the trees but the vigilante was gone.

I groaned, picking up my purse, I tucked it under my arm and that's when I noticed the rip in my jacket. I just bought this. Fuck. I walked over to where he lay unconscious and nudged him with my foot. Tonight was not my night, but it wasn't his, either.

He moaned and curled into a ball. I knelt beside him and pulled the bandana down. He was uninteresting, young, early thirties if I had to guess. There was nothing notable. I pulled out my phone and took a picture of his face.

I called the police and left an anonymous tip about a mugger in Central Park, then I went home.

When I reached my building, I pushed the doors open to the lobby and nodded at Giorgio, the door man. He knew more about my life than anyone else. I couldn't even explain how sad that was.

He'd known me well enough that he stopped questioning every time I'd come home with scuff marks, bruises or missing articles of clothing, instead he made light conversation of it.

If only he knew that half my nights were spent chasing down leads trying to find out everything I could about who Grimes was and where Alex was taken.

"Eventful night, Ms. Hart?"

I looked down at my jeans and the tears along my knees. "You could say that."

"Anything I can do for you?"

"No, thank you." I shook my head and clapped him on the back. "I'm fine. I just need a shower."

He smiled, bowing gently. "Good night."

"Good night."

The ride up to my room was quick, no one else got on which meant no one else would have to see this train wreck of an outfit.

I sighed as the elevator doors opened; Troy's shoes were placed neatly beside mine. I didn't feel like explaining myself to him tonight. All I wanted was a hot shower, a cup of hot chocolate, and bed. Maybe sex if he was in the mood.

Tip-toeing through my apartment, I managed to avoid making noise. I stripped, tossed the torn jeans in the trash and stepped into the hot stream. My body ached, my skin hurt, and my mind went to the vigilante in the park. I couldn't shake the feeling that he hadn't just happened upon the attack. If he did, did my attacker have anything to do with my past and the answers I was seeking?

No, I seriously doubted it. It was too convenient. But the vigilante, he was something else. How did he happen upon the attack? Did he know? I groaned at how ridiculous that was. How could someone know that something was about to happen? I rinsed the shampoo from my hair before turning the water off.

I draped the towel over myself, squeezing the excess water out. I was just shaken up. I was just attacked in the park. I was making something out of nothing.

Deciding that hot chocolate could wait, I padded my way across the floor and crept into my bedroom. Troy was fast asleep, his body twisted in the white satin sheets.

I crawled under the covers and slipped my hand over his waist. I closed my eyes and moved closer when I felt his hand slide over the curve of my hip and slide my leg up.

♥

There was a void, dark and endless, I couldn't see a way in or out, I just felt it. And deep inside, I saw myself, I was sitting in a dusty old warehouse, talking with someone, I didn't know who and I didn't know why.

All I did know was that I was afraid, I was so scared I could barely speak, but I was content; the man in the shadows, the man I was here to protect, was pleading for me to stop, to save myself.

But this was a necessary sacrifice, something I had to see through because it was all riding on me; this was my destiny.

The man with the knife stepped closer, and my heart cracked.

Behind him, someone shifted, someone who couldn't have been here. Alex?

"You need to run, baby. Don't do this."

"What?"

♥

I jolted awake. Again. These dreams were getting old; they were coming nearly every damn night now and each time, they got more detailed, but the faces never did, they were always shrouded in shadows or hidden by glaring light.

Something about the way the warehouse looked in my dream, the way the man shrouded by the shadows felt, put me on guard. It had

96

never been that vivid before. I almost tasted the sweat as he stepped closer to me.

I let out a breath and raked my fingers through the tangled mess of hair hanging over my shoulders.

Troy stirred beside me, bringing my attention to him. His exposed torso twisted in the tangled sheets before his arms snaked around my waist, pulling me closer.

"Bad dream?"

"Yeah," I muttered, finding a spot on the adjacent wall. I didn't have to turn to see him looking at me; I felt his gaze the whole time.

He brushed his fingers along my jaw, drawing my attention to him. I rolled over. His bright blue eyes warmed when he found the curve of my hip where he gently drew circles on my skin. "Do you want to talk about it?"

I shook my head, ignoring how his full lips curved up ever so slightly into a smile. "I think I need coffee."

"I'll make it, you rest," he murmured, kissing my forehead before disappearing into the kitchen.

As usual, he wore only a pair of red basketball shorts. Troy was tall and broad. His lightly tanned skin perfectly matched his tousled, light brown hair. He reminded me of the surfers you saw on Australian magazine covers—gorgeous in every sense of the word. He was loyal and faithful, even though he knew I wasn't. I should have walked away, but truthfully, I was selfish. He would always want more. The fact that he understood only made me feel worse.

I sighed and rubbed my face, returning my mind to my persistent nightmares.

The fear lingered as if I were still dreaming, still fighting. I hadn't felt that kind of fear since coming back from tour. I shivered, shaking the thought out of my head.

Those were long-forgotten memories for a reason. Alex always appeared in those dreams; he was always there, warning me of my impending demise, always telling me to run and I never did; every time I tried to help, I watched him die.

How long could I live like this before I finally snapped?

Not only were the dreams hindering my sleep, they were draining my energy. My fever spiked every night. I was no expert, but this wasn't normal.

When I heard Troy set down two cups, I pulled myself from bed and made a beeline for the bathroom. The reflection staring back at me was disconcerting. I was too pale, too clammy, too *different.*

I would never got used to what Grimes had left me with. The scar ran from the corner of my right eye, down across my cheek. The surgeons here said I was lucky he didn't nick my eye. *Lucky.* I sighed.

It had been two years since Alex died, since I lost my entire unit, my family, two years since I moved to New York and tried to start a new life.

Where I was used to dismantling bombs and assembling rifles, I was now setting up bows and tightening strings at the hunting counter in the camp store where Troy and I both worked.

I dragged myself away from the mirror and pulled on a pair of sweats, a plain black T-shirt, and some sneakers. I pulled my Yankees cap on and threaded my hair through the back.

Troy stood at the black marble bench buttering a piece of toast, his hip lazily resting against the edge.

"I made you coffee and toast, and I squeezed some juice." He stood shirtless in the kitchen, holding up the juice in one hand while he smoothed down a loose strand of hair from his face with the other.

"Thanks." I pulled out one of the heavy oak stools and took a bite out of the crispy bread. His eyes never left me.

"Is the toast good?"

"It's great," I replied, swallowing. "Thank you."

"I was thinking, if you're feeling up to it, we could go and see that exhibition you mentioned last week." He looked at me intently as I chowed down my food. "You know, the war memorial one. You love those."

"I don't know," I said as evenly as I could, ignoring the small, black gift box which appeared on the bench.

"That's fine, just thought you wanted to see it, maybe we can catch the Rangers game, they're playing the Canucks?"

He slid the box toward me.

I wasn't used to serving up my still-beating heart on a silver platter. But that's exactly what Troy wanted.

"I'm not sure—"

"I get it, no games, no exhibition...what about a quiet night in, just the two of us?"

"Troy..." I looked up, meeting his gaze. That same loose, wayward strand of hair fell over his eyes and I resisted the urge to reach up and rearrange it. "You know I care about you, but we agreed when we started this, no commitments."

He ignored my last comment and opened the small black box. Then he handed it to me.

The velvet lining held a small, diamond-encrusted "A." There must have been at least two carats of diamonds in the intricately designed pendant. Troy never paid for anything less than perfection. I took a deep breath and got up, still clutching the box.

Troy moved in a few months ago, not because we were official but because living in New York was damn expensive.

My parents had left me this apartment but even still, there were utilities, food, other expenses—it all added up.

Without a word, he took both my hands into his, box and all, and led me to the sofa pulling me down beside him.

"This is…it's too much," I said quietly.

"I'm not expecting you to marry me or anything, I just want this…this thing we have to be *us,* you know?"

"I'm sorry. I can't." I shook my head, carefully placing the box back in his hands. "I'm not ready for this."

"Is it because of Alex?"

His name brought fresh pain to the surface. How long did someone wait after the love of their life died? Two years? Ten? Forever? I sighed.

"I know it's stupid; it's been so long." I sighed.

"It isn't stupid, you miss him. There's no timeline for that." He reached over and gently squeezed my shoulder. "I want to be there for you. I want to be that person; you know?"

"I know and I appreciate you, but this isn't something I want, Troy." I closed my eyes and turned from him, damn him and those gorgeous, icy blue eyes. "I can't be that for you."

"You're happy with sex and breakfast?" he asked, without a hint of anger or annoyance.

"I can't give you what you need, Troy."

"What do I need?"

"Someone who treats you better than I do."

"I'm all for being here however you need me, Ace, but…" He paused, looking away for a moment.

"But what?"

"I hear you in your sleep, Ace, every night and when you think I'm sleeping, I hear you cry."

I remained silent. Those were private and intimate moments I never wanted anyone to see.

He pressed his hand over mine. "When I'm not here, it's worse, isn't it?"

When I didn't reply, he shook his head, sucking in a long breath. "Why won't you let me in? You know I'm here. I always have been."

I bit down, grinding my teeth. "Those are my issues."

"You don't need to deal with them alone," he replied, wrapping his arms around me.

"Troy, don't." I pulled back again. "I can't."

He sighed, removing his hands from me. "At least keep this."

I felt his breath on my cheek as he leaned across and fastened the necklace around my neck.

My hand instinctively reached up to touch the pendant feeling a pang of regret shoot through me.

"Maybe one day you'll change your mind and let someone in," he said, disappearing into the bedroom. When he returned a few minutes later he was dressed in dark jeans and a green polo, his bag of clothes slung over his shoulder. He leaned heavily against the door frame, and he nodded when I didn't say anything.

"Where are you going?"

"I can see you need some space; I'll crash at my brother's for a bit."

"You don't have to do that."

"Your place, Ace. I'll see you."

Moments later, my front door closed. I was alone in my apartment, and I felt unsure of my choices for the first time in months. Self-loathing was pointless, so I took my keys and phone and escaped the apartment.

Giorgio waved as I inserted my earbuds and got lost in the beat of the music. I ran for about twenty minutes before coming to a breathless stop just in front of the drinking fountain in Central Park. I had to force myself to stand up straight.

I pressed my palms against my thighs and sucked in the cold winter air.

A few passers-by gave me sympathetic looks, and I politely nodded to them before settling back into a slow jog.

I'd call Troy later and apologize for how our conversation ended. Maybe more than just sex could be on the cards for us, or perhaps I was kidding myself. I shook my head and pressed on. Either way, I didn't want him gone from my life.

The dreams and the lack of sleep were getting to me; I was cracking. Those sorts of things caught up with people; the *mandatory* psych evaluations were painful to say the least but necessary.

I had to run; I had to keep running. I had so much energy to burn. The exercise was cathartic. In school, I joined the kickboxing team and enjoyed fighting. The natural course for me post-graduation was the army. Special Forces found me, and I'd made my way up the ranks within six years.

The same, tangy taste of regret shot through me. I'd been responsible for so many deaths.

As I ran, I shook my head clear of the memories. So much had changed but that pain never did. The guilt ate at me just as freshly now as it did then.

I ground my jaw and pushed through the pain in my side as I sped up toward the fountain. My usual route took me through the snowy gardens and around the lake of Central Park. As usual, a perfectly styled woman sat on a park bench.

She was so out of place.

Last week, I chanced a look backward. That move earned me a collision with a stranger, he too was better than average looking and soon we were in his apartment discussing sports and weather as we warmed up under his five-thousand-dollar duvet.

Not my proudest moment but a girl has needs.

Today, however, as I rounded the lake for the second lap, she stood beside the next water fountain.

If I wasn't about to die of dehydration I would have continued and skipped the fountain altogether. I wasn't in the mood for conversation, nor did I want to talk to someone I didn't know. Increasing my speed slightly and continuing past the bench I slowed around the winding path stopping a few feet away from her.

She offered up a smile as dazzling as her expensive-looking coat and tucked her hands into the pockets. Her green eyes pierced mine. The familiarity in them nearly bowled me over. I couldn't tear my gaze from her.

"We have the answers you're looking for, Ace."

"What are you talking about?"

"If you're serious, we'll see you there." She held her hand out to me.

In it, there was a small, white business card with grey, embossed writing that glistened in the sun.

I accepted the card from her and read it.

Before I could say another word, she was gone.

"Oh, come on!" I shouted to the empty park.

Groaning, I let out an exasperated sigh and looked back down at the card in my hand.

All that was written on it was a date, a place, and a time under a name: *The Agency.*

How cliché.

Stuffing the card into my pocket I took off running down the winding path back to my apartment. I needed a drink, something strong. I sped up and something stirred in the pit of my stomach. What if they did have the answers I was looking for?

CHAPTER THREE

ACE

I squeezed the pink stress ball in my left hand focusing all my energy on the poor, deformed little blob which used to be a cute spotted thing.

I was doing this.

I couldn't believe it.

I must have taken too many hits in Iraq—that was the only explanation. I cracked. That had to be it.

"Ms. Hart, we're ready for you." A young woman who looked to be in her mid-thirties called me over. Her soft smile accentuating pretty features.

Observing her immaculately styled business attire I immediately felt pale in comparison.

Once upon a time, I was like her. The first girl with a new outfit and new shoes, but lately, I'd grown lazy.

Most mornings I'd shower and get dressed: jeans and t-shirt, perhaps a leather jacket and high heel boots to complete the look—if I was feeling adventurous. Then I'd throw my hair into a messy bun or loose ponytail and hide my face behind a pair of black shades. That is, until recently when even that had become a chore. My hair now sat just above my shoulders with the wispy ends framing my face.

I shrugged into my blazer. Despite my lack of trying to look like a lady, today I'd done a good job cleaning myself up—at least I'd thought so earlier. I gave myself a pep talk and walked into the office with a reaffirmed air of confidence.

"Right this way, through that door to your left." Before I could thank her, she was halfway back down the hall.

I marched forward, following her instructions.

The offices I passed were dotted with simple art and plain black desks. Almost all of them were otherwise empty except the last one. That room was filled with about fifteen people dressed in black suits, not unlike my own. I'd added a touch of color in the form of a silky red shirt.

They were paying attention to a man at the front of the room. He looked to be in his early thirties. Something about him stopped me; his dark hair was pulled back into a low bun, and a few strands of hair fell around his face.

As he turned to his left, we locked eyes, and I was forced to an abrupt halt.

There weren't enough words to explain the feeling that shot through me. It was almost as though the earth stopped spinning for an undetectable, unimaginable second and then realigned. Nothing had changed only everything felt utterly new. A sharp breath came out as I watched him.

Just as quickly as it happened, it was over, and I realized I had been staring. I pulled myself back and shook my head rushing away from the office.

Why did that feel so familiar? Why did I feel like this wasn't the first time I saw those eyes?

I chanced a quick look at my watch and sped up. Shit, I was late.

Skidding to a halt, I pushed open the door and prayed this was the correct room. I stopped just short of tripping over my own feet and salvaged whatever dignity I could by straightening up.

I was greeted by a trio. "Thank you for joining us, Ms. Hart."

The woman, whom I recognized from the park smiled first. She looked like a model from a bygone era in her floral blouse and pencil skirt, with her hair pinned in a chignon.

Beside her, there sat a man with dark silver hair who towered above everyone else in the room even when he was seated. His smile was wide and bright and his hands were folded neatly across his lap, next to him was a slightly shorter older gentleman, his grey hair was thinning but he too was handsome.

I shook his hand first and then the others.

He introduced himself as Michael and the other man as Raymond and finally Elena.

"Please sit," Michael said gesturing to the single chair placed in the middle of the room.

I sat and they followed suit. They watched me intently. I could only assume they were waiting for me to speak. Looking back and forth between the three of them, and judging from the way they carried themselves, Michael was the boss. Something about the interaction between Michael and Elena reminded me of my own mother and father—the way they glanced and nodded knowingly.

Elena cleared her throat and gracefully placed a tablet on her lap. Michael gripped a manila folder while Raymond had opted for an old-fashioned approach in the form of a leather-bound office pad and shiny gold pen.

If this interview got any more cliché, I hoped that pen was sharp and pointy so I could stab myself to death or maybe just enough to cause a distraction, so they'd release me from this nineties interrogation.

A slight, almost inaudible laugh came from Elena, as soon as I looked over at her. She regained her composure and glanced down at her tablet. Michael looked bemused—his attention darted between me and her.

I offered a fake smile and as much politeness as I could project.

"Ace Hart, twenty-seven years old, three successful tours in Iraq, and by the end of the third, you were picked up by Special Forces. You served two years with them and were sent home with an honorable discharge when your parents and unit died two years ago," Raymond opened.

Wow. Why did I even bother with the fake pleasantries?

I shifted in my seat trying to blink away my momentarily stunned expression I was sure I was wearing.

"That's right," I answered when I found my tongue.

"Since the death of your parents, you've been withdrawn," Michael continued, taking over from Raymond. He looked at me as he continued flicking through the manila folder. "You left your job at the camping store, you've been distanced from your relationship with Troy Johnson and you stopped attending your mandatory psych evaluations."

"It's been a difficult time." I cleared my throat. How the hell did they know I quit? I literally handed in my two weeks" notice, two days ago.

"Further to that, you've been quite busy with your late-night covert ops. Suffice it to say, you're now in a position that makes you both valuable and a liability."

I felt my cheeks heat with anger.

"You've stepped on some very important toes, Ms. Hart. And while we're quite forgiving, other parties may not be."

He closed the folder and looked across at me.

The "Classified" stamp plastered across the pages caught my attention as he flicked through them. They were military documents. Whoever they were, they had access to government sealed records. They weren't CIA, they weren't NSA either which told me they were something else, something more.

I inched forward on my chair, wetting my lips.

He looked at me for a moment, turning another page and stopped. Then he closed the folder and tossed it to the ground.

My eyes followed the flowing paper as it spilled out across the floor much like my life would if I got to that pen.

"You exhibited questionable behavior after your unit was killed."

"I needed to find out why they died—"

"The reasoning for your work doesn't interest me, Ms. Hart," Raymond cut me off. "The only thing I'm interested in, is the why? Why are you doing this alone?"

"Because I don't trust anyone."

He gave me a pointed look.

"I shouldn't have proceeded with the mission," I said truthfully. "That's on me. I should have aborted. Their deaths are on me, and it's on me now to find out why they were killed."

"Whatever happened was not your fault Ms. Hart," he said firmly.

My eyes snapped up to his.

"We can help you find your answers."

I looked between Raymond, Elena and Michael. Each member of this meeting looked sincere. I didn't know why I felt an urge to listen to them, but I did.

When I shifted in my chair and looked back at Raymond, he gave me a knowing look.

"I Don't care about your record; I know you weren't to blame for what happened to your team." He paused for a moment. "I know you've been blaming yourself."

That was a part of my life I never wanted to talk about again. I wet my lips, aware of the growing dryness.

"Regardless of your past, you are what the Agency needs." He pointed to the papers on the floor. "I've seen enough to know that what's in there is just some politician's way of saying he's afraid of what he cannot control. You did a great service to your country serving three times."

I remained silent.

"We want to utilize your skillset and in turn help you find the answers you seek."

This time I cleared my throat, scratching the back of my neck. "I'm sorry; I'm not sure what you're talking about. There are countless other soldiers who'd be ready to sign on, countless more probably better than me."

"We're not talking about your combat skills," Elena said.

When I didn't reply, she offered me the warmest smile and then suddenly I heard her speak, but not aloud and not in front of the others, she was *in my head*.

"You're like me and so few others my dear. We're known as Sensitives, you're not alone in this."

I jerked backward in my chair, my eyes darted from one face to the next.

"There are many wonderful gifts our world can offer. You just need to embrace them," Michael spoke.

I slowly turned my face to him. "How did she do that?"

"You must have thought you were losing your mind, after the ambush in Iraq?" His eyes found mine, boring into my soul, literally because I felt him in there poking and prodding at my feelings and memories. I tried to shake him, and the feeling was gone. I was me again, alone in my body.

He gave me a sympathetic smile before continuing. "What you did to those men, after they killed your team, no one holds it against you. Not many people would have survived what they did to you."

Looking down at my hands I closed my eyes, gathering my thoughts for a moment. I'd never spoken about that to anyone. The horrors that chased me in my sleep now, were my secret.

109

"You did what you had to—self-preservation, Ms. Hart."

I stared at them dumbfounded while they only looked amused.

"How did you—"

"You're part of an ancient line of exceptional people who have abilities beyond what the human mind can perceive, beyond what they can even imagine to be real."

"I'm not crazy." I whispered.

Elena shook her head, sympathy lacing her gentle movement.

Slowly, Michael stood up and handed me Elena's tablet, I wasn't sure what I was looking at so I looked up at him instead.

"We've been tracking you since you were born—your mother was one of us. Actually, her mother was one of the founding members of this Agency." Michael explained as he offered up file after file, until he stopped at a picture of my parents.

"Your mother was assigned to another like her and they fell in love which is extremely dangerous in this line of work and when you were born, the Collectors came after you."

My tongue grew heavy. "Collectors?"

Michael nodded, a sad smile found me. "Sensitives who kill others like them for their abilities."

"My parents were killed for their abilities?"

This time Elena spoke. "When they came for you, we fought and won, they didn't try again—"

"Until two years ago," I finished, knowing exactly where this was going.

Michael nodded with a weak smile. "You are important to us."

"To Grimes."

"He was just one."

I released a long breath. "That's why my parents died, because of me? That's why Corporal Westen was killed, my entire platoon?"

"I know this is a lot to take in," Elena said gently.

"No, this isn't a lot to take in," I ground out. "This is a fucking joke."

"Ms. Hart," Raymond's tone was filled with warning.

I shot to my feet. "I'm not interested, whatever this is, whoever you are. I don't want any part of it."

"You want answers," Michael reminded me.

"Not like this."

Every intuitive feeling I'd ever had, every prophetic dream I'd dreamt, every time I somehow survived when no one else should have, was all because of this thing my parents were killed for.

A knot formed deep within my chest and my heart ached, after so many months of being angry and bitter, I felt the sadness and it overwhelmed me.

"Was my family murdered?"

"We believe so."

"Why?"

"They needed you but couldn't get to you with your parents alive. Now you're out in the open, and we've done the best job we could in protecting you from afar, but now it's time to get you on board."

"Why am I important?"

"That is something we can only explain in time."

I scoffed, shaking my head. "Sounds like a load of BS to me."

"Ms. Hart," Elena said gently.

"No, I've heard enough. Thank you for your time, but this was a mistake."

"Please." Michael stepped toward me. "You will have all the answers, but we must be tactical about this. Please understand, we've gone to great lengths to keep you safe."

"It was you, the other night at the park?"

"Not me personally," he said. "But one of our agents, yes."

I didn't get a good look at him, but damn, his moves were unlike anything I'd ever seen.

The thing that stuck out the most was the feeling that washed over me. I'd gone from full-blown panic attack to complete calm. I didn't question it at the time, not until I got home and tossed my blood-stained clothes did I realize I could have died, and I should have been more disturbed by that. It was the same feeling I had just before when I saw the man in the board room who gave me the weird earth-slowing moment.

"Tell me one thing," I said, shooting Raymond a look.

"What might that be?"

"What am I?"

To that, he smiled and launched into a long and detailed explanation about the existence of all the different Sensitives and what they could do. He explained that there were people who could get into your mind and speak with you there, others could get into your heart forcing you to remember and feel whatever they wanted you to feel, some could make you feel physical pain, while others could make you relive your nightmares. Some could even read your thoughts and steal them without you ever realizing they were there. Then there were the more attuned class, the Trackers and Watchers. They guarded high up officials, protected the Director, and even the President of the United States.

"But you." He said pausing and looking at me intently. "You can do all of these things; you're a Divine Sensitive, that is what you are."

My heart pounded so loudly in my chest I thought it would crack my ribs. I sat back down quietly looking at Michael. Neither he, nor anyone else broke the silence, hundreds of thoughts rattled around in my skull but the one thing that kept repeating was what he'd called me. *A Divine Sensitive.* Could it just have been a coincidence that Alex had said something similar to me? No. I didn't believe in coincidence.

"It's important you come on board as soon as possible. I understand this is a lot to take in, take your time, but not too much time." Raymond added after a long silence on my part.

"I'm not ready to agree to anything yet."

"That's understandable. Take the night. We'll have one of our agents escort you home."

"Are there others like this agency?"

Raymond smiled. "We're just one of thirteen around the world. Each one has men and women who've dedicated their lives to protecting the world and the people in it."

Twelve other Agencies?

My mind reeled.

"Are they all run by the same people?" I asked, looking to Raymond for the answers.

This time he shook his head. "Every Agency has their own Director. But they all answer to the head of their country."

Michael stood, gesturing to the door. "Agent Lazarev will escort you home."

I knotted my brows. "Agent Lazarev?"

"He's the gentleman you saw earlier."

"You two will be assigned as partners should you choose to work for us," Raymond said.

"I'm not agreeing to anything, least of all working arrangements. I'm not ready for that," I said.

"You would help to take down the people who killed your family, the same people who terrorize others like us every day. If you still want to know more in the morning, we'll talk," Michael said, definitively ending that conversation.

"Fine."

Elena stood and nodded at the door. "Here comes Agent Lazarev, perfect timing."

I pulled my shoulders back, not that I thought it would make any difference now, as he'd already seen me make a fool of myself.

But he had stopped, too; he was looking at me the same way I was looking at him. Our eyes connected and I held my breath waiting for the same earth stopping feeling to wash over me, but nothing happened. As he neared me I noticed the intoxicating aroma surrounding him, he smelled like cologne and gunpowder and I was losing my mind to be thinking about how good he smelled.

"Nice to meet you," he said with a smile.

I tore my gaze away without saying anything.

He handed Elena something, and when he spoke to her, I perked up listening to his voice. He had a faint Russian accent.

"I trust there won't be a repeat of Operation Lullaby?" Raymond spoke quietly to Agent Lazarev.

Operation Lullaby? I kept my eyes averted and my ears perked.

"No, Sir," Agent Lazarev replied, standing tall.

A heavy, forced tension now blanketed the room. His eyes swung to me, a moment of hesitation passed across his features, and as soon as I'd seen it, it was gone. He turned his attention back to Raymond.

"Good," he replied. "Now if you'd please escort Ms. Hart home, we'll continue tomorrow."

"Of course." Agent Lazarev nodded, turning to me with a half-smile.

I kept my expression neutral.

He was tall, immaculately presented, dressed in what had to be a tailored suit that fit his body like a glove. He was hands down the most beautiful person I had ever met.

Before I could even let out the breath I was holding, he turned his attention back to me, his lips quirked up into a subtle smile.

Prior to Iraq and my "make-under" I had an impeccable record when it came to talking to cute guys and much to my dismay my old ways did not kick in and save me from a world of embarrassment.

Instead I stood with my sweaty hands clenched at my side, gaping at him like a horny teenager at prom.

His lip curled up in an almost amused smirk. When I got my higher functioning back I reached for my bag, and slung it over my shoulder.

"I'll bring Ms. Hart back here, tomorrow morning." His voice was melodic and commanding all at once.

"It's settled," Michael chimed in.

"We'll see you tomorrow and you can give us your answer."

With the meeting concluded, we headed toward the exit, into the underground parking lot where I'd left my car.

"That was presumptuous of you," I said.

"What was?" he asked without looking at me.

"Assuming I'm coming back here."

"Assuming you want answers for the deaths of those you love isn't a far reach."

"No, it isn't. But what makes you think I haven't found leads during my own recon?"

"You would acted on them by now."

I closed my mouth and followed him down.

"Agent Lazarev?"

He walked ahead, turning his head slightly to meet my eyes. "Illarion is fine."

"What Sense did you evolve in?"

He cast me a sideways glance just as we reached my car. "Feelings."

Of course, he did.

A smile flitted across his face briefly before his serious expression was back in full form, sensing my mood shift. I unlocked the car with a sigh and climbed in. Illarion stood beside me, one arm resting on the roof while he leaned down.

"I don't have any control of these powers," I said.

"It will come in time. What you have is rare and when you can control it, very powerful."

"That's why they want me?"

He nodded, solemnly pulling the door open further and letting me slip inside. "Yes, because you can be used as a powerful weapon."

My head swam. They could do so many bad things if they got to me, how could I stop them? Would I even be able to? Would I be strong enough? Would I succumb to them? I caught myself stopping the chain of thoughts mid-way, feeling self-conscious.

"I won't let that happen," he said firmly, his dark eyes narrowing.

Somehow with those few words almost everything I was worrying about seemed to fade away. It was still there but tucked far away enough that it wasn't an immediate worry to me. *Interesting.*

"You need some rest." He gently nudged the door shut. "I'll see you in the morning."

♥

Illarion was waiting outside at seven sharp. I couldn't believe I was going through with this.

He stepped around to my side of the car and pulled the door open handing me a coffee.

I sat and pulled my sunglasses on, taking a drink of the coffee.

When Illarion was back in the car, I turned to face him. "I thought about what you said."

"And?"

"I'm not the person you think I am."

"Why do you say that?"

"I'm done with this life. I don't want to be part of another team; I don't want to run missions and ops. I want to close this chapter of my life."

"You want answers. You want to know what happened to your team. We can help you."

"I don't want your help."

"How many answers have you gotten so far?" he tested. "Have you been able find the classified documents we have on you and your team?"

I ground my jaw.

"You need us, just as much as we need you."

"I've heard enough." I pushed the door open.

"You've tormented yourself for two years, swearing that you would do whatever it takes to get justice for Alex and the rest of your unit." He said making me turn in my seat.

"You should consider your next words wisely, Illarion."

"I know what it's like, Ace. To have something like that over you. I also know how consuming it can be."

"I'm sure you do."

"Just hear them out, see what they can do for you. If you don't see any benefit, leave."

"Fine," I shot back, closing the door.

♥

"So, Ms. Hart, have you made a decision?" Raymond asked.

I looked across at Illarion. He had his hands folded neatly behind his back and he stood tall waiting for my answer.

I sighed. "I have, sir, I accept your offer to join the Agency."

A broad smile formed on Raymond's face. "Welcome to the Agency, Agent Hart."

Agent Hart. God. Here we go again.

"Please sit." He said to us both.

Illarion took a seat beside me at the end of the table, facing Raymond.

He slid two files our way, one for each of us. A brief glance through the documents told me it was our mission brief, including our working arrangements and codenames. "Specter?"

Illarion lowered his gaze, "We thought it was appropriate."

"How so?" I turned my attention back to Raymond.

"I'm sure Agent Lazarev will be more than happy to explain later."

"Of course."

"Now these are the missions you've been tasked to over the next three weeks. Some of these will include travel. I understand this won't be a problem?"

Shaking my head, I flicked through the brief. "No problem at all, Sir."

"Good," he said. "Now Agents, I'd suggest you get some rest and prepare for your week."

Illarion stood and I followed. "Thank you, sir."

I followed him out. Once we were outside in the cool air, I let myself relax. The mission was simple enough, but the timing and covers we'd been given were a little out of my depth.

"How do you feel, Agent Hart?" Illarion asked softly, as we walked down the steps and out to the sidewalk.

"I'll let you know."

"You've been a soldier for a long time, now you're a soldier undercover. It's different but you'll pick it up."

"You seem to have a lot of confidence in me, Agent Lazarev."

"I was part of the offshore team that watched you in Iraq. I have no doubt you're capable."

I wet my lips. "Assuming you remember the part where I let my squad die."

"You didn't let them die," he shot, without looking at me, and hailing a cab.

♥

"So, you have to fly out again?" Troy asked, standing in the kitchen wearing nothing but a low hanging pair of pajama pants.

We'd made up for the most part. He moved back in but the tension was still there.

"You know it's part of the job,"

This was the third week on the job with the Agency, which meant my cover to Troy was a sparkly new corporate job. I was a marketing assistant to a startup tech firm.

Troy looked across at me when I remained quiet.

"What do you guys do on the West Coast so much?"

"Mostly help the tech guys pitch their products to clients, you know, make it more palatable for the sales guys." When he didn't reply, I looked back down at my plate of toast and cream cheese. I took another bite, taking care not to drop crumbs on my new silk blouse.

"They send you away every few days," he muttered. "How can they expect a work-life balance?"

"I knew that was part of the deal."

"And you're cool with that?"

"I wasn't aware that I needed to consult you about my working arrangements."

His mouth twitched into a straight, taut line and immediately I felt like an ass.

"I don't expect you to consult me, Ace. But I thought that since we decided to try and live together again, you would have considered us."

Sucking in a slow, calculated breath, I stopped what I was doing and faced him. "There is no *us*, Troy. Please stop pushing."

He didn't say a word, but the hurt on his face was a punch in the gut. *God.* I ran my fingers through my hair.

"I'm sorry," I said, exhaling. "It's just hard having someone else in my life, you know? And now this job, my new boss is a hardass, it's tough. I shouldn't have snapped like that."

"Yeah, it's fine." He turned away, grabbing a slice of toast for himself. "I don't want you to feel suffocated by me, but I want this to be a thing. I want to be your thing, you know. Someone you can talk to and rely on."

He turned to move, and I dropped my fork and quickly stepped around the counter, stopping him from leaving.

"Hey, I'm sorry."

"Don't be. I get it."

"I am, and I was out of line. Can we try this again?"

"Which part?"

"The part where I'm not a constant bitch to you. When I come back can we hang out?"

"You're not a constant bitch. You're guarded and I can see it for what it is. I don't want to suffocate you."

"You're not suffocating me. There are just too many skeletons in my closet. It's literally like a horror movie in there."

"Everyone has skeletons, and secrets, Ace," he added, cupping my cheek and tipping my face up to his.

When I closed my eyes against his touch, he dropped his other hand to my hip and tugged me closer.

I lowered my forehead to his chest and expelled a long breath, wrapping my arms around his waist. "I don't want to hurt you, Troy. You're important to me."

"I get it," he said softly. "We won't talk about the things you're hiding from. I'll see you when you get home."

"Yes, you will, and then we're going to have a normal night in. I promise."

He kissed the top of my head and when I pulled back to look up at him, he pressed a soft kiss to my lips and left to get changed for work.

I finished the rest of my toast in silence, eager to get back to the Agency. I needed some familiarity in my life, some normalcy. Leaving the army was hard and being confined to a *normal* life was about as painful as getting shot. As I swallowed the last bite of my breakfast, I stuffed everything into the sink and started packing my overnight bag.

Just like clockwork, eleven came around and a knock on the door alerted me to the fact that the Agency's drivers were as skilled as the agents themselves in the art of stealth.

I pulled the door open and let him come in. He had the same, disinterested look on his face. I left him at the door to continue packing.

"Nice to see you, Con."

Con was one of the Agency's finest, he was a driver and a bodyguard. Luckily for me, he was also quite the brooding older uncle type. He reminded me of my dad. Serious with a soft spot for my jokes. I missed my parents infinitely.

"You should take more care, Agent," he said firmly.

Smirking, I grabbed another towel and stuffed it into my bag. "Yeah, so you've said."

"You didn't even check your door." He stood with his arms behind his back, looking at the street below.

I slung my bag over my shoulder, took a final sip of my coffee and turned back to him. "You know I don't need to check. I can tell who it is."

"What if they're using a cloak or shield?"

I pondered his question for a moment as he guided me outside and locked up behind me. I'd gotten better at using my abilities for things like recognizing familiar people and whether they were Sensitives or not.

"Well then, I'm screwed, aren't I?"

He wasn't impressed with my answer, and I could have sworn he'd scoffed as we entered the elevator.

"You never know when someone using a shield will try to infiltrate," he said. "You need to take more care and you need to ensure you take your safety seriously."

"Fine," I conceded. "I will check the door, and make sure no one is using a cloak or shield."

He nodded, as professionally as they were all trained to do. "One day it might even save your life."

"Whatever you say."

He threw me a sideways glance and shook his head.

I slipped out as soon as the elevator doors opened, much to Con's dismay. I felt the irritation radiating from him as he followed behind until we both reached the limo.

"You know, since we're in the business of espionage, you'd think that we'd have a more inconspicuous vehicle."

"Please get in the car," he muttered, taking my bag from me.

Grinning, I slipped inside, slamming the door shut. I wondered how much longer before he quit as my driver.

As soon as he was seated, he accelerated down the street ignoring my teasing. I didn't have any issues with him. It was all good fun. Though I doubted he felt the same.

"Have a safe trip, Agent," he said as we pulled into the same, familiar underground Agency parking lot.

I nodded with a smile. "Thanks, Con, see you next week."

"Yes, you will, unfortunately." He scoffed. But I saw the smallest hint of a smile.

"Ah, you'll miss me."

"Be safe." He nodded once more; this time his voice was void of the previous disinterested tone.

I waved him off with a smile and made my way through the main entrance of the parking lot and circled the block toward the front of the building.

We hadn't found all the answers I was looking for yet but I had seen enough to know that Illarion wasn't bluffing when he said that the Agency could help me. I worked the smaller jobs and operations they gave us, and I stopped grilling him every day.

The working relationship was pleasant. I even felt myself warming up to him. It was familiar, kind of like the banter Alex and I shared.

Up ahead I spotted Illarion. The same familiar sensation of butter-flies in my stomach flurried to life and then stopped abruptly when I saw that he wasn't alone.

A tall, blonde woman in a sleek business skirt and blazer was hold-ing his attention. Every few seconds or so, she'd press her hand to his bicep and then laugh. As I neared them, he stopped and turned his attention to me.

I froze, I was still far away enough to be out of his line of sight but he was looking right at me. Before I looked like a tool, I walked again and noticed he'd stepped away from the blonde. I carried my bag to the main steps of the building where Illarion was waiting with his own duffel bag.

"Everything alright?" he asked, stepping down a few steps to meet me.

As usual, his dark hair was pulled back in a ponytail and a few, uncooperative strands of hair fell over his eyes touching the white col-lar of his tailored shirt. A black pinstriped suit jacket hugged his torso with such care I only imagined how soft the fabric was against his skin. I needed to stop thinking about him like that. I cleared my throat and turned from him.

I dropped the bag at my feet. "Fine, you?"

"Fine," he replied dryly. "Ace, this is Donna." He introduced us when she took the steps down to meet us.

She was even more stunning up close. I ground my molars and shook her hand.

"So nice to meet you but I have to run, I'm so sorry," she said with a big smile. "See you next Tuesday, do not forget our date, I'm not rescheduling again." She said to Illarion before running off.

I hated that my mind hung on what she said.

"Looking forward to it," he said.

Somehow, I didn't get that vibe, but I didn't push it. I dropped the conversation and turned my attention to the outside world.

"You seem distracted today," he stated softly, nodding down at my bag. "Sure everything's okay?"

I followed his gaze and spotted the half-in-half-out embarrassing display of my underwear.

"Oh my God."

He shielded a smirk, kneeling to help me zip up the overflowing bag.

"What's going on?"

I shook my head, absolutely mortified, annoyed and jealous.

"Ace?" His hand closed over mine which was still furiously attempting to work the zipper.

"Nothing," I lied, snatching my hand back.

Nothing aside from the fact that I'd just paraded my Victoria's Secret collection to half of midtown New York and that I was jealous of a super-hot, super-perfect blonde woman.

"You can't be that mortified about your underwear hanging out of your bag," he said softly. "What's going on? Are you stressed about the trip?"

"No, not at all," I said, happy to change the topic. I got to my feet, turning my face away from him.

"Anything you want to talk about? Is it your boyfriend?"

I breathed in deeply. "We're not having this conversation, Illarion."

"Just thought you wanted to talk about it, you seem distracted."

"I appreciate it. But it's not Troy and I'm not distracted. Doubt your girlfriend would want you talking to me about that sort of thing anyway."

He turned to me about to say something but the horn from the driver pulling up to the curb stopped him.

I took my duffle bag and made my way down the stairs to the waiting sedan.

Okay, Ace. It's time to shine.

CHAPTER FOUR

ACE

Illarion and I stepped through the revolving doors at the Ritz, arm in arm nodding at the doorman who came to greet us. This was our first undercover mission together. Elena had briefed us before we left—all the usual information provided. Aliases, rendezvous points, guidelines.

I gripped his arm and focused on taking deep, calculated breaths. *Husband and wife.* My stomach twisted on itself with each step. Somehow, he slipped into this role so much easier than me. He turned his head toward me and gave me a warm, sympathetic smile. "You're doing great, darling."

I smiled reading between the lines. "Thank you, sweetheart."

He led me through the foyer where we were stopped by a man in a sharp three-piece suit.

In my ear, Raymond spoke calmly, "Keep focused, Specter."

Nodding at his reminder, we both greeted the man and responded to Raymond. He was the only board member who was still actively involved in field work, so coupling his experience and Illarion's skill, we were pretty much unstoppable. I straightened in Illarion's arm; mentally turning my attention to the man we were meeting.

"Mr. and Mrs. Xavier," he called, smiling. He offered his hand to me and then to Illarion.

"It's a pleasure Mr. Fox," Illarion said with an English accent. I almost stumbled over my own words—he was so good and so sexy.

Christ almighty, I had to rein it in. The fact that Illarion could feel what I was feeling didn't elude me.

The man smiled back and returned his attention to me. "The pleasure is all mine, I'm sure."

Stepping forward with the most innocent smile I could I leaned into Illarion.

"This is my wife, Helen." Illarion softly ran his hand across my lower back. I bit my lip, genuine surprise spreading through me.

"You two are a stunning couple," Fox said turning his attention to me. "You are obviously the better half."

I chuckled.

Illarion's moods were contradicting. Inside he was all but vibrating with disgust at Fox, yet on the surface he remained completely placid.

Illarion's eyes swept over me before he looked back at Fox. "She makes me a better man."

Shifting my butt into gear, I playfully nudged him in the side and turned to Fox. "He always says that; it's quite the opposite I assure you."

"Oh, we have ourselves a southern belle?" he said to Illarion. "You're one lucky man."

"I know."

Fox grinned wildly before gesturing for both of us to follow him.

I let out the nervous breath I was holding and gripped the fabric around Illarion's arm tighter. A soft, gentle touch drew my eyes up to his as we walked.

"Just breathe."

His voice was soothing in my head.

"I don't know what's wrong with me."

He smiled at me and then at Fox. "*You're doing fine, Ace, just follow my lead.*"

Having him beside me, able to communicate thanks to our connection was literally my lifeline right now. I wasn't able to hold it for long and I wasn't able to initiate it myself.

"We're right through here, Mr. Xavier." Fox gestured to a frosted set of doors bringing my attention back to the mission.

"I'll wait out here for you, sweetheart." I pulled my arm free, motioning for the two men to go on.

As Illarion left and Fox closed the door, I let out the breath I'd been holding and slowly made my way over to the sofa.

As I sat down, I swept my gaze across the room memorizing the locations of all the cameras in my line of sight. When I was sure I was clear, I pulled out my cell phone and locked on to the internal security. *Got you.*

The whole grid came to life on my screen showing me where everyone was positioned and what they were up to. On the fifth floor, I spotted our target. A large, black briefcase. My heart thundered in my chest. I always got such a rush when I was out in the field, the adrenaline coursed through me. It was different to being out in Iraq, but the anticipation was always exciting. I brushed my hand across my left ear leaning into it gently, hiding my face from the camera.

"Arrow, are you reading this?"

Raymond replied, "Reading you, Specter, I need two minutes to copy the files. Stand by."

I focused my attention on the guards coming and going from the small room. As long as no one made their way inside, no one would ever see me remote accessing the files right under their noses.

Moments later, Illarion and Fox stepped out of the room, shaking hands with a smile.

"Specter, we need more time. Keep them busy."

We'd planned and gone over this mission a dozen times; we'd timed it. Illarion should have been in there for another two minutes at least. Shit. I kept my expression neutral and pondered the best way to stall.

"Your husband is quite the businessman, Mrs. Xavier," Fox said with a grin.

"Oh, I know." I smiled, stepping toward the two men. "Did you boys come to an agreement?"

"Oh yes," Fox replied, a wild grin on his face. "Mr. Xavier will be a brilliant investment in the firm."

I smiled, basking in a wife's boastful pride.

Illarion nodded to my cell with a smile. "Are we on for lunch with the Joneses?"

"Absolutely. They're just running a little late. I thought maybe we could do a little shopping on the way."

Illarion smiled and looked to Fox. "You know how it is. Have to keep the wife happy."

Fox laughed a hearty laugh, clapping Illarion on the back. "Ah yes, I certainly do, but with a wife as lovely as yours I imagine it's a treat to shower her in all the finer things."

"Oh, I'm the lucky one to have a husband who likes to sit around and watch me try on shoes all day long." I smiled linking my arm through Illarion's.

Fox led us down the hall to the elevator and I purposely took my time. Before we stepped in, I turned to Fox, the wheels turning in my head, which topic might best engage him. "You know, we'd love to have you and your wife over for dinner one evening, wouldn't that be lovely, sweetheart?"

Illarion nodded. "Absolutely, let us sort out the business first and we'll make a date. Deal?"

Fox grinned. "It would be a pleasure."

I was about to begin questioning him with regards to his wife's favorite dishes when Raymond spoke up in my ear again. "Got it, Specter. Get out of there."

I nodded to Fox and gently squeezed Illarion's arm. "It's settled then. We should let Mr. Fox get back to work now. I've taken enough of his time."

"Not at all."

Illarion smiled at me and then shook Fox's hand again. "Where would I be without her?"

Fox laughed loudly and motioned to the elevator, once we stepped inside and said our goodbyes, he pushed the button to the ground floor.

When the doors closed, Illarion and I remained in character, completely immersed in our cover, but inside he was reeling. Whatever happened behind those closed doors had him on edge, he wasn't happy, and it didn't take much digging to figure out what it was about.

Fox wasn't a good man. The seedy grin was just the tip of the iceberg. Whatever he said to Illarion made him livid.

I did what I could. I stepped closer to him, aware that the cameras in the elevator were getting reviewed right now. Men like Fox didn't become billionaires dealing in clean business, nor did they survive on top without being suspicious of everyone. I wrapped my arm around his waist, nuzzling closer to him, willing him to calm down. His body stiffened at my touch and then slowly his muscles relaxed.

"I'm sorry."

"Forget him," I replied.

His eyes remained fixed on the wall dead ahead.

"He's not worth it, Illarion."

His arm fell to my waist pulling me against him.

He bowed his head, shielding his face and mine from the camera above us in the elevator. A steely gaze met me and something about the way his dark eyes looked, hit me hard. His expressive lips parted letting out the weakest sigh like something inside him was desperately trying to break free.

This felt like a lot more than acting on our part.

"Forget him, he isn't worth it," I repeated. This time with a lot more emphasis.

I saw the rage pulsing through him. I didn't need to have any kind of supernatural ability to know that.

Before he could say anything more, the doors opened to a bustling foyer. I smiled, firmly taking his hand in mine, and leading him out.

If I hadn't seen the pain in his eyes moments ago, I wouldn't have believed it was there. Because he was the same, cheerful Mr. Xavier who stepped into the elevator just minutes ago.

As soon as his mask slipped into place, mine did too. We smiled and waved at the doorman and left the same way we came. We got into the waiting limo which was cleverly being driven by Raymond who was also keeping tabs on us through the Agency's state-of-the-art surveillance equipment.

Before we broke cover, Raymond tossed a small black device into the back seat which Illarion took and swept over me first and then himself. When he was certain we hadn't been bugged, he turned from me and muttered something in Russian under his breath.

I hadn't realized I'd been holding my breath until it came out in a low, shaky whisper.

"I'm sorry," he said, turning to me.

"Mind telling me what happened back there?" Raymond called from the front.

Good question, I wanted to know what happened to our timing. Illarion had five minutes with Fox, by my count he was out in less than two.

"Not now," Illarion warned.

131

I toyed with the idea of comforting him, but we weren't under cover anymore, he wasn't my husband and I wasn't his wife. We were nothing more than partners and he didn't have to explain anything to me.

I bit down on my lip and drew my attention to the world outside my window.

Raymond pulled the limo into the underground carpark reserved for the Agency, and I watched as Illarion scooped up my bags and stormed toward the doors.

What the hell was with the attitude?

Raymond looked like he was about to say something but at the last minute he closed his mouth.

A frown tugged on my lips but I followed them into the elevator which suddenly seemed cramped. Illarion was every bit as intimidating when he was speaking as he was when he was silent. When the doors opened, I followed behind them like a student getting sent to the head-master's office.

Illarion pushed his way into a meeting which was obviously not meant to be interrupted. Elena and Michael got to their feet, mouths gaping.

"This isn't going to work," he said before anyone else had a chance to speak. "I can't work like this with her."

My mouth dropped. "I'm sorry, what—"

"Please excuse us for a moment." She spoke softly before throwing a steely-eyed look at Illarion.

Elena smiled apologetically to the suits sitting across from them. Before I could protest, I was shoved out of the room, the door almost hitting me on the way out.

Shaking my head in pure disbelief, I stalked past Raymond unable to contain my anger.

If I stayed, I'd say and do something stupid. So, I found myself walking down the corridor, taking the stairs rather than the elevator. I must have spent a good thirty minutes navigating the seven flights, questioning the meaning of my life and my current situation.

As I rounded the corner coming out at the fire escape, I literally ran into Illarion.

"Can we talk?" he asked.

"Do I have a choice?"

"No."

Exasperated, I threw my hands up and followed him.

Great. Back up the stairs.

When the agony of walking an equivalent of the Empire State settled into my jelly legs and the awkward silence wore off, we reached the top landing and I was so happy to see that it was an open rooftop.

My lungs sucked in the cool New York breeze.

"I didn't mean for you to see that. It was wrong of me, and I'm sorry." His apology startled me.

"That's what you're sorry about?"

"And for what I said."

"Unbelievable," I muttered, pissed at how he managed to make me feel so small.

He stood with his eyes firmly glued to mine. "I wanted to explain myself."

"Good because I'm starting to get a real urge to test your combat skills."

His lip curved up into a smile. "You misunderstand."

"You're going to have to explain it to me then."

Slowly, tentatively he took a few steps forward. His hand grazed my cheek, tucking a strand of hair behind my ear. I froze.

As quickly as the sensation found me, it was gone and I found myself aching for it, for his touch. I was stricken, what the hell just happened? We weren't in character anymore; he wasn't playing a part.

It was nothing, just a friendly gesture. Get it together. I swallowed hard and evened my breathing out.

"When I said this wasn't going to work, I didn't mean because I couldn't work with you, and certainly not for the reasons you think."

Letting him talk it out, I remained silent.

His dark, lashes lowered as he inhaled a sharp breath. "Fox riled me up. It was inappropriate…I shouldn't have let my feelings get in the way."

I ignored almost everything else he said at that point. Is that why he broke our timing and got out before we got what we needed?

He leaned against the railing as the wind picked up his hair, blowing it around his face, completely consuming me.

"Fox said something to me which I'm sure in his world is acceptable to say about a man's wife, but to me it wasn't," He began. "I'm sorry for how I reacted."

Words failed me. I stood in silence, listening.

"When I said what I did, I meant that it was hard suddenly having these feelings and another person to…" He exhaled. "I'm used to working alone, I have been for a while."

"I know all about that." Having someone invade a space you'd kept private for so long was hard.

Was that how he felt about me? That I was invading his space?

"It won't happen again," he said. "I enjoy working with you. I don't want to jeopardize that."

"I appreciate your apology." I didn't know what else to say.

He smiled and motioned for me to follow. "Let's go over what happens next."

CHAPTER FIVE

ACE

The morning came swiftly, much to my relief. Weird dreams kept waking me up throughout the night, most of which were of my own death, again. Some were gruesome, some were just plain impossible and the one constant which kept twisting through the images was Illarion. It was no longer just Alex making an appearance now.

His face was always there, solemn and panicked and the one dream which kept repeating was where I was trapped, but Illarion never came to me. The same feelings I felt in the parking lot the first night we met, when he walked me to my car, they flitted through my head almost like déjà vu. His panic, sadness and hopelessness radiated through me so intensely I thought my heart was going to explode. Were these my feelings or his? I couldn't tell the difference since...well since I first laid eyes on him.

At the same time I started feeling all of this, I asked Troy to move out definitively. He couldn't stay over. I wouldn't keep leading him on.

I broke his heart and I couldn't even tell him why because even I didn't understand it.

Frustrated, I kicked the covers off and lay in bed looking up at the ceiling. I wondered whether Illarion was still below keeping watch. I imagined how his dark eyes looked in the dim lighting of the garage and how his hair fell in such a way that it looked as if it were styled like that.

Deciding that I was wasting time *imagining* him when I could see the real thing, I dragged myself out of bed.

After a quick shower, I dried off and dressed and grabbed a jacket before heading out the door.

Expectantly, I found Illarion sitting in his car which was parked just beside mine, though the Hummer towered over my tiny Audi.

Giving him a quick smile, I climbed into the truck. The drive was long and slow but seeing him in person was way better.

Noticing we were driving in a different direction; I glanced over at him. "We're not going back to the Agency?"

"We're going to visit the Director."

"And we're staying there?" I asked. Looking across at the back seat, loaded with what looked like ten days' worth of supplies.

"No, we're just visiting."

"Oh."

After that, the rest of the drive was silent. Despite that, my head was not quiet. My dreams bothered me and the strong feelings associated with them felt way too real to shake. Why would I have dreamt that or more importantly why did I *keep* dreaming it?

"We're here," he announced pulling up to a gate blocking off a large, white house surrounded by huge oak trees.

The gravel driveway continued past the gate and just as soon as Illarion spoke into the intercom the gate opened for us and we passed through. I caught a glimpse of what looked like piles of rocks, stacked neatly atop each other in perfect formation. From what I could see, there were markings all over them. A look at Illarion told me not to ask.

I looked behind us and watched the gates close.

Illarion pulled the car off to the right and parked it beside another. He gave me a quick smile and motioned for me to follow him down the path, past a large row of oak trees.

We stopped just outside the front door and Illarion turned to face me, he pressed a hand to my arm, turning me toward him.

"Michael and Elena are here." He looked like he wanted to say more, and finally, after a few edgy moments, he did. "The Director likes to test new agents. He can delve into your thoughts. Keep them safe."

Was the Director more powerful than Michael and Elena?

"Should I be worried?"

He released my arm. "I'll be right there with you."

"Okay. That's not really answering my question."

Illarion opened his mouth then promptly closed it.

"Keep your thoughts safe," he repeated before walking up to the door.

Michael greeted us and led us through the house. We walked down hallway after hallway until I lost count. This was the biggest mansion I'd ever seen. The government obviously paid well.

"They're waiting for us upstairs," he explained as we took another turn and reached a staircase.

Once we'd reached the top of the stairs, we hooked a left and headed toward an outdoor room where we were met by Michael.

"Illarion, should I be worried?" I asked again, so Michael couldn't hear.

Before Illarion could answer, footsteps sounded behind us. I whipped around coming face to face with Raymond.

"You don't have anything to worry about with us."

I glanced at Illarion. He just nodded ahead. Raymond gestured to a door. "We're just through here."

The room we walked into was an outdoor oasis built within the house and it was almost enough to make me forget my uneasiness.

We walked through two more doors before Elena and Michael excused themselves, leaving me and Illarion alone.

"Agent Hart, it's a pleasure."

I jerked my head in the direction of the voice that was laced in an Irish accent. I was met by a man in his early thirties with a fair complexion and jet-black hair. His bright green eyes contrasted brilliantly. A large scar cut across his cheek, and I found myself staring.

I held my hand out returning his gesture. As soon as our hands connected, I felt a rush of energy flow through me and right into my head making me double over in pain. Illarion's warning echoed in my head fighting against the intrusion, all the while I couldn't tell whether I was screaming or crying or both.

"*This pain will end when you learn to control it. You are powerful enough to do it, but are you willing to?*"

The agony ripped through my skull, expanding, twisting, and colliding with my thoughts and then it stopped.

Blinking through the haze, I saw myself, not through my own eyes, but as though I was watching from the outside. Illarion was there, his eyes wide with horror as he watched on, he was strapped to a chair, hurt and bleeding. I wanted to go to him, I wanted to help and in one swift, mind-stopping moment, a sharp blade sliced into me.

Before a scream could be ripped from my lips, I was back in the room, his hand around mine and I was panting, scrambling for breath.

As soon as his grip loosened on my hand and my mind, I staggered forward and straight toward the floor. I braced myself for the impact only it didn't come, instead I felt two strong arms around me pulling me back to safety and my world slowly realigned again.

"Interesting." His brows rose.

"You did well, Ace," Illarion whispered in my ear.

Through all the rushing of blood in my ears I didn't miss the wavering of his voice. A quick look across at him told me the scowl on his face wasn't aimed at me, but at the man.

While being this close to him would have normally made me giddy, right now I had much more important things on my mind. What the hell did he do to me and how was he so powerful?

"I'm Director Damon Cale," I heard him say, taking a few steps closer to me.

"Your Sense is Thought…" I bit, still reeling from the shock of our connection.

"Yes," he answered with a grin. "It's a pleasure to meet someone as unique as yourself." He added gesturing toward the leather outdoor lounge in the corner of the courtyard.

Much to my relief, Illarion sat down beside me while Raymond excused himself and joined a group of men talking by the cocktail bar.

"She's never been subjected to such examinations before; I would suggest you take it easy, Director," Illarion offered once we were all seated.

His polite words masked the venom in his voice. Underneath the surface, both men were sizing each other up. It took almost all the self-control I could muster to stay silent and out of it. But the curiosity was eating away at me, and I was desperate to know why there was such hostility there.

The two men looked at each other before Damon conceded and turned his attention back to me.

Illarion relaxed slightly in his seat and calmness washed over him.

"I would like to apologize for that, it was rude of me, but you understand that you've been somewhat of a myth, and meeting you is quite a treat," Damon spoke directly to me, ignoring Illarion.

I nodded in reply and tried to focus on reading him like Illarion said I would one day be able to, to hone in on my skills and learn to use them at will.

"You're every bit as brilliant as they said you were," he added. "No one has ever managed to push me out the way you just did. You should be happy with that, Agent Hart."

"Thanks," I managed.

Though I doubted that his compliment came from a warm fuzzy place in his heart.

Beside me, Illarion shifted slightly, and I could see from the corner of my eye that he had turned to look at me.

"I'm not sure what you think I can offer you when I'm constantly being assigned these menial operations?"

"Shall we walk?" Damon asked, gesturing to the door and heading outside.

Illarion stood and I followed.

"Sure." I nodded.

Damon's grin widened but deep inside I felt darkness. Something about it was so familiar. "Each operation is a piece to a much larger puzzle. Surely you can understand that?"

"In this line of work, sure. But when I signed up it was under the assumption that I would be working on jobs that would lead to answers."

"Your answers are part of a bigger equation. One we're all working on. That's worthy of your time, is it not?"

Illarion's mood shifted and felt almost completely aligned to my own, at least I wasn't the only one who was increasingly suspicious. Was I losing it? Everyone else was eating out of his hand—he had them all under some sort of compulsion, like he wasn't a total jerk. Raymond practically kissed the ground he walked on.

Elena and Michael were up ahead, talking to Raymond and another person I didn't recognize. As we neared, the other man left.

Damon cleared his throat.

Working for these people suddenly seemed like a bad idea. *Take your things and leave, Ace.* But I knew that if I left, I'd be walking away from any chance of finding out who killed my parents and why my squad was exterminated.

"You're right," I said.

"Good," Damon said cheerfully with an overly enthusiastic spring in his step.

Michael walked over joining us. "Thank you for your time, Director Cale. I trust everything went well?"

"It was a treat," he beamed.

I couldn't shake the feeling that something was wrong with this picture. I didn't know what yet, but I wouldn't give up until I figured it out.

Illarion looked at the exchange between Michael and Damon with a concentrated expression before finally gesturing for me to follow.

"Let's go," he said throwing one last glance at the two men.

Raymond and Elena stood silently in the background, keeping their attention averted.

I mouthed a wordless goodbye and followed Illarion out.

He led me though the house down the stairs, and outside toward our waiting car, which I noticed had been moved by the valet. It now sat across the lawn near the large trees we'd walked by.

"What was all that about?" I asked, breaking the silence.

Illarion walked ahead, his speed picking up as I struggled to keep up behind him.

When he didn't reply, I broke into a jog to catch up. "Illarion, what did he mean back there?"

"He didn't mean anything."

"Bullshit," I said catching him by the arm. "Don't lie to me."

When he stopped, he closed his eyes and rubbed the edges of his jaw, turning to me. "Are you alright?"

Our eyes briefly met. He saw what Damon made me see, or at least, he felt it.

"He had no right to do that," he continued when I didn't answer, shaking his head, annoyance evident in his voice. The same fury as before was raging through him. "I thought he might, but he had no right."

"It's okay," I lied. "It had to be done. They had to test me, right? Make sure I'm who you say I am."

"Doesn't make it acceptable, it was dangerous and careless."

He turned from me and picked up his pace again. I followed him until we reached the SUV and climbed inside.

As he took off down the road, I turned slightly in my seat to look at him; he had his eyes firmly focused on the road ahead, the steering wheel in a death grip. His knuckles were about to crack under the pressure. He was growing more tense as the minutes passed.

"How is it dangerous?"

"Delving that deeply into someone's mind can cause irreparable damage."

"Why did he do it?"

This time he turned his head slightly to face me. "To find your fears and weaknesses, anything that could make you a target, anything they could use against you."

"They want to see if I'm a liability."

He responded with a nod, "And from Damon's reaction, I'm guessing he found what he was looking for."

"What is that supposed to mean?"

"It means you need to learn to control everything inside you or you're just going to be in the way." He let out a long sigh and rubbed his jaw. "I told you to keep your thoughts safe. Whatever he made you see, were your own fears, understand? He was fishing."

My heart sank. Is that what my heart feared the most? I couldn't say a single word. My tongue was heavy in my mouth.

"You're careless."

"How the hell does that make me careless? I had no idea he was going to do that, let alone fight it!"

"You let your infatuation make you a target."

"Infatuation?" I balked, sinking right into the seat. "Who the hell do you think you are?"

"Right now, I'm your boss, and if you're serious about getting your answers then I'd suggest you get your thoughts on par with the job."

Ouch. I refused to let him see how much that hurt.

He was right. Of course, he was right. I was inexperienced and completely untrained for this. I shouldn't have thought otherwise and I shouldn't have deluded myself with thoughts about him, that we could ever be anything other than what we were now. That was on me. I blinked back the annoying haze of tears that coated my eyes and turned from him. I was naïve to think this was going to be a cake walk.

"Where are we going?" I asked, keeping my voice as even as I could.

"Back to the Agency, we need to debrief."

CHAPTER SIX

ACE

The stopover at the Agency was a quick one.

I watched from the other end of the room, leaning back in my chair. Illarion was passionate and concise. He didn't say a single word which didn't need to be said. He didn't waste any time, nor did he beat around the bush. Everything was to the point. Everything had a purpose. Which made what he said earlier, hurt even more.

If I couldn't hold my own against friendly fire, how was I expected to stand my ground against the Collectors if they ever came?

As he wound up the meeting, he motioned for me to follow him.

We were heading out on our own this time.

He tried to talk to me a couple of times on the way to the parking lot, but I didn't want to hear it. Truth be told, I was still licking my wounds and I was still incredibly embarrassed.

When we reached the Hummer, he tossed over the keys.

As we pulled out onto the main road, I turned my attention outside the window. Much like yesterday, it had been snowing overnight and remnants of the fury still held its hold over the grass and the trees above us.

Ice clung to the overhanging branches of the willows lining the road and the crystalline skies expanding around us were clear and deceptively welcoming. Outside, away from the comfort of the blazing heater of the SUV, it was below freezing. I gripped the wheel as we drove down the highway, occasionally passing another lone car.

Times like these were when I thought about my parents the most. We'd done so many winter trips, Aspen, Whistler and Thredbo.

My dad loved the snow, he wasn't the greatest at skiing, but it was the family time that he loved. He'd always make comments about how the weather was so miraculously deceiving, how death would find you in an instant if you weren't prepared.

He also believed there was poetry in death. Dying for a cause, dying for love, dying for religion...dying was always surrounded by a purpose of some kind. Whether it was something as beautiful as dying for someone you loved or dying to keep the natural circle of life afloat. Either way, we were all just pawns in the massive game of unequivocally unfair chess.

As much as I hated to admit it, I was kind of nervous. Illarion stirred beside me, and I felt his eyes on me.

My palms barely gripped the steering wheel of the huge Hummer, though I didn't tell Illarion that. He would have started sweating bullets and forced me out of the driver's seat.

"You haven't said a word since we left."

"Neither have you," I countered, keeping my eyes straight ahead.

I could feel his gaze intensifying. The papers he was previously preoccupied with were tucked into the glove compartment and suddenly, all his attention was on me.

I didn't need to be a Sensitive to tell what was going through his mind. Fortunately, I was, and I heard snippets of the thoughts churning in his head. Slowly more and more of my senses were developing, just like he said they would. I started feeling that inkling of control over them as they ran through me.

He was worried about hurting me and that he'd upset me. I didn't want to let on that I was unwillingly intruding on his personal

145

thoughts, so I just stayed silent. I swallowed hard and kept my eyes dead ahead.

"I upset you," he said suddenly.

"You didn't."

"It wasn't my intention. I was out of line."

"I understand. You were right."

"Ace—"

"Drop it. Please."

He gave me a curt nod and as much as I wanted to tell him how I felt, I knew it wasn't the right thing to do and his sudden changes in mood were giving me whiplash.

Much to my relief he dropped it. Whether he believed me or not I didn't know, he had shut himself off from me. One day I'd be able to do that too.

"The job we're getting assigned to is away from the Agency," he said after a few minutes of silence.

"Do you know what it is?"

"Not yet, but we'll be briefed and given a full run down." He said turning to look at me. "And you'll get to meet Josh, he prides himself on weaponry."

"Is he like the Da Vinci of warfare?" I asked, looking across at him.

"Something like that." He smiled. "He's the tech and weapons specialist at the Agency, whenever we need anything, we go straight to him."

I was so used to having a weapon, from years of being on tour. It became a part of you.

"Ask for anything you need; he can make it happen," Illarion said after a few moments.

"Looking forward to it, boss."

Illarion returned his attention back to the paperwork he'd fished out.

"So how does it work now?"

"We'll have regular contact with our handler. Someone in Josh's team, since they work the tech."

I nodded, turning back to the road. I couldn't bite back the question. "Why are we paired?"

"Sometimes there are Sensitives who complete the other, which is the usual pairing. Then there are Sensitives who amplify the other's gifts."

"Every Sensitive works in pairs?" I asked.

"In the field, yes."

"Have you had other partners?"

He remained silent but nodded and turned back to the window. He didn't elaborate and the way he looked away, told me not to ask.

Sighing, I turned on the radio and continued driving.

We drove for another hour before he told me to take a left and we pulled up to a cabin surrounded by ancient pine trees.

The surrounding ground was covered in a white substance, circling the whole building while just outside were the same strategically placed piles of rock I'd seen at Damon's. Around those rocks there were geometric patterns painted onto them and the soil around them.

"What is all this?"

"Protective measures," he said softly, placing a hand on my back leading me down the path.

"Like witchcraft?"

"Not really."

He stopped walking for a moment before he turned to look at me with an almost pained expression. "In our world, there's a belief in a Divine pair of Celestial Beings who basically rule over us, kind of like the Christian Jesus or God. They keep the balance of good and evil in check."

"So, it's a religious thing?" I looked around at the patterns.

Some were perfect outlines of triangles or hexagons while others were super complex, triangles within hexagons and squares.

"Most Sensitives preach it like a religion, yes, but to others it's more like a bedtime story to help make sense of who we are and why we exist."

I nodded slowly, taking a look at one which stood out at me. It was a large shape made up of three triangles. One was inverted, the tip crossing the center of the middle one while the third triangle sat above it, open at the top. A small, hollow circle sat within the tip. A chill ran through me.

"There are dozens of books about the Celestial Beings. I'll give them to you one day if you're bored."

"What do those things actually do?"

"They're wards, to protect borders and Sensitives within those borders. Others can stop the use of our abilities."

"Like a shield?"

He nodded.

"The Beings set them?" I asked, looking back at the patterns.

"No, not them physically, they're not of this world or plane," he replied, his jaw set in a hard line. "They have Sensitives who practice their craft and they're the ones who do it."

"Has anyone seen them?"

"Has anyone seen Jesus?"

Touché.

When I didn't say anything else, he smiled. "No one can see them. They appear to those with the same bloodline, and since no one like that exists...well you get the point."

"Yeah." I nodded. I'd never been an overly religious person. Mom and Dad went to church, but knowing what I know now, they were probably going to some church dedicated to these Beings.

"It's important to our people," he added once we'd reached the door. "They're our Gods."

"But not yours?" I looked up into his brown eyes. There was a lot more there, under the surface. "You don't believe in any of it?"

"No," he said simply. "If one day they decide to do something for us, then I'll believe in them."

"What happened?" I dared to ask.

"They failed me."

His voice was low, and I knew there would be no more talk about the Beings. Eventually, he'd tell me everything I wanted to know. But for now, I'd have to settle for a few snippets of information whenever he offered them up.

We walked up to the door and Illarion pushed it open. We were immediately hit with a dramatic contrast to the exterior.

It was completely white and sterile, lined almost wall to wall with computers. Tablets and monitoring equipment and at least a dozen men and women in sharp suits occupied the space. They were all answering to a man at the back of the room that I recognized as Damon.

"Ace, Illarion; the agents of the hour," he said holding his arms out in a grand gesture. "Welcome."

As if I just had to pretend this jerk didn't probe my brain only twenty-four hours ago.

I put forward a smile and looked as calm as possible.

Beside me, Illarion stood in silence, he didn't have to speak; I could feel him. He hated Damon

As Damon approached me, Illarion tensed at my side. I stepped forward and held my hand out to him, this time I braced myself making sure to build a barrier around my mind and block him.

Damon ate it all up and shook my hand. "Wouldn't have it any other way."

Illarion shook his hand after I stepped back and the two men looked to me and gestured to follow.

When the tension was diffused, I let out the breath I was holding and followed them.

Damon explained that the men and women here were already running the back end of the operation Illarion and I were tasked to. He also went on to explain that we were going to be radio silent for at least seventy-two hours and once we broke that, we would still be alone for the better part of the day. When we finished and checked in with our handler, whom we would meet later on, we'd have our next instructions.

He continued to explain that we would only have back-up for absolute emergencies in which we would call for help through a device which would be given to us when we had our briefing with Josh.

Once we were seated in a closed off section of the cabin, Damon handed us a folder each and closed the door behind him.

I was pleasantly surprised that this room wasn't as cold as the others, and it held a resemblance to a holiday inn. The chairs were heavy-set wood with large, green cushions which oddly enough matched the plush green rug under the coffee table we were seated around.

"The files you've got there are your mission outline. The information you recovered at the Ritz has directly led to this lead. Well done." Damon nodded to us. "You're going in under cover of complete darkness. No one will know you're there."

I looked through the file and spotted the target, a balding, older looking guy going by the alias of *Bob*. Apparently, he was making his big bucks through the assassination of smaller time Collectors around the city. I knew a lot about scum like this, obviously not with the supernatural-freak label they had, but criminals, nonetheless. By the look of the file notes, he was also a Collector.

"What do you want us to do?" Illarion asked, going through his file.

Damon crossed his legs and placed his hands neatly across the crisp fabric of his black trousers. "Seize and eliminate."

"Are we gathering Intel?" I asked.

"He won't be a talker, I can tell you that now," he said with a glint of something in his eyes, something which made me uneasy.

"He's one of us, gone bad," Illarion explained to me. "It happens sometimes, and they're dangerous, almost impossible to kill."

"But they're still people, like us, right?"

Illarion shook his head, and I felt a wave of sympathy rush through him. "Not anymore, Ace, they're bad people, and they hunt people like us, who are still good."

"If you hesitate, he won't," Damon supplied, showing genuine remorse for the first time. As much as he may have been a jerk, he still hated that the blood of our people was spilled.

What made people traitors to their own kind? I quietened my thoughts and looked across to Illarion who had the same, poised looked on his face.

A quick tap on the door drew Damon to his feet and he offered a nod to the man who stood there. "Josh is ready for you both," he said turning to us.

"You'll enjoy this," Illarion said brushing past me just out of Damon's earshot.

I followed them through the main part of the facility again and through the back into what looked like a garden shed.

"Wow, you guys like the whole cloak and dagger thing, huh?"

"Keeps it above suspicion," Damon explained, pushing the door open.

"A little cliché, isn't it?"

"Cliché, perhaps, but completely practical to hide from civilians."
He smiled.

My surprise didn't stop there, I was expecting another rush of people with high-tech equipment to be swarming this small space but instead, all I saw were tools, flowerpots, bags of soil, some rusty looking work benches and a wheelbarrow missing its wheels.

Illarion softly nudged me toward it.

Once all three of us stepped around it, Damon applied pressure on its handle and the ground beneath us moved. I stumbled slightly, grabbing hold of Illarion's arm to stop myself from falling. I didn't imagine the fact that he stilled, his arm tensed under my touch, and I quickly straightened, pulling my hand back.

The makeshift elevator descended at a slow pace through the earth which I was happy to see was protected by four walls of glass.

"Are all your facilities like this?" I asked.

So far I'd just been exposed to the Agency in New York. Everything else I'd experienced seemed a far cry from that.

Damon nodded. "Some are hidden in plain sight such as hotdog stands or diners, some are like this, underground and in the woods." He turned to me with a smile. "Others are on the move like our Hummers and vans."

The elevator came to a stop and this time I braced myself.

When the doors opened, I was met with a lot more of what I was expecting; white lab walls and desks stationed every few feet or so, manned by technicians and scientists working on God only knew what.

"Right this way," Damon said nodding down the hall.

"Josh always works down here?" I asked Illarion.

"No, Josh is one of our travelling techs, he goes wherever we need him, he's incredibly gifted with surveillance and tracking," he explained. "Michael and Elena believe him to be invaluable to our operation."

"So, he goes wherever we need him?" I asked, trying to understand the setup of our working relationships.

"Correct, and since we're starting you up and you're new to the Agency, we need to have the best facility possible to set you up with what you need," Damon cut in.

"And as Damon said, this is our best facility," Illarion added, stepping around me to shake hands with a man who had waved him down as we were walking. "I'll catch up with you later, Dan," he said as the man walked past.

"There's Josh," Damon announced.

Josh was rushing around with a group of guys having a loud conversation about something I couldn't quite make out. Beside all the guys, there was the tall, incredibly attractive Donna.

She was talking to another woman with much shorter, fiery red hair. I felt Illarion stiffen beside me as I stopped walking. I didn't need another lecture from him, so I forced my eyes away from her and back to Josh. He was tall and fair skinned with messy blond hair. Thick, square glasses framed his face and when I got closer, I noticed how attractive his smile was and how bright his blue eyes were.

Did this Agency just hire the world's most attractive people? I ignored the fact that Donna was looking our way and instead moved toward Josh.

His eyes went directly to me, and he held his hand out. "So nice to meet you, Ace."

"You too, I've actually heard a lot about you."

He looked surprised but took it in his stride, glancing up at Illarion and Damon. "Well, I'm not a complete nuisance to you guys after all."

"Not completely, no." Illarion chuckled, clapping him on the back.

Josh feigned offence before turning back to me with an overly exaggerated smile, he linked his arm through mine and dragged me off. "Please come with me, my lady, we have much to discuss."

I couldn't help but laugh. "Where are we going?"

"To my lair," he said, attempting a mock evil grin.

"Lair?"

He shrugged. "Lair, lab, wherever handsome, genius scientists hang out."

"Well then, lead on," I added.

He pushed open the door at the end of the lab. It led to another smaller room which was brimming with weapons, ammunition and a whole bunch of things I didn't recognize.

My eyes darted around the room.

"Like it?" he asked, holding his arms out proudly.

I nodded wordlessly.

"Ah, so she's a weapons kind of girl," he said, more to himself than to me. "We'll find something for you in here," he said taking my hand in his. He turned my hand over, quietly examining it. "Right-handed, no gun use, preferably something light but powerful."

I pulled my hand back. Since coming back from my last tour I just couldn't hold another gun.

He held his hands up in surrender, sensing that he'd hit a sore point. "I'm sorry, I didn't mean to pry."

"It's fine, what do you have in mind?"

"I'm glad you asked, come with me."

He pulled me over to a stool and gestured for me to sit. As he rushed around looking through the clutter of weapons and books littering his desk, I glanced around while his back was turned and was happy to see that he had a somewhat impressive Marvel collection stacked beside an Alienware PC, yeah, we would be good friends.

"Can I ask you something?" I asked, looking around, spotting all the security cameras covering every inch of this place.

"Shoot," he replied, rummaging through a pile of paper, ignoring the boxes and stationery that fell off the desk, cluttering to the floor.

"You guys are huge on the tech, I've figured that part out myself on the jobs I've done, but what's the security like out here when we're not reliant on the Agency?"

He stopped once he picked up a large, black case. "As in field backup?"

"Facility security," I clarified.

He came over to me and leaned against the bench behind him. "Well, the Agency itself has a hard lockdown protocol. If both entrance points are breached simultaneously, they force all the elevators and internal doors to lock down. You have fifteen seconds to get out before the Agency's finest go all ninja on your ass."

"Is that the case across each agency?"

"It is. Each campus operates on the same system, independently owned of course. It's about compartmentalization."

"That's intense."

"It is, but it's necessary." He stepped over the pile of papers on the floor. "If anything gets tripped here, the other campuses are alerted, and they go into a lockdown too. No one gets in or out. All the safes are shut down and data gets backed up onto an offsite server."

"Where's the server?"

"No one without top clearance knows, but I suspect it's somewhere out in the Atlantic, on a giant ship or something."

"What the hell is on there?"

"Again, without top clearance it's impossible to say but there is some important stuff in there. Mostly about who we are, who knows about us. Who we protect on and off the books. That kind of thing."

"Is it protected by any backups? If someone hits the ship even by mistake it's a problem."

"Sure. The location and the servers are just one part of it, to gain access you need a code. There are four Sensitives out there somewhere who have a portion of the code, each set of codes is one quarter of the key and they're independent of each other."

"So none of the four know who the other is?"

"Exactly." He blew out a long breath and nodded. "Compartmentalization." He placed the case beside me. "Anyway, that's boring shit. I heard you rocked your first official month running missions with the dreamy Agent Lazarev?"

I nodded, choking on a laugh. "Yeah, it was good. Successful, so I've been told."

"And that was using basic, run of the mill tech. Imagine how astounding you'll be when you're all decked out, with my gear."

He turned his back to me for a moment, retrieved another case and presented them both to me, opening them. Both were small, lightweight pistol bows. Small enough to keep concealed in a duffle bag.

"This is a Strykezone 350, absolutely light weight, well balanced and beautifully accurate."

I held it in my hand turning the piece in my hand, before I had a chance to open my mouth Josh took it out of my hands and handed me the second case.

"Now I know love at first sight when I see it, and you're not in love, check this one out." He opened the dark grey case in my lap. "This is Excalibur Matrix Mega 405."

This bow was even prettier. My eyes widened at the design. I gingerly pulled the bow out of the case and felt each of the taught strings. I could get well acquainted with this.

Josh once again pulled it out of my grasp.

156

I opened my mouth to protest but he held up his hand. "I understand, a woman should never settle for second best, the Excalibur shall be yours as a backup weapon, try this for me." He retrieved a third, slightly larger case and slowly unzipped it.

I tried to suppress my astonishment at the piece which sat in the velvet lined case.

He crossed his arms and looked at me. "It's a prototype, just a little something, something I've been working on. Interested?"

Tentatively I took the bow from the case and immediately felt a connection to it. My eyes flicked up to his.

"Sexy, isn't it?" he asked.

"Yeah." I drew my fingers over the intricate markings. "It's a Vulcan?"

"It was, now it's an original work of art by the one and only Joshua Walters," he proclaimed excitedly. "Tidied up the tensioners and customized the sight, accurate to three-thousand feet. Plus we can load Serum laced tips without affecting the accuracy."

"Serum laced?" It didn't elude me that Grimes had insinuated that Alex knew something about this.

"We need to back ourselves; we have a specially designed serum that can take Sensitives out or neutralize us." He wet his lips. "It's not ideal, I hate that something like that exists, but we need it."

"I get it. It's warfare."

"Right. In any case, we had to work around ways to administer it, bullets are one thing but with this weapon." He nodded to the bow. "It was harder to get the potency right in such a small tip to deliver something effective."

"How does it work?"

"Well, I don't know the chemical compounds of it, but it's used to subdue Sensitives and render them compliant. "

"Jesus, that sounds messed up."

"It is. But, necessary. Anyway, we don't use them often, it's reserved for last resort kind of deals."

"Well, I'm glad, and I'm impressed with this bow. When can you get one ready for me?" I looked up at him eagerly and within minutes he replaced the Vulcan in its case, zipped it back up and handed it to me. "It's yours, Ace, may it bring you many, many years of happiness."

"Seriously?"

"Hell yes, I'm serious. To see that baby bring as much joy to you as it's brought to me, is all I've ever wanted for it," he said with a huge smile. "Besides, it's a shame for it to sit in a box down here."

"I don't know what to say," I said, suddenly feeling a pang of sadness.

Josh was someone I could have been friends with in another life, a life where I wasn't constantly on the move, constantly living mission to mission. We wouldn't get chances to hang out and just go to the movies. The only times we'd meet would be in a room like this, discussing the weapons I'd use to kill people.

"Don't let this life get you down, Ace," he said, leaning back against the bench directly behind him. "It's easier to say than to do, but believe me." He paused looking at me intently, his eyes vibrant, determined. "If you let yourself fall, you'll never get back up."

"It feels different here somehow."

"Compared to when you were in the army?"

"Yeah."

"Because it was live warfare out there, you saw the enemy running at you. Here they're hidden in suits and fancy restaurants, hiding behind admirable jobs and titles. The evil is still the same, just dressed differently."

"You're right."

"I am, trust me on this. It's them or us," he said, suddenly reminding me a lot of what Damon had said.

We remained quiet for a few moments before he got up and pushed away from the bench. He swiped a small folder from the table and handed it to me. I gave him a quizzical look before he smiled.

"I'm your handler by the way, at least for this mission. Those are my details, if you need anything."

My eyes widened, that was an awesome bit of news.

"Thanks for Spock," I said, deciding there and then to take his advice.

"Spock?" he asked with a grin. "I like how your mind works."

"Likewise." I hopped up from my stool and hugged him.

He helped me with the two cases and sent me back to Illarion who was thankfully waiting alone for me. He took a case from me.

"I saw you found something you liked?" he asked, walking me back to the elevator.

"I did," I said with a smile feeling much happier having met Josh. "He's great."

"He is." He nodded pushing the button and closing the door. "He's the only non-Sensitive we have working here."

CHAPTER SEVEN

ACE

Illarion and I were dropped off and given our identifications for the coming mission. We made our way to our room and set up headquarters. The small bungalow was good for staying out of view of passers-by and the only sign of civilization we saw were headlights in the distance. I couldn't make them out, but I imagined they were semi-trailers delivering and transporting goods throughout the state.

I walked around, looking through each of the small windows taking in as much as I could. It was the best way to secure a location, to know where to go if you had to leave in a hurry. That was a habit I never broke, even at home in my apartment. I always checked and checked again, making sure I had full view of my surrounds.

Illarion returned from his perimeter check and allocated the main room to me while he promised he would be fine on the sofa in the living room.

"All the entrances are secure," he announced emptying the contents of the bag Josh had given us before we left.

I pulled my gaze from the door and stood beside him, so I could get a better look at everything he'd given us.

"What's that?" I asked pointing to a small box with a flashing green light and single red switch.

He picked up the small device and handed it to me. "It's the transmitter to send out our location should we need immediate extraction."

"Have you ever had to use it before?" I asked, placing it back on the table.

He shook his head putting everything back in its place. "I haven't, no. Other agents have had to when their covers were blown but it's not a common occurrence," he explained, moving between rooms to evenly space out our collection of weapons. "There isn't much that we aren't trained for, so we tend to deal with it before calling in reinforcements."

"Got it," I said following him around, watching in awe at the swift method in which he concealed guns in inconspicuous places, you'd never think to look.

Once he placed the last gun in a tea box by the stove we walked over to the small desk where I'd started setting up. He took a seat and picked up the file Damon had given us. He flicked through it before dropping it back on the table.

"Do you want to shower first?"

"No, it's okay, you go, I want to familiarize myself with as much of this as I can."

"Good." He offered me a hint of a smile before heading to the bathroom.

I dropped into the small chair and picked up the file and read through it a few more times. According to the information here, Bob was last seen at an address a few miles away.

With Josh's help, I broke into the surveillance grid of all the nearby traffic cameras. I opened the laptop we brought and logged into the main server of the security feed. The screen lit up with a satellite view of the whole town and its surroundings and the little blue dot on the screen informed me that Bob was still stationary.

We had a good few hours before daylight broke through and we needed to move. I locked into his location, set up a live trace, and turned my attention back to the file.

He was always surrounded by people, whether he was traveling to and from meetings or entertaining at home. Once I was done running through it for the fourth time, I dropped it on the table and leaned back in the chair, throwing my head back to stretch my neck out.

I stayed like that for at least ten minutes before the door to the bathroom opened and Illarion stepped out, surrounded by a cloud of steam. *Damn.* I raised my eyebrows at him and straightened up in my chair. "Did you just boil away the day?"

"I like hot showers."

"Me too, but that is boiling."

He smirked and nudged me out of the chair.

"Thanks for setting this up." He nodded to the laptop.

"No problem, boss," I muttered, rolling my eyes.

As he returned to work, I was quick to notice the slight shimmer on his skin as the hot water still held its mark on him; small droplets fell from the ends of his hair slightly wetting the tank top he was wearing.

I cleared my throat, turning away to regain my composure. Thankfully, he didn't notice and instead just remained seated looking through the paperwork on the table.

"Does any of this seem off to you?" he asked, interrupting my deep observation of his muscular structure.

"Off?" I looked back at him and tried to ignore the biceps staring me in the face.

"This operation," he clarified. "All the information we've been given."

"Why? Do you feel like something isn't right?"

"I don't know."

"You don't strike me as someone who questions directives, Illarion."

"Not usually. No."

I sat beside him. "Then I'd say you have your answer."

He considered what I said for a moment, then closed the laptop and turned his whole body to face me.

"What did you feel about Damon?"

Ah, there it was—the question burning between us for the last thirty-six hours.

How could I answer that question honestly, about a man who was held on the Agency's pedestal? He was the *Director*. There was literally no one higher than him, other than the President of the United States.

"Why are you asking me this now? You made it clear that I was a liability in that sense," I warned.

"You know something, and I need you to tell me."

"Know what? That I was thinking about you? Christ, do you want to humiliate me to the point of quitting?"

He remained quiet for a moment before folding his arms across his chest. "I didn't mean to humiliate you."

"Bullshit. You roasted me and you made no attempt to hide it."

Something flashed across his eyes. "It wasn't my intention."

"Maybe it wasn't but it doesn't change the fact that's what you did. That's why you were pissed right?" I paused, looking at him. "Because I was thinking about you? Because you're embarrassed, because it makes you look unprofessional?"

"Why did he see that?"

"How am I meant to answer that?"

He didn't say a word and after what seemed like an eternal minute, he spoke again. "He's planning something."

"That much is obvious, but I don't know why he would target me like that," I said in the firmest voice I could while trying to ignore the dangerous Darkness emanating from him.

"You know more than you're letting on. Your input is important here, Ace." And when I didn't give him what he wanted, he ran a hand over his jaw. "I need to know."

"You can feel it too, better than I can, so you tell me."

"I want to hear it from you," he countered.

His quick change in temperament shocked me and yet again I felt something stir inside me, it was a Darkness which swarmed around us. I'd never felt anything like it.

There were glimpses of it before, of course. How could I have missed it? After Damon's house, in the courtyard. I sucked in a breath and looked over at him. Whatever this was, was affecting both of us and I'd figured by now that he had no control over it.

"I'm not saying anything until you calm down, whatever this is, it's dangerous and you're getting consumed by it."

And just like that, he jerked back in his seat and looked at me like I just punched him in the gut. His shoulders sagged in defeat and he looked at me with pleading eyes. "Ace...I'm so sorry."

"What's going on with you?" I asked, recovering from the roller-coaster of emotion that just sped through me.

"I don't know."

"And you want me to tell you the truth?" I threw my hands up and stood, avoiding his attempt to take hold of my arm.

"Ace, I'm sorry."

"I'm taking a shower. Get some air."

Something was off and it wasn't just with Damon, whatever *it* was, it was creeping into both of us. His moods flipped in seconds and when they did, so did mine.

I stood with my back against the door. I focused on him and opened myself up to his feelings. His head was busy and his heart was heavy, I could hear him pacing up and down.

Fed up with the constant toxic feelings rushing through me, I pushed away from the door and crossed the small room in two strides. I entered the shower and turned on the water. At least a shower would drown out the noise in my head. And right now, there was a lot of noise.

It had never been this bad, not with Alex, not in Iraq. Why was I suddenly feeling so much?

I grabbed the towel hanging on the shower door and wrapped it around my body while I stepped across to the basin and rummaged through the supplied toiletries. There were two small bottles of shampoo and conditioner and a pack of vanilla-scented soaps which smelled more like dead flowers than anything you'd put in a cake.

They would have to do. I needed to wash myself and this was better than nothing, so I scooped the soaps into my hand and stepped back into the hot stream of water, arranging them neatly on the tiles.

Illarion's words burned through me.

Whatever was making his moods oscillate between the scales of normal to complete freak-out mode was a complete mystery to me, but he seemed to know what was causing it. Unfortunately for me, he was being less than forthcoming. It was something I would have to talk to him about.

I let out a heavy sigh, washed all the shampoo out of my hair and leaned heavily against the tiled wall. *What had I gotten myself into?*

A quick movement from the corner of my eye caught my attention. I had just enough time to glance across to the window before I spotted a laser pointed at my chest, reflected through the shower glass.

I threw myself out of the way and missed the speeding bullet which sent half the shower screen spraying across me. I was so happy I left the towel close by. Just as I wrapped myself in it, Illarion came busting through the door and dropped beside me.

Another two shots echoed through the small bathroom, narrowly missing Illarion as he threw himself to the ground to cover me. His body was hard against mine as his hand protected my face from the falling shards.

"Are you hurt?" he asked, urgently over the loud shattering of bullets around us.

I looked up at him, still in shock.

His eyes were wide and looking me over, then realized I must have been covered in blood when I threw myself out of the shower cutting myself on the jagged shards.

"Ace, are you hurt?" he asked again, this time grabbing my arm but keeping low as the spray of bullets continued.

"No," I managed. "No, I'm okay."

"Good, we have to go." He wrapped his arm around me and dragged me to my knees. "Stay low."

"Who the hell are they?"

He stopped just before we reached the door to the main room. "I don't know, but they've got us surrounded." He knelt and loaded his gun. "Stay here."

"I'm not letting you go out there alone, are you crazy?"

"You're wearing a towel and you're unarmed."

Suddenly aware of my less than battle-ready attire, I tightened the towel around me and tied it into a knot.

"I'm fine," I muttered pushing past him and the broken in door. I remembered I had left the cases Josh had given me on the bedside table and I was only a few feet away. A few feet too far.

I hated guns but right now I had no choice, I crawled the other way and reached for one of the guns Illarion stashed inside a flowerpot. As the cool metal brushed my skin, I cringed. This was something I never wanted to do again. Damn it.

Behind me, Illarion hissed for me to come back but he remained in his position covering me, shooting out of the window every so often when they stopped shooting at us.

"I'm covering you, go!" I loaded the clip.

He nodded, and we immediately formed a two-person formation.

The towel now firmly tied around me freed both of my hands. I made my way to the shattered window and slightly peeled back the curtain just enough so I could stick the barrel of the gun out, once I'd lined the shooter in my sight I fired, he went down and, in an instant, an assault of bullets flew my way and a rush of memories flooded back.

Forcing them away, I swallowed hard and ducked down just in time and prepared myself for my next shot.

Outside, adrenaline coursed through Illarion, his heart raced as he rounded the corner. The cool wind rushed in as he crept outside leaving the door open. He stayed low to the ground, gun out and ready. Shots echoed around him and right through me as our feelings collided again. It was wild getting this kind of insight into a teammate, one that made the job so much easier and gave me more confidence. I knew what he was planning, when he was about to execute and where he needed me.

He found the main shooter who was still shooting in my direction and took him out, freeing up my window of opportunity to make a run for the back door. I lined up another shooter and slowed my breathing down taking my shot successfully.

As he went down, I moved on to the next window, peeled back the shredded blind and trained my gun on the next gunman, a split second later, I fired, and he dropped.

In the cover of night, I had the advantage of my better than average sight. This allowed me to slip out of the back door and across the lawn behind a growth of shrubs, all whilst maintaining a full view of the men hiding in the dark. That, paired with my previous combat experience was a recipe for my success and ultimately their demise.

My feet were freezing in the wet grass and my hair was dripping wet, making this the most uncomfortable I'd been in a long time, and I'd been in some pretty unsavory situations in my life.

A pang of hurt shot through me. Alex and I had joked about running around together in jobs like these and how great we were at being a normal couple. We'd never made it official though, and that would continue to haunt me. I'd wasted so much time.

Crouching behind a rose bush I moved into a better position.

A sudden urge to laugh washed over me. I was running around, practically stark nude with a gun in my hand. I didn't anticipate this is how I'd be spending my evening.

But I remained as focused as I could in a situation like this and made my way across the field clutching my towel and gun.

Illarion ran across the driveway taking cover behind a large oak tree, he was glancing around, looking deeply concentrated and focused.

Silence enveloped us, and I knew they were waiting to see where we were hiding. I couldn't take the chance that I'd be made so I took it into my own hands and made a run for it across the field and behind the back part of the cabin.

More movement to my right caught my attention and thankfully I was more than prepared for the assault which came at me.

With a forceful jerk, I pushed my elbow up and into my attacker's jaw, he was momentarily stunned but regained his composure and came at me again. This time his foot connected with my stomach and threw me off balance.

For a moment, I stumbled, grabbing for his arm and when I felt it in my grasp, I pulled him down and threw all my weight into him, knocking us both to the ground.

He overpowered me instantly, flipped me over and pinned me down, pressing his arm against my throat.

Panic was not an option. I reached up as far around him as my arms would allow. We grappled, fighting for the upper hand.

I saw my moment. I dug my nails into his neck and thrust my knee into his gut. He yelled out in pain and released me. That gave me a momentary advantage to retrieve my gun which fell about a foot away. In one quick motion I cocked the pistol and fired into his chest. He slumped over me, crushing my body beneath his.

A relieved breath escaped my lips as our battle ended, but that was short-lived as I heard a quick rustle of leaves crunching beneath feet as another started heading toward me.

Using all the strength I had I pushed the body off me and wiped away the smear his blood left on my face. As I regained my coordination, I scrambled to my feet, still clutching my towel.

Illarion's fear rushed into me almost bowling me over but I kept running, pushing him out of my head as much as I could. This feeling was new. So far, I'd worked out that serious emotions triggered whatever ran between us and his fear was on a serious level. Pushing that aside, I brought my head back into the game. If he could feel that I was okay, he'd be safer too. I couldn't let him get hurt because he was worrying about me.

As I reached the cabin, I slipped inside and took cover by the back door and waited for the guy who was on my tail.

A few minutes later I heard his steps slow down and circle the back.

Catching him by surprise was easy since he was completely oblivious to my location. I used that to my advantage and sprung him through the door by elbowing him in the face. I knocked him backwards, giving me enough room to raise my gun and shoot.

He dropped to the ground and I ran around to the front, coming face to face with Illarion.

"Are you okay?" he asked breathlessly.

"I'm fine."

"We need to leave," he said tucking the gun into the back of his jeans.

Small snippets of what was running through his head, about me and the state I was in, came through our connection.

Suddenly, I felt incredibly self-conscious. He was so neat and precise and almost clinical in the way he fought. I, on the other hand, looked like a jungle freak who'd mauled someone to death in an alley.

A dirt-stained towel with my victim's blood was wrapped around me. The scuffs on my legs and feet didn't do me any justice either.

All I wanted to do was curl up into a ball and hide. I broke away from him, rushed into what was left of the bathroom and slammed the rickety door shut.

"Ace."

"Just cleaning myself up," I called back, trying to hide the shakiness in my voice.

"Are you sure you're alright?" he asked through the door. "Are you hurt?"

"I'm okay, just give me a minute."

"Ace."

"I'm okay," I muttered, not sure whether he could even hear me, and honestly, I didn't know who I was trying to convince.

Pressing a hand to either side of the shot-out basin, I focused on taking deep, steady breaths. I looked up at myself in the cracked mirror and winced. I reached for a small washcloth from the busted rack and wet it under the flowing water of the broken faucet. I swallowed back the lump in my throat as I dabbed away the blood on my face thankful for the faster than usual healing my body gave me.

The cuts would go within a few days and the scars would minimize over time.

"Ace, open the door." His voice was calm and inviting and I almost forgot why I was feeling the way I was. "Please."

Sucking in a deep breath, I tossed the small towel aside and pulled the door open.

He stood with a pile of folded clothes in his hands. "Here, we have to go."

"I know, I'm sorry."

"Don't be."

I smiled in return and left to get changed into the fresh clothes while he packed away our equipment and weapons.

When we were both ready, he led me down the path, past our Hummer which I noticed had its tires shot out, and into the woods.

"We're going to have to find our own accommodation, I don't trust what they've set up," he explained as we hiked through the woods, guided only by the light from the moon above.

I stumbled a few times following him while he led the way and navigated the rough terrain effortlessly.

"You think they set us up?"

"I don't know. I've left a vehicle parked a few miles from here."

"Have you always been suspicious of Damon?" I asked, remembering that Illarion had been under their employment for more than ten years.

"About as suspicious as you. A friend of mine left for that reason, my old partner."

The way his shoulders sagged told me this was a conversation for another time.

"How much farther?" I asked, realizing now just how sore I was and how much the cuts and grazes were burning underneath the fabric.

"At least another two hours."

I nodded, falling into step with him.

We walked silently taking turns carrying the bag and keeping the rear perimeter watch.

We needed no words for what we needed to do and when. I guess that's what he meant when he said some pairs amplified each other. I took the bag from him and let him fall back to take watch.

"We're not safe, are we?"

He paused ever so slightly before continuing up and through the shrubbery grazing our legs. "No."

"Where are we going?"

"To the safest place I know."

CHAPTER EIGHT

ACE

Illarion's house was even more of a mansion than Damon's and I made no effort to hide my amazement. When we pulled up to the large black gate I was blown away.

"Agency pays well."

He chuckled. "This isn't Agency, this is inheritance."

"Oh."

"My family was big in business back in Russia."

"Was?"

"They're no longer around."

I nodded to myself taking in the sight.

From the walls to the paintings and the ceilings, every bit of furniture accentuated the rooms. Illarion came to stand beside me while I looked up at the intricate ceiling design.

"I've had Elsa ready a room for you on the third floor. It's just down the hall from mine," he explained.

"Elsa?"

Illarion nodded, coming to stand beside me. "My housekeeper and my weapons provider."

He led me through the house and up the stairs which went up along the edges of the walls. It was a preserved Victorian property. The interior was as beautiful as the exterior.

There were pieces of classic art hung neatly along the walls every few feet or so, and on the landing of every floor we passed, there were small, dark shelves that were adorned with first-edition books.

The hardwood floors were deep chocolate, and they complimented the warmth of the walls.

"Let Elsa know what else you need, and she'll get it for you," he said softly, coming to a stop in front of a large, timber door.

He pushed it open and gestured for me to enter.

"You didn't have to do all this."

The bed was larger than my apartment's bedroom, as was the modified floor-to-ceiling window which overlooked a beautiful courtyard. Overgrown vines crept across the garden beds and up the side of the house. Far across the grounds, on the edge of the perimeter, there was a clearing, I couldn't quite make out what it was, but my attention fell back on a small garden with what looked like hundreds of lanterns and fairy lights.

Turning my attention back to the room, I spotted a desk in the far corner and nearly choked in surprise, everything I needed was right here and *he* did that.

I clasped my hand across my mouth and walked in absorbing everything I could.

"It's not what you had, but I hope that for now, it will do," he said coming to stand beside me and brushing his fingers along the delicate fabric of the crisp, black bed sheet.

There were few times in my life that rendered me speechless, one such time was in fourth grade when Bobby Kindel threw my matchbox cars in the fire. Another time was now, when Illarion, the man whom I'd known for less than a month recreated my entire life in less than a day.

"This is…it's…"

"You're welcome." He smiled, stepping closer, but only just.

"I can't go back to my apartment, can I?"

"No, unfortunately," he answered softly.

"Ever?"

He shook his head glancing over at me. "I'm sorry, it's not safe and I'd rather not compromise your safety or mine."

My whole life was there. Everything I'd built for myself, everything I'd worked toward. When my parents died, it became my salvation. How was I meant to just leave that behind? I hadn't even spoken to Troy, hadn't even said goodbye. What would he think of me?

Numbness settled over me. Everything would be different now. I blinked as the back of my eyes started to sting.

Clearing my throat, I looked at him. "What about my things?"

"We've made sure nothing can be traced to you."

"My apartment?"

"I've made sure all the bills have been set up for automatic deduction. Nothing will seem out of place."

"Right."

By now I was sure he'd felt how everything affected me, but he made no mention of it. From what I'd already learned about him, he was a gentleman like that.

I conceded, knowing there was nothing else I could say.

I sucked in a shaky breath, knowing that if I didn't move away from him and break this proximity, I wouldn't be able to stop myself from doing what I wanted to do so badly. Despite the dangers, I turned to face him and looked up into his eyes. God, how I wanted to feel his skin, feel how his lips would feel on mine. Forcing an even breath out, I reined in my emotions.

Where the hell was this all coming from? It's not like I'd never been around good-looking men in my life. This was more than that though. This felt deeper like it was less about want and more about a lack of control. Everything driving me came from a spot I couldn't pinpoint;

it was wild and totally out of my grasp and it was pulling me toward him and I had no control over it.

Up until now I could always feel or read people without really knowing that's what I was doing, which of course now made sense in hindsight, but with him it seemed amplified. Especially now, it was stronger, clearer. He felt like the piece of my life that'd been missing, as cliché as that sounded.

But an insidious voice reminded me that I was just his partner, and all these thoughts were irrelevant. I wasn't the tall, beautiful blonde. I wasn't the woman who matched him in every way and fit by his side. I wasn't Donna.

"Where are you right now?" he asked.

"Thinking that I need to get some rest."

He didn't believe me.

His hand gently circled my wrist, his breath was hot on my skin. "What's really going through your head?"

Taking in a deep, uncertain breath, I looked away. There was no way I could say anything. He already thought I was being unprofessional with the thoughts Damon was privy to. I couldn't make that mistake again. Whatever Damon did see put us both at risk now. I knew that much.

"Ace, I need to ask you about what Damon saw."

"I don't know what to tell you."

Whatever Damon had done made feel like I was a lab rat being poked and prodded and the memory still lingered making me sick. The feeling of being close to Illarion was similar in the sense that his presence invaded every part of me too, but in a different way.

Illarion was much stronger than Damon was, he could see more of me than anyone else, but in the short time we'd known each other, he had never violated me that way—he was just there, like my mind opened to him willingly.

"What did Damon see, when he took your hand?" he asked again, reading where my mind went right away.

"Darkness and pain. I've never felt anything like it."

"Tell me."

I wrapped my arms around myself. How could I tell him that I saw my own death while Illarion watched on? How was I meant to put that into words anyway? By the way, I had a vision that I was dying and there was nothing you or anyone else could do about it, oh, and the ghost of my dead boyfriend was there too.

He watched me intently and I exhaled wondering how I was meant to do this?

The only thing he knew already was that it was to do with him. That's all he needed to know.

His emotions were powerful. They flooded through me and mixed with my own. I could hardly tell which feelings were mine, and which were his. My skull throbbed with the invasion, and I could feel the onset of a particularly nasty migraine coming on.

"I think I need some rest," I repeated not daring to see his face or those eyes looking at me. "Thank you for all this."

"You don't have to thank me. Rest and we'll speak tomorrow."

He turned and left, shutting the door with a soft thud and with it, my resolve faded.

A tired and shaky sigh escaped my lips as I took everything in.

How would I ever learn to control all of this? I couldn't stand to be around him because every part of him flowed into me and every part of me was confused by what I was feeling.

Christ. I ran a hand over my tired eyes and eyed the bed. Luckily, most of the day had passed so I didn't feel bad.

Even if I had wanted to stay awake and explore there was no way I could. My body was exhausted beyond belief and my mind was already half asleep.

I staggered to the shower and stepped into the stream, letting the hot water wash over me. I pressed my hands above my head and leaned heavily against the tiles. I was quick to notice the wide array of soaps and shampoos, all vanilla and coconut scented. I smiled to myself as I opened one and smelled it. Illarion had noticed that these were my favorite fragrances.

Once I was done, I dried myself off and crawled into bed under the fluffy thick covers and landed heavily on the pillow with a sigh, God that felt good.

Usually, I was good at calming myself before bed and letting silence envelop me but tonight would obviously not be the case.

Illarion's fragmented thoughts ran through my mind, entwining with mine while my own feelings of despair and worry grew and grew. I squeezed my eyes shut trying to force as much of his thoughts out as I could until finally, like a switch, it was gone, my mind was clear, and sleep came swiftly.

"I won't let her die and you won't get anywhere near her." His voice was cold and calm and sent a range of mixed feelings through me. "You can do whatever you want to me, but I will not let you hurt her!" he shouted, stepping closer to the man holding a gun.

Why the hell would you step closer? I panicked. I tried to run to move closer to him, but something held me firmly in place.

I looked around at the warehouse, it was large and dusty, cluttered and filled with unfinished cars. Tarps and rags lay scattered across the floor which was also dotted with crimson spots.

A fist connected with Illarion's face, and a sharp pain shot through me. The man subdued Illarion, but he didn't even fight back. The man pushed Illarion backward into a chair and tied him down. My heart hammered in my chest.

He cast a sideways glance at me. My breath caught.

Then without warning the man lowered the safety of his weapon and fired.

Sweat drenched my clothes as I shot up in bed panting and gasping for breath. I threw the covers off myself and peeled my top off.

"Oh God," I moaned into my hand trying to recall all the vivid details of my dream, only the more I thought about it I realized it wasn't *my* dream, but it *was* a dream I had so many times before.

Did he shoot me or Illarion? My heart hammered as an afterthought.

I quickly pulled on a pair of sweatpants and a fresh T-shirt and ran down the hall stopping in front of what I assumed was Illarion's door. I knocked loudly.

A minute later he pulled the door open and looked battle ready in a pair of dark pants and a black tank top, which accentuated his physique beautifully. For a moment, I stood transfixed, almost forgetting why I had come. He didn't look like he'd just been asleep, but I knew he had been.

"What happened, are you okay?" he asked almost breathlessly.

"I'm fine, but your dream," I stammered. "What was it? Have you had it before?"

He stood mere inches from me and his confused expression suddenly turned dark. "What did you see?"

"What was your dream about? Did you have it before you met me?"

A few awkward moments later, he grabbed my arm and pulled me into his room. The walls inside were a dark brown color, giving the whole room a sixteenth century feel. It was adorned with floor to ceiling bookshelves which were filled to their entirety.

His bed was a large four-poster with a luxurious maroon bed spread and I found myself wondering what it would be like to sleep beside him, to feel his warmth encasing me and as the thoughts formed, I shot them down.

He gestured for me to sit and once I obliged he sat opposite me in a matching chesterfield arm-chair, eyes firmly focused on mine.

179

"What was your dream about?" I whispered looking into his dark eyes.

Something stirred deep within him which eerily resembled the same fear I had felt when I watched him die in the dream.

"You were being tortured, and I couldn't do anything to stop it."

"I saw myself die."

A thoughtful expression crossed his features before he spoke again. "Was that my dream or yours?"

"I can't tell."

"Does it feel like it's yours?"

"I don't know," I admitted looking up. "I can't tell the difference."

"You will learn to tell the difference. But this was just a dream…" He paused looking across at me, his features illuminated by the moon shining through the window. "That's all it was, Ace. Just a dream."

But his voice shook, contrasting drastically with the words he just spoke.

"Then why are you so terrified?"

He had no answer for me.

"You expect me to be honest with you, Illarion but you can't even look me in the eyes when you lie."

I got to my feet and briskly turned from him.

"Ace, wait!"

I had already crossed the length of the room and reached the door. "Get some sleep."

I walked back to my room, mesmerized by the moon as it lit up all the beautiful artwork on the walls. One in particular drew my attention. It was of a young bride in bed while her groom sat at her side weeping. I remembered art class when we learned about eighteenth century artists, I think this one was by an artist called *Barker*, it was morbid but serenely beautiful. He managed to capture the beauty of eternal love and the painful sorrow of death.

My mind returned to Illarion's terrified pleas and instinctively shivered beneath the painting. The similarities were too eerie.

I gave it one last look and entered my room completely awake; I didn't think I'd be getting any more sleep tonight.

It was nearly four in the morning, and I had missed at least three days of jogging, so instead I opted for some exercise.

I began with my usual reps of push-ups and sit-ups, then some high intensity cardio and finally some shadow boxing rounds.

A full two hours had passed before I decided I'd had enough. I still had the whole mansion and grounds to explore.

I rummaged through the closet and decided to see just how resourceful Elsa had been.

There were dark denims much like the pair I'd come in with, a huge array of T-shirts, plain and patterned and at least a dozen pairs of leather boots, ranging in style from ankle to knee length. Some even had a cute heel while most were flat.

I pulled out a pair of black jeans and a grey T-shirt and threw them on the bed. There was another closet filled with undergarments. I pulled out a black bra and smiled to myself. "You are good, Elsa."

It was the perfect size, simple and practical just the way I liked. There were days I missed the old Ace, the one who loved fashion and shopped at Victoria's Secret religiously, picking out all the sexy lacey items I could get my hands on. But that Ace was slowly slipping away, she was lost in a catacomb of self-pity and PTSD way back in the sands of Iraq.

The select items I still had that resembled *sexy*, were paraded to everyone last week, including Illarion which of course, made me cringe again. I'd have to buy some new stuff, maybe something a little prettier.

Annoyance flushed through me. No, Ace. You don't need pretty bras, no one's going to see them, especially not Illarion.

Shoving the closet door shut, I made my way to the bathroom.

Once I'd showered and completed my outfit, I dried my hair and left it out for a change. The sun was out, and the birds were singing. Some of the birds were eating the small grapes growing on the vines, which had grown all the way around the house.

I walked along the gravel, brushing my fingers through the shrubbery absorbing every detail I could. The trees were colored in brilliant hues of red and gold and beneath them were vibrant pink and purple flowers. The air was crisp, much cooler than a usual winter day in Long Island. I watched the dark bleed away from the sky as the light chased it away, coming up and over the horizon. The wooded grounds reached all the way to the edge of the perimeter and there stood a huge, towering gate which circled the property.

He liked his privacy, I thought to myself as I made my way farther down the path and toward the main gate we came through last night.

A quick glance around the main pillars holding it all together confirmed my theory. Josh must have been directly involved in the set up here, which also meant that Illarion trusted him wholeheartedly. Several high-definition cameras were placed strategically around the property and an intercom box fitted with retina and fingerprint scanners at this entrance and all the others I didn't know about.

"Does it meet your standards?" Illarion's voice came from behind, making me jump.

"It's pretty thorough." I turned to face him, catching my breath.

He offered me a smile.

"It needs to be, especially in our line of work." He folded his arms behind his back and nodded toward the path motioning for me to follow.

As we walked together, the familiar feeling of warmth I felt when I first met him started to come through again. Whatever last night was, it was awful, and I hoped I wouldn't have to see it again.

We walked down a winding garden path which was surrounded by weeping willows and cherry blossoms, the small petals fluttered around us, making it look like snow.

"I'm sorry about last night," he said at last.

"It's okay."

We kept walking and reached a small garden which was by far the prettiest thing I'd ever seen.

Two concrete benches were placed underneath a large oak tree and all around were smaller ones. A long chain of fairy lights was strung around forming a circle of light; this must look so beautiful at night.

In front of us there was a tall, wall garden, with hundreds of roses growing across it. This was the garden I saw from my room. I smiled looking up at it all.

He led us to the benches and took a seat. "I was out of line."

"I'm a big girl, Ila, I'm fine, I can handle it." I shrugged sitting down on the other. "And besides, it wasn't something you just talk about with someone you barely know. I get that."

"Ila," he replied softly.

I shielded a smile.

"Sorry, I guess we're not at that stage yet, huh?"

"No, that's not it," he began then stopped. I felt hesitation flit through our connection and then dissolve. "*Ila* is fine, just never been given a nickname before, that's all."

That wasn't all, not by a long shot.

"What are we going to do now?" I asked, looking directly ahead embracing the gentle breeze that carried the little white petals around us.

"As soon as we get word, we leave. I've put some questions out there, now we wait."

"It's beautiful out here."

"It's even nicer at night," he added reaching over and pulling a petal out of my hair.

Looking across at him, my heart raced, sending furious streams of blood to my head making me dizzy.

"What does it mean?" I asked. "Us, that we're connected?"

"I don't know, to be completely honest. There hasn't been much information about you."

That was still so strange to hear, that somewhere out there, there were books written about me, stories told, legends inspired.

"But it's dangerous?"

"It is, it makes you more powerful to them."

"Is it dangerous for you?"

"It is."

"Because they'll use you against me. It's what Damon saw."

He turned his face, he looked surprised that I'd said anything.

"Is that what the dream was about?" I added. "Part of the same problem?"

He sighed, scrubbing his jaw. "You've had the same dream before, you tell me."

That, I did not expect. I looked at him for a moment before clearing my throat.

"How can we have the same dream? And how can I keep having it? What does that even mean?"

"It means that you know a lot more than you're leading me to believe…and you're already a lot more powerful that you know."

How could he know that? I was always careful when I let my mind wander.

I clamped down on the tightness in the back of my throat and wet my lips, buying myself more time, more time to think about my next choice of words.

"It doesn't matter, it's just a dream, right? What do we do now?"

"Don't change the subject, you wanted to talk and we're talking. What did the dream mean to you?" he asked, firmly.

It was faint, barely there but I felt the Darkness creeping in. This topic was obviously something he didn't want to talk about, I got the feeling he'd rather go through a root canal.

Anxiety started forming at the sudden change in his mood. "It was a warning."

"Exactly."

And there in that one simple word I understood why he got so wound up. Us being together was dangerous because if they came after me he would try to stop them, and I would try to stop him. Although we were destined to be together, we could never be *together*. That and the fact that he had blondie.

♥

Illarion and I weren't strangers to working in uncomfortable conditions. As much as he may have been stoic and uber professional, his feelings didn't line up to the emotions I felt pulsing between us. Having said that, I still had to remain professional, I still had to rein my feelings in, because we were still partners, he was still my boss, and I was still so far from being ready for any of this it wasn't funny.

We'd walked back to his house with small chatter filling the void and unspoken awkwardness.

"Elena came through," he said softly as we stepped into the kitchen. "I'll make coffee."

Taking a seat, I nodded and waited patiently until he came back and sat beside me with a fresh cup.

"Here."

"What's the plan?" I drank half the cup in a single go and leaned back in the chair looking up at him.

185

"We'll head out tonight, there's a car a few miles I from here I keep for emergencies."

"A personal vehicle?"

"Yeah. It's registered under an alias should the Agency ever come across it."

"You really don't trust them."

"No, not everyone," he agreed. "It shouldn't take us long to get to."

"Fair call, so I take it we're going ahead with the mission?"

"At this stage, yes. We need to get to this guy, he knows something."

"When do we leave?"

He glanced down at is watch. "Eleven. That should give us enough time to work out what the deal is before contacting Michael and Elena."

"Okay."

"Get some rest, I'll see you tonight."

CHAPTER NINE

ACE

Four hours later, I saw the glint of the headlight glass through a clearing in the woods about two yards away.

Thank God.

I took the bag from Illarion so he could move the shrubbery out of the way. It was a modern SUV fully lined with all the comforts one would need.

"Are we heading straight there?"

"No, we're going to a safe house."

"A safe house?" I questioned, as I played with the music dial.

He pulled the car out of the bush and onto the road. "We need supplies and weapons, and a phone."

Right. We'd discarded both our cell phones and were travelling completely off the grid.

Great. Hopefully, the safe house would have a shower and food. I'd kill for a Big Mac right about now.

I continued to run through the radio stations which earned me a look from Illarion.

"How do we know this Bob guy is bad?" I asked, finally switching the radio off. There were no good options.

"Intel."

"Intel that was given to us by Damon's people." I paused, carefully contemplating my next choice of words. "Who are we killing? How do we know if their intel is legit?"

"He's killed people like us, Ace."

"How do we know *they* weren't bad?" I asked, raising an eyebrow. "You said it yourself—people like us sometimes go bad."

Illarion looked at me thoughtfully but didn't say a word.

"That is unless they told us this story. Don't get me wrong, Bob is bad, but maybe Damon is trying to cover something up, by getting us to kill him? I mean it would make sense. Send us to kill him, and send them to kill us…"

"What do you suggest we do?"

He pulled the car over onto the side of the road.

"We do surveillance, make sure we're positive we know who we're killing and why, and if we find the Agency's file notes are conclusive then we finish the job like we were meant to."

He considered my words for a few moments before throwing the car back into gear and pulling onto the road again.

"Start organizing the specifics and when we get to the safe house, we'll go over it together."

"Okay."

We drove in silence for at least fifteen minutes before I turned the radio back on and flicked though five or six stations before reluctantly admitting defeat once again.

I slumped back in my seat and looked out the window—darkness and snow and absolutely nothing notable to see. Spring was nearly here, but winter was still relentlessly holding on.

"Can I ask you something?"

He nodded without looking away from the road.

"What's your specialty?"

What I saw back at the cabin was a badass killing machine who single-handedly took out at least seven highly trained and armed men. And *that* was more impressive than anything supernatural.

He regarded my question for a few moments before answering.

"Mostly hand to hand, but I can't pass up a Smith and Wesson."

"I didn't recognize the style."

"It's a Russian taught specialty, something only those in Spetsnaz know. I can show you some day?"

"I'd like that."

"Can I ask you something?"

"Sure."

"I noticed that you opted for bows, can I ask why?"

My heart did a flip in my chest as I pondered my answer. I wasn't ready for him to see the dark secrets lining my soul.

"I was too good with guns. Too much of a proficient killer," I murmured, sick at the words coming out of my mouth.

"You did what you had to."

"I did it because I was good at it. I enjoyed the job."

"It's normal."

"Normal?" I ground my jaw. "No, there's nothing normal about killing people and enjoying it."

"Not the act itself, the weight it carries. Knowing why you're doing it, protecting people and the country they belong to."

"That's both incredibly diplomatic and patriotic, Illarion."

"It's my truth." He briefly met my eyes. "Everyone has skeletons in their closet, Ace, it doesn't make you a bad person."

I cringed at the choice of words. It was the same thing Troy had said to me. God I was a shitty person. He deserved so much more than the way I treated him.

"Those choices and actions don't make you a bad person."

"It sure as hell doesn't make me a good person."

"Sometimes the worst things we do are the most necessary ones."

"You sound like you're speaking from experience."

"In a way."

I nodded, reading between the lines.

"Does your girlfriend know about this part of your life?" I asked.

For a moment he looked confused, his head tipped to the side slightly. "Girlfriend?"

"Donna," I reminded him. "When I met you before we went on this job, she told you about your date which was this week sometime right? Only we're out here on the run. How do you explain this side of the job to her?"

"She's not my girlfriend, she's my doctor. Actually, she's on the Agency's payroll. We entrust her with our secrets and she's read into some of our operations."

"Oh."

"I have a standing appointment with her for my shoulder. I was shot on the job six months ago. She checks in with me every few weeks."

"Well, this is embarrassing."

He shielded a smile. "You did a good job back there."

"I did what I had to."

"You know how to look after yourself and I'm happy to have you watch my back."

"So why do I feel like that was a struggle for you to say?"

"It isn't a struggle, it's the truth."

"Ila," I tried to be as gentle as I could. "What is it?"

"When I saw you and all the blood, I didn't know what happened."

My heart started pounding fiercely in my chest.

"We're meant to be partners, level on the playing field, and I don't know if we can be," he said finally, keeping his eyes on the road.

"What is that supposed to mean?"

This is not where I thought this was going. What was he saying? That I wasn't good enough and that he'd always have to run in and rescue me? I rescued myself damn it. And didn't he just say he was happy to have me watching his back?

Anger heated up my cheeks. An outburst would only cement his impression of me; impulsive and reckless. So, I reined it in and calmed myself but before I could prepare an argument, I felt his hand softly fold across mine.

Calm down, Ace. Remember that thing called breathing.

"You misunderstand, it's not because you need rescuing, it's because I'd want to be there for you first, above any mission, above any job."

His admission forced my mouth shut.

"Can you hear my thoughts?"

"No. Just your feelings, I can read them and bring calmness over you."

"It was you." The pieces suddenly clicked into place. "You were at the park that night?"

A weak smile crossed his lips, and he squeezed my hand before letting it go and turning back to the road. "Your emotions were lighting up Central Park. It wasn't hard to find you."

"You were the reason I got knocked down. You distracted me..."

"I apologize. It wasn't my intention."

Damn, I knew there was something odd about the way I came home that night, barely giving the mugging a second thought and then it was the feeling, the almost familiar hum I'd never forgotten.

"It was you in the desert?"

He nodded.

"You were the one who brought me back to base? You saved my life."

"I did what I had to."

"How did you know where to find me?"

"I've told you before that I was on your offshore protection detail, Corporal Alex Westen was stationed with you."

Then, like a punch to the gut that knocked all the air from me, I realized. "You were friends."

Illarion's eyes flicked down to the wheel for a moment before he returned his attention to the road.

"Oh my God, and I was such a jerk to you."

"It's fine, Ace. You were hurting."

"Were you close?"

"We were, we were good friends, old friends," he added with a small laugh.

My hand went to my mouth. "I'm so sorry."

It was Alex I'd always felt inside my head, the warm sliver of calm that started in my toes and spread throughout me entirely, encasing me in a cocoon of warmth. Just like Alex had kept me safe all those years in the desert, Illarion did the same here. It was why the feeling was so safe, so familiar.

Tears burned my eyes. "Tell me everything?"

Illarion smiled. "We worked together here in the States, we crossed paths on some operations, but he was tasked to Iraq, and we remained in touch only for briefing purposes."

"Did he, did he talk about me?"

"All the time."

"Bet he told you all about my endless complaining."

"He didn't say it was endless. He did say you were impartial to some of the food."

I laughed through the tightening in my throat.

For a moment, neither of us said anything as Alex's memory settled between us.

"They never found his body."

"I arranged for him to be brought home, Ace. Simmons couldn't know about it."

"Oh…"

Illarion looked at me for a second before turning away again. He wet his lips and then spoke. "He was serious about leaving the army with you. You should know how much he cared about you."

I couldn't stop the tears from falling. I swatted them away with the back of my hand and nodded.

"I'm sorry I couldn't save him."

"Oh, Ace. You've carried this guilt for years, and it wasn't your burden to carry."

"How is it not?" I released a broken breath. "He died because of me."

"He died because he knew it would save your life."

"He shouldn't have done that."

"You know better than anyone what love will make you do."

I looked across at him. I did know. It was dangerous and raw. The pure, unadulterated anger that had raged through me when I saw Alex die was unrivaled and nothing had ever come close save for the dreams I had of Illarion's death. I knew what I was willing to do.

He tore his gaze away. "I know how hard it is, trying to hold on to your own feelings while experiencing mine as well, but you will learn to control it, I'll help you. You just have to be honest with me. I can't help if you hold things back."

"Do they know that we are alike?"

"The Agency?"

"People interested in me."

"Some do, yes. But no one is like you."

"But they know what I am?"

"Yes, and when they found out, they knew you would be in danger, they knew interested parties would come looking."

"So they tasked you to watch me?"

"Yes."

"Damon?" I asked.

"Not just him," he bit. "I don't know who we can trust, Ace. I don't want to be wrong and put you in danger. I've been watching out for you a long time—since you went on tour."

"And Alex?"

"Alex knew who you were. He knew how important it was to keep you safe. Everyone invested in protecting your interests knows the risks."

I nodded to myself.

After a moment, he shook his head like the weight of everything he knew was ready to come tumbling out. I couldn't comprehend the kind of pressure he must have been under all these years.

"What changed?"

"When your parents were killed, the people who were after you, became bold, dauntless, they didn't care who had eyes on you. That put us on edge, and we knew we had to bring you in."

"Why am I so important? You're as powerful as I am, right? It's why we're paired."

"I'm not, Ace, not even close, but together we're more powerful than any of them could anticipate."

I shook my head trying to understand.

"Collectors gain powers from every Sensitive they kill, you know that."

"Right."

"But if they get to us, they hit the jackpot. Adding me to your abilities is like the missing piece of this elaborate puzzle."

"Because we're connected."

"Exactly. They'll have all the power they could need, what runs through you is rare and powerful, but I amplify it."

I looked over at him.

"What do we do? How do we stop that?"

"We can't stop it, but we can stay off the radar."

We were no longer under the cover or protection of the Agency, nor did we have backup ready to run in when we got into shit, we were alone.

"And do what?"

"We're going to track the target. We'll get whatever we can from him. If he's high on their list then he knows something, so that's where we start."

"Assuming you have someone you trust?"

He gave me a half smile before turning back to the road. "I've got it covered. That's where we're going now."

"Good." I settled back in the seat. "Some help would be good."

"You get some rest. We're still a while out."

"Okay," I murmured, feeling my body growing heavier and sleepier. "I'm just going to close my eyes for a bit."

❤

Illarion swerved off the road, coming to an abrupt halt waking me in the process. I'd been dreaming and there had been a bright flash of light at the end.

"What was that?" I jerked in my seat looking around, but all I could see was darkness and snow.

He didn't reply but his tense posture said enough. He was concentrating on the dark woods surrounding the road.

"Someone's out there." He spoke low and fast, loading his gun.

"Shit." I reached back for my gun too, slipping low into the seat just as he was. I cringed as I loaded the clip.

"They fired some kind of EMP, immobilized the car."

"Do you think they made us already?"

He shook his head, concentrating on the tree line off to our right. There was nothing.

"I don't think whoever's out there is from the Agency." He looked at me before pulling me down lower into the seat.

"What are you doing?"

"Stay down and do not move, I mean it."

He slipped out quietly and closed the door with a soft thud, I watched as he disappeared into the darkness.

The comms given to us by Josh were in the seat behind. Why didn't we put them in before he decided to run off and leave me alone? Then, like a slap to the face I remembered that the EMP would have fried them too.

We were literally in the middle of nowhere and we were alone.

Subtle noises outside the vehicle drew my attention. My eyes moved across the black expanse of nothingness. I checked behind me. There was no one there.

Before I could take another breath, the door I was resting against was yanked open and I was roughly pulled outside by my hair. I instinctively reached up for the hands holding me and before I could inflict any damage I was dropped onto wet ground.

Snow fell, drenching me in a matter of seconds. I rolled over, trying to get control back but the second I made a move, I was thrown back down. I heard my skull crack against the ground sending starbursts exploding across my vision. Then a sensation came over me.

Something like sleep paralysis. I was awake and aware but unable to move.

Before the scream building in my throat could escape, I was silenced. A heavy blanket of dread forced my mouth shut.

I tried to crane my neck, but nothing moved. I was paralyzed with fear, as cold as the layer of thin ice that coated the ground. I gasped helplessly, focusing on my chest, trying in vain to open my lungs. My eyes watered, and hot tears spilled out across my cheeks.

Black dots assaulted my vision, and a harsh suffocating silence enveloped me. The burning in my throat subsided. I wasn't struggling with every impossible breath, and I wasn't afraid like I had been. It was slowly getting darker. I was warm now; the cold was gone.

My head lolled to the side, and I was met by two men neither of whom I recognized. One was much younger, maybe in his early twenties, standing watch and the other was holding me, his eyes were locked onto mine, yet his face came in and out of focus. Slowly, he moved closer to me and his lips moved but it was too low for me to hear. He whispered words that didn't sound like English…maybe they were Macedonian or Serbian…no, no they were Romanian.

Through the blood rushing in my head and the deafening silence, I could barely make anything out, but I heard my name. I heard the desperate edge to the voice I recognized and knew I loved.

The man who was holding me silently placed me on the ground and got up. As my head lolled to the side and my cheek fell to the snowy ground, I got a look at his shoes. They were hideous—a combination of animal skin, and material, with two-inch soles the color of mustard. They were custom.

As Illarion got closer, they both left, rushing away but I remained glued to the spot where the ugly shoes had left their imprint.

Still unable to move, I squeezed my eyes shut, forcing the tears free. The hold over me was dissipating, and coherent thoughts formed freely once again in my mind. I felt the dampness of my clothes as they clung to my wet skin and the sheet of ice beneath my body. As my tears fell mixing in with the snowflakes, I opened my eyes trying to focus. In the distance, from the corner of my eye, I saw Illarion running toward me.

He shouted my name as he dropped to his knees, skidding in the snow and mud.

"Can you hear me?" He pulled me up off the ground and into his arms.

I tried to nod. I tried to give any sign of being able to hear him, but my body refused to respond. My limbs felt heavy in his arms, void of life and control.

"Hold on," he begged, and I heard that usually powerfully, sweet voice of his break. "Ace, hold on."

He cradled me against his body until I felt myself leave the ground. Then he carried me to the car.

Distantly, I heard the engine spark to life and moments later we were on our way.

How did he get the car started?

Wasn't it fried?

I felt my heart slowing.

The tires screeched against the wet road as Illarion floored the SUV and there, through all the Darkness clouding my mind I knew there and then what Illarion felt toward me. The whole time we had danced around each other, only slivers of his true feelings spilled into me, now there was no hiding it.

My eyes struggled to stay open and the only thing keeping me focused was seeing his eyes flick to me every so often as he drove with a panicked expression on his face and a calming hand on my cheek.

Despite my best effort, the exhaustion won out.

♥

Warmth. Comfort. Safety.

My eyes opened, with a slight struggle, and I saw that I was now under a soft and fluffy blanket and in different clothes. Everything seemed to be so difficult at first, then my arms moved again and finally, all the events of last night came back.

A low groan escaped my lips as I realized that the light flooding the window was doing my massive headache no favors.

"Ace?" I heard the familiar accent draw me back into the room.

His feelings ran through me as his hand found mine.

I dared to crack my eyes open again, only this time I wasn't blinded by the sun and instead, I was met with a comfortably dimmed room.

"Tell me you're alright."

"I'm practically doing backflips," I whispered.

"Easy," he murmured, linking his arm under mine and helping me up.

"What happened?" I groaned.

He sat down on the bed beside me. "I imagine Damon's henchmen—off the books of course."

"How did you get the car going?" I murmured, pressing my fingers to my temple.

He handed me a small device no larger than a pen. "It was some kind of rocket-propelled immobilizer. Turns out it didn't short-circuit the electronics, just temporarily disabled them. I've sent pictures to Josh, and he should be able to work out what it was from there."

"That was some serious compulsion." I rubbed my head.

"I know." He handed me a glass of water. "I'm sorry I left you alone."

"Don't be, you can't be around all the time." I shook my head taking a sip of water. Although privately I had chills. Whoever had ripped me from the truck had terrified the hell out of me. "I'm not your charge, I'm your partner."

"I know that. I also know that it's my job to keep you safe."

"You can't let that stop you from doing your job, neither of us can."

He didn't reply, instead he sat looking at me with a solemn expression before he got up.

"I'm glad you're okay."

"It's good to be alive." I held up my arm, nodding to the striped pink and grey sweater. "Did you dress me?"

"The housekeeper did."

"What I felt last night. Did you mean it?"

A line in his jaw feathered as he bit down and averted his gaze. There were words on the tip of his tongue, but he remained silent.

He was shutting himself off from me. He paused for a moment, and I almost thought he'd say something, anything, and then he didn't.

"Ila?"

He got up, fighting some sort of internal battle before he walked over to the door and let his hand hover above the handle for a moment before he spoke.

"We're at my contact's house. We're safe here. Breakfast is ready whenever you want to come down."

The door closed with a thud.

I dropped my head in my hands, my heart got the memo, and this damn headache was slowly getting worse by the minute. At this point I was lucky to see anything through the black patches in front of my eyes.

Dragging myself from the bed, I stumbled to the bathroom.

There were new clothes and shoes stacked neatly by the window. Apparently efficient housekeepers were popular here too.

CHAPTER TEN

ACE

The house we were in was extravagant to say the least. Not in the same way as Illarion's but amazing nonetheless.

Where Illarion's was a marvel of modern technology aside from his antique styled room, this house looked as though it was plucked straight out of a vampire movie. Dark, plush rugs lined the hallways covering the dark floorboards beneath them. Timeless oil paintings adorned the walls every couple of feet or so; they ranged from morbid battle scenes to creepy portraits, and around me, heavyset wooden furniture filled each room in an extraordinary array of color and style.

The hallway was just as intricate. I walked trailing my fingers along the roughly finished surface of the walls and I had to admit that the unpolished wood gave it character. Something about the darkness surrounding me felt safe and almost familiar.

As I crossed the threshold from the main living quarters and reached the landing of the stairs, the smell of freshly cooked eggs and freshly baked bread hit. My stomach grumbled and my feet took me straight toward the food.

Illarion was seated in one of the heavyset kitchen chairs drinking a coffee and reading a newspaper.

The dining table was a large, Edwardian period style and it looked immovable. The open plan of the space had a floor-to-ceiling window, overlooking spectacular gardens.

"Anything notable going on?" I sat down opposite him.

The table could seat at least six people, but with the distance I put between us, you could practically fit another ten.

He shook his head closing the paper; he folded it in half and placed it back on the table to look up at me.

"Did you eat?" I asked, not turning to look at him.

I put two heaps of scrambled eggs on my plate and cut two thick slices of fresh bread from the loaf.

"I did, thank you."

I stood at the stove with my back to him deciding that standing and eating was more comfortable than sitting face-to-face with him.

"Where's your contact?"

"He stepped out to do a perimeter check."

"He does perimeter checks around his own property?"

"Force of habit, I guess."

"Cool." I nodded. "Cooks, bakes and runs perimeter checks."

Illarion scoffed behind me. "His housekeeper does most of the cooking."

Well, no one could deny we were good at avoiding the elephant in the room. It was clear that he didn't want to discuss anything that happened last night, least of all what he let slip.

Once I'd chewed enough to be able to talk again, I asked how long I was asleep and where we were. At least we could talk about that.

He explained that this was the home of his ex-partner, who'd gotten out of the Agency a few years ago, due to conflicting interests. I didn't need it spelled out, Damon was the conflicting interest.

"He'll be back soon and you can meet him," he said.

I heaped another fork full of eggs into my mouth.

He stood, and I reluctantly turned to face him.

He towered above me, his dark hair was pulled back into a low bun, but a few stray hairs still escaped, falling over his eyes.

His proximity and the intoxicating aroma of the aftershave he wore made me light-headed.

He crossed his arms and leaned lazily against the bench with his hip, waiting for me to finish eating.

"We have to talk," he said simply.

"Yeah, we do." I mirrored his stance.

Unamused, he furrowed his brow.

"You felt something last night, you asked me about it this morning."

"I did and you shut me down. And whatever *it* was, you've made it pretty damn clear you didn't want to talk about it."

He flinched.

Being cold and distant was better and safer for him. I took a deep breath and tried to close myself off. I wouldn't make the same mistake he did. There would be no accidental sharing of feelings here.

The door behind us opened, saving me from this conversation. His contact walked in carrying brown grocery bags. An array of tattoos covered his arms. His whole upper body must have been covered in Olympus. The black T-shirt hid some of the artwork but I saw clouds peeking through the collar.

Once he put everything away he turned to me, icy blue eyes locked onto mine.

"She lives," he said comically stepping forward and holding his hand out.

"You did a perimeter check carrying bags of food?"

He raised an eyebrow at me, his lips quirked up into a smirk. "I like her."

I fought the urge to grin.

"Did he leave you any food? He's always had the worst table manners—doesn't entertain much."

I wanted to correct him and say that Illarion had the best manners of anyone I've ever met. If he didn't entertain, it was because he was too busy with work.

"I had plenty. Thanks."

"No worries. Just help yourself."

An awkward moment passed as he looked from Illarion to me, I looked away before bringing my eyes back to his.

"You were with the Agency?"

He nodded, grabbing a cup from the top shelf. The back of his shirt came up revealing the skin on his lower back. It was scarred up and faint, pinkish lines marked his skin. I was glad to see I wasn't the only patchwork doll around here.

He poured two cups of coffee and handed me one.

"Sure was, left a few years back, moved to Australia for a while."

That was the faint accent I detected before. "Have you been back?"

"Nah, never really got the chance."

"I've only been to the mountains a few times, skied in New South Wales. That where you lived?"

"That's cool. Great spots up there but no, I was a Melbourne boy."

"Isn't there a huge rivalry between Melbourne and Sydney?"

He nodded, smirking. "Yeah, but everyone knows Melbourne's better."

"Spoken like a true…Melbournite?"

"Melburnian, but yes." He chuckled.

The sound was warm and welcoming, and I could see how he and Illarion were good friends.

"I'm Aurel, by the way," he said, retrieving a tub of yogurt from the fridge.

"Nice to meet you."

Illarion shifted beside me, he was relaxed for a change.

"How long are we staying?"

"A few days at least, we're close to the target and we don't have to worry about being made here."

"It's a fortress." Aurel nodded at the house taking another spoonful of yogurt.

"At least it's not a dingy fortress."

He nodded and took a spoonful before clearing his throat.

"So, uh, the tension is about as thick as this yogurt." He dipped the spoon again and motioned it in a circle above the tub to demonstrate the texture.

I cringed.

"Don't take life so seriously, you'll regret it," he said wisely before finishing off the yogurt and tossing it in the trash.

Both Illarion and I remained silent.

"I want to show you something. Come with me," Aurel said forcefully, not leaving me with much choice.

"I'll get our trace set up," Illarion said before we left.

"Don't do anything too exciting, brother," Aurel muttered with a chuckle. "Wouldn't want to have to sober you up or anything."

"Keep walking," he called back over his shoulder only eliciting another laugh from Aurel.

"What was that about?" I asked, as we stepped outside into the cool spring air.

"He's too serious, that's all."

"Yeah, no kidding. How long have you known each other?" I asked, falling into step with him.

The grounds weren't as serene as Illarion's but it was still beautiful in its own way.

It was the same kind of look he was going for, rough around the edges. The band T-shirt and ripped jeans complimented his style. He wore his light brown hair in a half ponytail, some of the shorter strands fell over his eyes.

"More than twenty years I would say, we grew up together, his parents really helped when mine died and then I trained him."

"I'm sorry, I didn't know…"

"It's fine," he smiled. "It was a long time ago."

Illarion carried a lot on his shoulders, I knew that and it killed me to see the constant internal battle he was waging with himself. But God, it was hard, it was hard on me too.

"You're a Sensitive too?"

"Sure am, punk."

I rolled my eyes, following him up and over a few jagged boulders before we jumped down into a clearing of soft, green grass. The blades were still wet with the dew that settled over night.

Aurel took my hand in his and helped me across a large gap in the ground. Down below, a trickle of water rushed through the soil.

"Do you have someone, a friend you connect with?" I pressed my palm to my face.

He laughed and shook his head opening a small gate. "No, I don't. No one is connected the way you and Illarion are; it's rare."

"How did you know?"

"I saw it when he carried you through the door."

"That's your Sense."

"It is. I see people and their gifts, sicknesses, fears, worries, the whole lot."

"That must be difficult, sensing that someone is ill."

"It gets easier with time when you learn to control what you let in and out."

"I wish I could control mine."

"That would drive me nuts—other people's emotions and visions buzzing around in my head." He kicked a small stone up ahead of us and my eyes followed it until it disappeared behind a patch of grass.

"I don't know how to control it as well as Illarion does, but I guess he hasn't mastered it either."

"Something slip out that shouldn't have?"

"Yeah, you could say that."

We stopped walking. He placed his hand on my shoulder and gently squeezed it.

"Illarion is strong, the strongest Feeling Sensitive around, if it slipped out, then it slipped out for a reason."

"I don't know, it's confusing, I don't think it's a possibility."

"It is, if you both feel the same."

"It's not possible."

He shrugged. "If you say so."

I turned away from him and continued walking the perimeter of the grounds staying close to the fence.

"Come on." He motioned down another, small path.

Once we reached a clearing, I noticed two wooden benches side by side and a whole bunch of sticks and training swords.

"Illarion said you wanted to be better at hand-to-hand combat?" he asked, standing with his hands stuffed into his pockets.

"Yeah."

"Good, then let's get started."

CHAPTER ELEVEN

ACE

We left the training pitch covered in blood and sweat and little bits of tree and grass. Correction, *I* was covered in blood; the only thing Aurel was covered in was a smirk.

"You did well." Aurel patted my shoulder and I felt like a kid who'd just fallen off her bike while learning to ride.

I held my hand up to my face tenderly examining it to make sure nothing was broken.

"For a novice, of course."

"Gee thanks." I rolled my eyes and did my best not to limp.

I thought I was decent at hand-to-hand combat, but this guy was a machine. I pulled a twig from my hair and sighed.

"A little more training and you could take anyone on."

I smiled to myself. I had managed to land a few good blows on him in the form of an uppercut punch, a few annoying jabs and a right hook. But it didn't do nearly as much damage to him as it did to my hand.

"Under the age of twelve."

There it was. I groaned and kicked at the grass. It hurt to lift my foot and make the quick motion, but it did feel good to release the annoyance.

"Don't you ever get tired of talking?"

"It's actually one of my favorite pastimes."

"I can tell," I muttered.

"Sarcasm is obviously yours."

He led the way through the gate and we were back on the familiar grounds surrounding his home. When we reached the stairs, I involuntarily groaned with every step.

He clapped me on the back, forcing another irritated groan to surface.

"Tomorrow we'll run through the same drills but with a little more design on your fighting form. I have a feeling you'd suit the more aggressive style."

"If you're going to get more aggressive, I don't know that I want to get involved."

"Nothing you won't be able to handle. Now get showered and dressed."

"Why?"

"We're going on a stake out."

"Me and you?" I asked.

"I think you and Illarion need some time apart, the tension is giving me a migraine. You should also learn from the best, so like I said, you're coming with me."

This was going to be a long night.

I stopped at the bottom of the main staircase preparing myself. I slowly lifted my foot. Yep, this was *torture*. I whimpered taking the steps one at a time until at last I reached my room.

Collapsing onto the tiled floor, I lay there for a few minutes until I could move again. Then I checked myself over the mirror wincing at every movement which involved stretching the skin around the cuts I'd acquired.

A nasty purple bruise was forming rapidly under my left eye and across my cheek. At least it covered the scar. *Great.* That was attractive. It was a good thing I healed faster than the average person, and my social life was limited to these guys and a tech-nerd at the Agency, none of whom would even look twice at it.

Focusing on gently applying concealer to the bruise, I dressed for the second time today and made my way down the stairs, coming face to face with Illarion who was on his way up.

I narrowly missed running right into him and was saved only by my quick reaction to move out of his way. His eyes skimmed over the bruises on my face and neck.

I sighed. Despite my best contouring efforts, he still saw the bruise. A cord in his neck popped as he took a few steps down. He didn't look impressed. Clearly, he'd been expecting more from me.

I peeled my eyes away from him.

"I was just coming to get you."

"Here I am," I said, wondering whether he was coming up to hurry me or if he wanted to come along. "I'm not sure I can stand to listen to Aurel boast all night. Why don't you join us?"

He smiled at that and shook his head. "I'd love nothing more than to see you put him in his place, but I can't," He motioned downstairs, and I followed him. "I wanted to show you the encryption software we're using to track our target."

He handed me a small envelope with two black chips in it.

I tipped the contents into my hand. "Tracking devices?"

He gave me a quick nod before dropping into the chair in the makeshift office he'd set up. Files brimming with papers filled the space on the kitchen table, two laptops and a couple of notebooks sat neatly beside it.

"As soon as you plant them, it'll activate this and we'll start a trace." Illarion nodded to the laptop he pulled toward him.

He opened it and showed me a screen which came to life with the street view of Bob's house.

"Does Aurel know?" I asked, suddenly curious just how much trust lay between the two men.

"He knows what he needs to."

"Do you trust him?"

"I trust him."

"Okay then," I said softly, tucking the envelope into my leather jacket. "I'll see you in a bit."

He'd given me everything I needed and he'd said everything he needed to. Yet neither of us moved. His eyes were focused on mine, his dark lashes low hiding undeniably intoxicating whisky eyes. My breath was caught in my chest. There were words on the tip of his tongue, just there, under the surface but he remained silent.

Before he could say anything, I got up. I felt the apprehension rushing through his heart. If he was this unsure about me, I wasn't going to make this any harder for him.

"Be careful," he said.

"Always am."

After I'd gathered a few more things Illarion had prepared for me I made my way outside to where Aurel was leaning against the porch with a cigarette in his hand.

"Ready punk?" he took a last haul and blew ringlets into the air.

"Sure am."

"Let's go," he agreed, tossing the butt on the ground. "When we get there, we'll do a drive around, find a spot to stake out and when we spot him you get your trackers on," he explained. "Nice and simple. No heroics, got it?"

"Got it." I nodded, pulling out everything I would need when we got there.

Illarion was right when he said that we would be closer to the target here because we only drove for about fifteen minutes before we were sweeping the surrounding streets and looking out for a spot to park.

211

Aurel decided on a large tree which cast a heavy shadow in the afternoon sun and sheltered us.

A few kids were playing outside throwing a ball around which made me miss being a normal person. Would I ever have that? Kids and a house with a white picket fence? Probably not.

"Can I ask you something?" I turned my body to face him.

"Sure, punk." He nodded, throwing up a kernel of popcorn into the air, catching it in his mouth.

"What is Operation Lullaby?"

His eyes narrowed as though I'd caught him by surprise. "It's classified."

"Classified?"

"Operation Lullaby is need to know only."

"I need to know. I'm working on this team. I'm working with Illarion. What is Operation Lullaby?"

His body stiffened as he took my question in.

"Aurel?"

He turned his attention outside, no doubt keeping an eye on the house we were watching.

"Operation Lullaby is about you," he said keeping his eyes on the street.

"What? What do you mean it's about me?"

"It's the name the Agency gave to *Operation watch Ace*. It's been around since you were born. Illarion was read into it ten years ago, before him, there were others, Michael, Elena…"

"Damon," I bit.

"Yes."

"When I came in for the interview, Raymond said something to Illarion, he asked him whether there would be a repeat of Operation Lullaby. What did he mean by that?"

Aurel ran his hand through his hair. "Illarion can tell you about that."

"What happened?"

"Ask Illarion."

"I'm asking you."

"You're a pain in the ass."

"I've been told. Don't deflect."

Before he could respond he straightened up and spoke. "Here he comes."

"Earlier than expected?"

"Maybe he was bored at home."

My eyes followed his but I couldn't see anything. I looked back at him dusting off a kernel of corn which had found its way into my ponytail.

"Trust me, he's there."

Right. His sense was sight. How could I forget? He probably saw him through the walls or something.

"You ready?"

"Double around the block, meet me in ten."

"Go get 'em, Specter."

I took the envelope and dropped the trackers in my hand, rushing across the street. I tried to blend in with the residents walking around as much as I could.

No one paid me any attention as I stepped up onto the sidewalk and up to his car. I ran into the driveway before he could reverse. I hit the trunk with my hand and shouted.

The brakes engaged and he got out of the car.

He came at me with fury until he spotted me. Then his scowl turned into a full blown, pervy grin.

"Are you alright, miss?" he asked, looking at me and then his car.

I looked up at him with the most seductive look I could muster. I fanned my chest with the side of the jacket and watched as his eyes lowered until they fell on my chest. I knew how to use my assets. I'd been gifted with a lean, athletic build as well as D cup breasts. Given that his attention was on my cleavage, it didn't matter that my make-up didn't completely cover the bruise spanning the whole left side of my face.

"I'm sorry. I wasn't paying attention." I swayed gently on my feet leaning against his car giving him a better look at my chest.

"No, no, my darling, I should have seen you there."

A smile spread across his lips, now while his attention was on me, I reached behind me and planted the trackers. Bob was one creepy dude.

Much to my advantage, I'd learned that apparently seedy old criminals loved young women in tight jeans and leather jackets.

"Love your style, Specter," Aurel said, and I could tell he was smirking. I rolled my eyes when I turned away from Bob.

He offered to take me out for dinner, to apologize for nearly running me over. I smiled and thanked him for his kind offer but politely declined.

He wasn't happy with my answer, but he sent me on my way no doubt checking out my ass as I left.

I watched his car pull out onto the street and drive away and around the corner, when I was sure I was clear I casually walked back around and got into Aurel's car.

"Are we up and running?" I asked, closing the door.

He nodded and pulled out onto the road. "Illarion has the feed, good work, rookie."

"Thanks."

He handed me the tablet Illarion had set up to track the car and I brought up the screen.

"When do we engage?"

"We need to collect data for at least twenty-four hours; we need to know what his movements are before we attempt anything."

"Twenty-four hours, damn." We were cutting it close. They'd be expecting to hear from us by then.

"I know, but believe me, rushing these kinds of ops is a bad idea."

"What do we do now?"

"We track who he sees, when and where, how many people he travels with, when he stops to eat and sleep, everything," he explained.

I nodded.

"When we know all of that, we can plan our attack."

"Illarion told you we're not killing him, right?" I asked, needing to be sure we were planning the same mission. Bob was a total creep, but right now, there was nothing pointing to us needing to eliminate him.

He nodded taking the car through a back road to his place. I noticed how Aurel's eyes flicked to the rear view mirror every so often; he was no doubt making sure we had no tail. He was still alive out here on his own because he was good.

"Illarion told me you think you can get information from Bob," he said.

"Do you think that's naive of me?"

"Not at all, a great agent always questions their orders."

I gave a half laugh. "I heard the opposite."

"That's the difference between good operatives and great ones."

I beamed.

"You're going to be the latter."

Now that was as sincere as he had been with me since we met.

"You'll have your answers soon. Then you'll be on your way with prince boring."

"He's not boring." I laughed this time, shaking my head.

"He's pretty boring."

I continued monitoring the movement of the blue dot on the screen.

After a few moments of silence, he added, "He'll protect you no matter the cost."

"That's what scares me."

His eyes went back to the road. "You'll come to know that when Illarion wants to do something, no one can change his mind or stop him."

That's exactly what worried me.

"In all my years of working in the field, I've never known anyone as stubborn as him. If you're worried about choices he may or may not make in the future, then you're wasting your time. You can't live on what ifs."

"Infinite wisdom from Aurel," I muttered.

"Don't knock it. I swear it's true."

"I bet it is."

We pulled up to the gate and keyed in his pin. The pad was also coded to his fingerprints. He had some serious security out here.

"So, big night for the two of you," he said, parking the car.

"I guess so, have to look over everything, get some plans in motion."

He nudged me in the ribs.

"What was that for?"

"Don't forget what I said." He pushed the door open and disappeared up the stairs.

I sighed. Of course he would leave me to wrestle the door and bags of equipment on my own. I rolled my eyes.

"Hey, need help?" Illarion called out appearing before me.

"Yes, please." I handed him the heavy bag and followed him back through the house.

"Sorry about that, Aurel's not the chivalrous type."

"That's okay, I'm sure it's some kind of training in patience or feminism," I added sitting down beside him.

"You're probably right. Good job by the way."

He nodded to the map up on screen.

The blue dot travelled through winding roads.

"Thanks."

"We need to find the best window of opportunity to execute the plan. We won't have any room for error." He moved closer to me to reach across for the equipment I brought in.

The mix of cologne and sweat on his skin was gentle yet intoxicating and I almost had to remind myself to breathe because for a moment, I stopped. His arm brushed across mine and I felt myself tense in response.

He tensed as well. Shit.

Looking back down at the tablet in front of me, I cleared my throat and fiddled around with the settings. Damn it. Why was the screen so bright?

If there had been any time to try and block out my feelings, it was now. My heart was pounding against my ribs and my brain was about to explode as I imagined his muscular arms holding me, and his breath dancing on my neck.

He continued working and I continued telling myself every few minutes or so to stop staring.

I couldn't get a read on anything he was feeling and I wasn't sure whether I wanted to know at that point.

I bowed my head and focused on the work.

We were going to have a long, difficult road if we were right about the situation. How would we take on Damon, the Director of the Agency? Would anyone believe us?

I glanced across at Illarion before bringing my attention back to my laptop.

CHAPTER TWELVE

ACE

Illarion monitored the screen and our target while I busied myself with menial tasks. Ones that he'd assigned to me, no doubt trying to keep me out of his way. Not that it bothered me, I needed to keep my distance from him.

"Aurel is going to join us," he said.

"To do surveillance?"

"I'm changing the objective. I want him. I want to know what he knows."

"You want to bring him in."

"Yes." He leaned back in his chair, stretching his neck out, making his shirt came up slightly.

I couldn't stop my eyes from going down across to the taut lines of his abdomen. A myriad of faint scars lined his skin, quickly, I pulled my attention away.

"Who's infiltrating?" I asked, hoping that he didn't notice my little intrusion.

"You and I." His mouth curved into a smile. "Aurel is running surveillance a few streets away—the usual formation."

I nodded, recalling that's exactly how we played it when Raymond was with us for our visit to the office of Mr. Fox.

He looked down at his watch. "We should get some rest. We need to be on the ball tomorrow."

As I was turning to leave he gently took a hold of my wrist.

My heart fluttered at the slight contact but I reminded myself that this was a job and he was my boss. I calmed my heart and offered him a smile.

"Maybe a walk first would be good," he said quietly. "To get some air."

"Good idea." I dropped everything back on the table and followed him out. God knew I needed some fresh air and probably a cold shower.

We walked along the same path Aurel and I took earlier today only there wasn't any back and forth banter this time. All that surrounded us was silence until he spoke.

"I need you to know that this is dangerous, what we're involved in," he said.

Looking at him side on, I considered his words for a few moments and then cleared my throat. "I know but it needs to be done though, right?"

"Yes. It does."

"We'll be fine. I trust this team."

He responded with a soft laugh, and it was the most comforting thing I'd heard all day. It just felt right. He looked down at the ground, his hair falling over his face, shielding him from me.

I focused my attention on him and was surprised at what I found there, he was nervous. Prying into someone's head like that was frowned upon. Especially since I felt like my skull was going to explode when Damon poked and prodded inside there.

Moments later, he turned to me stopping. "If things go bad, I need you to get yourself out."

"Okay."

His eyes darkened. "You know the dreams are a warning. You know what they mean."

"We can't live on what ifs." I surprised myself at how easy Aurel's words came to mind.

He had been right. Annoying attitude aside, he was a smart guy, too smart.

"I need you safe, do you understand?"

His vulnerability seared me to the core.

"I'm sure you'll do a good job keeping me in line."

He didn't even crack a smile. "I'm serious, Ace. I need you safe."

I began analyzing his words almost immediately; he *needed* me safe. What did that even mean?

"If things go bad, run. Promise me you won't try to be a hero. Not for Aurel, not for me."

He looked at me intently, obviously waiting for my answer but I didn't know what to give him.

I swallowed hard and took a step forward closing the gap between us. I didn't know what I was doing, my head and heart had stopped communicating the second his eyes fell to mine. Somewhere between the mild air turning cold, I found myself daring to imagine what it would be like to feel those full lips on mine.

He stood at least a foot taller than me and looking up at his rich eyes in the light of the moon was almost as intoxicating as the mixture of cologne and sweat which adorned him.

Adding to all of that, the air was alive with electricity between us.

I heard his breath catch.

"Ace…"

My name was barely a whisper on his lips. But the pleading in the one word was more than I could take. My body knew what it wanted, and my heart was yearning to be close. God, I wanted to feel him and feel his arms around me.

Slowly, I moved closer, emotions rushed through his eyes, every nerve was burning within him and as much as he tried to close his mind, he couldn't shut off what I saw in his eyes.

There, through the unspoken truth, I felt it. What he'd been hiding. He was afraid, terrified of me. Of my love and what I made him feel.

He lowered his gaze and gently raised his hand tucking a strand of hair behind my ear. I had to remind myself to breathe before I passed out.

"We shouldn't..." he whispered.

"No, we shouldn't."

Neither of us moved. The moonlight danced upon his skin. His eyes were alive, fire and passion flashed behind them, but he didn't act.

For moments, we lingered in the silent garden standing so close we were breathing the same air, almost touching but not needing to because I felt him course through me more than I had ever felt anyone before. This wasn't infatuation, it wasn't anything I'd ever felt before. He couldn't deny that he didn't feel the same.

He moved closer to me, and I moved closer to him. His lips parted and the softest sigh filled the air between us. I closed my eyes against the soft caress of his hand cupping my cheek. His breath was hot on my lips and my heart raged to life, and just before our lips met, he took my hands in his and pushed me back.

My eyes snapped open, confusion flushing my cheeks, reddening them.

"I can't lose you." He let out a breath.

"I don't understand."

He paused, looking away from me. "You and I, we can't. I can't."

"You're pushing me away? I think I have a right to know why."

"Ace—"

"Tell me."

"We can't, there are things you don't know, Ace, please understand."

"Then help me understand. Explain it to me." I stared at him, wide eyed. I swallowed, hating how my voice shook.

"One day I will…right now, I can't. It's not the right time."

"When is the right time?"

"I don't know."

"Fine. Got it. Loud and clear."

He tried to stop me as I turned to walk away but my stride was much quicker than his. I didn't stop to give him an opportunity to speak again.

Without caring that I was acting like a child, I stormed my way up the garden path and back into the house. My heart was heavy as I walked up to the front door and pushed it open.

As I rounded the corner and slammed the door shut I ran right into Aurel who looked slightly amused but thankfully said nothing letting me sulk away to be alone in my room.

I dropped face first into the bed and let the fluffy pillow take the brunt of my groan. Once I was done and felt remotely satisfied, albeit petty, I kicked off my shoes and crawled under the covers.

Pulling my hair out of the ponytail, I threw the elastic to the ground. I didn't need that shit in my life, not when I was just learning to develop my senses.

Love was a made-up emotion anyway and I didn't need that lingering around when I needed to be one hundred per cent focused and ready to fight.

So, in a way I should have been grateful for his help in realizing that.

Reaching down, I retrieved my phone from my pocket and glanced over the emails from the Agency. Amongst them were a few text messages from Aurel.

There was information about some calls we were going to monitor tomorrow before the job and some pictures of the surveillance equipment we would be using. I sighed, homework.

Once I'd gone through all the business messages, I noticed one at the end about Illarion.

"He doesn't know how to respond to you, he'll come around. See you tomorrow, punk."

I rolled my eyes and tossed the phone across the bed and dropped back into the pillow.

Yeah, you got that right. He has *no* idea.

I got stuck into the information he'd given me and began researching.

♥

The next day came quickly. I dressed in black slacks and a black tank top throwing on a leather jacket to match the plain combat boots. The more I stalled, the more I felt myself growing nervous about seeing Illarion after last night. *Maybe I could just call in sick.*

"Get yourself together, Ace," I muttered at my reflection.

Reining my nerves in, I made my way downstairs and collected the things I prepared last night and swiftly walked past the two men chatting in the kitchen. Ignoring them, I walked outside, and into the cold.

Illarion was regretful and frustrated, I couldn't tell at whom, but I didn't care, he proved to me last night he didn't know himself, so that was out of my mind now. Aurel was confused and a little annoyed and he wasn't hiding the fact that Illarion was the source of that annoyance. I shook my head; both their emotions were as confusing as hell.

Neither of them said anything about it during the drive and I was happy that we could maintain a professional relationship discussing the mission and the facts without any unnecessary words.

The feelings, however, were still there, twisting and turning beneath the surface of calm. That annoyed me more than if he were to just be upfront about it. At least if he told me that he wasn't interested then I could move on. But he was interested, and he was lying, why? I had no idea because he didn't want to talk to me about it.

As we pulled up, I got to work. Aurel let Illarion and me out while he drove the van around the block and parked a few streets away.

Illarion handed me a walkie and a small satchel.

"The signal is still the same?" I asked.

He nodded. "You're on as soon as I cut my line. Good luck and stay safe."

I slung the satchel over my shoulder and ran along the edges of the fence. Thankfully, we were partially hidden in shadows from the tall oak trees that lined the streets. Glad that we had done our initial drive around during the day, I ran confidently, knowing exactly where I needed to go from here.

The cover of darkness was just enough to let me pass through the secured gate unnoticed; as I slipped in, the guard returned to his post.

"I'm in," I spoke into the earpiece staying low to the ground getting my equipment ready.

Aurel had gone over the details. How to get in, where to go from there and how much time I had between the change of guards. My role would be to get in and find the information on the computers inside the office, upload it to a portable hard drive and get out. The Agency wanted this guy dead, but Illarion wanted him alive and in our custody. Most of what we were here to get today would be information surrounding who he was working for, what he was hiding and why the Agency wanted him dead.

Somehow the cover of him being a drug dealer and Collector didn't sit well with me. There had to be more, and soon, we'd know.

Illarion would be in charge of monitoring the lines of external communication so that he could locate and apprehend the target. The thug was going by the alias of, *Bob*—the guy who loved young women in tight jeans and leather jackets.

Aurel would make sure we were both clear to do these things.

I ran across the field, dodging randomly placed sprinklers until I reached the wall. I crouched down and waited.

"You're looking good, Specter, Nighthawk is about to make the cut. Wait for my mark," Aurel announced in my ear.

Readying myself, I slowly got to my feet and got ready to make the run.

I spotted the signal which was a strategically timed flash of lights and sprinted across the yard toward the south side of the house. Leaping over an array of rose bushes and planter boxes, I commando rolled into a soft patch of grass right underneath the first-floor balcony and pressed myself flat against the wall.

Satisfied that I was safe, and no one was alerted to my presence, I reached for the window and hoisted myself up and over the ledge and squeezed into the room through the window.

"Good work," Aurel commented. "Wait for my mark to make the next move."

Nodding to myself, I crouched low to the ground, sweeping the room. It was quiet and unoccupied. It looked to be a small office of sorts, not the one we needed sadly.

Aurel's voice came through the small device in my ear again. "You're clear all the way down the hall, first door on your left."

I proceeded across the room to the door, cracking it open slightly waiting on Aurel's word.

I took a deep breath and slipped out of the room gently closing the door behind me. I made my way down the hall and located the door.

"The door is locked, I need a minute," I spoke quietly to Illarion.

"You're clear. Take your time," he responded promptly.

It took a few moments of tinkering before I heard the lock give way. I slipped in through the door and closed it behind me before moving to the desk at the far end of the room.

"And tell me again why I couldn't have just crept in through this window?" I asked, while setting up my hard drive ready to copy across the data from the computer.

The room was large, almost as big as Illarion's study—only this one had a more Edwardian feel to it. There were bookcases stacked from floor to ceiling with old, antique books while the floorboards were a dark mahogany protected by a large, thick Persian rug. I gave it a quick appreciative look before bringing my attention back to the computer.

"Because it's directly in view of the main guards."

"Fair enough," I said, getting to work on the external and internal surveillance. Once the feed was looped, I cut it. "You're clear to come up."

My encryption software locked into the main server and shut down the surveillance in the house. *Damn I was good.*

"Copy that," he replied. "Nighthawk, you're up. I'm keeping a tab on the external surveillance, but the looped feed looks good."

"Stay alert everyone," Illarion's voice came through the channel.

Just as he moved on his end, I made my way into the next file we needed, I started to copy across all the information, narrowly avoiding the virus which would be set off if the information was disturbed. I sucked in a breath and worked around it. Crisis averted. As soon as the first copy was done, I tucked it into my pocket and moved onto the second copy.

"I'm in position," Illarion said.

Aurel didn't have internal surveillance of this part of the house, which was another reason I needed to be here to guide Illarion down to where he needed to be. I pulled the USB free from the laptop and stuffed everything back into the satchel. I pulled open a large closet door, revealing eight large monitors.

"How did you know they'd be in here?" I asked. My question was to no one in particular, but Aurel's smartass response was exactly what I expected it to be.

"Because they always are. Don't you watch movies?"

I snorted.

Focusing my attention back on the monitors, I looked at the feeds and followed a few guards walking around the lower levels of the house.

I looked over the internal surveillance. "You're clear to go. You've got one down the hall to your left."

"Copy that."

Once he was clear, I made my way out of the room and down the hall taking the elaborate staircase two steps at a time.

I took a sharp left and rounded the corner into the large living area we'd seen on the schematics of the building. I made my way straight across the floor into the butler's pantry, which held a good amount of food and more importantly, Twizzlers. I considered taking one but decided against it. All the way at the back there was a door to another room—the office—all the information I needed was right through there.

Grinning at my success I pushed the door open. What I didn't expect was a person in there and my ego quickly came down at least ten notches. Not good.

He lunged at me, and before I had a second to think, he took a hold of my wrist and pulled a restraining maneuver on me. He pulled my arm behind my back, threatening to break it at any moment if I struggled. I screamed out in pain before I could stop the sound.

I had to think.

I had to get myself out.

The momentary surprise threw me off before my training kicked in. I snapped my head backwards, effectively breaking his nose. As painful as it was for me I managed to get him to release my arm, giving me the advantage I needed.

He must have been my age. His eyes were completely black, anger poured off him as he hissed through his teeth. I couldn't look away. *What the hell was wrong with his eyes?*

Distracted by the shocking appearance of my sparring partner, he threw a left-hand jab, stunning me and finished it off with a right hook right in the eye socket right in the already bruised, delicate flesh. I dropped to my knee clutching my face and as he came again. This time I launched my foot at his knee and dropped him. He was only down for a few seconds before he was coming at me again. The tight fighting quarters was making this a whole lot harder than it should have been, that coupled with the fact that he was so much stronger than anyone I'd ever fought before. I bit down on my molars and lunged at him. My fist met with his jaw making him stumble back slightly before he regained his composure and threw an equally effective punch at my face.

I recovered, spun around on the spot and kicked. My foot connected with his knee and as I'd hoped, I heard a loud crack as the bone gave way. I didn't take any chances. I did a switch kick and slammed my shin into the side of his head. He dropped in a painful, graceless heap.

He tried to shout out, but I lunged forward and closed one hand over his mouth pushing him down, into the ground. Had I not broken his leg, his sheer size would have overpowered me, and this would have ended a lot differently for me.

I pressed my forearm down on his throat until he went limp. I didn't kill him, but he wouldn't be down for long.

Expelling a shaky breath, I gathered myself and rushed over to the desk. I threw a quick glance back at the unconscious man. *What the hell was he?*

The fact that he didn't have surveillance in this room was something to mention to Aurel when we met up again.

"I'm here, I've got it, Nighthawk."

"Copy that, Specter. Subject has been acquired, heading to the rendezvous point now," he replied.

I nodded to myself and made my way out of there.

The rest of the mission was simple. I made it back to the rendezvous point unseen. I pulled open the door to the van and climbed in surprised to see that I was there before Illarion.

As Aurel's eyes fell on my face, his features hardened. "Jesus, what happened?"

I'd forgotten about the rapidly forming bruise across my face. I reached up and touched it gingerly. "Just a scuffle."

"Are you okay?" he asked, not dropping the concerned look.

No. I wasn't fine. Not by a long shot. I fought some dude with demon style pupils who had a right hook Sam and Dean would have been proud of. I shook the image aside and lied. "I'm fine, where's Illarion?"

"He's heading up now he had to take the long way back."

"Is everything okay?"

"He's just being cautious," he explained, looking back at my face. The look in his eyes shook me. What did he know that I didn't?

"Let me see," he said firmly. "That cheek was already injured from our training session; it could be fractured now."

"Probably is, it hurts like a bitch."

"Let me see."

"It's fine. I'll ice it when I get back."

I pulled away, shaking my head.

"I think you'll need a lot more than ice."

"It's just a scratch. Perks of the job, right?" As I touched it again, I realized that it wasn't just a bruise, the bastard had split my cheek.

I sighed, rolling my eyes. Aurel was right, that cheek was already hurt, and it could actually be fractured now. I wasn't a stranger to pain or scars and bruises.

He reached behind him and retrieved a white first aid box. He flicked it open, rummaged through the contents before fishing out a fresh gauze. He tossed it over to me and I wasted no time peeling the packet open and pressing it to my cheek. It was hardly the worst thing I'd experienced but damn it still hurt.

Iraq hadn't been kind to me. I went in feeling confident, proud, ready to stand tall, and when I came out, I was anything but. The gunshots, torture, and the nightmares that never ended—those were the perks of being a *hero*. I hated the term. I refused to entertain it. I was not a hero. I was a killer.

As he looked at me, eyes narrowing, I tried to add a lopsided smile but got no reaction from him at all.

I turned my face away from him pulling my hair out of the elastic, letting it fall over the latest injury.

The door at the back of the van opened and Illarion dragged Bob into the back with him and dumped him on the floor of the van.

From what I managed to see before I turned around, he looked fine with no signs of struggle at all. I guess that's why he was the boss.

"Let's get this gentleman home and see if we can get a few answers from him," he said softly in an almost melodic tone.

Aurel gave him a quick nod and pushed past me to get to the driver's seat. He turned the engine on and moments later, we were driving back to his house.

Behind me, Illarion pulled out a syringe filled with a pretty blue liquid and injected it into Bob's neck, he struggled momentarily, his face twisting in agony before falling still.

He held up the syringe and watched at the man's eyes widened, looking at it.

"Do you know what this is, Bob?" Illarion asked calmly.

He shook his head, eyes focused on every word Illarion was speaking. I didn't know either.

"This Serum will immobilize your evolved Sense so don't bother fighting it. You won't be able to break through. No one has ever broken through the Serum."

The Serum, that's what Josh was talking about. That's what Grimes mentioned. The fact that Illarion was using this meant this was serious.

Bob's eyes shot up and looked at me and then Illarion. Terror seized him and then he was out like a light. His eyes were open, but they were vacant.

With Bob taken care of, Illarion shifted from business to rage in a manner of seconds when he looked at me.

"What happened to your face?" he asked, moving across the van to kneel directly in front of me.

I tried to shake my hair over the bruise, but he took a hold of my wrist stopping my movement and much like last night my heart raced and my anger at him disappeared. Would he always be able to just melt all of my resolve?

"Just ran into some trouble, but I took care of it," I said softly.

A muscle in his jaw worked as his emotions ran wild. I felt anger coursing through his veins. His hand was still holding mine, heat radiating between us.

He gritted his teeth and spoke to Aurel without turning. "I thought you were watching her."

Annoyed with myself for feeling what I was, I pulled my hand out of his, not able to deal with my own stupid reaction to his touch. I wanted no involvement in the feud between the two friends.

"It's not his fault; there weren't any cameras in the guy's pantry."

Illarion ignored me. Something told me that my words wouldn't make a difference. He moved to me again and his voice softened.

"We have to get this cleaned up."

"It's fine," I insisted.

He ignored me and gently placed his fingers under my chin and tilted my head up.

"Ila..." I began trying to get him to stop.

He did, for a moment and looked me in the eyes. *"I need to do this Ace, please let me."*

His voice inside my head consumed me. He was inside holding on to every fiber, every nerve. Every cell lit up to his voice and his touch. My breath caught in my lungs, failing to come out.

"Fine," I muttered out loud.

I turned my face while I chewed my bottom lip pretending that the physical pain was worse than the emotions churning through my heart.

He peeled away the gauze which I now saw was soaked through. He tossed it in a trash bag and pulled open the same box Aurel had.

He got to work cleaning the cut all while I held my breath.

His voice was low. "Nearly done."

I swallowed hard and let him finish the job while I tried to push out the feelings flowing into me from not only him, but Aurel too.

His were mixed with what I could only describe as anger and fury, while Illarion was just plain furious.

As much as I just wanted to let it go, the illogical girl who wanted answers, deep inside me, was strong. *"What is this?"*

Aurel, oblivious to our conversation, continued driving silently keeping to himself but not keeping his feelings hidden.

Illarion paused before dabbing more antiseptic on my cut. I stifled a hiss.

"What's what?" he asked, avoiding my gaze.

I rolled my eyes and lowered my face so he had no choice but to look at me.

"You look at me with longing, but you push me away. You let your feelings suffocate me then you hide. Just tell me. What is this?" I bowed my head, and suddenly that powerful, confident resolve was gone. *"Why are you dragging me along?"*

He stopped what he was doing and dropped his hands into his lap. He sucked in a deep breath and found my eyes.

"Ace...I—"

"Be honest with me, damn it. Or stop dragging me behind you."

"Being with you is dangerous..." He trailed off looking down at his hands.

"Because you think I'll get hurt?" I asked, feeling stupid as soon as the words escaped me.

Much to my surprise, he shook his head and looked up at me. His warm, brown eyes were full of sadness. *"No. I'm afraid I'll lose you. I'm afraid that you'll be in danger because of me."*

"Don't you think I'm safer with you?"

"If I'm with you Ace, and things go bad, I will endanger everyone under our protection because my thoughts are on you," He admitted hanging his head.

And that was it. The noble spiel I couldn't fight. It wasn't about us alone; it was about everyone else and the job.

Finally understanding, I nodded.

An almost definitive end to a life we'd never really had.

CHAPTER THIRTEEN

ACE

My face hurt and my muscles were still recovering from the previous day's work out. So, as we pulled up to Aurel's house, I silently walked past the two men making a bee line for my room.

Illarion tried to stop me but the look I shot him must have been convincing enough to make him reconsider.

The moment I reached my room I slumped into the bed once more and cried.

What he said made perfect sense, but it sucked. My heart felt like it was in my throat and my stomach did somersaults as I played his words over and over, in my head.

His nobility made him a better person and it only made me feel more selfish.

I got up, moping wouldn't do me any good. He told me the reality of the situation and he meant it. There was no denying we couldn't be together. I felt his pain but I also felt his unwavering belief. That was certain.

The day had taken its toll on me. I cringed as I moved my aching body, I needed a shower. I stripped off my bloodied clothes and dropped them in the wash basket. My bones protested each movement until I stepped into the stream of hot water. I'd let myself soak for a good fifteen minutes before my skin started to tingle.

Once I was dried and dressed, I took out the laptop Illarion had provided and I retrieved the copy I'd made for myself from Bob's house.

I sat on the bed under the covers and slowly began sifting through all the information. I came across a name that was familiar. Damon Cale. These were his case notes, all his work. It suddenly begged the question. How did Bob have this information? And was he working for Damon?

"What are you planning?" I whispered.

I opened the folder which brought up at least a dozen more. I skimmed over several locked files until one stuck out at me. It was a peculiar name; it was simply labeled: The Taker. I couldn't open that file, just like others attached to it, they were encrypted, far more advanced than anything I knew how to break through.

My mind raced, the *Taker*. The Taker of what? The taker of life? The taker of money? My blood chilled. There were far too many unanswered questions. Far too much which made no sense.

The back of my throat grew dry and curiosity settled in the back of my mind. As I read through the rest of the files, another one caught my eye. It was labeled, *Cale*.

The moment I read the name my heart sunk and knew it wasn't a coincidence.

I deliberated whether I wanted to read it for a good fifteen minutes before I opened it. On the one hand these were the answers I needed, on the other, I believed that sometimes ignorance was bliss. I was terrified. What if it was something I couldn't live up to, what if it was something I couldn't face? I sucked in a breath and began.

The first file was dated almost thirty years ago. It seemed to be some sort of birth extract linked to a police report.

"I received instructions to respond to a distress call from the Cale residence at approximately 19:00. Dispatch advised the caller was male.

Upon my arrival, the male identified himself as the victim's father, Joe Cale. He confessed that he had found a male, approximately 23 years outside his daughter's window. Upon further investigating Joe admitted that his daughter fifteen-year-old Mariah had been raped by the intruder and in a blind fit of rage, he hit the intruder with a snow shovel while he was attempting to escape."

I sucked in a deep breath. The second police report had the same police officer's handwriting, roughly ten months later.

"I was on duty as a uniformed police officer when Mariah Cale, a young woman I met more than ten months ago contacted me. She asked me to witness her adoption papers. The rape resulted in a pregnancy she refused to terminate. Upon recommendation from her psychiatrist and her parents, she gave the baby boy up for adoption. The birth certificate was completed by the mother and witnessed by me. The child's name is Damon Cale."

Tears stung my eyes. I suppressed a sob, pressing my hand to my mouth, Mariah was my mother's name, she'd never told me her maiden name. But could this have been her? The coincidences were just too many not to be. Was Damon Cale my half-brother?

How the hell was I meant to process that? How could she never tell me? How could she keep such a huge secret knowing that this asshole was going to come after me some day? Anger and confusion swept through me and along with it, a torrent of tears which would never stop. Swatting away the tears from my cheeks, I opened the next document. It was dated ten years later. September ten. My birthday.

"Operation Lullaby is in force."

My mouth grew dry as I opened the next document.

A lump formed in my throat. These looked like they were still on an official level but not from the police. These looked like they belonged to the Agency. Upon closer inspection, I recognized the signature at the bottom from the mission briefs we'd been given. It was

Damon's, these were written by him, dated many years later, on my first year on tour.

"*Agent Illarion Lazarev has been read into Operation Lullaby. His duties are strictly observation. Agent Lazarev will not be required to engage any targets unless they're deemed an immediate threat.*"

The next case note beneath it was dated two years later.

"*Upon further review of submitted agent reports it has been decided that Agent Lazarev will remain suspended. Psychological evaluation pending.*"

My heart lurched. Psych-eval? Illarion? I shook my head clicking onto the next one.

It was dated almost four years later.

"*Mariah and Robert Hart deceased following fatal collision. Reports indicate Acacia Hart is protected by the Military. The Agency cannot get within two miles of her without raising suspicion. We need her on board now.*"

I blinked away the burning in my eyes and looked away from the computer. Nothing about this made sense, surely my parents would have sensed something was off about him. He was hiding in plain sight. Slowly, after what seemed like the longest time, I brought my eyes back to the screen.

This case note was dated six months later, around the time of my recruitment.

"*The Agency has been devising a plan. However, she must come willingly. She cannot be taken. By ensuring that her life is in danger, we will force the Agency into reckless action. It is imperative that they believe the threat to her life is real. The Taker thinks he's controlling this, he doesn't have a clue about how important she is.*"

I wiped my eyes with the heels of my palms. Who the hell was he talking about? I shook with rage as I read.

"*Agent Elena Somers will be tasked with bringing Agent Lazarev and Acacia Hart together. Agent Lazarev's familiarity will unite them while eliminating the people he deems a risk to Agent Hart's life. Agent Lazarev is key, without him access to her will be limited."*

I kicked off the blanket and paced up and down the room. My heart was thundering in my chest. Deep inside I felt the shift. A Darkness—much like the glimpses I caught in Illarion—flitted to the surface. It fueled me as the searing heat spread through my fingers and toes. Around me, the subtlest shift of air moved as though it came from me. Like static it burned in the air and just as it came, it was gone.

Anger boiled inside; it was a setup. All those years ago, they had set Illarion up. They knew he'd do whatever he needed to, to keep me safe. I ground my teeth. They made him kill, for me. Christ. I needed answers. After tonight's conversation, I knew it was the right thing to do and I knew he would have done the same.

Pulling on a sweater and a pair of jeans, I slung my satchel over my shoulder and quietly slid open the window. Carefully, I slipped out onto the edge of the sill.

Damon's words echoed in my head repeatedly, sounding more and more messed up the longer they rattled around in there.

As I stood on the ledge, I brought myself back to the present. The drop was at least ten feet and if I landed badly, I'd most likely break a leg, or if I didn't I could very well sprain an ankle which would be just as bad.

Aurel's house wasn't as big as Illarion's but he had a great landscaper. I needed something to climb down, or perhaps something useful that would cushion my landing.

They'd definitely hear me throw a mattress out the window.

I spotted a small garden bed made up of a box hedge and some shrubbery. It would do. I maneuvered myself out onto the ledge, scoped out my best angle and jumped.

The ground came hard and fast.

With a groan, I collected myself from the ground and stumbled my way across the yard carefully avoiding the locations with cameras and sensors, extremely grateful for the great memory I had.

As I made my way through the maze of cameras, I kept checking in with Aurel and Illarion to make sure they were oblivious to my movement. I could have been wrong, but I could have sworn that I made the air inside the room move as I mentally moved among them, or maybe I was losing it. Surprised that it didn't alert them, I picked up speed.

The gate was about a yard away. My ankle screamed in protest with every excruciating step.

When I reached the wall, I took a few moments to catch my breath and pulled myself up and over. The road stretched far ahead of me.

With no place in mind and no one to ask for help I did the only think a young woman could do out on the open road, alone; I hitch-hiked. I gripped the strap of my satchel and stayed closed to the edge; close enough to be spotted, far away enough not to get run over in case the wrong person came speeding along.

It didn't take long for a creepy, balding trucker to pull up and offer me a ride flashing me his toothless grin.

I tried to offer up a genuine smile as I climbed in; checking one more time to make sure Spock was in the bag. Satisfied that I was protected enough, I closed the door and told him to drive to Alabama.

He looked over at me every so often checking out my face, wondering who's been beating me up, while I held onto my bag as tightly as I could.

"You running away?" he asked, suddenly.

"Yeah, people suck."

"They sure do, doll. Do you know where you're running to?" he asked, changing the station a few times before settling on a country song.

"Anywhere but home," I lied.

He turned back to the wheel with a nod. "That sounds like a good plan."

We drove for another hour before he pulled off at an interstate exit and onto another highway.

"You have money?" he asked.

I shook my head.

We drove for another three hours before he finally pulled over.

"Where are we?"

"Just outside Alabama."

He reached into the glove box. I tightened my grip on Spock, wondering if I was about to use it.

From the corner of my eye I spotted a small, faded photograph. It looked like him, twenty years ago, and a young, happy girl.

"Is, is that your daughter?" I nodded to the glove box. The young girl had the widest, happiest smile on her face, her eyes shielded slightly by her dark blonde bangs.

He nodded, taking it out.

"She's pretty."

He looked back and smiled at it, "She was, until her boyfriend beat her to death."

Jesus. I swallowed hard. "I'm sorry."

"I am too. Every damn day. Just take care of yourself and keep running."

He pulled out his wallet, fished out two, hundred-dollar bills, and held them out.

"Here."

I looked at him dumbfounded and then back at the money. "I can't take that."

"Sure you can." He smiled and his hand shook ever so slightly. "You won't get far without money, trust me."

I accepted the bills and thanked him.

"I hope you find home one day."

I jumped out of the truck with a heavy heart.

"Keep running. Don't ever stop."

"Thank you." I smiled as he pulled onto the highway again.

Shrugging into my jacket, I wrapped my arms tighter around myself, and continued to walk with a heavy heart.

I quickened my pace and headed toward a seedy looking diner and snuck inside taking a seat in a corner booth which was poorly lit much to my relief. The walls were peeling with yellow and red paint, at some point I'm sure this looked like a cool place. Like one of those sixties diners where couples came to drink milkshakes and eat burgers. Today, it looked like anything but a place you'd bring a date to, unless she was paid by the hour.

The waitress who looked as bad as I felt took my order of a cheeseburger and chili fries and came back with a milkshake on the house. Grateful for her hospitality, I inhaled my meal and sunk back into the seat. I was exhausted, my feet ached, my head was splitting, and my insides felt like they went through a shredder. I was barely holding my emotions in place.

And then, it came to me. I shot upright and pulled out a few coins and asked for the pay phone. Surprisingly, no one questioned my need of an archaic technology in a world of modern miracles and instead just pointed me to the back of the diner to a phone box. No one even looked up from their cold, stale meals and week-old newspapers. At least I wouldn't be bothered here.

I fed the machine my coins and wiped the phone down before I pressed it to my ear and dialed a number I had committed to memory.

Seconds later, a familiar and friendly voice answered.

"Vanessa, it's me. I need to call in that favor."

Vanessa was one of my oldest friends and she was also one of the most resourceful women on the east coast. Being a former military resource, off the books of course, she could get anyone anything they wanted it. She was also insanely paranoid. There were rules in place as to how you had to approach her, and I respected that. Once upon a time I'd helped her out of a jam. She'd went through some traumatic stuff with a jerk from Langley and when the system failed, I hadn't. Now she always came through for me—we girls stuck together.

She agreed to meet me at the diner in two hours leaving me with a lot of time to set my plan in motion and get everything ready.

I made my way back to the counter and waited for the waitress to come back. Now in the full light she looked me over and stopped her gaze on my bruised face, which looked worse, especially given the rest of me was blue from the blizzard outside.

"You need to me to call anyone for you, hon?" she asked, quietly leaning across the counter, keeping her voice low.

As much as I hated the idea of exploiting people, that was part of my job and I'd become exceptionally good at it. This was going to work to my advantage and playing it up was going to help me a lot more than telling her to mind her own business. *I was so going to hell for this.*

I leaned across and whispered back, "I just need someplace to stay for a few hours. My friend is on her way."

She nodded and ushered me to a booth farther in the back, which I assumed was reserved for the employees to have their lunch during peak hours. "No one will bother you here."

I thanked her profusely and took my seat in the booth accepting the free coffee she kept bringing out. I downed each cup with a new-found respect for truckers and late-night workers. These coffees were awful.

Guilt gnawed at me for lying to her about such a serious thing, but it had to be done. Across the table, I set out the things I had brought trying to figure out exactly how I was going to make this work. I had my contact in mind. He was a horrible and dangerous man, but at this point he was all I had. I'd read about him in a few files that Aurel had forced me to read. I was meant to understand the dark side of our world. This guy was apparently right up there. He'd been accused of using his abilities to lure women to his room. I shuddered thinking what took place there. He'd even been known to use his Sense to force people into giving him money, drugs, and information. I cringed, I had no choice. If the other lowkey contacts proved to be a waste of time, I had to go in and brave it and hope that I was as good as people said.

Before I knew it, more than an hour and a half had passed and the waitress only checked up on me a grand total of six times and introduced herself to me as, Amy.

When Amy left, I looked up at the clock and right on time a car pulled into the empty parking lot.

What I didn't expect to see was Illarion instead of Vanessa.

Damn it.

I restrained myself from slamming my fist against the table. How'd he track me? I'd been so careful; I didn't even use my own cell phone. The booth was placed so I could see the entrance but whoever walked in couldn't see me.

I shoved everything back into the bag and rushed over behind the counter and ducked.

"Amy," I whispered. "I need to get out through the back."

She looked at me with a confused expression before putting two and two, together.

"I'll call the police."

"No, please. I'll just get out of here and then I'll call them myself. I need to do it. It should be me."

"Running won't make him stop, hon."

I shook my head and took a hold of her wrist. I added a tiny sprinkle of compulsion for good measure, not enough to completely control her, but enough to make her listen.

"Please, just help me."

"Honey, this isn't going to get better if you keep running away."

Shaking my head, I gave her the most pleading look I could muster, all while trying to keep my mind as clear and blocked off from Illarion as possible.

If he got a read on me this would end so badly. I didn't want her to call the cops and cause trouble for him. The last thing we needed was to be pegged on the radar.

The compulsion took hold, and she eased up and pointed behind her keeping her hand out of Illarion's line of sight. I couldn't risk opening myself up to him to ascertain his next move, so I was blind on this escape so to speak.

Keeping low to the ground, I made my way out the back door. I was as silent as possible, keeping away from anything that I could potentially knock over.

Once I was clear of the diner, I made my way across the parking lot and located Illarion's car, remembering my badass, not so orthodox method of borrowing cars, I picked the lock of an old grey sedan beside it. When the lock gave way, I slipped inside and got to work hotwiring the car. As the engine kicked and spluttered to life Illarion turned in my direction. I had just enough notice to shift into drive and take off.

Pressing my cell to my ear, I grit my teeth. I had no time to wait for Vanessa. "We need to change locations."

In the rearview mirror, I saw him, and in the briefest moment our eyes locked my control over blocking my mind was gone and he broke into my head.

"Ace, don't do this, please."

Sadness and anger roiled inside me. There were so many things I wanted to tell him, about us, about Damon, about all the shit that had been predetermined before we even had a say. But this wasn't the time. Instead, I calmed myself and spoke firmly through our connection. *"I'm sorry, Ila."*

And when I was able to push him out again, I managed to block him off completely until I didn't feel him anymore.

I was still learning about our telepathic abilities, but I had figured out that distance didn't impact the ability to *feel* one another but we did need to make eye contact to be able to speak through the connection, for now. Who knew what levels my abilities could stretch to once I hit my peak.

That was a sobering thought.

CHAPTER FOURTEEN

ACE

The highway exit for Boston came into view a few miles ahead. Following the road signs down to the city center I parked the car a few yards from the hotel building, I took everything with me and checked more than twice to make sure no one had followed me.

Certain that the men sitting on the bench across the road weren't Damon's henchmen, I slung my bag over my shoulder and crossed.

The hotel looked more like a motel and more teenagers filled the foyer than adults. Shrugging into my coat I smiled as a group of boys walked past me. This would work to my advantage. If anyone could help me, it would be these guys.

Off to my left I spotted the concierge. "Hi there," I said smiling widely. "I need a room please."

The lady behind the desk smiled in return handing me a clipboard with a form attached to it. "How long are you staying?"

"Not sure. I'm thinking of doing some sightseeing, so it could be a while."

"It's forty-five dollars a night and we require a credit card for holding."

Focusing on her, I took a steady breath and focused on the woman's eyes. Her violet aura intensified and then stopped pulsating as my power took hold.

"That's fine, however, you won't require a credit card in my case."

"We don't need your credit card.

"Great."

I handed her the cash and released the breath I'd been holding.

"Here are your keys and details for the Wi-Fi."

I took the paperwork and signed my creative alias of Sydney Vaughn. I handed her the clipboard and happily took the key from her.

Making my way to the elevators, I pushed the button for the seventh floor and disembarked with a group of tourists from the UK.

I smiled as each of them walked past me. I waited until they rounded the corner before entering my room.

Sucking in a deep breath I turned on all the lights, closed and locked the door behind me and leaned heavily against the wooden frame. Securing the room took less than a minute considering it was the size of a shoebox.

This was going to be hard, I mused, looking around at my surroundings. I was alone, low on cash and out of my depth.

There had to be a way to get to the guy who had the information, I remembered Illarion mentioning something about rumored sightings of Sensitives. Sometimes they were spotted around bars, sometimes the underground papers made mention of us. Maybe that would be my way in. Maybe I'd finally get in touch with the elusive creep who knew more than he should have.

Laying out the minimal clothing I'd brought with me, I scoffed. None of these would get me into any bars. I needed something nice, something sexy.

Taking the cash I had, I locked up and jogged down the stairs, taking them two at a time.

A store just across the road caught my eye. I smirked; sexy, daring and exactly what I needed.

There were backless gowns, strapless dresses, fabric which didn't cover more than my navel.

"Can I help you?" a woman in a gold, tube dress approached me.

Holding a black, strapless mini dress, I smiled. "Have you got this in red?"

♥

Leaning against the bar, I sipped my Mimosa watching the dance floor fill with scantily clad women and men who respected no one. They were grinding against each other, lost in the beat of the music and the sweat drenching their bodies. I looked away, this was not my scene. But I was trained to fit in, to disappear when I needed to, and stand out when it counted.

So as a guy a few years older than me came to stand at the bar, I smiled, biting down on my lip producing a seductive smile.

"Are you alone?" he asked, his eyes wandering down across my body, stopping on my breasts, my legs and then coming back up to meet my face.

I smiled.

He cleared his throat.

"And if I am?" I asked, tipping my face in his direction.

"You shouldn't be."

"Well then I'm lucky you're here, aren't I?" I whispered, leaning into him.

As I took the last sip from my glass, he took it from me and placed it back on the bar. "Dance?"

Nodding, I followed him, keeping my eyes focused on his as much as possible. His thoughts were a real treat to endure. He loved the way the red fabric hung on my hips and the way my breasts looked in the bodice.

I wanted to roll my eyes. Instead, I stood in front of him and let him put his hands on my hips. He pulled me toward him and somehow his knee ended up between my legs, ready for some sort of grinding dance move. I cringed but went with the flow.

We moved in time to the music and occasionally he'd grope my butt and when I snatched his hand away, he'd smirk before pulling me in for a kiss. I went with it for the first few times, careful to keep my temper in check until I couldn't stand his face on mine anymore.

Before he opened his mouth to complain, I pushed him backwards into the wall, close to the exit of the bar. He looked up at me excitedly and took it as a hint that I wanted to leave. Well, he wasn't wrong.

We did leave, only I didn't want to go anywhere with him. He followed me like a lost puppy for the first few yards until he swore at me and left. I didn't hear all of his creative remarks but I heard tease and bitch a few times.

Sighing, I pulled on my coat and headed back to the hotel.

"Everything okay?" a voice spoke, drawing my attention.

"Sure," I muttered turning to the sound.

It belonged to a young, blond man. He stood against the wall, puffing a cigarette.

"You're new here," he said matter-of-factly.

"Yeah." I nodded, pulling off my heels and replacing them with a pair of flats I'd kept in my bag.

"You look like you had a bad night," he mused, dropping the butt at his feet, snuffing it.

"My night was fine. I went out dancing, and met some jackass and that was not so fine."

"Did he hurt you?"

My eyes narrowed.

"Did the guy hurt you?" he repeated.

"Why do you say that?"

"Maybe the look on your face is a different sort of pain, or angst."

Was this guy a Sensitive? His aura looked normal, usually I could tell if there were gifts within someone. Lately I'd become much better at it, more in tune.

"I'm not in pain," I said flatly.

"Well, then," he said softly. "I apologize, I'm obviously mistaken, but if you need a drink, I'm hanging by the bar. God knows, I need it."

"Fine, let's drink."

"I'm Chris," he said softly.

"Sydney." I nodded, shaking his hand.

Together we spent the better part of the evening drinking. He spent a lot of time asking questions trying to get information from me. I, however, spent most of my time avoiding answering him. He wasn't a Sensitive, but he knew about us. He was my ticket.

♥

The same knock I'd heard every night for the past two weeks, came again at precisely seven o'clock.

"Ready, Syd?" he called from the door.

"Yeah, come in, just getting my shoes," I muttered, pulling the second, black stiletto on.

"So, tell me again why we're going to the same, boring club?"

"Because I need to find who this source is," I explained, nudging him with my foot. "Come on, VIP is only letting us in until eight."

He nodded getting up. "You never told me why this was so important."

"I told you. I'm working for this guy. He needs the info, that's all I know."

"So, you're not one of them?" he asked, raising his brow.

Scoffing, I pushed him out of the room. "Nope. I'm just a normal gal, probably boring."

"You're not boring. You're pretty cool."

Laughing, I pushed the elevator button to ground. "Thanks, appreciate it."

"Seriously, the stories about this guy aren't good. Are you sure you want to go digging around for him?"

How could I tell him the truth? I turned to him and frowned.

"The guy I work for...he doesn't care how I get the info. My butt is on the line here. One way or another, I have to do this—with or without your help. I'd prefer your help."

"I'm with you, but you're nuts, you know that, right?"

Laughing, I smoothed down my dress and kept walking. "Come on, I'm cold."

We rushed to the door of the VIP line, thankfully we only waited a few minutes before the bouncer let us in.

"I'll hang back."

I spotted my target and moved. I couldn't believe my luck. We'd been coming here night after night and he was here, finally.

I nodded without turning back.

There had been more than three occasions where I'd heard whispers in this bar about the creepy, balding dude who sat by the fireplace. Now I saw him, his name was Larry, and he made my skin crawl. He was a convicted criminal, apparently, he did time for some serious stuff.

Swallowing the nausea, I moved toward him, sauntering like I wasn't walking toward the worst decision of my life.

He stopped groping the waitress as I neared and looked up and around until he spotted me. His eyes widened.

"To what do I owe the pleasure?" he asked, pushing the waitress away.

Forcing myself to remain calm, I looked across at the man beside him. "Tell your bodyguard to take a walk."

He smirked, but he did as I said. "Mike, we're fine."

As Mike left, I moved toward Larry's table.

"What can I do for you, baby?" he asked, giving me all his attention.

His aura reeked, and he didn't smell any better. I cleared my throat and looked at him, ensuring I was shielding my identity as much as possible. He didn't need to know who I was, not if my anonymity could work to my advantage.

"I need to know about Sensitives."

"You know more than you're leading me to believe, Sydney, is it?" he asked, cocking his head.

"I know enough, but I need to know more."

"More?" He laughed, drawing the attention of a few people around him. "I think you're lying to me."

"I don't care what you think. Where can I get information about the Divine Sensitive? Where can I find out about the others?"

He considered my question for a moment before laughing again. "There's another club near here, Zion. It's a hub, loaded with everything you need to know. But it's a waste of time."

"Why?"

"Because no one there will know anything more than me. Now, if you want any more information, I'll be expecting payment."

"Forget it." I shoved away from the table.

He laughed again, calling the waitress back over, signaling the end of our conversation.

Chris met me halfway across the dance floor and stopped me. He pressed both hands on my shoulders. "What happened?"

"It's a dead end."

I pushed past him, heading for the door.

"Syd, wait."

I paused while he caught up.

"We'll keep trying. There have to be more leads."

"There aren't." I turned on my heel. "It was all a waste of time."

He pressed his hand to my waist, pulling me toward him. "It doesn't all have to be a waste."

I wanted to pull back, but this week had taken its toll on me. I was exhausted and I was alone.

Noticing my hesitation, he stepped back. "Come on, I heard there was a cool club around here."

"I don't want to go to any more clubs, I'm tired."

"It's not even ten, plus you look awesome in that dress and I'm not done drinking, something tells me you're not either."

"I really just want to go to bed."

"Zion is meant to be insane, you won't regret it."

My ears perked up. "Zion?"

CHAPTER FIFTEEN

ACE

Chris and I walked along the dark, plush green carpet into the underground of Zion. The club was dark—death metal pounded through the walls. People were either high on drugs or compulsion.

I wasn't alone in here. There were loads of other Sensitives. I swallowed hard and looked around. It was getting easier to spot auras and differentiate them from the non-Sensitives.

Chris followed me as we roamed the cobblestone club. Up above us, cast iron lanterns swung to the beat of the overhead rail system. Electric green neon lights lined the edges of the bars and the walkways. My eyes drew everything in, as did Chris's.

"This is crazy," he shouted.

All I could do was nod wordlessly. This was unlike anything I'd ever seen before.

A woman stopped in front of me.

"First time?" she asked, toying seductively with a lock of her hair.

I nodded.

"Follow me."

I glanced sideways at Chris who appeared ready and willing to follow. I rolled my eyes.

"A drink?" she said as we reached the end of the bar.

"Sure." I followed her further behind a dark drape.

"This is your private booth."

Chris and I glanced at each other.

"We offer the seats to first timers. Take a seat, and we'll bring the drinks out."

As she left, we both sat down in the velvet, U shaped lounge while Chris took the opportunity to lounge across it like he owned the place.

"Huh." He said, looking around like he was impressed. "VIP twice in one night."

"Doesn't this seem odd to you?" I asked, looking around the room and up at all the cameras.

"You're just paranoid. We both know that."

"You're right." I nodded. "Sorry."

"Don't apologize, just have some fun. Relax." He smiled, patting my hand.

Never once in the six weeks I'd known him had he tried anything more than to be my friend. I couldn't express how good that felt. I needed someone in my life but not like that. I never fell asleep without thinking about Illarion. I never woke without him on my mind. But God, I was lonely. Troy was out there somewhere thinking I ghosted him, Illarion was God knew where, hopefully not in trouble and I was galivanting around like some secret agent I had no business acting like.

Sighing, I smiled as the waitress came back with a vibrant green drink in a tall challis and copper goblets to match.

Chris grinned as he poured me a drink and then himself.

We drank more than three cups each as I felt the dizziness start to wash over me.

"I need the washroom, I'll be back." I laughed as I got up and stumbled over my feet.

Chris nodded, leaning back in the lounge. "I'll be right here."

Walking through the club I averted my eyes as much as possible. Girls winked at me, boys tried to call me over, but all I wanted to do was find the toilet. What the hell had they loaded the cocktails with? It wasn't roofies, I knew that much.

As I pushed the door open to the washroom another woman followed me in and shut the door, locking it.

It took two seconds flat for my guard to go up. I spun on the spot, holding my arms out, ready for a fight. The woman held up her hands in surrender and then she spoke, in my head.

"We're on the same team, Agent Hart."

My breath caught. I'd been careful.

"You've been a hard woman to track down, took me more than four weeks to pinpoint you."

"What do you want?"

"I want to help you; you've been asking around for information. I think I may have it."

Her eyes were warm, and kind and the orange hue of her aura pulsed steadily, she wasn't lying but I wasn't new to this game.

"Your friend sent me."

No one should know me here. I'd been careful. Keeping my expression as neutral as possible I folded my arms across my chest, stepping back.

She smiled. *"Vanessa said you would be reluctant to believe us. She also said that if we didn't convince you, you'd be happy to know that Agent Lazarev got home safe after the diner."*

Tears burned the back of my eyes and I let my guard down.

"The information you need is in these documents, but for the sake of your safety, and all you're meant to be protecting, take it and stay low. Do not get involved."

She handed me a shiny black USB.

When I took it and looked up at her the woman smiled.

"Be careful."

I agreed, turning my attention to the USB in my hand. When I looked up, she was gone.

I returned to the lounge, happy to see Chris. He was drinking another glass of the freaky green liquid.

"Thought you bailed."

"As if I'd leave your sorry ass here alone, come on. I'm bored."

He got up and followed me. I tucked the USB safely in my bag and started to move through the bodies on the dance floor. As I neared the door, I felt a gentle tug on my wrist. The dizziness of the alcohol caught up with me as I turned back.

Chris stood a foot away from me but a moment of hesitation on my part, cost me my space. He stepped closer and closer, and before I could talk myself out of it, I brought my hand to his cheek and kissed him.

For a moment he didn't react, and I felt the urge to pull away but as I was about to apologize, I felt his arm around my waist pulling me closer and he kissed me back.

I closed my eyes against his touch, desperate to feel something, anything other than the constant numbness inside me and the constant desire for Illarion, which I knew would never be anything other than that.

He swept his hand through my hair lowering his other to the curve of my hip. I moved closer to him, aching to feel his body against mine.

As his tongue pushed past my parted lips, I felt him sigh, pulling me closer.

"We shouldn't do this," I breathed as we parted for air, conscious of all the people doing the same thing we were—getting lost in the beat of the music pounding around us.

"Why?" he breathed back, pulling me closer to him.

"I don't know."

"Let's get out of here."

♥

Hours went past as I lay beside him listening to his breathing. My heart knew what we'd done was wrong. I hated myself for it. I hated that I'd led him on all because I couldn't stop thinking about Illarion. I ran my hands through my hair and wrapped my arms around my stomach burying my head under the soft, fleece blanket.

The sun began to rise, and I knew it was time to go. This would be the day I did what I'd come here to do. I pressed a soft kiss to his cheek before I pulled on last night's red dress and stilettos and wrapped my coat tightly around my shoulders. Then I crept away as fast as I could.

The Uber took me back to my motel, where I changed into a pair of jeans, a black tank top, and traded my stilettos for boots.

As I left the shelter of my motel's foyer, I shrugged into my leather coat and headed in the direction of the sunrise, which also happened to be the way to creepy Larry's apartment.

I was sure now that the rumors were true. I'd heard stories in the bar about how he'd used his abilities to control people to get what he wanted. I shuddered to think of the kinds of things he made people do. Battling both the proverbial and literal chill, I took a deep breath. Before I neared the entrance to the dilapidated building, I checked my possessions again and verified that Spock was there. Feeling somewhat prepared I entered through the gate. His apartment was on the seventh floor—uneasiness washed over me.

A quick glance at the exits told me there were few options. Jumping from the window was out of the question, and climbing down the water pipes wasn't the best idea either since they were corroded.

I would just have to take my chances and deal with whatever came. Piece of cake. I slung my bag over my shoulder and pulled my hair into a ponytail, it was longer nowadays, making it hard to do anything without it getting in my way and the last thing I wanted was an enemy to grab my hair and overpower me.

The main door creaked open, and I stepped over the shot-out glass littering the floor. Slowly, I made my way across to the stairwell ignoring the elevators all together. I highly doubted they would be in working order.

Seven flights of stairs later, I reached Larry's floor and spotted his room at the end of the dark corridor. Overhead, the lights flickered. *Oh, come on.*

I shrugged into my jacket and gripped the strap of my bag in my hand.

Aside from sensing Darkness, I was also able to tell if there were other Sensitives in the area. My heart raced. There were two of them. I had no doubt that he had his bodyguard with him. Nausea filled the pit of my stomach, my warning system, I was grateful for the advantage my senses gave me.

I walked forward, bow in bag and head held high. I was going to get my answers one way or another.

I knocked three times before the latches on the door opened.

A quiet, almost undetectable voice in my head told me to turn around and leave. I pushed it far into the back of my mind and stood my ground.

Larry was one of the worst, most unappealing people I had ever had the displeasure of meeting and his whole aura reeked of rotten eggs and wrongdoing.

The door opened and the stench from inside nearly bowled me over. I had to force myself not to gag. The last time I saw him he was in the midst of fondling a waitress.

"Baby, you're looking good, the scar is a nice touch." He grinned from ear to ear. "I could hardly believe my luck when I heard you wanted to see me."

I'd used a bunch of drugstore makeup to hide my scar and make me less recognizable at the club, now he was seeing me for what I really was. I shuddered, feeling vulnerable beneath his gaze.

He grinned—he'd lost a few more teeth since I'd last seen him—and wiped his hands on his grease-stained T-shirt. "You know; I've heard a lot about you. I mean the real you, Ace Hart. Rumors mostly, but they don't do you justice. You're much prettier in person especially without all the makeup."

I cringed sidestepping a nasty looking stain. There was no point trying to hide my identity now, he already knew I'd been using an alias. "Glad I made the front page."

"Ah, you're making a lot more than the front page—you're talk of the town."

Mike got up and grinned at me, and then back at Larry.

Shit.

I swallowed my anxiety.

"Here to party?" he asked, cocking his eyebrows at Larry.

"Tell your lap dog to back up!"

He smirked.

I pushed past him. He seemed to have no problems with female domination and grinned even more. The creep was loving this.

I clenched my fists and walked around the apartment carefully trying to avoid stepping on anything that looked like it may have been alive at some point. Finding a spot that was clear of any carcasses, I stopped and turned around.

There was literally shit everywhere, clothes, food, rubbish and dead things, but on the table on the far right, which housed his weapons, there wasn't so much as a speck of dust, and I made a quick observation of exactly what was there in case I needed to utilize any of it.

"How can I help you?" he asked smugly, bringing my attention back to him.

He loved the power trip, knowing that I was here asking for his help.

"I'm sure you already know why I wanted to see you. I need information," I said with my feet planted firmly in my spot carefully keeping an eye on both men.

He smiled his toothless smile telling me that his contacts had told him why I was here. He was playing games.

"Do I look like a library to you?"

"You look like a lot of things, none as pleasant as a library." I stood my ground.

"Feisty and sexy."

Then he took a step toward me. I swallowed hard but remained in my spot.

"I know you have the information I need." I eyed the other man who was slowly moving toward me from the other direction with a smile creepier than Larry's.

He shrugged, still looking at me. "And what kind of information would that be?"

Pulling out a picture from the file, Vanessa had given me. I held it up showing him. "Damon Cale. I need whatever you can get on him."

"Couldn't find it yourself?" he asked, moving closer. "Is the Director hiding his skeletons in places you're too afraid to look?"

I cleared my throat hiding the nausea that welled inside of me. *Hold it together Ace, you've got this.* And just like before, the small, nagging voice was there in my head, telling me to leave. I pushed it back and shook my head in response to his last comment.

"Not the right information, he's a saint on the surface, I need the real story," I admitted which earned me another pleased grin. "Someone has that information. I've heard that someone is you."

He stepped closer and closer until he forced me to step backwards and into the wall behind me.

I was going to have to throw this jacket out. There was no chance I would get the grime off the fabric now. I held my breath as he brought his face close to mine and whispered.

"He's a bad egg. Someone you should not be involved with."

"Do you have the information or not?" I hissed, fighting the panic.

"What are you going to give me for it? I warned you that I'd expect payment the next time I helped."

He cast his glance between me, and his friend.

I reached into my back pocket and pulled out a stash of bills.

His eyes widened greedily at my offer, and then he reached for the large pile of manila folders.

It only took a minute for him to flick through them before he pulled one out. He tossed the rest back on the table knocking over a bottle of what could have once been ketchup.

"Damon Cale," he stated.

I swallowed hard and walked toward him locking my eyes on the folder.

"Twenty pages of pure evil."

I didn't want to know why or how he had all this information. He held the file up, waving it at me.

As I approached him, I felt a wave of something I couldn't quite pinpoint but realized that I was starting to feel a lot less like leaving and I couldn't remember why I was in such a rush. I forgot the folder and focused my attention on him.

His friend walked over to me with a smirk and motioned for me to follow.

Deep down inside, I felt fear, but I didn't know why, so I obeyed and casually followed the man feeling quite relaxed.

"Have a seat, doll," Larry said gently guiding me toward the bedroom where I sat down on the edge of the bed. "Mike and I are going to show you a real good time."

263

The white, floral sheets were stained yellow in random places and clothes littered the surface. Larry scraped off the contents and smiled at me.

That same voice deep inside me urged me to get up and leave but I didn't.

I was warm and if I left, I wouldn't be.

"Why don't you get comfortable?" he suggested, and I wondered why I didn't think of that first.

Mike helped me up and then he helped me out of my jacket. I was left standing in my black tank top.

"Much better, isn't it?" he asked, tracing his fingers along the bare skin of my shoulders.

I nodded wordlessly.

"Why don't you take that off too and lie down? You'll be much more comfortable."

A wave of quiet and calm washed over me, and I obeyed only this time Mike moved over to me and helped me out of my tank top leaving me in my plain sports bra before he pushed me down onto the bed.

"No baby, lay down on your stomach."

I rolled over.

I heard Larry thank him before sitting down beside me. He ran his fingers through my hair, pulling it out of the elastic. He let his fingers hover on my skin, tracing lines up and down my back.

Again, I heard the voice and ignored the faint yelling inside me which was telling me to get up and run.

"That's a good girl, much better, now close your eyes," he ordered.

I closed my eyes, but I could still feel his presence. The mattress moved under his weight.

"Now we're going to have a little fun, the three of us." His voice was much rougher now and the voice in my head louder.

Only, I still couldn't remember why I was in a rush to leave.

Mike knelt on the other side of me. He pulled the straps of my bra down and off my shoulders.

"Look at that milky skin, I can't wait to see the rest," Larry whispered huskily in my ear.

I shivered. The nausea in the pit of my stomach grew. I knew I had to get up, but I didn't know why. The persistent voice in my head was getting louder while my own thoughts were barely a whisper.

His hands snaked over my skin, flat against my back sliding down and across to the front of my body. His palm was rough on my stomach as his hand slipped lower and lower.

And then, as if a switch was flipped, the calming haze which entranced me was gone and I realized what was happening.

My eyes snapped open, and another hand immediately closed around the back of my neck pushing my face down into the pillow.

"Get off me!" I screamed, trying to kick at him and free myself.

All that I managed to do was excite them more. I heard Larry's shrill laughter in my ear as he pressed his body against mine. His hand was flat against the lower part of my stomach. He was reaching for the button on my jeans.

The weight on top of me was too much, I couldn't move, whatever I did, however I struggled it seemed to only give him opportunities to get closer.

He ripped the button and zipper which forced a scream from me.

Throughout it all, the voice that had warned me earlier became more prominent. I heard the familiarity in it now, Illarion.

Tears sprung to my eyes as the reality of the situation dawned on me. Illarion must be close by if he knew what was happening, but was he close enough to help in time?

My body thrashed in protest. No, God no. This couldn't be happening.

I continued my attempts to free myself, thrashing against the disgusting men—their bodies pressed too tightly against mine for me to escape.

My screams echoed around me as Larry pulled my jeans down. I felt the cool air of the apartment brush across my skin where there was nothing but underwear and my bra.

Mike had me up against him—my back was flat against his stomach. He pulled my arms behind, locking me in place and Larry yanked my jeans down to my ankles.

The hum in my heart told me Illarion was getting closer, and the anger inside me was rising. I felt the heat building in my stomach, burning through my veins.

Larry moved closer, wiping the sweat off his forehead. He grunted as he moved over to us. Before my brain could register what he was doing, a thick rag was pushed into my mouth and a rough piece of fabric tied it into place.

Larry's foul breath assaulted my nostrils as his laugh roared in my ears. I forced myself to calm down and think. *Think God damn it.* Tears stung the back of my eyes but I ignored them.

I threw my head back, bracing myself for the impact. My head connected with his friend's face, breaking his nose.

He released me suddenly and yelled out. Giving me the only opportunity I needed.

One of them would be incapacitated but the other could still do a lot of damage.

I launched my fist into Larry's face and while he was stunned, I threw myself off the bed and tripped over my jeans that were still bunched around my ankles coming dangerously close to a rotting pack of fries. Not letting it deter me, I scrambled to my feet, making it as far as the living room before I felt a hand grip my wrist and tug me back.

I screamed into my gag trying to rip it off and thrashed again only this time Mike pulled me toward him. With one, swift swing of his arm he slapped me across the face sending me backward, into the floor. Black dots exploded across my vision and I felt something warm on the back of my head. I wasn't naive enough to think it was anything but my blood pouring out of my cracked skull.

A shallow breath escaped my lips as I lay in pile realizing that I had blown it. I tried not to cry but my attempts of putting on a brave front crumbled before my eyes. I couldn't get my bearings, I couldn't get up, my vision dimmed around the edges and a metallic taste rapidly filled the back of my throat.

Footsteps came closer and closer, and I dared to look. Mike stood above me unbuckling his pants grinning that sickly grin. I barely had the energy to keep my eyes open let alone fight. All I could do was try to cover myself as much as possible. Not that it would do anything to stop what was about to happen. I painfully drew my arm over my chest, using the other to try and pull my jeans up. He laughed at that point as he pulled my arm down.

He crouched down in front of me and roughly pulled me toward him. He grabbed my face and squeezed it. "I want you to *feel* everything we're going to do to you, bitch. Do you understand?"

Reluctantly I let my tears fall. God, I didn't want to cry, not in front of them, not like this.

Larry stalked around me pulling me up by my wrists; painfully, he pulled them behind my back, dragging me up to my knees.

"You think you just get to walk in here, demand information without payment?"

Larry laughed. "He doesn't mean payment of the green bill variety, if you know what I mean."

My arrogance brought me here. I thought I'd be strong enough to fight. God was I wrong.

When he forced my body around, I saw Mike, grinning and grunting. Blood poured from his broken nose as he started undoing his belt.

I closed my eyes ignoring the sickening communication between the two.

Larry dragged me back to the bed and forced me down onto it. My face was crushed into the sheets as my legs were pushed apart and I felt someone's hands on the waistband of my underwear. Tears erupted. No.

Seconds later, his rough hand was on my stomach, he was toying with me. I wanted to scream but all that came out were muffled whimpers drowned out by the gag. He traced his callused finger along the band of my underwear and before I had a chance to shout again, the sound of splintering wood cracked through the apartment as the door was kicked in.

In a blur, Larry was sent flying, landing against and breaking the bedroom's wooden door into a hundred pieces.

He fell into a heap. I forced myself off the bed and through hooded eyes I made out the figure standing over him. One loud pop later, Larry was dead.

Mike, in a panicked rush, grabbed my arms pulling me up to my feet and backwards toward the door. "I'll kill her, stay back!" He had a gun pointed at Illarion.

My head hurt and my vision blurred.

Illarion dropped the gun and stepped toward us.

"Stay back!" the man yelled from behind me, painfully pulling my arms tighter behind my back. I wanted to scream, this was bullshit. How dare he point a gun at Illarion? How dare he be holding me hostage, almost naked in this filthy apartment? The gun was now pressed at my back.

Through our connection, I felt Illarion warning me, he knew what was simmering inside, but I couldn't stop it. I couldn't. Not after all the bullshit these two morons put me through and everything they would have done to me. I could hear the sick, fucked up shit they were planning. If they didn't kill me I would have begged for my own death. Illarion remained silent alternating his gaze between my terrified and furious eyes and the man behind me.

"I will shoot her right in the spine, stay the hell back!"

Illarion's eyes met mine, but I was blind with rage. A sudden jolt of energy ran through me.

No. I balled my fists and welcomed the dark, dangerous feeling spreading through my veins. I welcomed the consuming hatred pulsing through me and for a split-second I couldn't see the vibrant brown warmth of Illarion's eyes, all I could see was red, red pure rage.

"Don't do this Ace…just look into my eyes.., let it go."

I couldn't stop. I *had* to do this. I pictured everything I would do to this idiot holding me, the pain and torture I would inflict, I thought about every nerve lighting up inside his body, every blood vessel exploding as his eyes filled with blood. I imagined how he would go down with gargled screams consuming him.

As the thoughts formed, his hold on me tensed, I felt the shift in atmosphere, that same shift of air I'd experienced in Aurel's house happened again and his hands froze. It was like static charging the air around us. His body convulsed as violent tremors shifted the electrified air behind me. Guttural screams erupted from within him and I felt the slick, hot blood drip from his body and wet mine. My eyes focused on Illarion but I wasn't seeing him. Sonic pulses of energy ripped through my skin, frying anything that made contact with it. I didn't need to look at him to know what I'd done.

As silence descended, Mike's body fell and landed with a heavy thud. Only then did I let out the breath I was holding and I met Illarion's dark, stormy eyes.

"It's okay, it's over."

269

Exhaustion took over and I stumbled forward on shaky legs and right into his arms.

He pulled off his jacket and wrapped it gingerly around me. Slowly he began untying the fabric around my head releasing me from the gag. I winced as he gently pulled my jeans up and located my tank top and helped me back into it. His hands trembled with every breath, and I did the best I could not to react.

Then he picked me up, letting my head fall against his chest.

"The folder, please get the folder," I asked, as he moved.

Illarion stopped and turned. He made his way over to the counter and pulled my bag into his arms. He collected the folder before rushing us out of the building.

He walked silently, at some point I'd closed my eyes and only opened them again when I heard the familiar sound of a car door opening.

As gently as everything else he did, he lowered me into the seat and buckled me up. He brushed his fingers across my hand letting his touch linger.

His heart raced a million miles an hour, but he was calming down, the hum inside my heart never lied. I felt it as clearly as I felt his hand on mine as he knelt down beside the car.

"Are you hurt?" he asked softly.

Despite the massive headache, possible concussion, and embarrassment, I wasn't hurt.

"Ace..." He looked at me intently.

"I'm fine."

Before he could say anything else, my breath faltered.

I heard him let out a shaky sigh and then he was on his feet, the speed at which he got into the car and drove off was dizzying. We drove in silence for more than an hour, neither of us saying a word until we came to a stop just outside a small cabin which I assumed was some kind of Airbnb, which was conveniently right beside a gas station.

He roughly threw the door open and then slammed it shut leaving me to watch his body shaking just outside the car. He walked around to my side and pulled opened the door.

God. I must've looked like hell, I felt like hell. I turned away swallowing the lump in my throat. I didn't want him to see me like this.

"Look at me," he said firmly.

How could I? How could I face him after that? It was my own stupidity that landed me there in the first place.

"Look at me, please," he said again. I felt his soft hand on mine, all the years of training had left his fingers calloused but that made his touch sweeter. "Ace."

His voice was as gentle as his caress, and I couldn't refuse him. I turned my head slightly, painfully aware of the burning in my cheeks.

His eyes found mine and that was all it took to undo me, without warning I burst into tears and not a second later his arms were around me pulling me closer.

"I thought I was too late."

His voice cracked, which was not something I expected to hear. He was always so strong and so fierce. The change terrified me.

I didn't know what to say, that I was an idiot? That much was obvious.

"What were you doing there?" he asked, keeping his hands on mine.

I couldn't even manage to form the words in my head let alone explain it to him. I pulled back and looked away again unable to face him.

"Damon was playing you. I wanted to find out why. I wanted to know what he was planning to do with me, to us."

"The folder?" he asked, knotting his brow.

"I got some information from a friend. But it wasn't enough, I needed more," I said, keeping my eyes averted.

Without even realizing it I cringed when a wave of stabbing pain hit me. Illarion pressed his hand to mine.

"You need a hospital."

"No—"

"Ace."

"Please don't make me."

He ran his hand through his hair.

"Okay, alright, but you can't go to sleep, you've got a concussion," he said, not letting me answer but instead, he got to his feet and helped me out of the car.

My vision was beginning to double and the nausea was intensifying more than I cared to admit.

"Slowly," he murmured wrapping his arm around my shoulder helping me to the door.

My body ached, and the cuts stung under the fabric of his jacket. He unlocked the door and pushed it open leading me to the bedroom, but not to the bed for which I silently thanked him.

"You've been staying here?" I looked around spotting the immediate tell-tale signs of his work, precise positioning of his weapons, his computer, the bags he travelled with by the door.

A quick nod answered my question. I could only imagine the hell he was going through trying to track me all over the country.

"Sit down, let me see your eyes." He knelt beside me.

I turned my head and avoided meeting his gaze. He gently brushed my hair off my cheek then disappeared, returning with a bowl of water, several small washcloths, and a tube of what I guessed was antiseptic lotion.

"I don't think you should have a shower just yet."

He spoke softly but his voice was thick. He dabbed the washcloth into the water gently bringing it to my face while I forced myself to keep my eyes on a far point across the room and away from him.

"I need to dissolve the smell of those pigs off me."

"You're not stable on your feet just yet."

As he dabbed away the dried blood and whatever else was mixed in there I bit back the tears when they started to form again.

"I should have been there sooner," he said quietly, shaking his head.

His voice cracked and I couldn't help the tears as they fell. So much guilt coursed through him. Through our connection in my heart, every fiber of his being was blaming himself.

"I'm so sorry, Ace," he whispered again wiping my tears away with his thumb.

I shook my head and turned to look at him.

"Don't..." I managed, wanting so desperately to just pull him against me, I couldn't bare the pain he was carrying on the account of me. "It was my fault."

"I shouldn't have let you leave. I should have followed you. I should have..." He bowed his head rubbing his face before bringing his eyes back to mine.

The intensity in his gaze was intoxicating and I found myself struggling to breathe, I was shaky and still getting my bearings back. But I couldn't stand the dizziness his proximity gave me, and truth be told, the concussion was less painful and easier to accept than wanting someone so badly whom you knew you could never have.

I turned away and bit down on my lip. I couldn't be this close to him.

"Ace..."

And the way my name rolled off his tongue in that subtle accent was just too much.

"I need space," I said quietly, not even knowing if he heard me.

"Okay."

I carefully got to my feet and walked into the adjoining bathroom closing the door heading straight for the shower, despite being advised against it.

I pulled the dirty tank top away and my jeans tossing them into the wastebasket. I stepped into the hot stream and leaned against the cold tiles, sliding down against the wall. I let the water wash away the blood and the pain and I cried. I cried so hard I curled in on myself and collapsed into a ball against the cold, wet floor.

I tried to put up my walls and block him out. I didn't want him to feel what I was feeling. But the more I tried to block him out, the more I felt the strain and the inability to do so—I was drained.

After an hour soaking and crying, I got out and dried myself off. There wasn't much in the way of clothing so I opted for the white robe which hung on the back of the bathroom door. I'd have to ask if he had brought anything for me, knowing Illarion, he'd be prepared.

The pale, washed-out expression that reflected back at me through the small bathroom mirror shocked me. I ran my fingers along the cut on my cheek and winced. My face was already scarred and this would be the cherry on top. But like with most Sensitive things, the healing was already kicking in. The cut in my head was almost healed over and soon my face would be too.

I leaned heavily on the counter and sucked in a breath.

Once I collected myself, I opened the door and as I did he got to his feet but stayed put.

Apprehension coursed through him.

Instead of letting him stand there contemplating his next move, I stepped toward him and wrapped my arms around his waist and let my head fall against his chest. To hell with caution, I couldn't care less right now. All I wanted was to feel his arms around me and a few tentative moments later, he did. He wrapped his arms around my waist, and I felt his heart hammering.

"I brought some clothes for you," he said, smoothing my wet hair down my back.

Since leaving him, this was the closest I'd ever been to him. We never even got that close during our training sessions. I imagined how he would feel against me body, but it was nothing compared to what it was like.

His arms were strong as they held me and the intoxicating aroma from his warm skin flooded my senses.

I closed my eyes against his touch, my heart raced in time with his, why did I have to feel like this?

"How do you feel?" His voice was so smooth, so perfect.

"I feel like I need to lie down," I murmured, forcing thoughts of him out of my heart.

"Okay, but you can't fall asleep."

"I won't."

Illarion walked me over to the bed and pulled back the covers. I fell into the soft mattress and let out a loud groan as my bones and muscles protested the movement.

Once I made myself comfortable, he sat down beside me but kept a conservative foot between us.

Before I could stop it, my eyes closed, they were so heavy and I was so tired. I curled up on my side letting out a long, relieved sigh.

"Ace." His voice floated over me. "Don't fall asleep," he reminded me, moving closer.

My heart fluttered but my eyes were heavy.

"I'll try not to."

"Ace." He shook my shoulders turning me on my back. "Stay awake."

"I'm not sleeping."

His hand gently cupped my cheek. "I mean it Ace, don't fall asleep."

"So tired," I murmured opening my eyes.

He brushed my cheek letting his fingers linger for far too long. "I know. Keep your eyes on me."

I nodded against the pillow and slowly opened my eyes and looked up into his.

He cupped my cheek in his hand, brushing his thumb across the cut.

"When I felt your fear, I thought that I was too late."

"I'm sorry."

"Why didn't you come to me with this?" he asked, not hiding the hurt in his eyes.

Blinking back my tears, I looked away for a moment. "I wanted to help. They played you, and I just wanted to fix it."

He bowed his head.

"Lie with me."

"I don't think that's a good idea."

"Please."

He chewed his bottom lip before he pulled the cover back and lay beside me. "I would have helped you. I will always help you."

"I'm sorry."

Slowly, he took my hands in his. He remained still for a moment, apprehension coursing through him until he broke the silence. "I want you to feel this."

Before I could speak, he pressed a kiss to my forehead and brought his eyes to mine.

"My intention was to stay away from you because it was too dangerous. But I don't want to stay away anymore."

The words flowed off his tongue as smoothly as the warm flood of emotions which flowed into me.

"Ila…"

"I wanted to pretend that I didn't feel what I did. I wanted to pretend that I didn't care how my heart beats only for you. I wanted to lie to myself, but I couldn't." He brushed my hair behind my ears and that was all it took.

I saw it the moment it happened in his eyes, his resolve was gone and slowly he lowered himself until his lips were over mine.

My breath caught as his tongue brushed mine and he deepened the kiss.

He knotted his fingers through my hair and he brought my face closer to his. And just as my body arched to feel him, he pulled back.

"Ila?"

"When you're feeling better," he said gently.

"I'm feeling fine."

A smile crept across his face. "You were just falling asleep."

"Now I'm not."

He chuckled. "Make no mistake, I want this, more than you could imagine." He swallowed hard and narrowed his eyes. "I want you, but right now is not the time."

"Why? Because of what happened?"

"Yes, because you nearly died in there. You need to rest."

"I don't want to rest."

"I can tell."

"Then?" I whined.

He kissed me again and I stopped talking. He wrapped his arm around me and lowered me onto the sheets. His dark eyes looked right into my soul. He carefully pulled off my robe and I took my time removing his clothes. Minutes later we were skin to skin, the heat from his tense muscles ignited every nerve within me.

For what felt like a lifetime, I let myself be close to him—allowed myself to feel everything.

His hands roamed across my body as if devoting every scar to memory.

He brought his eyes to mine and cautiously searched for permission. I gripped his forearm and brought his lips to mine giving him the answer he needed.

Gently he slipped his hand to the small of my back and eased me toward him.

I didn't waste time pulling his T-shirt off and he didn't dance around letting his hands slide under the robe.

I was breathless as I hooked my thumbs under the waistband of his sweats and release him.

I groaned and his hands coasted across my breasts and across my stomach dipping lower and lower until his fingers slipped inside.

My heart slammed against my ribcage as he worked his magic drawing broken gasps from my lips.

"Ila..."

"When you say my name like that." He chuckled, lowering his body over mine before he hung his head with a sigh. "Shit, I don't have condoms."

"I'm on the pill."

"Incredible." He chuckled.

He held me tight as we became whole.

The movements were frenzied, wild and raw.

A breathless gasp left my lips as his legs tangled with mine. He moved with me. His soul was *inside* me, unravelling as each breath expelled was a reminder of how much we had been keeping inside, hidden.

As he traced lines across my ribcage and over my hips, he flattened his palm across my stomach. He dipped his mouth to my neck and pressed his lips to my wildly beating pulse.

He threaded his fingers through mine, pressing our hands above my head, tangled amongst the sheets.

The sound of my name on his lips undid me as both our bodies snapped releasing the pent-up tension. Not just from tonight, but all the times we chanced a touch or brush of skin but denied the way our bodies needed to be close, in sync.

Slowly, he circled me in his arms. His uneven breaths matched mine and his lips brushed against my ear.

"Stay awake."

Chapter Sixteen

Ace

The sun chased the night away. Illarion had refused to let me sleep and instead he stayed up all night, sitting with me. Words weren't needed when the connection pulsing between us said everything.

Last night was a welcome relief for the both of us. Illarion turned his head toward me slowly and pressed a kiss to my forehead letting his lips linger for a moment. It had been all the small, unspoken things which were missing. The slight touch, the lingering kiss, the whispered words.

His hand drew lazy marks on my skin stopping across each and every scar across my back. I was so self-conscious about them even within myself that I would have died had it been anyone else doing what he was. But with him it was okay. I still flinched whenever I remembered the way they came to be there, but I knew that Illarion would make it okay, he'd chase away my demons and tame them.

"How do you feel?" he asked, brushing away strands of hair from my cheek. His touch left my skin on fire.

"My head isn't pounding as fiercely as it was," I murmured against the pillow and moved closer to him.

"You should be safe to sleep tonight."

"I don't think I'll be getting much sleep if you're around. What time is it? Shouldn't we be up and working?"

He smiled and planted a kiss on my forehead. "Just after seven."

We had so much to do. I was about to protest when he swept his finger along the curve of my lip. I shivered in response immediately feeling all warm and fuzzy again.

"Everything can wait. I just want to be here. I wanted to feel you. I never thought I would. I thought I lost you."

I never imagined that I would get to see this man, a war machine capable of disarming and battling dozens of men at once, so peaceful and content. He was open and vulnerable, and there was nothing sexier than the fact that he was letting me see him like that. A warm tingle spread through my heart and he must have felt it because he squeezed my shoulder and pulled me closer so that my cheek was resting on his chest.

A few more kisses landed on my face while he busied himself with running his fingers along the feint lines on my arms. Whenever Troy came close to touching me like that, I jumped. Then the guilt settled in. Christ I was a shit person.

"What's going through your head?" He pressed a few more kisses to my cheek while his other hand cupped my elbow.

"Nothing," I lied sucking in a nervous breath.

I forced my barriers up again.

His hand on my elbow tensed and then he was up on his side. He gently eased me down onto my back and his dark eyes found mine.

"Don't do that," he whispered leaning down to kiss me.

I melted under his gaze and then when he kissed me like that.

"Don't do what?"

I reached up and tangled my fingers through the dark strands of hair, which had fallen over his eyes.

"Don't hide yourself from me," he clarified trailing kisses along my cheek and down to the dangerous spot under my ear where my pulse thundered. His voice rolled over me in waves sending chills over my skin.

"Look at me," he said softly, and I did.

His hooded eyes looked down at me, drinking me in.

"Don't hide from me," he said again holding my wrist in his hand.

I swallowed hard and nodded.

"Ila…"

My words were lost when that same, dark look flitted across his eyes for the briefest moment. His dark lashes fanned across his cheeks as he closed his eyes.

"You're too beautiful to feel like that."

He ran his fingers along my arms and then across the long, shiny mark across my face letting his thumb linger on the curve of my parted lip.

Then I understood. He got the whole Troy thing, how I felt so ashamed of my scars not that Troy had ever made me feel bad about them. He was perfect and kind and I was a bitch.

"I'm a terrible person."

"You're not."

"I didn't even say goodbye to Troy. I didn't even end things properly."

"Did you love him?"

"Not the way I should have, not the way he deserves."

"And this, with us? Do you regret it?"

"No."

"Then you will get to explain everything to him when the time comes. You're not a terrible person."

I sighed. I needed to learn how to keep my thoughts hidden from him. Especially thoughts like that.

"I'm still not used to this." I held my breath, looking up at him, in that moment, he wasn't guarded at all—he was open and vulnerable.

"It will get easier."

"Aurel said the same."

"He makes valid points sometimes."

I grinned. "Sometimes?"

"When he's a not a pain in the ass."

I laughed.

Illarion drew my face up to his before kissing me deeply again. "I think we should get up, we do have a lot to do."

"I know we do, glad we did *that* first though."

He laughed holding his hand out to me. He pulled me out of the bed and pressed another kiss to my lips.

"Did you want to shower first?"

"No, you go. I'm heading out for supplies. When I come back, we'll get started on the file."

A knot formed in my stomach. *The file.* I forced my gaze away from the lean, built statue of a man standing before me in all his glory. His tracksuit pants hung so dangerously low on his hips and the shirtless state of his body winded me.

I stepped away reeling in my emotions again. He handed me the discarded robe and gave me a quick smile before disappearing from the bedroom.

I walked to the bathroom on shaky legs and allowed the steam to fill the small room before stepping into the hot stream of water. I had to rein in my wild emotions, but the way his body left mine wanting was inhuman. I couldn't shake the touches he left on my skin and the searing hot kisses on my lips.

Once I'd cooled down, I stepped out, dried myself off and was pleased to see that he did in fact have clothes ready for me. I smiled at the thought that he stood in my room picking out which underwear to bring me. I pulled on the black jeans and grey t-shirt and pulled my wet hair into a ponytail.

The browning, floral wallpaper gave the old cabin, an authentic, vintage feel. If I wasn't so anti old lady charm, I would have quite liked it. It was quaint.

The matching brown leather couches worked well with the small rectangle table positioned right in the center of the room. I scanned the rest of the area noting that there were several tall, wooden shelves stacked with old board games, books and magazines. Some of the shelves were overflowing with old newspapers and underneath there was a shelf with two large vases of colored marbles. Yuck. Such tacky decor. I walked over to the shelf farthest on the left beside a large bay window and picked out a random book. I scowled. Oedipus Rex. How ironic, me and prophecies just weren't meant to work.

I sat down and leaned my elbow on the window ledge. Opening the book, I immersed myself and began reading. The story was so tragic but something about it resonated with me.

Sometime later I heard Illarion's car pull up on the small gravel driveway crushing the rocks beneath the large tires. The better part of the afternoon was already gone.

He carried two large bags into the cabin, and I heard him unpacking them in the kitchen. The fridge opened and closed a few times and the rest of the items seemed to go in the overhead cabinets.

"Ace?" he called from the kitchen.

I put the book down on the coffee table and made my way to join him. He was already preparing two coffees.

"What was on the USB you got from the club?" he asked, jogging my memory back to it.

"Information about Sensitive's, rumors about other Divines, stuff they documented throughout history."

"Anything we can use?"

Shaking my head, I took another sip of coffee. "I don't think so, it seems pretty farfetched."

"Want me to take a look?"

Shrugging, I plugged the USB into the laptop and brought up the files. For a moment, I held in a breath, letting my fingers hover over the keys.

"Ace?

"I don't know, Ila, a lot of it just seems…"

"What?"

"Disturbingly accurate."

He looked at me thoughtfully. "What are we talking?"

"It says that there is a pair of Celestial Beings, joined by blood. They each give their essence to a Divine Sensitive to carry out their work in the mortal realm."

Illarion nodded, encouraging me to continue.

"They always focus on balance, right?"

"Right."

"And if it's all about balance it's got to be good and bad, light and dark. That sort of thing."

"Go on."

"This speaks about Aaryon, the Moon Being and Solaris the Sun Being. One harnesses the darkness and the other, blinding light."

Illarion's eyes narrowed.

"What if there's something in this, Ila? It says one is a Giver and the other, a Taker."

"The Taker, you're sure?"

"I'm sure. Ila, what if Damon is this person everyone's been warning me about? What if he's the Taker?"

"No, Ace. It's not possible."

"Why not?" I asked, straightening up in my seat. "You said so yourself, there's no way he could have been strong enough to have everyone under that amount of compulsion."

Illarion stayed quiet, but I'd struck a chord. His posture stiffened as he looked at me intently.

"It says Celestial Beings and the Divine Sensitives share blood. Damon and I share blood."

"I don't know Ace."

"All I'm saying is that we should consider this. What if he's much stronger than we thought?"

"Then it changes everything."

Letting out a long breath, I bowed my head and Illarion's arms were around me in a matter of seconds.

Our connection hummed a lot more intensely and I wondered whether this whole being connected thing was starting to affect both our moods.

At some point, I had to confront him about that. Right now, though, didn't seem like the right time. I wanted to just be here, see him relaxed somewhat and enjoy his company. Last night had been a huge shift for us, both of us had been holding out for so long, and the way he kissed me and made love to me, proved that point.

The more I trained myself in my abilities, the better I became at keeping my own secrets while digging for others.

"There's something else," I said softly, bringing his eyes back to mine.

I brought up the file and read it out loud.

"The Divine Sensitive is born of Celestial Blood, there reins one until the balance is tipped in favor of the sun or the moon. When the scale falls, the second is born."

Illarion bowed his head.

"It makes sense, right?" I whispered, hating that my voice shook. "But no one ever mentioned there would be more than one. Elena never told me there was another Divine."

Illarion nodded, squeezing my hand. "Maybe they didn't know?"

"I don't know. Maybe they didn't want me to worry." It sounded stupid as soon as the words left my lips.

"There has to be a reason you weren't told."

"Damon was born before me, he's tipping the scale. I was born to bring the balance back."

If this was going to work, and I was going to live long enough to live up to my task. I had to work on my barrier, I had to work on keeping myself grounded. Yesterday I lost control and I didn't like what I became. I pushed down the lingering feelings of the dark power that coursed through me. I couldn't lose control like that again. Being a Divine Sensitive meant that I was a pressure cooker ready to blow at any time if I wasn't careful. Yesterday was just a taste and it scared me.

All this information was weighing me down. Illarion was much better at keeping a lid on it than I was of course, but he was as emotionally compromised as I was and most of it was because of me.

He stopped what he was doing and twisted his body to face me. "What did you tell Aurel?"

"I told him you were hurt and that we needed to take some time for you to get better before heading home." His lips thinned.

"I guess he's on his way then?"

Illarion shook his head and threaded his fingers through mine, pressing a kiss to each of my knuckles.

"No, I told him we had a lead, and we'd call if we needed someone with expertise in paranoia and security."

"Oh my God, was that a joke?"

"Don't get used to it, you know I love brooding." He smirked.

"I don't know, I kind of like this version of you."

He laughed softly and turned back to the file in front of him and the open laptop.

His laugh was so warm that it filled me and only now did I realize how empty I'd been for so long, since Iraq, since my parents, since *Alex*. My insides felt gooey and a dopey smile spread across my face.

I pulled out my own laptop from the case which he'd brought along. I had work to do as well. Gawking at him was nice, but it wouldn't get the job done.

I tried to remember back to the first time I met Damon. He took my hand and probed inside my head. The feeling was sickening and it took everything I had to hold in the bile which lurched in my stomach. He was looking for something. What the hell was it? I forced myself back to that moment, I had to remember it.

He was looking through my memories, but nothing struck me as important in my past. What would he need with any of that information? He touched the part of my soul that mourned my old life and my comrades in Iraq, he sliced open the part of my soul that screamed when I got the phone call about my parents' death. But that wasn't it. He kept probing, forcing himself deeper into the darkest recesses of my memories. I pressed my palms flat against the table, using it to ground myself, not only here physically, but I needed an anchor to pull myself out of my head.

What was it that he said to me? That I was *good*? He seemed surprised, but if he knew who I was and he set all this in motion years ago, why would he have been surprised?

Something told me that wasn't what he was talking about. I pushed harder forcing my mind back to that exact moment. A flash of white consumed me and then I was there. Not really of course, I knew my body was grounded in the small kitchen beside Illarion. I still felt the cool marble table beneath my palms and the rigid plastic of the chair. My nostrils pricked at the familiar scent of Illarion's cologne mixed with the distinct smell of the guns and bullets he handled so often. These were the things that kept me grounded.

I walked through the doors just like I had the first time I was there. Only this time there was no one around. No chatter seeped through from around the corners, no Illarion beside me keeping me strong. I swallowed hard at the eerie, thick air and walked up the stairs trailing my fingers along the banister. It was dark, almost dense. White, smoky air floated around me in the stagnate environment. I pushed forward.

Memories of people and conversations buzzed in the air like echoes of the past. I felt them in my fingertips in everything I touched. The sensation was growing stronger; I was growing stronger.

The last step came into view, this was it. This was the room I was looking for. Locked away in here is where I would find what I needed.

The light from outside slowly started to leave the sky dipping the room into darkness.

Hushed whispers circled me, but I stayed frozen in my spot. They were just echoes. I swallowed the uneasy feeling fluttering in the pit of my stomach and sucked in a deep breath.

"Where are you?" I whispered aloud.

The air behind me shifted and the heavy atmosphere became denser.

A thick hand closed around my throat, panic rose inside but I pushed it back. I had to stay calm. I had to. Damon was here. *In my head.*

"This pain will end when you learn to control it. You are powerful enough, but are you willing?"

Those words again.

He circled around me. *"I'm flattered that you're here."*

"I want to know what you want from me. I want to know how you had everyone fooled."

"I want what's inside you." He smiled though there was nothing kind or genuine in the gesture. *"As for the compulsion, that's my little*

secret, and one day soon you'll even have the pleasure of finding out for yourself."

"You're not going to win, and you know I'm not just going to hand myself over to you."

He laughed squeezing my throat a little tighter. "I think when you realize your lack of options you will be more than willing, little sister. That choice will be your only out since all your others will be taken."

"What are you talking about? What choice?"

"An inevitable choice."

"I'm sure that works well in Bond movies. But you sound like a douche."

"I hope you never lose your sense of humor, even when the worst days come for you." He disappeared and then appeared a few feet in front of me. "And there will be dark days, mark my words."

I sucked in a deep breath and before I could ask him to elaborate I was back in the kitchen. The asshole pushed me out. The next time I saw him, I'd be sure to knock him on his ass. I looked across at Illarion, glad that he was oblivious to my little trip.

What the hell did he mean by an inevitable choice?

I pressed the heels of my palms to my eyes and rubbed my face.

When he noticed that I was looking at him, he stopped what he was doing and turned to me.

"The abilities we have, are there adverse effects, things that start going bad?"

He looked at me intently for a few moments before answering.

"Are there?" I questioned.

"Are you asking because of what happened yesterday?"

That caught me completely off guard though it shouldn't have because of course he would know. He was there; he saw my lowest point when I became a monster.

"Yeah."

There were times when it was prominent inside him and I felt rage and anger which I wouldn't have been able to control, but he was better than me. He held it together when I wouldn't have been able to.

He remained quiet for a moment and looked as though he was contemplating what he would say to me. A muscle worked in his jaw before he looked back at me.

"I won't hurt you, Ace."

"What? God, no, that's not why I'm asking. Ila, I would never think that you would hurt me. God, if anything, I thought I was going to hurt you back at the apartment."

His eyes left mine briefly. The words burned on his tongue I could almost taste them. "I lose control of it sometimes."

"I lost control…you didn't."

"Believe me, it wasn't easy."

"But you still did it."

He took a deep breath and looked at me thoughtfully. "When you get a taste of the power, it hooks you and you fight it, but it gets harder as each day passes."

"Is it possible to be completely taken by it?"

"Yes. It's something we usually train early in life but since you've only been shown your power now, it's much harder to learn how to stop it from taking over."

"Why?"

"Because to you it's natural and you don't know any different."

"That's why you tried to stop me, to stop it from taking hold."

We sat in silence letting the heaviness of that statement hover over us. I sucked in a breath and for a moment he didn't say anything or do anything.

He looked back at me and threaded his fingers through mine and something in his eyes told me that something deep within his soul came undone. He squeezed my hands in his like he was afraid that if he let go it would all be over.

"I didn't want you to feel what I felt." I closed my eyes as the words left me. "The shame and anger, it didn't feel like me. It didn't feel like any part of me."

"What happened back there was terrifying, no one would ever pass judgment on what you felt and did."

The Darkness that lingered in the pit of my stomach burned. I sighed.

My *powers* were burning inside me almost begging to be released. What would happen if I ever succumbed? He brushed his fingers across my cheek, chasing the thought away.

"You need to be careful; you can't let it take over like that again, Ace. Do you understand?"

"What happens if I can't fight it?"

"It will continue to grow until it consumes you. The Darkness inside you will not stop until your soul is black, and your aura is darkened."

"But…you're fine."

He shook his head dropping his gaze from me. An unnaturally humorless laugh left his lips. "Acacia, I'm not, you know I'm not."

Then, like a light clicked in my head I knew. I understood why he didn't want to allow himself to fall for me and why he didn't want us to connect like that. Because I would draw from his Darkness—I would pull it out and amplify it. I knew I was right because the power inside me surged as the thought formed. It was reacting to him. It loved the way he made me feel, *it* seemed to feed off the emotions.

Shivering, I pressed my fingers together in my lap. I needed to think.

"We need each other. There's Darkness inside me, there always has been I know that, but you helped me. I felt it, at Damon's house, you drew it away from me."

"You wouldn't have needed that if you weren't involved in all of this."

"But I am involved, and I need you. You said we're connected for a reason, that we were put together for a reason. So, I say we see this through. Use each other to stay alive and stay sane."

"You're placing a lot of trust on the unknown."

"I trust my gut feelings."

"What is your gut telling you?"

"That something bigger than us, even bigger than Damon is out there."

"Are you talking about your dreams?"

"Yes."

"Tell me."

"For years I've been having dreams that seem too real to be dreams, too visceral to be mind junk. Sometimes, they come true."

"Premonitions."

"If that's what you'd label it. Is that normal for someone like me?"

"Not that I know. There is little known about you."

"Then whatever it is, is bigger. The dreams that have started lately are more violent and more detailed. They scare me, Ila."

"You're allowed to be scared."

"Fear is pointless. You know that as much as I do."

"Perhaps, but it is a natural emotion."

"I know," I said. "More reason to trust my gut."

Confessing that aloud was as frightening as the concept itself. I *needed* him. I shuddered thinking about the alternative. If he didn't stop the rage building inside me I would have lost control completely. Who knows what else I would have done? I'd felt the shift of energy, the static charge as it erupted from me. What if I didn't stop myself, what if I brought the whole building down around us? Was that even a possibility?

The muscles in his arms twitched as he clenched and unclenched his fists. "This relationship, it's dangerous for you."

"Then it's a good thing I can handle myself."

His jaw tightened and then he reached toward me pulling me against him. "It was selfish of me, but I'm not sorry."

"Good, because if you apologize for last night, I will have to hurt you."

"That's something I'll never be sorry for. Only thing I am sorry for is taking so damn long." He released me and sat back in his chair. "This won't be an easy road."

"But you'll be there with me, I'll be fine."

A few moments of silence passed between us then he spoke with his voice full of conviction and promise. "I won't let it take you."

"I trust you."

All at once, I felt like the previous things that occupied my mind were so trivial and completely redundant. I would be lying if I said I wasn't scared. I'd end up institutionalized if I didn't end up dead for destroying half the known world. That's exactly what Damon wanted me for.

"I won't let you lose yourself. I'll always lead you back."

His words brought a smile to my face. Who would have thought, sentimental and sweet?

"I'll hold you to it, as soon as I start singing the *Sound of Music*, I'm coming after you," I said with a grin.

"If you start singing that, *I'll* come after me."

"Oh, I don't doubt it."

He laughed again and turned back to the papers on the desk. "Damon knows what you're capable of."

"So what is his real goal?

"Damon is a Collector," he said looking at me.

"You're sure?"

"Yes."

"Well shit."

That was not good. Collectors were once like us, but somewhere along the line they lost themselves for whatever reason and killed other Sensitives for their abilities. Damon had seemed off, and Illarion had an aversion to him, but a Collector? That was a lot to take in. That meant he didn't just want me to do the dirty work—he wanted to steal my abilities and do it himself.

"If he gets his hands on you, he'll be unstoppable," he added.

Like I needed any more reason to be afraid of him. I sucked in a deep breath and ran my fingers through my ponytail.

"And hiring us both was not a coincidence I'm guessing."

He shook his head.

"Did you know that he was my half-brother?"

Illarion nodded, a passing look of sympathy flashed across his eyes.

"Did he?" I asked.

His jaw was set in a hard line. "Damon knew when he assigned Alex to watch you in Iraq and me from afar."

Turning away from him, I sat for a moment looking at the papers between us. There were a thousand things or more in this life that I hadn't done yet. *Would I ever get the chance to?* I stopped myself mid-thought. *Don't go there, Ace. Not yet. There was still time.*

A few moments passed before Illarion held out a paper that he'd highlighted. It was a photocopy from a book, an old book from the look of it.

I was desperately trying to piece everything together in my head. I guess he was pissed that I was ultimately more powerful—the better sibling. I looked down at the files strewn across the small kitchen table.

"I'm sorry," he said.

"He killed my parents to get to me. He killed Alex."

"Your mother kept you away from this world to protect you."

I pulled one knee up and draped my arm over it. I rubbed my eyes and looked at him. "Did he get their abilities when he killed them?"

His steely eyes were on mine but he remained quiet.

"Tell me," I insisted reading the apprehension on his face. "I need to know."

"Yes."

"What were they?" I asked biting back the anger and the building burning behind my eyes.

"Your mother had an evolved sense of Sight and your father was evolved in Smell. They called him a Tracker."

"A Tracker?"

"Gifted Sensitives who can use their ability to look for others like us. Something went wrong on their way to meet the General. They were ambushed."

She had the foresight to know what would happen and she tried to come for me anyway.

I stood and turned from him rubbing my eyes with the heels of my palms. "How did I become what I am?"

"It's complicated; a lot has to do with genetics and the way certain genes dominate others. But it's rare. There are rumors about Divine's and how they're created. We don't know anything concrete."

"Were your parents Sensitives?"

"They were."

"Tell me about them," I said.

"My father was a Hearing Sensitive; my mother was a Feeling Sensitive. They fell in love on a mission when they met in a small town on the Croatian Coast." He tucked a strand of hair behind my ear and continued. "They were infiltrating an organization which preyed on young Sensitives who didn't know about their abilities. He always said that he fell in love with her the moment he saw her loading a semi-automatic in a boat."

He laughed that wonderful laugh, and I watched his eyes lighten as the words continued. "He loved her more than anything, she was his world."

"What happened?" I asked, quietly squeezing his hand.

"When I was sixteen, they left for a job, they were gone for months, I stayed with Aurel's aunt and uncle while they were gone. I hacked into my mom's work emails and found out that they were spies. They were on a mission in Neive. I didn't find out much more until after she came back."

"They were betrayed."

"Yes. They were ambushed, they got to my father and tortured him and my mother fought, she knew how much the Darkness would consume her but she faced no other choice, she managed to kill the men who were holding them, but my father was already dead and the effects of the Darkness had already taken hold. When they brought her back she was locked away inside her own head, I haven't been able to speak with her again."

My heart hammered in my chest, hurting for him.

"She's in LaGuardia Hospital now, I try to visit as much as I can, but it's not always possible."

"I'm so sorry."

He smiled cupping my cheek in his hand. "It's alright, *moya zvezda.*"

My heart spluttered like a rapid-fire machine gun. I'd never heard him speak Russian before. His voice seared me to the core.

"What does it mean?" I whispered, leaning into his touch closing my eyes.

"My star."

I fought the stinging in my eyes. This beautiful man could completely undo me.

After a few moments, he pulled away and smiled. He took a drink from his cup and leaned back in the chair.

"You understand the dangers of the power, you've felt it yourself. Do you understand why I need to keep you safe?"

"We're going to keep each other safe," I countered.

"We have to keep you away from Damon."

"We need to know what he's planning."

"Yes. There must be an end game here, a reason," he muttered flicking through all the documents on the table again. I watched as his eyes scanned everything before him as a muscle twitched in his jaw.

"Maybe he's just a power-hungry bastard?" I suggested turning away.

"No. There has to be more, another reason. There must be something he's working towards."

For a moment, I sat, thoughtfully looking back down at the array of documents scattered across the table.

"I found the ancient prophecy," he said quietly, handing me the photocopied sheet. "I don't think Damon knows this."

I came across the final line which was highlighted in an overly cheery orange color. "The Divine Sensitive cannot be collected; her powers will be used when she is introduced as a catalyst using strong compulsion."

"Well to add to that, Damon said something to me in my head when I saw him, and again just before."

"You spoke to him again?"

"I managed to find him somehow, like I was meditating. I pushed myself into his head somehow."

"Ace, that is incredibly dangerous."

"I figured that part out myself. Believe me, I won't be doing it again, it was horrid. Anyway, he said that I will have the ability to end it all if I could make the choice. Then, I found some files on the drive we took from Bob, Damon was writing about me coming willingly and that I would make the choice."

"Why the hell would you make that choice?"

"Why did your mom sacrifice everything for your dad?"

Illarion stilled.

"You said he was searching through my head for a weakness, something to exploit. What if that's it? What if he will make me choose you?"

He scrubbed his jaw, saying nothing.

"Illarion, if that's what this is about, I don't know how we're meant to fight this."

"We'll figure this out, I won't let him get anywhere near you, so none of this matters."

I nodded, letting myself believe that this would work out and that Illarion in all his glory could beat and outsmart an ancient prophecy which had been in the making for a thousand years.

CHAPTER SEVENTEEN

ACE

I balled my fists in my lap. As much as I prided myself on being tough, I was freaking out and quite honestly, close to a full breakdown. Hearing how you would be the tool used as a go between for a psycho and his victim, well that didn't make me giddy inside.

I must have started to hyperventilate or turn green because one minute I was leaning back on the chair trying to hold my shit together and the next Illarion was kneeling beside me.

"You okay?" he asked with a subtle tone of seriousness, his dark eyes meeting mine.

"Yeah, fine."

He tucked a loose strand of hair behind my ear. "Give it time, you'll learn to control it and it won't take you by surprise."

"How do you even begin to control it?" I sighed looking at him.

"It's not easy, but you learn to pick up on the signs before they become too much, and you learn to recognize the triggers and how to respond." He looked at me intently and then he pressed his hand to my knee. I hadn't even realized I'd been nervously tapping my foot.

"I feel like they're getting more intense," I admitted quietly, cheeks burning.

"You're not weak. I know that's where your mind is," he said. "You're evolving, your mind and body are letting more in. I won't lie, sometimes it will be overwhelming but you will learn control."

"I don't know if I'll ever be in control."

"Believe me, we'll teach you."

"Have you always known I'd be like this?"

He turned his head slightly. "What do you mean?"

"Operation Lullaby."

"You caught that."

"I did." I smiled. "I also caught that it rattled you."

"Rattled would be an understatement."

"What happened?"

"I will tell you, Ace, I swear, but not now." His expression softened as he looked away.

I tried to hold onto his feelings as much as I could, but damn he was good at blocking them all away. I couldn't break through the shield he pulled up, over himself. I leaned back in my chair and looked down at my hands.

He pulled his chair beside mine and turned me to face him, a mischievous smile met me. "Try to read me."

"What?"

"You said you wanted to get better? You want to learn how to control what you can read and what you put out."

"Yes."

"Then try to read me."

I wet my lips, taking a breath.

Our eyes met and I forced as much concentration as I could into what his thoughts were. Moments later I had a clear idea about how he was feeling and how light his mood was and there, through all the cluttered chains of thoughts and waves of feelings I caught a hold of a single feeling and followed it.

It was like a single silver thread weaving in and out of a black and gold fabric tangled in thousands of other colors and textures.

I covered my mouth suppressing a surprised gasp. "I did it."

A proud smile found his lips.

"Let's try something else." I shifted in the chair until we were sitting as close as possible without touching.

"Okay, try this." He held out his hand slowly. "You should feel me pushing my feelings into you. I want you to try to block it and push yours into me, if you can."

The look in his eyes made me smirk. This was going to be interesting. I nodded slowly taking hold of his hand.

"Ready?" he asked.

My heart caught in my chest. Was I ready? He was one of the best Sensitives evolved in the field of Feelings in the Agency, maybe even the country.

"Ready."

For a few moments, we sat like that hand in hand. I started to think he wasn't doing anything at all. I straightened in my seat. That's when I felt it.

It was a warm, almost undetectable feeling. All the pieces fell into place. I immediately took hold of the thought which looked almost like a gold sliver this time and blocked it off pushing my own thoughts back toward him.

I pushed every thought I had about how I needed him and how he couldn't fight me on this. I made him feel how deeply my emotions ranged from Alex's death to feeling guilty about Troy to the utter earth-shattering emotions I felt whenever Illarion was around.

Seconds later his eyes narrowed, and I noticed the muscle in his jaw work. He dropped my hand and looked at me curiously.

"Did it work?" I asked.

He nodded silently.

"What's wrong?"

He got to his feet. The chair scraped across the tiles loudly as he did.

"What just happened?" I got up after him.

"Just leave it."

"Ila." I reached out and grabbed his wrist.

"Drop it Ace."

"What the hell did I do?"

"You didn't do anything." His voice was low and dangerous. "I did."

"I don't understand."

He turned briskly on his feet and moved toward me. I had no time to react as he pushed me back and pinned me to the wall.

His hand gently found the curve of my neck, the other pressing into my hip, clutching me like a lifeline.

My breath caught in my chest and words failed me. Inside, my heart was hammering against my ribs and if he didn't move away from me, it would explode. His breath was hot against my face as he lowered his lips to my forehead.

I felt his fingers tense against my skin as his dark lashes lowered until I could only see the tiniest amount of brown. His dark hair fell over his face as he moved closer to me.

His heart was racing but I was close, too close to stop now. Despite the wrongness of prying I delved deep into his mind and looked for the answers. Since he wouldn't provide them I had to find them myself. What was he so afraid of?

"Stop," he whispered.

He lowered his head until his forehead rested on mine.

"Stop what?" I knew that he hated how I could so easily look into his heart and soul like that.

His breath danced on my lips as he inched his mouth closer to mine. We were close, too close and my body just wanted him closer.

"Ace…" His hooded eyes found mine.

Slowly the fury faded. I felt the corner of his lips brush mine leaving a ghost of a kiss in its wake.

"We need to stop," he whispered.

"Why?"

"Because it is dangerous."

"I don't care."

"You should."

He pulled back and looked at me and I was sure my heart was going to stop beating this time.

Before I could respond he slid his hands down my arms and stopped at my wrists circling his fingers around them. His dark eyes set on mine. I couldn't read him, I couldn't feel anything through the connection anymore, he was fighting back.

Startled, I gasped as he pushed me back against the wall. Moments later his walls crashed down and I felt *everything* his heart was holding back. My skin burned under his touch. All my senses were ignited.

"I can't lose you," he whispered. "I can't stand losing you every night in my dreams…"

"You don't believe in the dreams," I reminded him.

He shook his head and tightened his hold on me. "I can't afford not to take anything seriously, we have to be so careful, Ace."

The way the words came out in painful, staggered breaths shattered me. Each word chipped a part of his heart away, each word weighed him down.

"You won't lose me."

I moved closer to him, closing the last, tiny gap between us. With the abilities I knew I had control over, I focused on everything I felt, all the heartache of waiting for him, all the love and unrequited passion, and lowered my own walls.

I looked up into his eyes, watching as each emotion registered in his head and with each touch his eyes widened, wetting with tears I felt within myself.

What happened to us was not love at first sight or sparks flying between people, we were literally two halves destined to meet and *connect* and when that connection happened it was an experience that could hardly be described. And I'm pretty sure last night had everything to do with it.

"I only read about what it would be like connecting with you."

I couldn't reply. But I guess I didn't have to. He felt me and everything that coursed through me.

"We're a myth," I whispered, leaning into his touch as his hands tightened around my wrists.

His lips formed a half-smile. "It feels real to me."

"Don't fight me anymore."

He smiled and moments later his lips were on mine again setting in stone every feeling we just shared and experienced.

"We should do some work," he breathed against my lips, his hot breath tickling my cheek.

"But this is much more fun," I murmured, snaking my arm to the nape of his neck deepening the kiss.

He pulled back again. His dark hair fell over his eyes and his ragged breathing suggested that my idea tempted him.

"You're making this hard…"

"I can tell." I grinned against his mouth.

I slipped my hand up under his shirt and skimmed the ripples on his stomach with the palm of my hand. He tensed letting out a deep growl before he pushed us back toward the bedroom.

Now this was the kind of work I could get behind.

Hours turned into the rest of the day and eventually the night and before either of us knew it, the day was gone. We lay tangled among the sheets holding onto each other, constantly touching and caressing. Sleep claimed me first as we drifted off in each other's arms.

CHAPTER EIGHTEEN

ACE

I woke up when the nightmare I'd been having for the past few weeks returned and ripped the last shred of sleep from me. I sat up panting, trying desperately to slow my breathing. This one was worse than before. The fear lingered where usually I could shake it. I couldn't do a damned thing to calm myself down this time.

Illarion shot up beside me. He gently ran his hand across my back pulling my hair away from my shoulders.

Sweat slicked my whole body, I was completely drenched and the sheets suffocated me. I couldn't get them off me quick enough. I'd figured it was still sometime in the early morning because it was pitch black in the room and I could only make everything out because of my super freak gifts.

I didn't mean to flinch, but the reaction happened before I could stop it and I immediately sensed his regret as his thoughts went back to Larry's apartment. He leaned back down propping himself up on his elbow.

"It was just a bad dream," I managed slowly. I took his hand and squeezed it.

"Tell me," he said, trailing soft lines across my back as I turned on my side, facing him. His voice was light, but I felt the uneasiness inside him.

"It's nothing, don't worry about it."

"Are they always this bad?"

"This has been the worst one."

"What happened?" He propped himself up higher and cupped my cheek, drawing my attention to him.

"It's nothing."

"A dream is a way to get into someone's head, especially if the Sensitive's ability is Feeling and if they've collected someone who had developed the ability to dream walk. There's a good chance they're trying to get into your head."

"I've had this dream before. It's always the same thing, you fail to save me and then I see myself die through your eyes, only now..."

"What?"

"Now I can see that it's you. All these months, I've just seen a silhouette."

He nodded slowly encouraging me to continue. He kept his hands on my skin, tracing soft lines. But deep in his eyes I saw fear.

"I'm suffering, there's pain and I always see you desperately trying to come to me. But for some reason you don't, I think it's me, I think I'm forcing you back." Our eyes connected again and I shook my head. "I don't know. It doesn't make any sense."

"Is the location always the same?"

"The first time it was in a warehouse, and then it was a boat shed with the ocean raging around us and the next few times the location seemed hazy like I couldn't quite make out the details."

"And this time?" he asked curiously.

"The warehouse." I sat up beside him. "What does it mean?"

"Was anyone else in the dream?"

"Yes," I whispered. "Damon is there with his henchman."

"What does he look like?"

"I don't know, I can't remember."

"Ace, I need you to think, what did he look like?"

"I can never make out his face. I keep seeing his feet, he's always got these hideous shoes on. I feel like I've seen them somewhere before."

"We need to go," he said getting to his feet. "Now."

I barely had time to register what he said. He was already off the bed, pulling on his jeans and t-shirt before he threw my clothes to me.

I got dressed, watching Illarion shove our belongings into the large duffle bag he kept by the door.

"What's going on?"

"They're connecting with you in your dreams trying to see where we are and what we know, every time you've had that dream they've visited you. That's how they found us before and they'll be coming again."

"How is that possible?"

"A few more sinister abilities the Collectors have," he said with a hint of venom in his voice.

He slammed the cabinets shut after he retrieved his stashed weapons.

I flinched as each wave of anger rolled off him and flooded me. Oh God. They're doing what I did when I visited Damon's house. If I could do it untrained, then I could only imagine what they could do with years of experience backing them.

My heart sped up as the pieces clicked into place. When we were attacked on our way to Aurel's house, there had been two men, the one keeping watch and the one suffocating me. He stood when Illarion called out and I saw his shoes.

It didn't make sense though. I was alone, Illarion wasn't there. If he wanted to kill me, he could have taken me right there, but he let me go. *Why?*

"Where are we going to go?" I demanded.

He continued to furiously throw everything into the bag stopping only to zip up compartments and load more things. "Anywhere, we just have to get out of here."

"Ila. They're coming after us." I stood still, watching him work furiously.

"Yes."

"*Us,*" I said again.

"Yes, us."

"Ila, stop."

He turned to look at me.

"They're coming for us because of me," I said.

"Ace, no."

"You're in danger because of me."

"Ace." He was right in front of me now.

Heat radiated off him. He stepped closer and pressed his hands on my arms.

"Don't." I folded my hands across my chest and stepped back. *Stand your ground Ace.*

"You have to go, they're going to find us and then we're both screwed."

He looked at me silently, his jaw working as I felt the turmoil between our connection spark. He knew I was right. His eyes caught mine again and just like before he shook his head.

"I'm not leaving you, Ace."

"Ila…"

"No. Not a chance." He shook his head stepping even closer.

"You said so yourself, if they get to both of us, they hit the jackpot and its game over."

"We can fight."

"We can't fight them." I shook my head.

I wanted nothing more than to pull him against me and just stay here, together, but I knew and so did he, it wasn't possible.

"We'll make it work," he said.

"How?"

"I don't know. Somehow."

"Somehow?" I shook my head sadly. "Come on, Illarion. You're smarter than that."

"You're asking me to abandon you."

"I'm asking you to think logically."

He closed the gap between us and gingerly wrapped one hand around the small of my back and with the other pulled my face closer to his and kissed me like he'd never kissed me before.

My heart sped up and the tears spilled over the dam.

When he broke the kiss, he brushed my hair behind my ears and kissed the top of my head.

"You know I'm right."

"You are. But I'm not letting you do this alone." He brushed his thumb across my cheeks and wiped away my tears. "I will die fighting them if that's what I must do, but I'm not leaving you."

That's exactly what I was afraid of. His mother and her sacrifice came to my mind. I wouldn't let him die.

I balled my fists and closed my eyes. I did the one thing I never wanted to do. I focused my energy on him.

Through his touch, I followed his emotions, through his shaky breaths I followed his fear and, when I opened my eyes I pictured what I wanted, and I forced him back. I pushed so hard I saw the change take hold. His eyes understood what I had done but he couldn't do anything about it.

"I'm sorry," I whispered. I reached up and grazed my fingers across his cheek. "I'm so sorry."

Then I ran.

I couldn't hold him for long, so I ran as fast as I could into the darkness and into the cover of the woods in the night. Hauling the bag, he'd prepared only minutes earlier proved to be a hindrance, but I ran on.

The woods grew denser as I navigated the small patches of clear path and jumped over the smaller shrubs that were in my way.

My breath grew ragged as each step drew more energy from me. My eyes stung and my heart was heavy. I couldn't keep my head clear; his eyes would haunt me forever.

He taught me how to block him and everyone else out, and despite how sick it made me to use it against him I had no choice. I knew what he would do to save me and I couldn't let that happen.

Tears clouded my vision, and I ran harder not daring to stop. The sun lightened the sky ahead, but it did nothing for my mood. It was still dark inside my heart.

Through our connection, I felt him. He was fighting hard to break my hold. He was right, I was much stronger than I thought I could be, but he was strong too.

I gritted my teeth and spotted a wide enough gap in the trees to fit through and get out into the open.

My hold on him was weakening, and his own resilience was over-powering me. *No, not yet, don't let him take over yet. Just a little bit longer. Please.*

I ran as fast as my body would allow. Only once I was clear of the woods did I stop. I felt like I'd been running for hours. Hours of adrenaline rushed through me until there was nothing left. I stopped and collapsed against a tree.

When I recovered, I pulled the bag up and over my shoulder and walked until a clearing opened onto a road, taking it east I began my long walk. I had to get there before Illarion did and I was sure that by now he'd have contacted Aurel and soon they'd both be tracking me.

312

I'd be naïve to think otherwise, especially given what happened the last time I was away from them both.

This time would be different. I had a plan and I could protect myself.

A few miles down the road, a passing car stopped and picked me up. The elderly couple didn't question my appearance though I could hear the woman's thoughts loud and clear. Each time she looked across at me, her aura brightened with worry and pulsed with questions and when I looked over at her, it dimmed as I soothed her busy mind.

Without drawing any more attention to myself, I convinced them both I was heading somewhere safe and once the compulsion took hold, I closed my eyes and pressed my cheek to the cool window allowing myself a moment to rest.

Illarion would have broken free by now and I needed to know what he knew.

♥

ILLARION

My body broke free from her hold. I cast the clock on the wall a quick glance, shocked that more than three hours had passed.

"Shit!" I slammed my palm against the kitchen table and brought the phone to my ear, dialing Aurel's number.

"She's gone."

"Why did you let her leave?"

"Obviously, I didn't let her go of my own free will," I spat, running my free hand through my hair.

"She got in your head?" he asked incredulously.

"She's strong, Aurel."

"Where is she going?"

"After Damon and he's going to kill her, he knows she's coming."

"Stay where you are, I'm on my way."

I bowed my head after we disconnected and placed the phone beside me.

♥

ACE

As I brought myself back to the present, I leaned back in my seat, letting a heavy breath settle. This was going to be much harder than I'd anticipated.

The elderly couple were still driving, oblivious to my internal battle. When I saw my stop approaching I instructed them to pull over and once they let me out, continue down the road forgetting they'd seen me. The pale red aura surrounding the man sparked to life at my instruction and eventually solidified as my compulsion took effect.

Once I was out in the cold winter air I tightened my coat around my body and pulled up my collar to protect my ears as much as I could. It must have been close to six in the morning by now and the sky had opened up and let out the mother of all snowfalls.

I walked on, spotting the lights ahead, marking the beginning of a small town.

Between the darkness and the snow, I could barely make out the Cedar Motel vacancy sign. But it shone dimly among the snowflakes and the icy night making it ten times creepier than it should have been.

Hurrying toward the entrance, I didn't expect to find the front desk manned. As the door swung open, my previous suspicions were confirmed. There was no one in sight.

Grabbing hold of the door, I struggled for a few seconds before I reclaimed it from the wind's clutches and shut it. Letting out a breath, I leaned against the frame taking a moment to adjust to the dark. I rubbed my hands together scanning the room, taking in my surroundings.

The shelter was a welcome relief from the bitter cold, and I was really happy that I wouldn't be dying in the snow tonight.

Once I was warmed up, I moved around the wonky unattended front desk and found a small box containing the room keys. The lock was a piece of cake and seconds later, I was in.

"Here we go," I muttered, grabbing a key to room thirteen, looking at the number suspiciously before tucking it safely into my pocket reminding myself that I wasn't superstitious.

The carpeted stairwell cushioned my steps and I quietly made my way up the stairs, avoiding the attention of other patrons, if there were any.

The lock gave way to room thirteen and I stepped inside, securing it behind me.

It wasn't pretty, but it would do. The windows hadn't been cleaned for years and the blinds weren't any better. Some of the slats had been broken and some were altogether missing.

The only source of light aside from the seedy light bulb that dangled above me was the glint of the moon through the broken blinds. *Get to work, Ace.* I walked the room, scanning each piece of furniture making a mental note of what was here in case I needed to utilize anything.

Beside me, the small cabinets housing changes of sheets and towels had paint blistering and peeling off the sides which no one had bothered to vacuum as it fell onto the carpet.

Blue and green wallpaper surrounded me in a dizzying kaleidoscope of hideous, seventies decor. *Yuck.* I trailed my fingers across the pale, wooden table in the middle of the room. There were no chairs save for one on the far right which was tucked under a bench that came off the kitchen in an L shape.

There was a sofa, a single bed with the linens folded at the foot, a few cabinets, and a stool by the kitchen. My stomach grumbled at the prospect. *God, I was hungry.*

But heating was more important right now. I spotted the thermostat on the wall and flicked it on.

"Okay heater," I whispered through chattering teeth. "Work your magic."

I backed into the wall and slid down. Curling up into a ball I leaned against one of the heating panels in the floor and waited for warmth.

Cold, shaky breaths escaped my lips making small clouds of steam in front of my face and suddenly I felt alone. It was suffocating. My chest ached and my arms were numb around my body. I just wanted to be at home, in my warm bed, maybe even Illarion's bed. I squeezed my eyes shut and tried to slow my breathing down.

Pulling my knees against my chest I began crying, again. I'd made this choice. *Damn it.* I decided that this is what I needed to do. I couldn't stop now. Despite how much I wanted to call him and tell him to come and get me.

The story he told me about his parents struck a chord. I knew what she would have faced. The knowledge and certainty of what she was planning on doing must have been suffocating. But she did it. She didn't cower away because she was scared. She must have known the probability of her walking away was minimal. Just like I knew now.

Sighing. I peeled myself away from the floor, feeling less popsicle and more human. As soon as I could move my fingers properly, I got up and scoped out the rest of the room. I didn't hold my breath that I would find food.

At least I wouldn't run out of caffeine. And weapons. The kitchen was stocked to the brim with coffee and cast-iron pots and pans. I took a skillet for good measure and brought it with me.

As a lonely thought dawned on me, tears pricked the back of my eyes. I wrapped my arms around myself blinking back the haze of tears.

This would be the last place I spent a night in. Not beside Illarion and not in his bed in his house, not in his arms listening to his breathing as he slept. But here. In this lonely, broken motel room in the middle of nowhere.

I dropped my gaze to the discolored red rug beneath me and forced myself to snap out of it.

This room wasn't going to secure itself.

Chapter Nineteen

ACE

I looked around at the boathouse. Familiarity struck me. There were a few oil barrels marred with years and years of weather damage, and far against the back wall was a large sign with a name I couldn't quite make out. James...Jamie...Jameson. It was too hazy to tell. It didn't matter.

I jolted awake in a cold sweat, Damn it, again. My heart raced, hammering inside my chest, sweat dotted my forehead plastering my hair to my face.

There was no way I could fall asleep after that, so I got up and washed my face in the small bathroom mentally prepping for the day ahead. If I was going to get the information I wanted, I had to stop putting off the inevitable. I needed to see Bob.

He knew a lot more than he let on and a lot more than Illarion suspected. As much as I hated what I was about to do I knew had to get there before he did. And at this point it was the only plan I had.

Sighing, I forced myself to stop sulking. When all of this was over, I'd see him again and it wouldn't be under such shitty circumstances. Maybe.

The sun had just started to peek through the horizon chasing away the last remnants of night as my thoughts were chased to the present. I gave the room one quick look before I took my belongings and ventured outside.

My bag hung heavily on my back as I prepared for the long trek in the cold.

Deep inside I felt our connection buzzing. Illarion had been uneasy the whole time I was gone, stopping short of losing his composure.

Outside, the snow was falling, and kids were making snow-angels in the park. I smiled to myself as I passed them and some young mothers who had taken their place on the sheltered park benches. I guess this wasn't two in the morning room thirteen kind of creepy, when you saw it during the day.

One lady even waved at me as I walked past with my massive bag. Reluctantly, I waved back and snuggled into my jacket. It would work to my advantage looking like an average tourist, especially considering that my only form of transport now would be hitchhiking.

I took the same path out of the town that I followed last night and I was pleased to see that the woods were much less daunting with rays of sun shining through the canopy of trees.

Confident that I wouldn't trip over a log as I walked, I took this as my moment of serenity to clear my mind and check in with Illarion via our connection.

♥

ILLARION

"We'll find her," Aurel said sitting down opposite me cradling a Corona in his hand.

I closed my eyes, pressing my fingers to my temple.

"Brother," he said calmly. "We will find her."

"You didn't see her," I managed, rubbing my face with both hands.

"She's stronger now. You have to trust that she'll be fine," Aurel said. He got to his feet and made a fresh pot of coffee.

Moments of silence passed between us before he handed me a cup of coffee. "Thanks."

"No problem."

"She's going after Damon," I said.

"You two know something I don't?"

"Ace was given information which leads us to believe that Damon is the Taker."

"By whom?"

"An unknown source."

"Then it could be wrong."

My brows rose. "You don't believe that, do you?"

"No. I don't."

"The more we looked into it, the more it seemed plausible. The prophecy said that if there were two Divine Sensitives in existence at the same time it was because, the original had tipped the balance of the scales in their favor."

"Damon was born well before Ace."

"If we're right about this, then she's walking into a trap, he wants her to go after him. We need to get there before she does."

Aurel shook his head. "That's obvious, but the problem is that we don't know where the hell he is."

"She'll lead us to him. I hate it but it's our only choice."

I balled my fists and looked across the table at him. I still couldn't shake the image of her crying, when I found her last time.

"Something else is on your mind," Aurel said, bringing my attention back to him.

"I killed one of the men when I found her."

"I know you, Illarion, you did what you had to."

"She killed the other man. It was." I paused looking for the right word. "It was terrifying."

Aurel stirred but remained quiet. I didn't have to elaborate, part of me was thankful for these abilities and the other part worried about Ace and my mother and the things that were wrong with people like us. Suddenly, those thoughts were chased away by a nagging, indescribable panic which set in almost immediately.

The image of Ace beneath that filthy bastard's body, her blood mixed in with her tears made every nerve in my body light up. The way her heart raced when they ripped her clothes off…I couldn't bear to ever feel that again. I couldn't bear to see that look of terror in her eyes again.

I put the cup back on the table letting my shaking hands settle.

"Brother, listen to me," Aurel spoke, remaining seated across from me. "I know you hate that she's using her abilities like that but if she didn't, those assholes would have raped and killed her. She was scared and she did what she had to. You know this."

"I know."

"I would have done the same if I'm completely honest." A muscle twitched in his jaw. "Where would she go first?"

"She's going after Bob."

♥

ACE

Damn. I pulled myself back to my own mind and to the morning sun. Illarion worked it out much sooner than I anticipated, though I shouldn't have been surprised.

Illarion was the smartest person I'd ever come across. He was a genius so I shouldn't have been surprised that he'd worked it out.

I sped up my pace.

Illarion's pain hurt. I felt it inside me as though it were my own. Illarion and Aurel would be heading over there now and by my count, I was about three hours away, they were five.

The trees grew sparse giving me a better view of the road and a car in the distance caught my attention.

Perfect timing.

I ran faster through the last patch of thinning forest and out onto the road waving the car down.

The blue SUV came to a slow right beside me opening the passenger window.

"Where are you heading?" the driver asked, leaning over.

Once I managed to catch my breath I leaned against the window locking eyes with him. I didn't need to try as hard anymore. I was getting better at it as each day went by.

"I need your car, take me to the nearest service station and I'll take it from there."

He nodded, unlocking the door letting me in. As my compulsion took hold, his light green aura intensified and grew solid like a blanket was thrown over him.

I placed my bag down at my feet and leaned back lowering the seat. I had to take extra precautions now. I didn't know if they had other agents watching me. Or whether Damon had his men out there looking for me now. One man in particular with particularly bad taste in shoes.

The sun had come up completely now and yesterday seemed like a bad memory, but I still couldn't shake the fear. I swallowed hard and closed my eyes. I needed to check in with Illarion again and see what I was working with.

♥

ILLARION

"We're not going to get there before she does." I shook my head as I drove down the highway toward Aurel's house.

I was already pushing the Hummer; I couldn't risk getting pulled over now, it would cost us time we couldn't afford to lose.

"I'll get in touch with my contacts and make sure we get to her before she does something stupid."

"I didn't think she'd evolve this fast."

"Gifts develop as emotions change. What's triggering hers?"

I let out a sigh. I had no choice but to tell him. My carelessness was inexcusable. If she died, it would be because of me. If I just stayed away this wouldn't have happened, at least not so soon. We would have had more time.

"When her parents died, it triggered the change, and when her team died in Iraq she grew stronger," Aurel pushed. "So, was it your presence that triggered the change this time?"

"Yes. I shouldn't have allowed myself to get close to her."

"You couldn't hide your feelings forever, Illarion."

"I should have tried harder to suppress them."

♥

ACE

I opened my eyes as the SUV pulled into the service station, the driver got out and handed me the keys.

"Catch the next bus and head home, report your car stolen tomorrow morning and forget you saw me."

The driver nodded yet again and began walking toward the bus stop. I took his place in the driver's seat and took off down the road.

By my estimation of my previous travel, Aurel's house was less than thirty minutes away which gave me about ten minutes to get the information I needed from Bob.

After that, I would be on my own. No more clues or help from anyone else.

Thirty minutes later the tall, grand gates surrounding Aurel's property came into view.

Firstly, I needed to figure out how to bypass his killer security.

I pulled up to the gate and left the SUV there as a barricade, even if it bought me a few extra minutes it was still a few minutes I wouldn't have had otherwise. And at this point, looking up at the intricate piece of tech on the gate, I needed every bit of help I could get.

"Time to shine."

The keypad was complex, and as far as *my* hacking skills went, apparently impenetrable—one other choice left—jump the gate and remember where the blind spots were. *Piece of cake.*

I secured the bag across my body and tracked back to the spot I jumped over last time. I sighed pushing back the thoughts of what made me run in the first place, the gruesome discovery of what the son of a bitch had done to my parents. It made it a whole lot easier knowing that this would end with Damon lying at my feet with a shiny gold arrow lodged right between his eyes.

Up ahead the mansion came into view. I maneuvered my way around the blind spots confident in my memory of where the cameras were. As I neared the rose bushes that barely cushioned my fall last time, I caught a glimpse of something I hadn't noticed then. A long, narrow stone with a brass plaque fastened to it. The inscription read:

"War does not determine who is right, only who is left—Bertrand Russell."

The small, intricately engraved name underneath was a sobering reminder of the world we lived in.

"*Adelina and Adrian Arcos.*"

Aurel's parents. I bowed my head. He was only a kid when they died. I couldn't imagine how that felt, being left alone here, in this mansion with the weight of the world on his shoulders.

More and more people like us were falling because of people like Bob and the men he worked for.

I imagined a young, blond boy with tears in his blue eyes standing at this stone. His choices were ripped from him when he was thrust into this world of darkness and deceit.

Was that the moment when his gifts evolved?

Like he said, every emotionally prominent moment in our lives was responsible for unlocking more of our gifts. God knew I had *a lot* of those moments.

Watching my team get killed because of me, watching Alex die, watching my life changing before I could hold on.

I pushed myself to my feet throwing one last glance at the names, I promised myself this would end. No more kids would grow up too fast because some power hungry, jackass wanted more.

I scaled the wall.

The window opened just as it did last time and I slipped inside. The room remained untouched, just as I had left it. Almost making it feel like a memorialized tomb. I felt him in here. His presence lingered, suffocating me. The anguish fill the air and his pain was etched into the fabric in the bed, in the paint on the walls.

This is what Illarion felt when I left. Guilt gnawed at the pit of my stomach again. I was going to make it up to him…if I got out of this alive.

Heading straight for Aurel's makeshift holding cell, I made my way down the stairs.

I'd only spent two nights here, but the feelings anchored me to the floor, like I belonged. I pushed that away. I didn't deserve to belong or to have a home where someone loved me. People like us didn't get happy endings.

I slung my bag over my shoulder and tightened my grip on it. The stairs led right down into the basement and the lock presented no problem. I picked it in record time and pushed the door open.

Bob sat at the far end of the cell, cross legged with his head leaning on the wall behind him. A small, stupid grin adorned his face. He looked like he was stoned, or worse.

He was still there, almost coherent but not quite. And like a tiny reminder on the side of my neck, my mind travelled back to my time with Grimes.

"I remember you," he said jogging my mind back to him. "I hit you with my car…you have a great ass."

I rolled my eyes and made my way to the desk beside the cell. I felt a strong pull toward a small tin box, so I followed my senses. Illarion was right, I was getting stronger.

A small, silver key sat in the bottom. *Bingo.*

Bob immediately perked up as I walked toward the cell, key in hand. He opened his mouth to speak but I stunned him into silence just by thinking it.

"Don't get too excited. I've had a bad couple of days, and I'm not in the mood for chatting."

He immediately shut his mouth and looked at me curiously instead. He lowered his eyes.

The lock clicked and I pushed the cell door open. I knelt in front of him, and it didn't take much to persuade Bob to do what I wanted him to do. I heard it was much easier on people who were easily impressionable, or brainless. Or in this case, already drugged.

Slowly he got to his feet and stood obediently while I brought in a chair and nodded for him to sit.

It took a moment for me to bind his hands to the chair behind his back before I felt it, for the first time.

My head was fuzzy, like I was hung-over after a massive three-day bender. I swayed on my feet using Bob's chair to steady myself. I sucked in a deep breath and bowed my head looking down at my feet. Things were a lot more serious than I thought. Tiny droplets of blood speckled the floor between my white Converse.

"Feeling a bit sick cupcake?" he asked, craning his neck.

"Shut up," I hissed, pressing my hand to my stomach.

My knuckles bleached under the pressure, and I swallowed back the nausea.

"You know the more you use these powers of yours, the more you welcome the Darkness."

"Keep talking," I warned, trying to focus on taking deep, slow breaths.

"The more you use it, the more it affects you. Before you know it, you'll be sharing a room with lover boy's mom."

I froze and Bob laughed.

"Shut the hell up," I hissed trying to force my heart rate down and steady myself on my feet. My vision dimmed, I had to make this quick.

I straightened and walked around him. I left the cell momentarily and pulled up another chair for myself.

Once I brought it back and sat down, I opened my bag and retrieved Spock and a switchblade. I needed to control him, but his words echoed as a warning in my head.

Our eyes briefly met, and in that moment, he knew exactly what I was thinking.

A smile crept across his face.

I gripped Spock in my hands and cleared my head.

Collectors like him went on a massive withdrawal like a junkie missing his drugs. The only thing on his mind was the next, intoxicating hit.

That's how addictive killing Sensitives was. We gave them a high and I was ready to beat that expression off his face.

"Tell me what I want to know, and I won't ruin those jeans." I pointed Spock at him and gripped the blade in my other hand.

"I don't care what you think you can do to me." He squeezed his eyes shut.

Like that would stop me. *Idiot.*

"Bob, you don't want to make me use this knife. I mean I will, it's not like it bothers me or anything."

"You were way more fun the first time I saw you."

"I'm having a lot more fun now."

Bob kept his eyes shut but it didn't stop him from grinning at me. "I'm sure your boss won't be happy that you took me."

"Who said anything about taking you?"

His eyes shot open, confusion briefly sweeping his wrinkled face. He spat a ball of saliva in my direction narrowly missing my foot.

I felt my face heat up and it took a lot of self-control not to lose it now.

"Oh, Bob, that wasn't nice." I stood and moved closer to him until my face was inches away from his. I felt the depths of my soul roaring to life with that familiar, terrifying Darkness. "You're going to tell me what I want to know. Look at me."

"Like I said lady, I don't care, whatever you can do to me is nothing compared to what he will do."

Why wasn't my compulsion taking hold?

"Do you even know who I am?" I asked, looking at him incredulously. His fight was dying down and I felt him slowly weakening, he was stronger than I thought. Or was I growing weaker?

328

"Should I?"

"Huh," I mused. "Thought the news would have reached everyone by now. Especially considering you were harboring all of Damon's case notes and personal files."

"You an angry ex-girlfriend or something?"

"Sister, actually."

That response earned me an open mouth stare. He was utterly dumbfounded but he knew.

One point for me. I got up and gently placed Spock on the chair. "You're *her.*"

"Now we're getting somewhere." I smiled and launched my foot into his chest throwing him backwards.

Two points for me. I grinned.

He landed with a grunt and the sound of his head hitting the ground made me flinch.

"You fucking bitch!"

I shrugged out of my jacket and placed it over the back of my chair. "It's a matter of opinion, Bob."

He heaved trying to struggle out of his ropes, but I did a good job on them. There was no way that he'd break free.

With confidence intact, I wrapped my hand around his throat and held my knife to his neck, crouching over him. This was something I had a lot of field experience in.

"Listen carefully," I said evenly. Knowing that I now had the upper hand, his resolve dissipated and he was completely compliant. "Tell me what I want to know."

He tried to struggle from my control and I could feel my grip on him slipping but I was still better than him. I couldn't let him beat me.

I focused on his mind and delved deeper, trying to get a better view inside the chaotic mess. He tried to squirm out of my hold, he struggled and his breathing sped up. I could feel the fear rippling through him and I grinned even more.

"Tell me what Damon wants with me."

He started bringing up old memories and recalling dates and times and then he spoke. "He wants what's inside you."

"I already know that. What does he want with it?"

"To beat The Taker."

For a few moments, I remained silent, looking at him dumbfounded. No, he had to be mistaken. Damon was the Taker. It all made sense...didn't it?

"Who is The Taker?"

"No one knows who he is," he said quietly.

"Is Damon the Taker?"

Bobs eyes remained fixed on mine, not seeing me at all. "He's the one who controls everything. The one who takes away your choices."

"I know that. But is Damon Cale the taker?"

"The Taker takes your choices. He takes your life."

"Why?"

"To beat them."

"Who?"

"The ones who want to keep us in the shadows and one day those shadows will grow, all around the world, everything will burn."

My jaw tightened causing my teeth to grind.

"But you will be there, among the flames...standing tall until you can stand no more."

A rush of chills crept across my skin.

"What choices were you talking about? Who is he?" I repeated.

"Your choices won't be your own, but your last choice will be the one that can end it."

Christ. All these cryptic answers were giving me a migraine.

"Where is he?"

"You'll see when you find him. Follow your dreams."

From the look on his face I wouldn't be getting anything else out of him. His mind was fading.

I rolled my eyes and got up. He writhed on the floor, frothing at the mouth. I wasn't sure how long my hold would last, so once I reached the front door of Aurel's house I sprinted across the yard, making sure to stay within the blind spots.

My heart lurched when I spotted Illarion's black Hummer pulling up behind my SUV.

"Shit."

I ran around the far, east side and climbed the wall there. It didn't matter whether Aurel's surveillance caught me now, I was out of options and I had to move. I landed as quietly as possible and waited a few seconds making sure I didn't alert them.

My head was throbbing, and my vision was getting hazier, not good…not good.

Being in such close vicinity of Illarion, my heart thundered in my chest. Our connection raged inside me. He was close, I could *feel* him. I could feel his anxiety and desperation. I almost gave in, but I couldn't back down.

He and Aurel came into view as they keyed in the code at the gate and both took off sprinting down the path, toward the house.

I let out a shaky sigh and got to my feet, at least I had a way out now. I jogged toward Illarion's Hummer and got in, throwing it into gear and taking off.

Ignoring the guilt creeping up on me I pushed his face into the back of my mind along with his pleas for me to come back.

"I'm sorry, Ila, I had no choice."

CHAPTER TWENTY

ILLARION

"She's gone," Aurel muttered looking around the holding cell and its pathetic occupant.

"She hasn't been gone long." I picked up the small silver key, which sat outside the metal tin.

Her energy lingered in the air like the scent of a summer day carried on the ocean. It was intoxicating. The vanilla and coconut imbedded itself into my memories, committing her to every thought.

I scanned the rest of the area and spotted crimson droplets, much too far from the prisoner to belong to him. My stomach twisted in tight coils.

"Aurel." I knelt, pressing a finger to one of the small droplets.

I looked up meeting his eyes.

"It doesn't mean anything; she could have cut her finger on something."

"I admire your optimism."

"Wouldn't hurt you to try it sometime."

I ground my jaw. He knew it as well as I did, she was using her abilities too fast, she didn't know how to control them yet, she didn't know how much damage they could do.

Aurel turned his attention to Bob and pulled him up roughly, "What did you tell the woman who was here?" Bob looked right past him, like he wasn't seeing him at all. "What did you tell her?"

He remained silent, completely unresponsive.

"This isn't helping and she's running out of time." I paced the small quarters.

"We just need this bastard to speak." He squeezed Bob's throat harder.

"Stop. That's not going to work. We need to get inside his head."

Aurel retreated. I stepped in front of Bob and clipped off the ties around his wrists, pulling him up off the ground and depositing him into the wooden chair.

I hated doing this but I had no other choice. I focused on his emotions and the slow rivers of fragmented thoughts churning through his head.

I sat down in the chair opposite his. "What did Ace want from you?"

When I asked the question, I saw the resolve in his eyes dissipate. He was under the hold of the Serum as well as the compulsion Ace had him under but my ability transcended both. It was something I was gifted with and in the beginning, in a past I rarely spoke about, used as a weapon.

He cleared his throat and spoke. "She wanted to know what Damon wants from her."

I ignored his answer delving deeper into his broken mind.

His body tensed as I pushed into his head ignoring the sick feeling inside me, whenever you pushed through someone's barriers like that. It was like destroying their free will, taking away their decisions. I hated the feeling, regardless of whether they deserved it or not. But Ace was more important to me. I would do anything; I would break any rules for her. I knew the moment I spotted her that I would be set on a dangerous road.

"She wanted to know what his end game was."

"What did you tell her?" I looked deeper. "Where did you send her?"

Aurel squeezed my shoulder. "Careful, Illarion."

I shrugged his hand away.

"Come on, Bob. What did you tell her?"

"The Taker will take all of her choices, he will take the life inside her…"

"Who is the Taker? Where did you send her?" I pushed, ignoring the last sentence.

His body tensed as I pushed, relentlessly ignoring the sickness forming in the back of my throat. I was losing him; I didn't have much time.

"Only he knows the truth about the Divine's powers. She can't be taken, she can't be collected."

My grip tightened around his forearm and I gritted my teeth. "Who does? The Taker?"

Bob nodded. "And now he'll get her exactly where he wanted."

"Where did you send her?"

"By the sea."

I pulled myself out of his head and got to my feet, without hesitation, I pulled my gun out, aimed and shot.

"What the hell are you doing?" Aurel shouted, surprised as I was at my own actions.

"She's walking into a trap!" I shouted, not stopping for a second to feel anything about the scum I just shot. "He sent her to Jameson Constructions."

Aurel processed my words before collecting his own things and following me up the stairs.

"Ace has been dreaming about that place for months, he fed her that information knowing Ace would piece it together."

♥

ACE

So, it was a trap. I should have figured as much; it was too easy. Didn't matter though, it was still the only way I would get my answers.

I focused my energy on the road ahead and continued driving toward the warehouse.

A wave of nausea washed over me. Illarion's mom knew how to take on powerful Sensitives. She had a lot more experience than some of the best agents around and I needed answers.

So, I picked up speed and keyed in the GPS to take me straight back to New York City. I didn't feel as relieved as I thought I would be heading back home. Maybe it was the possibility of seeing Troy again and having to explain my sudden disappearance from his life.

As I took another exit, I felt a faint hint of nausea returning. I pinched the bridge of my nose taking deep breaths, focusing on the road careful not to swerve into oncoming traffic.

I turned on the radio and tuned out.

Exactly two hours later, I pulled up to my old apartment building with a mix of emotions running through me.

I ditched Illarion's Hummer around the block and walked up to the front, greeting the doorman like I hadn't disappeared months ago.

"It's good to see you again, Ms. Hart," he greeted.

"It's good to be back."

The familiar ride up to the top floor was harder than I thought. I knew Illarion would be less than pleased to know I'd returned to an unsecured location, but then again, knowing him, he would already be on his way here as well.

I swallowed hard as I entered my apartment. *Home.* The furniture was arranged in much the same way I left it, save for a few things that had been packed up and stored, things that tied this place back to me.

I made my way over to my bedroom, retrieved a pair of jeans and a sweater and threw them on after a quick shower. I pulled out the laptop from my bag and sat down on the sofa overlooking the city. In the moment it took to power it up, I let my eyes wander.

I missed my apartment. The cool greys and slick blacks of the kitchen reminded me of the way everything was. Pots and pans hung suspended from the ceiling above the island bench. My makeup bag and several nail polish bottles sat haphazardly on the coffee table beside some uninteresting magazines and stationery. I peeled my eyes away from the memories and leaned back. They were all reminders of how everything had changed.

Balancing the laptop on my crossed legs I powered up Google.

"Okay, LaGuardia hospital," I spoke aloud looking through the results. "Patient search."

I clicked through the names searching for *"Lazarev."*

Only one result returned. *"Lazarev, Sonya."*

"Got you." I reached for the small notepad on the coffee table and wrote down the details and shoved the loose sheet in my pocket.

I didn't have to travel far, which was good for me since I wouldn't be going anywhere by car anymore, I couldn't risk using the SUV and I couldn't risk using my own car. I sighed. I missed my little Audi, summer was never going to be the same. The cool wind in my hair as I drove down the highway, leaving New York behind with the roof down.

Sighing, I looked back at the note in my hand, the subway was my only option. I cringed at the idea.

As I was about to leave a yellow sticky note on the fridge caught my eye. How had I missed that? A quick glance told me it was a phone number, Troy's new number. Of course he would have tried to find me, he had my key.

Guilt gnawed at me from every angle. I had to make things right with him. I had to explain. I snatched the note and shoved it in my pocket.

The pendant around my neck grew heavy.

Locking up, I took the elevator down to the basement level and made my way out through the service doors watching for anyone who might be keeping an eye on me. Two, maybe three pairs of men dressed in dark suits stood at various access points around the building.

If I wasn't trained in the art of surveillance, I wouldn't have glanced at them twice, but I was. So, I changed my route and took another exit, down the back of the long, dark alley where I crept between the dumpsters and discarded beer bottles.

The subway was off the cards now. When I was sure I was clear, I hailed a cab and got as far from there as possible.

LaGuardia would only be a short, fifteen-minute ride, so I needed to ensure I had a solid plan in place. Going in and trying to talk to someone in a vegetative state wasn't going to be easy.

I took the time to check in on Illarion.

❤

ILLARION

"New York City," I said to Aurel.

"Why would she go back there?" he asked, unlocking his car, tossing to keys to me.

Taking the back routes through the winding roads, I drove faster.

"It's home."

It was the only thing that made sense. I knew she would go there before she even left. Why though? That was something I didn't know yet.

"Do you think she would be ballsy enough to go back to her apartment?" Aurel asked.

"I have no doubt."

♥

ACE

Well, at least he didn't know why I was in New York. That made things a little easier for me. And, it bought me a little more time.

As the cab pulled out, I quickly tossed him a wad of cash and made my way up to the busy streets.

I flagged down a young man walking on his own and flashed a smile.

"Can you tell me where the hospital is?"

"LaGuardia?"

I nodded.

"Just down that road, it's a two-minute walk," he added.

I thanked him and hurried in the direction he sent me. Just as he said, it came into view and my heart raced.

The large glass doors slid open as I approached and I made my way across the cheap, blue carpet to the reception desk.

The stark white walls made me shiver. Hospitals were always grim. Regardless of the paintings and plants they scattered throughout to try and bring some life back into their halls.

"Excuse me," I flashed a smile, leaning with both elbows on the counter. "I'm here to see my aunt."

The redhead raised her eyebrows at me and tapped the sign taped to the side of the desk with her long, sparkly manicured nails. "Visiting hours ended two hours ago."

I looked at her nametag, *Meghan*. Alright Meghan, if you're going to play that way.

I took a deep breath calming myself and locked eyes with her. "You'll make an exception for me."

"And why would I do that?"

Damn, my compulsion wasn't up to scratch. I cleared my throat and tried again.

"Because I've had a long day, and I really just need to speak with my aunt. You're going to help me."

For a moment she stared at me. The obnoxious ticking of the clock on the wall behind her seemed amplified, slower somehow. Then, she returned her eyes to the monitor and nodded.

"What's your aunt's name?" she asked, looking at her computer.

"Sonya Lazarev."

"She's on the second floor, room sixty-three."

"Thank you, Meghan," I said firmly, taking off toward the nearest elevators.

My heart pounded in my chest bringing up the sickness tenfold. I took another deep breath and ignored it. Could the power use really be sucking me dry this badly?

The elevator stopped and opened at the second floor letting me and another woman out.

The plaque attached to the wall across from the elevator pointed me in the right direction, rooms thirty to sixty were to the left and rooms sixty to ninety were to the right. So, there I headed.

Three doors down, I saw it. Room sixty-three.

I took a deep breath and let myself in.

The woman remained completely unmoving until I closed the door and walked across to her bed.

She looked straight at me, and my heart caught in my chest, her eyes were the same rich shade as Illarion's. The same color of whiskey, golden and brown.

"You are Acacia."

"Yes, and I need your help, Sonya."

I kept my eyes on her while I pulled a chair closer to her bed.

"You're afraid but determined."

A frown tugged on my lips. Illarion did say that she was a powerful Sensitive. One of the best in her field. I shouldn't have been surprised that she could read me like an open book.

Looking into her honey eyes I sat up straight.

"Please, I need whatever information you have."

"You search for the Taker."

I nodded.

"You're afraid to use your gifts."

"How can I not be?" I hesitated. *"I saw what can happen. I'm afraid that letting Illarion in will harm him too."*

"You need each other. Regardless of the risk."

"Am I strong enough without him?"

"Perhaps, but it is not wise."

"So, I risk his life to save my own? I'm not okay with that."

"It is his choice to make, no?"

She was very matter of fact, just like her son, I guess I shouldn't have been surprised.

I wet my lips and shifted in the chair. *"You tried to save your husband, didn't you?"*

For a moment she remained silent in my mind, sending waves of something I couldn't quite understand into me. Courage? Clarity?

"You won't end up like me, malyshka. My son would never let that happen."

Her eyes searched mine.

"I tried to protect my husband and bring him back. I wasn't strong enough, but you are stronger than me, and my Illarion is stronger than his father."

"What if I'm not strong enough to save him?" I understood the gravity of what I was facing. *"What if he dies because of me."*

On the one hand, I needed to get into Damon's head, and I already knew how big that challenge would be, and on the other, I needed to make sure I could keep Illarion safe. *I needed him safe.* I couldn't face what was coming if he was in danger, because of me.

"Acacia."

Her voice drew my attention back to her.

"These challenges that await you are going to be hard. They will be life altering. But you must not doubt yourself. You are much more powerful than I ever was."

Much the same way Illarion let me see how he felt, she was able to do the same, only it wasn't through feelings, it was through sight. Through her power, she showed me the light shrouding me. It translated into strength and confidence.

"Do you know who the Taker is?"

"We don't know anything for certain, I'm sorry."

"How do I prepare to fight something I don't know?"

"You know how to find him."

"My dreams."

"Yes."

I released a small breath.

"Your self-doubt will hurt you, Acacia. I don't trust in anyone more than you, to protect my son. And I know you will find a way to end this. I've seen and felt your strength. You don't even know how powerful you can be."

"Can be?"

The glint in her eye told me she knew more than she let on.

"You're not there, not yet, but you will be, when the time is right, and stars align. You will be unlike anything anyone has ever seen."

Looking away as tears pricked my eyes, I kept my face down. This was too much.

"When the time comes you will face the Taker and anything you've faced until then will seem a distant memory. When that time comes, you must be strong. You won't have a choice."

"What does that mean? Why won't I have my own choices?"

"Because he will take them from you. That is what he does."

"So, whatever I do is for nothing? I'll end up with The Taker anyway? I'll end up with Damon."

Her mind was quiet, and for a moment I thought she was gone.

"You will face him, and you will die. That is the only way this ends. It is the only way you can become what you have always been destined to become. It's the only way you can become what we need."

Oh wow. My stomach churned.

"I have to die?"

"It's the only way you can grow."

"How can I grow if I'm dead?" I shot back.

"Ah, Acacia. You aren't like us; you aren't like anything. The same principles do not apply."

"This is absurd." My heart slammed into my ribs.

"You can do this."

"I don't know that I can."

"You can. But you must know, you must prepare yourself for the outcome. Not all three of you will survive."

My eyes shot up to hers. Three of us? Me, Illarion and Aurel. If I didn't die, then Illarion or Aurel would?

How could I keep them both out of this, it wasn't like I could lock them up, both were coming after me.

"You need to go now," she said, breaking my chain of thought. *"There isn't much time."*

"Will Ila be safe?" I dared to ask. My heart wasn't going to be in it if he didn't make it. *"If I do this, if I fight, will he be safe?"*

"It's the only way he will be safe."

And with that, the only answer I needed, I got up.

"Thank you."

She remained still, but her eyes conveyed all I needed to see. She was proud. She trusted me. My heart fluttered with pride.

"Acacia."

I turned.

"I am truly sorry for what is to come. I am sorry I cannot protect you from it."

I drew in a long breath. To say that fear eluded me would have been a total lie. I was terrified out of my mind but the desperation to protect them and do what was right to stop the Taker from killing more of our people, far outweighed the fear I had for myself.

I gave her a final smile and then left the room. Illarion would undoubtedly have worked out by now where I was and where I was going, which didn't give me much time to work with.

I took the stairwell back down to the lobby and hailed a cab once I was outside.

"Where you headed?" The driver asked to which I had no reply yet.

"Just drive toward the city, once we're close, I'll let you know."

"Works for me." He pulled out into the flow of traffic and I leaned back in the seat and checked in with Illarion.

♥

ILLARION

Aurel and I walked past the door attendant to the elevator before any questions could be asked,

"This is where she lives?"

I nodded in response to Aurel's question and pushed the button for the penthouse. She was here not long ago; I could still feel her energy in the air. It hummed like static.

When I was here last taking care of the apartment, her bills and everything else I needed to ensure it remained safe but not in her name, I found out that her parents had left it to her in their Will. I didn't know how they came upon that kind of money but a quick dive into her father's history confirmed he worked on some clandestine operations many years before she was born and they paid well.

"Nice building," Aurel mused.

It hadn't been that long since she left, but I already felt the separation.

"You okay?" he asked when the doors shut.

Was I okay? How could I be okay when I knew she was going on a suicide mission?

"I will be when I find her."

When the elevator stopped and the doors opened, a wave of emotions rushed into me.

I closed my eyes running my fingers across the counter: nostalgia, she missed this place and her old life. But she knew she couldn't go back.

Her essence drew me toward the kitchen, and I followed her trail to the fridge, there'd been a note, something that made her feelings pulse wildly. Digging through the essence of this space a little deeper, I worked it out. Troy.

It made me jealous, the second I saw it, which I was ashamed to admit.

My fists balled at my side.

"Get your contacts to find Troy Johnson. She might reach out to him for a place to stay."

"On it." He pulled out his phone and sent off a message.

I kept searching her apartment and stopped when I spotted a small notebook tucked away from the pile of stationery with a pen beside it.

I took the pad and held it up, a faint indentation was left on the sheets beneath the one she wrote on, I could barely make out what she'd written, but two words were as clear as day. As the realization hit me, my stomach lurched.

"What is it?" Aurel's voice sounded miles away.

"She's gone to see my mother."

♥

ACE

I pulled myself out of Illarion's mind, and back into my own. He had figured things out too fast. Time to change my plans.

"Take me to Central Park, please."

"You got it."

He knew where I had been, but he didn't know where I was going, not yet. I still had that advantage. I needed help if I was going to remain off the radar. Thankfully, I knew the perfect person to help. Illarion would be pissed. *Beyond pissed.* But it was my only choice. The word made me double back to what Sonya had said. Choice…my choices would be gone. It was all so cryptic.

I pulled out my cell phone and dialed the number scribbled on the crumpled yellow note in my pocket.

The voice on the other end answered after three rings.

"Troy, I know it's been a while."

CHAPTER TWENTY-ONE

ACE

I wrapped my arms around my chest trying to keep as warm as possible on this cold ass night in Central Park. The wind had died down which helped and the hot cup of coffee I cradled in my hand was a godsend. My stomach grew queasy waiting for Troy. I clutched the Starbucks cup like a lifeline and a source of liquid courage.

He'd agreed to meet me before I even asked him to come. He was so good like that.

I didn't explain why I'd left or why I was back, but I had no doubt that those questions would come.

Remembering the newly formed scar across my cheek, even though it was mostly healed, was going to raise some concerns. I patted myself down to look presentable, hoping that it would take attention from my face. I yanked my hair out of my ponytail and pulled some of it forward over my shoulder.

Kids and parents skated across the frozen lake; they had no idea about this world of mine—which threatened to take theirs. I swallowed the knot in my throat, my parents used to bring me here as a child. We were a normal family then. *God, I missed them.*

I took a sip of the hot liquid and leaned back against the park bench.

In the distance, I spotted Troy, gorgeous as always.

My heart tumbled in my chest making me feel like a massive jerk. He didn't deserve what I'd done to him.

"Ace," he said tentatively when he reached me.

"How are you?" I shook my hair over my cheek.

"What the fuck happened?"

He reached for my face and in a reactionary move I caught his hand and squeezed—apparently a little too hard.

He yanked his hand back and shook it.

"I'm sorry. It's a long story. But I need your help."

He looked wary of me for a moment, but then he moved closer once again and brushed the hair away from my face. He inhaled sharply and when I turned from him, he caught my cheek and turned my face back.

"Who the hell did this, Ace? Are you running from someone?"

I knew that I'd had to explain if I was going to get him on board. I closed my hand over his and gently pulled it away.

"It's complicated. I'm running *to* someone, the same someone who's responsible for a lot of shit in my life."

"You're not making sense."

"I know." I moved back giving myself a comfortable distance. "It's complicated. I can't go back to my apartment again. I need your help."

It was a lot to ask, and I felt bad, but I had no one else in this city to ask for help. Vanessa was amazing at this sort of thing, being in the CIA and all, but she couldn't pull strings here. It was strictly out of her jurisdiction, and I didn't want to put her out any more than I already had.

"You bailed…without a word."

"I'm sorry." I bowed my head. "A lot went on, a lot happened."

"You could have called."

"I couldn't, and that's the truth."

He didn't look like he bought it and I couldn't blame him. I wouldn't have either.

"You're going to have to explain this to me."

"I know, and I will. But right now, I need your help." I wet my lips. "Please, I don't have anyone else."

He stuffed his hands into his pockets nodding at my jacket. "We should go; you'll freeze out here."

I smiled and followed him.

We walked side by side while I did my best ignoring the lovey-dovey couples around us.

"Where have you been?" he asked, turning his face toward me.

"It's a long story."

He took his coat off and handed it to me. "We've got a long walk to my apartment. And I think you owe me at least that."

"I do. You're right."

I accepted the coat, and greedily wrapped it around myself. It was warm from his body and the familiar smell of sandalwood made my stomach twist in knots.

"So?" he prompted.

He kept his eyes on me—the sharp, angular lines of his face were set hard. I wouldn't get away with ignoring his questions. Damn. I could have compelled him. It would have been easier; no questions, nothing to answer for. But I wouldn't do that to him.

"There are a lot of things about me that you don't know."

"Then tell me," he said softly. "I came, I'm here. I want to help."

Troy always had the ability to make me feel like telling him all my issues would be alright, like he wouldn't judge me. I knew he was a good man, and he didn't think any less of me no matter the things he saw but it was me. I was the one who was afraid to let people in.

"You already know that I was in the army, three tours." I began gauging his reaction.

"You never wanted to speak about that."

"Because my unit was killed, on my last tour."

"Ace, I…"

"It was my operation and I failed them." I wet my lips. "You know I lost Alex. It was my fault he died."

"You never told me that."

"How could I tell you that I was responsible for so many lives? How would that conversation even have gone?"

"With sympathy." He looked across at me. "What happened?"

"My unit was taken by an ex-marine, he was disgruntled. He had my unit killed. Alex and I, we were spared. Left alive only to be tortured."

"Jesus Christ."

"I lost count of what they did to us and for how long. And in the end, it didn't matter. He killed Alex in front of me. A bullet to the chest. That's it. Snuffed out in less than a second."

Troy slowed and then stopped walking. I wrapped my arms around my chest.

"I got out of there; I walked through the desert for days until I passed out. Someone brought me back to the base. He saved my life."

His eyes were wide. His heart was so heavy it broke me in two.

I gestured to keep walking.

"My parents were on their way to meet my general, to launch a search party when they were killed."

"Oh my God."

"I left after that. Couldn't stay. There was no point for me."

"That's when you came to New York."

I nodded.

We'd reached his building and he let me in first where we greeted his doorman and took the elevator up to his floor.

When we were both safely inside his apartment, he gestured for me to sit on the sofa, motioning for me to go on.

"I realized when I came back that something happened to me then, I realized I was…different."

"Different how?"

"After the marine tortured me and I escaped, I used some kind of ability. I didn't know it then. But I know now."

"What are you talking about?"

I drew my knees to my chest. "You've heard the rumors about the people with gifts?"

"Yeah, Sensitives," he said looking at me curiously. "The word gets tossed around a lot at clubs and shit."

"They're real."

"You're one of them?"

"I'm not exactly like the rest of them. Turns out I'm something more and a lot of interested parties are after me now. It was the Agency who found me in the desert, who employ me now."

"The marketing job was a cover I take it."

"Yeah."

After a few moments of silence, it seemed to click. He sat on the coffee table in front of me.

He remained silent, absorbing everything I was throwing at him.

"Are they CIA?"

"No, they're not affiliated directly with any government body. They're their own entity, answering somewhat to the hierarchy."

"Who's after you?" He shifted in his spot.

"That's classified."

"Okay." He got to his feet. "Drink?" he asked, walking over the bar.

"Please."

He set two scotch glasses on the bench, filled them with ice and added just enough amber liquid to cover the cubes.

"I assume you have a team?" He walked back to me and handed me one of the glasses.

"Yes, I have a team."

"Where are they now?"

"It's complicated." I took a sip and leaned forward.

Clearly frustrated at my lack of answers he rubbed his face with his free hand and looked at me. "I'm hearing a lot of, it's complicated, and not a lot of answers. How can I help you if you're not telling me anything?"

"There are some things I can't tell you, Troy."

"I get that, God knows I do. But you called me, remember? You asked me for help. I ditched my family dinner, cancelled my nightshift to be here."

I cleared my throat. "I'm sorry you had to do that."

"I'm not saying it to make you feel bad, I'm just telling you, so you know I'm serious about helping but you have to give me more than *it's classified.*"

Our knees were almost touching and the tense atmosphere between us intensified.

"I want to help you, Ace, I do. But I need to know what I'm getting involved in. You just disappeared. I didn't know if you ran away, or if something happened on your work trip or…or if you died."

My stomach knotted and for a moment, he did nothing and I remained transfixed on those blue eyes burning holes into me.

"Your apartment was cleaned up and your car was still in the garage."

And when I didn't answer, he continued grilling me.

"You disappear for months, no call, no text, nothing. Then you call me out of the blue and ask for my help?" he inched closer until our knees were almost touching. "I want to help you. But you have to give me something."

"You're right. I'm sorry."

"I don't want you to apologize, just trust me enough to talk to me."

"I do trust you. That's why I called."

"And I'm glad you did. But why aren't you asking your team for help? Someone who's clearly authorized to know this information."

"When I found out my parents were killed to get to me, I realized that the information I found takes me down a path that my team can't follow."

"Can't or won't?"

"I won't let them."

"Why?"

"It's too dangerous," I said, shaking my head. "If they're after me and my abilities they'll be after them and theirs."

"Your unit is made up of people like you?"

"Similar."

He watched me with a clenched jaw.

"If they're like you, then they're skilled, trained with crazy ass abilities, right? So, who it is dangerous for?" He looked at me curiously. He wasn't naïve.

"For everyone."

He looked at me, sighing before he dropped his hands between his legs and held his scotch there.

"I was in love with you, Ace," he said shaking his head.

"I know."

"I would have done anything for you."

"I know. And you deserve so much better than I have given you."

"Damn straight."

I rubbed my face and looked at him, and when his eyes finally lifted and met mine, I forced a tight smile hoping he could see the pleading in them.

"Will you help me?"

"Of course I'll help you. You know there will never come a time you ask when I won't be there."

I wet my lips, hating that I was using him.

"So where do I come in? What can I do?" he asked quietly.

"I need to get some rest. I just need a safe place to stay, maybe a shower and some food."

"Of course. Money?"

"No, I don't need money. Thank you."

He drank the rest of his scotch and set the glass down on the coffee table behind him.

"What else can I do?"

"For now, nothing."

"Okay, I'll make us dinner. Help yourself to the shower, you can take the guest room."

He got up before I could say anything else or even thank him. I deserved that.

I headed for the bathroom and took my time. Once I was done, I sat down on the bed in the guest room. Rangers posters were stuck to the walls along with a framed and signed jersey. It brought a smile to my face. He really loved that team.

Turning my attention to the foot of the bed, I saw the clothes he'd left out for me to sleep in. I'd just stripped when he knocked and opened the door. I barely had a second to register that I was standing half naked.

"Shit, I'm sorry," he muttered stumbling to close the door.

"It's fine, relax, not like this is the first time you've seen me sans clothes." I took the hoodie he'd set out and started pulling it on.

I felt his eyes on me.

"Jesus, Ace. What happened to you?"

"When I said bad people were after me, I wasn't exaggerating."

"Yeah, but I wasn't expecting you to look like you just came out of a cage match either."

"You should see the other guy," I tried.

"That's not funny."

I flinched at the dark tone.

He stood by the door, his heart breaking with each moment he looked at me. I knew the bruises along my back from Larry's apartment were there. I knew the evidence of fighting the creep in Bob's pantry was there.

"You can't do this alone."

"I'm not alone, I have you," I tried.

He didn't crack a smile. He looked like he was going to be sick.

"Hey," I finished dressing and sat at the foot of the bed. "I've got this. They're just bruises. I can handle a bit of combat."

He hugged a bag to his chest. He was in shock.

"Hey," I tried.

"I'm sorry, I just came to give you this."

He placed the bag on the ground by the door and quickly closed it.

I frowned and slowly padded over to the door. When I noticed it was a care package, I smiled. It was filled with a couple of books and my favorite candy. He must have gone down to the corner store while I was cleaning up.

I put the bag beside the bed and climbed under the covers and welcomed sleep.

I ran and ran knowing that if I slowed, I would get killed. They were coming after me faster than I'd anticipated. The warehouse was just up ahead, and if I could make it, I would be safe. He would be safe.

The darkness around me grew heavier and suddenly my speed was irrelevant, nothing I did brought me any closer. And then came the silence.

There was nothing, not even the sound of crashing waves reverberated through the stillness of the night. It was thick and heavy like a fire blanket had been placed over the world.

I blinked and when I opened my eyes I was tied to a chair.

"It's good to see you." Damon's eyes glistened in the night.

I felt a warm pool of blood collecting around my wrists, dripping to the floor.

"What are you... what... what is this?" I choked, looking around.

"This..." He held his arms out. "This is your nightmare, my reality."

My mind reeled, how was this possible?

"It's possible because I can walk dreams," he said, reading my every thought. "I believe you're familiar with the gift?"

"What do you want?" I hardly recognized my voice as it echoed around us.

He stood above me with a blade in his hand.

"You've been in a position like this once before, have you not?"

My mind rushed back to Iraq.

"You were in the dark then, Ace, you can't run with that now."

"What do you know about that?"

He shrugged, circling me.

"What do you know about Grimes?"

"He was crazy, but he was right. They were looking for you."

"Why?"

"Because you, dear sister, are going to be the one to change everything. Without you, everything we do is for nothing."

"I don't understand."

A smirk spread across his thin lips, then he knelt, and my heart rate shot into overdrive. He drew the sharp blade along the insides of my wrist and slowed when my eyes shot to his.

"Let's see how good you really are."

"What?" my voice barely sounded.

"If you can't stop me in here, you'll have no hope out there." And with one sharp slice he cut open my wrist.

I screamed.

I couldn't stop the sound as it erupted from deep within me.

"Come on, Ace!" he taunted me. "You're not even trying."

Just like before he moved to my other arm and the blade made contact ripping my skin open.

Another scream escaped my lips.

And then there was silence, not even my voice sounded. The stillness was eerie; nothing made any noise, not even his shoes on the concrete below, all I could hear was my blood rushing inside my head.

As it poured out of me, pooling on the ground I realized that sound was amplified.

"I want you to fight," he said simply as he came to stand right in front of me running his fingers through my hair. "I want what's in here, you're not giving me any hope."

He folded the blade away and knelt in front of me, tilting my chin up.

"You will never get me."

"I've got you now…" he said.

"You're in my dream!"

"It's the perfect way for me to get what I want. And to get you to practice."

"What are you talking about?" I looked up at him.

"Look around."

My eyes darted around the darkness and fell on a tall, dark figure running toward me.

Although he was running, the darkness seemed to be slowing him down just like it did to me before.

Once my eyes adjusted to the blackness, I saw his face and my stomach fell through the floor.

"He's here to help you," Damon cooed. "But he'll fail."

No. He couldn't be here.

"He'll always be there, dear sister. He will always do what he can to keep you safe and he will always fail because that is how it needs to be."

"Ace!" Illarion's voice shot right through me and I noticed that sound had started to come back. "Fight him!"

"Yes," Damon suggested, standing back. "Fight me. If you can. Push me out. Wake up. Save yourself."

I struggled against the restraints feeling the sting of torn flesh rubbing against the rope. "Ila, you can't be here!"

His face twisted in agony as he ran, watching me and I couldn't look away. "Fight him, fight! Wake up!"

Damon stood and looked back at me with an amused expression on his face. "Fight me little sister. That's all you have to do. Just wake up."

My breathing hitched. I looked at Illarion again, he was closer now. "Fight him, Ace!"

"He can't save you in here," he said kneeling. "Only you can break free from this. Only you have the power to save yourself. So, will you? Will you manage to wake yourself up before you bleed to death?"

I heard screaming, which I quickly realized was my own. The strain was breaking my mind in two.

"You're strong enough to push me out, but you're failing, why?" Damon asked simply.

"Get out of my head!" I cried out.

"Make me. That's all I'm asking."

Illarion's voice grew louder in my head. "Fight him!"

"You really should listen to him," He swept my hair behind my ear, looking up at Illarion. "See how strong your Prince Charming is, see what

357

he's made of, did he tell you about his colorful past? Did he tell you about Operation Lullaby?"

I screamed as anger raged through me and his words threw my mind into overdrive.

"Focus on me, Ace!" Illarion yelled again and I desperately tried to hold onto his voice, but the darkness grew heavier again drawing him away from me. A tightness in my chest filled my body with fear.

"Ask him what happened in Iraq. Ask him what happened with Operation Lullaby," Damon cooed. "Ask him how you nearly died because of him."

As Illarion neared me, I grabbed onto the sliver connecting us as the edges around my vision darkened. I used him as my anchor. I pulled. Hard.

Damon's shrill laughter rapidly faded until I was sitting in the dark, no chair and no ropes. As my eyes closed, the sound went with it. Nothing but darkness and quiet surrounded me.

"Ace."

An urgent voice brought me back to the bed and back to Troy's apartment.

My eyes flew open, and I jerked back.

"Easy," he said softly. "Breathe, Ace, focus on my voice."

"Ila?" My throat was raw.

"I'm here, just focus on my voice," he breathed holding my wrists in his hands. "Look at me."

"What happened?"

"I need water; we need towels here," he shouted to someone.

When my head lolled to the side, his gentle voice brought me back to him.

"Ace." He leaned in closer to me, his eyes were wide and panic rolled through him and right into me. "Hold on."

"What…what are you doing here?" I tried to keep my eyes focused, but I couldn't.

"Here, let me see," Aurel spoke with urgency.

Illarion released my wrists and as he did, I felt the stinging come back full force along with a lot of blood.

I let out a sharp gasp and realized I was crying. Illarion left my side for a heartbeat and when he came back, he pressed his hand to my forehead.

"I need to dress the cuts, Ace," Aurel spoke slowly while he carefully handled my wrists. "She's bleeding out. Hold this here." He spoke, not to me but to Illarion. Then another hand, with a towel was holding my other wrist.

Illarion's heart was thundering in his chest, he didn't try to hide the fear rushing through his veins.

And there, by the door, a smorgasbord of feelings washed over Troy as he watched Illarion with me, he was conflicted, confused and scared.

I forgot that he didn't understand this world and only got thrust into it because of me.

"Check her," Aurel ordered. "Make sure she's okay."

Aurel finished bandaging up my arms and gently let them down. Illarion didn't wait for an invitation. He pulled me closer and cupped my face in his hands.

"Ace." His eyes searched mine. "Tell me you're okay. Tell me you're in there."

I flinched, my head felt like it was scrambled with an eggbeater and my arms hurt a whole lot more than I wanted to admit. But I was here. Mostly.

I clutched at the black fabric of his t-shirt and buried my face in his chest when I realized I couldn't stop the tears from falling. I cried more than I had ever cried in my life, and it hurt.

He held onto me so tightly I was certain he knew every single thought running through my mind.

"Come on, give them some space," I heard Aurel say to Troy.

Reluctantly the two left, closing the door.

Illarion's shallow breathing matched my own.

"You were in my dream," I said.

"I sensed it as soon as we left the hospital," he said quietly, caressing my arm.

"How did he do this to me?"

"He's powerful Ace, he won't stop until he gets you."

"You saved me," I said with a weak smile, again, I was useless. What did I even bring to this team aside from being the damsel in distress? "He said you would fail."

"You uncovered more than we had in weeks, Ace, don't discount that."

"And you're here saving my sorry ass again."

"Stop." His hands found mine. "We're a team, I'll always save you and you'd always save me."

His smile broke down the walls I was holding up and the tears flooded my eyes again.

"You did well."

"He nearly killed me."

"You fought back. You pushed him out."

I smiled feeling the love swell inside him.

"Why did you come here?" he asked, quietly rubbing his hand up and down my arms, carefully avoiding the bandaged areas.

Right. That was something I didn't know how to answer. I shrugged. "I needed a safe place to stay…"

"He cares about you," he said softly planting a kiss to my forehead.

"I know." I smiled looking into his eyes. "I care about him too."

He wrapped his arms around me.

"But I, what I feel for you is different."

"I know," he kissed the top of my head.

Aurel walked in and sat on the bed beside us. His eyes flicked over the bandages and then my face. His jaw hardened.

"You okay?" Something inside him silenced me.

He was seeing something, something he didn't let on. I wasn't sure even he knew what he was seeing. But he looked confused about it. Almost worried.

"The kid prepared another bed for you. You can't stay here," he said.

I looked down and realized that I was literally lying next to a pool of my own blood.

Illarion got up first and held his hand out. "I've got you."

He leaned down and then his strong arms wrapped around my waist and pulled me up against him. I slung my arm around his shoulder and pressed my cheek against the hard muscles in his chest.

CHAPTER TWENTY-TWO

ACE

I opened my eyes against the pounding in my head and the black dots blurring my vision. My head felt like someone had taken an ice pick and started hammering away at my skull. I was exhausted.

Easing myself up on my elbows, I took a deep breath and ignored the sharp pain in my wrists as they held my body up.

Slowly turning my arms, I examined the bandages. God. They reached up to my elbows. A shaky sigh left my lips. It was terrifying, I'd felt so helpless and if Illarion hadn't come when he did, I would have bled to death in my sleep.

Shivering, I inched closer to the edge of the bed and waited a moment, steadying myself. I looked around recognizing this room immediately. It was Troy's bedroom. A pang of sadness shot through me, I shouldn't have come here. I shouldn't have involved him. Shit. If Damon worked out where I was, Troy would be in danger.

I thrust my fingers into my hair and combed out the knots and pulled the thick mass into a messy knot.

I stopped just short of the kitchen. Illarion and Aurel were talking in low, determined voices. I pressed my cheek to the cold, exposed concrete finish and listened. Of course, I focused my remaining energy on blocking myself off from them.

Illarion let out a heavy sigh and I heard him push away from the chair he was sitting on. "If that son of a bitch touches her again-"

"He won't," Aurel cut in.

"I won't hesitate to put a bullet in his head."

"No one would stop you, least of all me, but we need to be smart about this."

"I'll get in touch with the Agency. They need to know about this," Illarion spoke again and Aurel's reply was a sarcastic laugh.

"Do you actually think they'd be involved in all of this? That they would intentionally put her in his hands if they knew what he wanted?" Aurel asked.

Illarion remained quiet for a moment. "He's had help. There's no way he is strong enough to have everyone under that amount of compulsion for that long."

"Agreed, we have to be careful about who we tell."

"We can trust Michael and Elena. I'll read them in." Illarion's voice was dangerously low. He didn't like what they had to do. But he agreed that we needed help. We needed more people on our side.

"What did you do about contacting them?" Aurel asked quietly.

"After extracting Bob?" Illarion's voice was low, muffled by the door.

No one said anything and I imagined Aurel just nodded.

"I contacted Josh, breaking radio silence. I had to ensure no one suspected anything," he replied.

"Good," Aurel said. "You should check on Ace."

Illarion moved and I felt the shift of energy coming my way. Shit.

I tried to move away from the door as quietly as possible but I must have sounded like an offbeat tap dancer because my attempt at a stealthy escape was anything but.

The door opened and I came face to face with him. His dark eyes found mine.

"You shouldn't be up."

"I'm fine." I breathed in his scent as he stepped closer.

"You're swaying on your feet; you don't look fine." He brushed my cheek with his thumb and led me to the kitchen.

Troy looked like he wanted to get up and come to me, but Illarion's expression deterred him. Illarion right now was a man who'd had his patience tested and tried. He wasn't about to yield to anyone.

"I'll set up the meeting now," he said, pulling out his phone.

Aurel nodded to him, and then handed me a cup of coffee. "Feeling better, punk?"

"Thanks for this." I held up my free hand.

"I'm just glad you didn't die," Aurel said with a wink.

"Who else would hand you your ass during training?"

I shoved him playfully.

Illarion pressed the cellphone to his ear and walked over to the corner of the apartment. His broad shoulders tensed as he leaned his body against the windowsill. One arm rested above his head slightly.

"Special Agent Lazarev identification code: Alpha-Charlie-Delta-seven-seven-nine-two. I need to speak with Acting Director Somers."

A few moments later, he spoke again. "Director Somers, can we meet?"

Nodding, he hung up the phone and stuffed it into his black jeans. He sat back down next to us.

"The meeting is set."

Through our connection, I felt him checking in on me while on the outside he was looking at Aurel as he spoke.

"When?"

"Wednesday."

Aurel nodded and looked back at me.

"Why didn't he kill me?"

Illarion gently took my hands in his and ran his hand across the bandages.

"He was trying to scare you."

I shivered. "Well he succeeded."

Aurel reached over and placed a reassuring hand on my shoulder. "We won't let him get to you."

If only it was that easy. I bowed my head letting my mind wander back to those words that continued to play over and over in my head. *"You will face him and you will die. That is the only way this ends."*

"You okay?" Illarion's hand found mine.

Swallowing back the bile, I nodded. I was terrified out of my mind.

He squeezed my hand in his, drawing my attention to him, when our eyes met, I saw a flash of sorrow. "I'm sorry I wasn't there sooner."

"You saved me, I'd say that's pretty good timing."

A quiet laugh left his lips.

"It's going to be okay," Aurel broke the silence again. "We're not going to stop until he's dead."

His blue eyes were wide. That look met me again, what the hell was that about? He was acting so weird.

"You've just been dying to shoot someone, haven't you?" I pushed it back again and smiled instead.

"Is it that obvious?"

All I could do was laugh.

Beside me Illarion relaxed slightly as did Troy, surprisingly.

"So, have you done any actual work while I was sleeping?"

Aurel's eyes narrowed, and a smirk appeared on his lips as he looked to Illarion. "Have we done any work? Who does she think she's talking to?"

His fingers worked on the keyboard until he found what he wanted to show me. He pushed the laptop over.

"We've been running a trace on the Jameson Warehouse, and I had Josh set up remote surveillance. Troy here also knew a little about the area so he helped narrow it down."

"Really?" I asked.

Troy nodded. "My old man did some consulting with a firm out that way. He mentioned the commissioning of that project."

"No shit," I said, impressed.

I continued scrolling through the information and Troy craned his neck so he could see what we were looking at.

"When I meet with Michael, I'll make sure we have back up," Illarion explained.

"We're infiltrating?" my eyes flicked up and met Illarion's.

He nodded. "As long as he's out there he's going to keep coming for you."

I knew that. But I also knew there was nothing that would end this without…well without ending me. My heart was heavy and my mind raced. Was there any point in doing any of this? Wasn't I going to end up fulfilling the prophecy anyway? Like Oedipus, only less gross, obviously.

With a sigh, I pulled my hand free from Illarion's and rubbed my eyes.

I looked up across the table and met Troy's blue eyes. His light lashes lowered looking away from me. When he got up and moved to the window, I followed. He sat at the loveseat under the window, and I sat beside him.

"Thank you for letting them work here."

He looked over at the two men and then back at me. "I didn't have a choice, Ace."

"You always have a choice," I said firmly. Suddenly remembering that I wouldn't have my own choices when all of this was done. Whatever that meant.

"They basically knocked down my door at two in the morning, going on about you being in trouble, and how they needed to help you. Like I would have refused them."

"I'm sorry about that."

"When I saw you…when he pushed that door open, there was so much blood, and you weren't breathing…"

Pulling my gaze away, I looked down at my hands. "I'm okay now."

He shook his head. "If he hadn't come here, you would have died in your sleep, and I would have found you tomorrow-"

"Troy—"

"You don't know how useless I felt."

"You weren't useless—"

"I felt pretty damn useless." He shook his head. "I can't compete with him, with them."

"You don't have to."

"The hell I don't. You asked me to help you, Ace. I was useless."

"Troy, it's okay. You helped, you let me stay, you gave me somewhere safe to sleep."

He pressed his hand on my knee. "I saw the way you were with him last night." He shook his head a little, as if he was confused by the words coming out of his mouth. "You held onto him. You were terrified and out of it but you knew you could count on him. I wish I could have been that person for you."

"I know you would do anything for the person you love."

"I would. Only, he would fight until the end, and I would die before the fight even began." His eyes found mine and they were filled with sadness.

"You can't compare yourself, he's a Sensitive and he's powerful, he's destined to be a part of my life, to protect me and work with me."

"And love you."

"And love me," I agreed.

"He's the one who saved you from the desert?"

"Yes."

"And you work with him now."

367

"Yeah, we do."

He nodded again. "I saw how happy you were then. I can see why."

"Thank you, for all of this. I mean it."

He got up and kissed my cheek. "You know I will always help you, with anything." He smiled and then he turned away. "You should get back to them and I should get to work—got to sell people their camping goods."

I smiled, shaking my head a little.

Once he was gone, I made my way back to the table and caught up on what they had learned and what our next move would be.

"What's our move?"

Aurel handed me a tablet. "The warehouse is covered, we'll know whatever's going on down there and, in the meantime, I suggest you stick with us until we make our move."

"Agreed." I nodded, handing back the tablet.

"We should go," Illarion said gently. "I'm sure Damon already knows where you are."

"Will Troy be safe?"

"I've asked Josh to put surveillance on him."

Illarion packed up the equipment while I collected my personal belongings—the books and Twizzlers being the most paramount.

And when we were done, the cab was waiting outside of Troy's building. As we settled in for our three-hour ride to Illarion's house, I leaned back, closed my eyes, and allowed sleep to claim me. I felt Illarion's arms pull me against him, fitting me against his body just before I drifted off.

That same, suffocating blackness surrounded me again and before I could utter a word, his hand shot out, tightening around my throat.

"Wherever you go little sister, I will find you."

I tried to turn my head from him, but he held me locked in place.

With the little movement I did have, my eyes darted around taking in my surroundings. I was still in the cab, the driver casually cruising while Aurel and Illarion were nowhere in sight.

What the hell...

"You're not going to survive this," he cooed, dragging my eyes back to his.

I could still feel Illarion's thigh nestled snugly against mine, I could still feel his warm breath disturbing the strands of hair on my head, but I couldn't see him.

"So you keep saying," I muttered.

"I was pleasantly surprised you managed to wake up during our last encounter."

"Glad I met your expectations."

He laughed while I strained my eyes in the dark trying to focus on where his voice was coming from. But it was everywhere. Like the black-ness. Suffocating. Endless. Consuming.

"He won't be able to save you next time, you will die and you will be mine."

"Yeah, I got that the first time you said it. This conversation is over."

I squeezed my eyes shut and forced him out of my head.

"Ace." Illarion's face hovered above me.

"I'm fine." My throat worked to let a soft breath free.

The fact that I was getting headaches almost every time I had any form of contact with my Senses or with Damon, didn't elude me.

"He's getting restless," Illarion muttered, brushing my hair away from my face. "And the brazen bastard is getting stronger."

"This is starting to piss me off." I massaged the back of my neck. "Have you got any Advil?"

Aurel tossed a box over and Illarion fished out a bottle of water from the glove box.

"Thanks." I downed two right away.

"We'll keep you safe," Illarion said, taking the bottle from me and setting it down in the cupholder.

"To what end? He always knows where I am."

"As long as I'm here I will do whatever it takes."

"You can't babysit me in my sleep, Ila, it's…"

"Listen to me Ace—"

"He's going to kill me."

"No." He cupped my face in his hands turning me to face him again. "I won't let that happen."

"You won't have a choice." My voice broke on the last word. "Remember the prophecy?"

He pulled back, studying my face.

"It's the only way this ends, that's what it said, that's what Damon said."

He bit down hard and without another word, he pulled me against him, resting his chin on my shoulder. "I will do everything I can to protect you."

"That's what I'm scared of," I whispered, breaking down completely.

Something inside me shattered.

My resolve was gone, and my stomach twisted in knots. Why was I so damn emotional?

"Hey." He moved closer. "What are you talking about?"

"I've seen it." I pulled back rubbing my face. "I see you die in my dreams every night."

"They're just dreams, Ace."

"I know you don't believe that."

His eyes darted away when I called him out.

He knew I was right, and it killed him.

The wave of his emotions burned inside me. Scenario after scenario ran through his mind on repeat. All the ways in which he would fail me, tormented him. The realization dawned on him, and it crashed into me like a thunderstorm. He knew there was no scenario in which I walked away from this.

Pulling free from his hold, I looked away knowing exactly how he felt. I watched him die every night knowing there wasn't a damned thing I could do about it.

"We'll figure this out," Aurel said when the silence in the car became a suffocating entity.

There was no point sugar coating the situation. We were screwed, on an epic scale. I silently turned my attention to the trees outside the window.

It was almost noon, and the sun was high on the horizon. A somber feeling spread through me, the darkness would always disappear once the light broke through and each night would end when the morning came. The world would continue when I died. That is why I was doing this.

No more kids would grow up orphans.

Smiling at the horizon coming to life, I closed my eyes, I would really miss seeing all of this.

CHAPTER TWENTY-THREE

ACE

My eyes settled on the large, opulent mansion ahead. I'd only been at Illarion's for a short while before we left months ago, but it still captivated me.

Illarion lingered beside me, letting Aurel walk up ahead of us with our belongings.

I scanned the grounds and my breath caught when I spotted the small, gravel path that led to the garden with the lights. The garden where he told me we could never be together. The garden which was filled with the prettiest flowers and the beautiful cherry blossom tree.

Illarion's steps slowed beside me and when I turned, he had stopped completely. His eyes found mine and for a moment, neither of us moved. His broad shoulders squared as his hands sat tucked in his black jeans. A wayward strand of hair fell over his eyes.

The cherry blossom's petals floated around us, caught in the breeze.

"What are you not telling me?" he asked softly, his voice was barely above a whisper and those rich, understanding eyes sought the truth I was afraid to share.

"What are you talking about?"

He stepped toward me, closing the gap.

The tiny pink petals fell, covering the blades of grass beneath our feet. Above us, the trees swayed in the breeze catching my hair, blowing it around me. Illarion's hand reached out and smoothed a wayward strand behind my ear.

His hands landed on my forearms and swept up until he gently cupped my elbows and pulled me closer.

"Don't hide things from me."

"I'm not hiding anything from you."

He didn't respond immediately. "I can see the fear inside you. I can *feel* it, Ace."

Closing his eyes, as though he was checking in on me, checking his Sense, his dark lashes grazed his cheeks until he opened them again and met mine.

"What are you hiding?" he repeated.

My lips parted but words failed to form.

Before I could stop him, he was inside my head. Pushing and prying for the information I refused to give in.

I tried to pull back and break free from his hold, he didn't like that. Not at all. His eyes flared and his grip on me tightened like he was afraid to break the contact, like he was desperately holding on and if he let go, he was letting me go, and in that split second between his mind opening and mine connecting, I felt where his fear truly lay; he was afraid of losing me.

When I finally pushed him out and stammered back, there was a sharp inhale I quickly realized belonged to Illarion.

"Stay out of my head," I whispered, pulling my arms free, my voice a lot darker than I had intended.

"What are you hiding?"

"You need to rein it in, Ila. You're losing control."

Something in his expression shifted.

This wasn't like him at all. I swallowed and stood my ground; I'd seen him react like this before. It was the Darkness inside him; it was the same Darkness that flowed through me only it was worse. It was feeding off mine. It was amplifying it.

This shouldn't be happening. I was meant to be the freak, he was meant to be okay, I was meant to draw it away from him.

Neither of us spoke before I forced myself to even out my breathing.

"I can't talk to you when you're like this."

His eyes darkened for a second before he took in a sharp breath and blinked. His arms trembled as realization flitted across his features. He stepped away from me.

"Ace, I, I'm—"

"Take a walk. Find me when your head is clear."

The pain in his eyes gutted me but I couldn't deal with his Darkness too.

Silently, I made my way up the path, back to the house and back to the room he had made mine.

It would be exactly as it was left and I counted on it. It was my haven, the only one I had left.

Taking the stairs two at a time I reached my room, pulled off my boots and tossed them against the side wall.

Stripping, I climbed into the bed and sat up against the wall, retrieving the tablet I'd brought with me. This was going to be a long, long day.

Aurel came by a few hours later and handed me a cup of coffee. My eyes bulged out of my head at his gesture.

He grinned and sat beside me cradling a bottle of Corona in his hand with a tiny wedge of lime sticking out the top.

"What? No beer for me?" I said, nodding at the drink.

He looked taken aback like he was searching for the right thing to say and when he started turning unnaturally pale, I chuckled, poking the lime down into the liquid.

"Relax. I'm joking. Coffee is good."

His shoulders dropped, and his blond hair fell over his eyes. He'd usually worn it in a messy bun, like Illarion, but today it was half up while the rest sat just above his collar.

"Find anything?" he asked, taking a long drink.

"Do pages of useless, boring shit count?"

"That good huh? Can I get you anything?"

"Looks like I've got everything I need right here." I tipped the cup in his direction.

"Good." He nodded, looking away from me. "I've got some stuff to take care of, so I'll see you later."

He turned to leave, then he stopped and looked at me, his eyes sweeping over my face, then searching my aura.

"Okay, this is just getting odd, Aurel." I got up but stood back.

"What is?"

"You keep looking at me with this look, what is going on?"

He sighed, rubbing the back of his head. He leaned heavily against the doorframe. "I think you should go and see a doctor."

"Am I...am I sick?"

He could *see* those kinds of things in people. He told me the first time we met, so, it wasn't improbable.

"It's not my place to say anything, not about this, but please, see a doctor, okay?"

I started to say something but the look that shot through his eyes as a wave of nausea rolled through me, told me he wouldn't tell me, not now.

Breathing through it, I looked up at him, but he'd already stepped back through the doorway.

"See a doctor, okay?"

I found myself nodding wordlessly.

The headaches had been getting worse, the nosebleeds too. And the nausea? God. I clutched my chest but before I could ask him to elaborate, he was gone.

I was dying, that had to be it. I was using my abilities too much, this could happen, Illarion and Bob had said as much.

I drew in another long breath and slowly exhaled before returning my attention to the work in front of me.

Aside from that conversation and my potential sucky health, I still had more pressing things to tend to. Like how I was meant to survive and see this through.

There were literally thousands if not more, pages about rumored sightings of Sensitives, where we hung out and what we did for fun. Some of these reports also included the seedy bars I'd had the unfortunate pleasure of meeting Larry at.

The information also linked many of the sightings to the other bars I'd been to. More than half of them mentioned a God-like individual who had evolved in not one, but all the senses. *A Divine Sensitive.*

My heart hammered in my chest. I was there, during those visits. Could they really have been referring to me? It would make sense, I mused.

Swiping through to the next file, I stopped when I reached the next few excerpts which were articles about Larry and his friend who were known to be violent and suspected of serious crimes against other Sensitives.

The next article reported the death of the creepy duo, *a violent supernatural act,* was the cause of death.

Rubbing the back of my neck I stood up and stretched. I pulled on a pair of shorts and a t-shirt, threw on my sneakers and carefully peeled off the bandages around my arms, glad to have my fast-healing ability. There was an angry scar on the insides of my arms but soon it would fade.

I made my way downstairs in search of exercise. I broke into a jog as soon as I stepped outside. I needed to clear my head, and nothing cleared my head like running.

In the distance, I spotted another building adjoining the large greenhouse. Steam had fogged up the windows so I couldn't make out exactly what was inside, but I assumed there would be a sauna and showers. All the usual gym stuff.

When I pushed open the door I nearly fell over my own feet. A giant, rectangle swimming pool filled the better part of the building. The tiles around and in the pool, were an opal white, while small, black diamonds separated every fourth tile creating a stunning mosaic.

There was a giant, black crest at the bottom of the pool. The lettering inside it was familiar, I'd seen it around Illarion's house. It was his family crest.

Two black daggers pointed downward, crossed at the tip and in front of it was an L. The Lazarev family crest was simple, but it was striking.

On the far wall, there was another smaller room. Two glass sliding doors showed that it housed towels, a pair of showers and a dressing room. I knew he had money, but wow. This was next level.

Beside the showers there was another set of sliding doors, and inside I spotted all the equipment a fully functioning gym would have.

Resisting the urge to dive into the pool, I walked over to the gym. Starting with the treadmill, I broke into a slow jog. Once I realized it was doing nothing to quieten my busy mind, I increased the speed to the point where I was nearly screaming just to keep up and still, my mind was loud.

Whatever I tried I just couldn't shut the thoughts out. I hit the stop button and dropped to my knees catching my breath.

My heart was racing, thundering a million miles an hour inside my chest. Reaching up, I grabbed onto the side of the treadmill and dragged myself to my feet.

After a quick shower to wash the sweat off, I made my way to the pool and looked around. When I spotted a tall set of storage units, I padded over to them clutching the towel wrapped around me. Bingo; rows upon rows of fresh white towels, black swimsuits and caps and goggles.

I took a swimsuit and stepped into the change room.

I dropped my sweaty clothes and towel into a neat pile by the steps before I dove in.

The water rushed around my ears, momentarily silencing everything inside my head. My hair smoothed behind me, pressing flat against my back as I breached the surface. I swam lap after lap pushing my body harder and harder until exhaustion threatened to stop my muscles from working.

Slowly, painfully I treaded across the pool to the shallow end and grabbed onto the edge. The water reached just over my stomach and a cool breeze caught my attention as it chilled my exposed skin.

"Feel better?" Illarion's voice boomed across the water.

"You can't just sneak up on people." I muttered, looking up at the tall, striking figure walking toward me.

He smiled and crouched down. I looked up at him. Painfully aware that I was in his gym, in his pool. I flinched, lowering my body into the water, as if that would hide the myriad of disappointing features marring me.

As much as I hated myself for even letting the thought cross my mind, I couldn't help but feel the ugly self-consciousness creeping up on me.

I pulled my hair forward, letting it fall over my shoulders, covering the top of my chest but Illarion moved quickly. He reached down and gently took my wrist.

Okay...Breathe, Ace...breathe. He's just holding your hand.

"Ace." My name rolled off his tongue like a bittersweet prayer. It was enough to make me drop my guard completely.

"I need to get some clothes on."

His hold on my hand tightened slightly and his voice was gentle. "I told you before that you don't ever have to hide from me."

His dark eyes narrowed and he gracefully got to his feet.

I was silenced when he started to take off his clothes. My heart spluttered and the only coherent thought that kept repeating was how good he looked. Chewing my bottom lip, I breathed in deeply. I couldn't pull my eyes away.

My heart sped up as he removed his t-shirt and the hard, taut lines of his abdomen were right there, in all their glory. He slowly removed his jeans and dropped them beside my clothes. I gripped the edge of the pool and relaxed.

Without breaking eye contact, he took the steps down into the water, one by one, and walked over to me. As the water rose and lapped around his thighs, wetting the black Calvin Klein's, images of chiseled gods filled my mind but they had nothing on him. He stopped when he reached me.

I swallowed the breath I was holding and leaned into his touch, his free hand drifted to my cheek, sweeping away the wet strands surrounding my face.

He brushed his thumb along the scar that lined my cheek leaving a fiery burn in its wake.

At this point, I had little self-control left. I wet my lips and my eyes drifted down to his. They were full and parted ever so slightly, his breaths were coming in low, sharp bursts and I was about a second from kissing him.

"We need to talk." His voice was low, and he was close. Too close. "About before."

His dark hair fell over his eyes framing his face and all I could do was nod.

"I wanted to apologize."

Apology accepted. My pulse sped up.

His dark eyes watched my every move as I found myself slowly backing away. My breath caught. I couldn't...we couldn't be this close. God. I needed to control myself. I knew it wasn't the time for this. His head was all over the place, and I had so many things clouding my mind. As though he read my apprehension, he spoke, backing up.

"Ace, I would never hurt you."

He pulled his hand away from my face, letting it hover like he was afraid to touch me. Something flashed in those eyes, moving me to my core.

"I saw your face, you were scared." When I didn't respond, he shook his head, shielding his gaze. "I hate myself for that, you know that I would never hurt you."

"I know." I closed my eyes for a moment, collecting myself, before facing him again. "I do, because you're a good person, Illarion. Such a good, and warm person."

His eyes flicked away from me for a moment before a small frown tugged on his lips.

This time, I moved closer, inching toward him, as he moved away. His heart was racing, mimicking mine. He wanted me as badly as I wanted him. But he was so doubtful of his own goodness it broke my heart.

When his body backed into the edge of the pool he stopped, looking into my eyes and searching my face.

"I believe in you," I whispered. "And I need you to believe it too."

A split second later, he'd moved forward and reversed our positions, he lowered his forehead to mine pressing one hand on either side of me.

"The Darkness sometimes takes hold; I told you I couldn't control it as well as you think," he whispered, lowering a hand to my hip.

God, I couldn't have this conversation when he was here, like this. I lifted my chin, meeting his gaze.

"But I could never hurt you, do you understand?"

"I know that."

As his other hand brushed across the scar again, I flinched.

"Why do you still hide from me?" he asked quietly.

When I remembered how to speak, I whispered, "You deserve better—"

"You are perfect." He cupped my cheek in is hand turning my head to face him. "You're all I want. You're all I'll ever want."

If his words got any sweeter, I would melt. I leaned into his touch closing my eyes.

"You always know what to say."

"Because it's the truth."

The words he said and the actions he showed spoke volumes. I couldn't think anymore.

When he moved, the water lapped around us until there was no room left.

His hands fell to my arms and for a moment his fingers circled my wrists. When I let out a long, whisper of a breath he slowly began tracing lines across my arms paying special attention to the marks that were left on my body.

My lips parted as my breathing faltered.

He brought his forehead to mine again, drawing in a ragged breath. Damn. The man had some serious self-control.

"Ila…"

He shook his head lowering his mouth to mine, but he didn't kiss me. He let his lips linger, painfully, frustratingly close.

My heart was racing. I couldn't speak.

Slowly, he pulled me toward him, while his arm snaked behind me bringing my right thigh up and around his hip.

A fine shiver rolled up my spine, sending goosebumps over my exposed skin.

He pushed me back into the wall and held my leg in place there. My breathing matched his and butterflies fluttered to life inside me.

His other hand slowly traveled up my arm and stopped, he twisted my hair around his fist where he dipped his mouth to my pulse and pressed a tender kiss.

After an excruciating wait, he trailed gentle kisses starting from my neck and working his way up, eventually he brought his lips to mine and kissed me. His tongue pushed past my parted lips and everything else was lost in the moment.

My legs grew weak, my knees faltered but he was right there, holding me up. His fingers skated across my thigh, slowly sweeping up higher and higher until my breath slowed when he slid his fingers inside. He took his time, he moved slowly, teasing and taunting until I couldn't take it anymore. I tipped my head back letting out a moan.

"I think we need a condom," I whispered. "Haven't had a chance to refill my pill script."

Illarion smiled against my mouth. "One moment."

He climbed out of the pool and rushed over to a cabinet attached to the wall. When he opened it, I noticed all sorts of first aid supplies, bottles of water and of course, condoms.

"Where were we?" He chuckled when he came back.

I chewed my bottom lip and looped my arm around his neck.

Illarion expertly unraveled me with each taunting, teasing flick of his fingers. But I needed more. I slid my hand down and found his hardening length and gently guided it to my core.

Before I could say another word, he pushed me back into the wall, caging me in with a hungry kiss. He brought our bodies together, enveloping me in his embrace.

My hands searched his body, feeling every ripple of every muscle as he moved with me. He too carried scars, much like my own, and I could see why he found mine beautiful. His were a work of art, not marring his features at all, if anything, I thought they made him look more incredible, if that was even possible.

"Ace." His voice was so quiet, I barely heard him.

He was so bare, so honest with me, every fiber of his being was opening up to me.

The water moved around us as he delved into me, ragged, breathless gasps left our lips. His grip on me tightened as his breathing sped up, matching mine. Surges of electricity coursed through my veins, under my skin, pushing me toward the precipice.

I dug my nails into his tense arms as a deep, fierce sound escaped his throat, pushing us both over the brink. I threw my head back, suppressing my cry.

After everything, he gently brought my face to his, kissing me deeply and long after our breathing had evened out and returned to normal, I still held onto him, afraid to let him go, afraid that if I did…this moment would be gone.

Because neither of us knew what tomorrow would be like, neither of us knew whether there would ever be another moment like this, and I think he'd had the same thought. A dark look found me before I could suck in a sharp breath. Maybe this would be it, the final night we'd ever get to share together.

Burying my face in his chest, I held onto him tightly and closed my eyes. I wanted to remember everything. I couldn't lose him; I couldn't lose this.

CHAPTER TWENTY-FOUR

ACE

As the morning came I woke up and stretched in the bed. A warm, hard chest was pressed firmly against my back, one leg tangled between mine and an arm lazily draped over my waist.

A dopey smile spread across my lips.

Turning slowly, I looked over his still face. Steady, deep breaths sounded while he was caught in the world of the dreaming, peaceful and content.

But as my eyes traveled over his chest, a small frown turned the corners of my lips.

Faint, pinkish lines stretched across the expanse of his body, criss-crossing over his chest, running down over the ribbed planes of his stomach and only now, in this light had I noticed them. I recognized those scars. I knew from the way they crossed his body that they were from an age-old favorite technique of torture. They'd hang you from the ceiling and whip you over and over, to break you. Judging from the amount of lines crossing his skin, I knew he couldn't be broken.

Deep inside, a pang of pain shot through me. Repressed memories of war were never easy. Especially when it had cost so many people so much. And guilt quickly replaced the sadness, my mind skated over the memories and stopped on Alex, his still face, a life cut far too short. I had been responsible, Grimes had ultimately pulled the trigger, but I led them there, I led him there to endure weeks and weeks of hell.

By the end of it, the whippings and beatings were nothing compared to the pain of watching him die.

Shuddering I traced my fingertips across the lines on his chest.

A few short moments later he stirred, capturing my hand in his pulling me closer.

"You're not sleeping."

When I didn't reply, he cracked his eyes open and studied my face.

"Ace?" His brow knotted, creasing his skin slightly with the movement. "What's wrong?"

"Sorry…"

"What's wrong?" he asked again, this time his striking eyes were full of focus, sleep a mere memory.

"Nothing, it's stupid."

"Hey." He brought my hand to his lips, kissing each knuckle. "Nothing is stupid, tell me."

Slowly, I returned my hand to the faint lines across his chest, I felt him inhale a sharp breath and then release it.

"It hurts to think what you've been through."

When he remained silent I looked up into his eyes, something in his gaze moved me.

"None of that matters when I'm with you. It doesn't matter what happens to me."

"Ila…"

He pulled back, there were words just on the tip of his tongue but he didn't say them, instead he smiled and pressed a kiss to the hollow of my cheek.

"Did you sleep at all?"

"For the first time in a while," I admitted.

"We can't stay much longer, unfortunately," he said softly, twisting ropes of my hair around his fingers.

The mission was simple. Let Damon get to me, before he got to Illarion. And after that…well I didn't want to think about that yet.

We knew where Damon did his work, and we knew that *his* end game was getting to me to Collect my abilities.

What he didn't know was that it wouldn't work with me. He would only succeed in killing me—my abilities would die with me. From what I'd read in the prophecy that Illarion found, it was like a failsafe, a handy built in kill switch should a Divine ever be captured.

What scared me was what came after that. I felt stupid for believing all the hype and the prophecies. But how could I not? Everything else that they said had been right. Everything I read prophesied that I would have to die for there to be any chance of stopping him and the men like him. I guess the whole *transcendence* thing only worked when I was fully evolved and to become fully evolved, I had to die.

Illarion and Aurel stayed up for hours looking into how to we were going to fight him. But I knew. And I couldn't tell him. I couldn't hurt him like that. He refused to tell me that he was scared that there was nothing, but the way he and I were connected, he didn't have to. I could see it in his eyes and feel the refusal of acceptance in the depths of his soul.

"Are we going to the Academy today?" I asked, combing my fingers through his dark hair.

He nodded kissing my forehead.

Last night before he fell asleep, he told me there was one other source of information he had to try. A school where people like us grew up and learned about their Senses.

"If there's anything to find, we'll find it there. Their library has the largest known archived information about us."

"Is it a part of the Agency?" I asked, reluctant to go anywhere where they held power. Who knew how far their hand reached?

"The Agency uses their facilities to store information because it's a fortress. Sensitives who are trained as Watchers are guardians there, they protect the next generation."

"Protect the youth, ensure the future. Right?"

"Right."

"Do the non-Sensitives know about it?" I asked.

That would be a weird thing to explain to teenagers.

"The Sensitives are enrolled into a certain set of classes which the non-Sensitives don't get to go to. That's where they keep the archived information."

Suddenly images of young Illarion rolling around a school, in his uniform made me all gooey inside. He was a jock, I decided, smiling to myself. "Did you go there?"

"No, I grew up in Russia and when I came here, I was placed in home school." He chuckled, probably sensing my imagination running wild.

Oh. The image dissipated in my head.

"So, there's a whole world of people like us living amongst the non-Sensitives and they have no idea about us?"

"There are many divisions around the world where we're utilized." Illarion said, reminding me of what I'd learned at the Agency. "FBI, CIA, sometimes NASA."

"NASA?"

"Space exploration has had many helpful progressions from Sensitives."

"Huh," I mused.

"Not to mention the fact that a lot of rumors get out," he explained. "And many non-Sensitives believe that we exist and lot of them even knew about us."

"But if they ever learned too much, the compulsion would take care of that, right?"

"Unfortunately, sometimes it's necessary."

"Doesn't always work though, does it?"

"No."

My mind wandered back to what I'd read earlier, everything was heightened for us. Love, pain, sex, drugs. You name it. Whatever we did was amplified and so I wasn't surprised that sometimes the ecstasy would be too great to set a proper compulsion in place.

"Our anonymity is the safest way," he said.

I guess it was.

"We'll find what we need there," he said breaking the silence. "I promise."

Nodding mindlessly, I let my hands smooth across his skin, digesting those last two words. He didn't know, and right now, he didn't need to.

♥

"So the lovebirds are up." Aurel smirked as we walked into the kitchen.

"What are you smirking at?" I asked, sitting down at the bench pulling out the books I'd brought from Troy's apartment.

"Nothing." He shrugged and poured two cups of coffee for us handing me mine. "Enjoy your swim yesterday?"

My eyes shot up.

He laughed, taking a sip of his coffee. "Like I didn't know you two were letting off some steam in the gym. Why do you think I didn't grace you with my presence?"

Illarion shrugged. "I was apologizing."

I felt Aurel's eyes burning a hole in the side of my head. "And did you accept his apology?"

Oh. My. God. I could feel my cheeks burning.

I cleared my throat and looked up at Aurel and then back at Illarion. "Yes, it was a good apology."

"Well, now that you've had your fix of humor for the day can we get on with the job?" Illarion spoke up, eyebrows raised at Aurel.

A ghost of a smile was on his lips.

He looked at me sideways with a wink and my heart fluttered like a schoolgirl's, reminding me a lot of the first day we met.

He turned his attention to Aurel. "We're going to the Academy."

Aurel took a gulp of coffee and leaned against the edge of the table, knotting his brows. "St Augustine's?"

"Yeah."

The concerned expression on Aurel's face instantly caught my curiosity and I stopped turning the pages of the trash mag.

"Sure that's a good idea, brother?" he asked, no hint of sarcasm or anything else which was normal for Aurel, and that made me uneasy.

Illarion remained quiet for a moment. "It's a last resort."

I looked back and forth between the two men getting a read on a laundry list of emotions and thoughts running between them. One in particular stuck out at me. Silent understanding. Of what? What were they secretly discussing?

Now I was intrigued. Surely a school full of teenagers couldn't be dangerous, so there was a different reason for him not wanting us to go there. And I needed to find this reason out.

"Can I talk to you for a minute?" Aurel spoke up. When he moved around the bench he grabbed Illarion by the arm and dragged him away to another room.

What the actual hell was going on? I focused on the faint waves of dialogue travelling through the space and without having to try that hard I managed to break through to the conversation.

Illarion tried to block me out, learning from last time. Between his struggle to do his part and mine to break through the barrier I only caught the tail end.

"You know she's going to be there," Aurel said, and I imagined Illarion just looked at him because it was quiet for a few moments.

"Are you really ready to see her again?" he spoke again.

"I have no choice."

"There are other ways, brother," Aurel said.

"Not anymore, not with this, we're running out of time and I'm doing this for her." The last word caught in his throat and I felt our connection buzz through me.

"This is a bad idea."

"This is the only idea," Illarion said flatly.

Aurel didn't like what he was hearing, his emotions were raging inside and he grew more and more annoyed at the prospect.

"I don't want to see her. I don't want to ask her for help, hell, I don't even want to be in the same building as her. But I need to do this. I will not lose Ace. Not if I have a chance to get answers."

"Brother," Aurel began.

"There is no other way."

"Fine." Aurel exhaled a sharp breath. "Call me if you need anything."

"I will."

I picked up my coffee cup and continued flicking through the magazine on the table.

My mind raged on, who was the woman Illarion didn't want to see?

When they walked back through the door, I smiled up at Illarion. He didn't need to know that I heard all that. If he wanted to talk about it, he would. Then again, if I waited for him to say anything...well we'd both be a lot less happy.

"If you need me, call," he said, taking one more sip of coffee before placing the cup in the sink and looking knowingly at Illarion.

He took off leaving me and Illarion and a whole lot of questions lingering between us.

We both took the moment to simply absorb the events of last night and drink our coffee without any more expectations. I didn't know what this *arrangement* was meant to be, but I sure as hell wasn't going to ruin it with questions. Besides, I had this mystery woman on my mind now. Why did she have them both so rattled?

"How do you feel, by the way?" he asked suddenly, breaking my chain of thought. "How do you feel after last night?"

I took a few moments to think about my answer and then spoke.

"I don't feel any different now but last night I did, it felt like a huge shift, I felt like I could feel more but not just on the level I was feeling before…does that make sense?"

He nodded.

"Before we…before the first time," I paused, looking into his eyes. "Well, I could sense what you were thinking or feeling and now, I can actually *feel* what you feel, as though you're a part of me." I hoped he wouldn't take that as a hint that I heard and felt his reluctance to go to St Augustine's.

"That's a part of it, being connected."

"It's weird. I feel like nothing has changed but the connection is stronger, it feels more alive. Will it continue to grow?"

He nodded. "For you everything will be amplified, I can feel you a lot more now too, which also means that soon the effects will start to show, and they'll come hard and fast."

No one had had experience with a real Divine Sensitive in over a century from what I'd learned and so what was true and what was rumored, was still a mystery to us. I sucked in a breath not knowing what to expect. I'd read enough during my sifting through pages upon pages of boring shit yesterday, to know that it was all still a grey area.

"The Darkness will grow too, won't it?"

"Unfortunately, yes and I can't protect you from that," he said.

Illarion's heart was heavy and his uneasiness radiated through me. Something in the way it felt definitive, seared me. Why did I get the feeling he was getting ready to say goodbye? I pushed the thought away and swallowed hard.

"We should get ready." I said quietly getting up.

He nodded following suit.

"Do we go as part of the Agency?"

"Yes." He smiled. "I'll meet you at the car. I'll put together our IDs."

Before I left, he stopped me. "Pack an overnight bag too, we're stopping by another one of my properties, there are a few things we need to get."

"You got it." I nodded and took off up the stairs, taking them two at a time feeling giddy. I was going to enjoy this.

I closed the door and made my way to the large, fully stocked closet of clothes. I chose a black pair of fitted pants and a tank top and completed the look with a black jacket. I looked in the mirror smiling at the tailored suit.

I pulled my hair into a sleek ponytail and applied a quick cover of makeup. I didn't need to look like I was going to a photo shoot, but I did need to look presentable.

Throwing the last few items together, I slung my purse over my shoulder, hooked the Agency badge to my shirt and jogged downstairs.

Illarion was already there, sporting a ridiculously well-tailored, three-piece suit.

My God. My knees weakened as I wobbled over to the car and sat myself down.

"I like that," he said softly.

"What?"

"Your hair like that."

"Oh." I smiled, my cheeks flushing hot.

He didn't reply to my awkwardness, thankfully, and instead he just drove.

A couple of minutes in, a quiet, peaceful song began on the radio and my heart immediately warmed. Illarion was a fan of Ella Fitzgerald, I smiled inwardly and shrugged into my coat. For a moment I was transported back to snow covered Christmases with my family in Canada.

Since they died, I don't recall ever stopping and actually mourning my mom and dad. My brave parents who knew all along what I was destined to become and had never once let me feel any different to any other kid in the world.

"Ace, are you okay?"

"My dad liked this song." I pressed my cheek against the cool leather and turned to look at him.

He reached for the dial. "I'll change it."

"No, it's okay…it's nice to hear." I cupped my hand over his. "It's like he's still here."

"I'm so sorry about your family."

"Yeah, me too."

The lyrics filled the car sending waves of sadness through me. Sensing the shift inside me, he took my hand in his and continued driving in silence.

In that moment, I realized that I had never loved anyone as much as I loved Illarion, not only for the way he made me feel, but for the ways in which he understood how I felt.

The car ride was painfully bittersweet. And with every new song that started more and more memories filled my eyes with unshed tears.

"We're here," he said quietly breaking me from my reverie.

Only at the last minute when we parked at the large, towering gates did he let go of my hand, and slightly turned his body to face me.

"I'm going to go and speak to the people we need information from, I want you to wait for me."

"You don't want my help?"

"Honestly Ace, I didn't want you here at all. These are not people I'm comfortable mixing you with."

"But you brought me, so you need me," I said matter-of-factly.

He nodded, the tiniest hint of a smile playing on his lips. "Not for the job, but for me."

"I'll keep you safe." I winked.

Despite the churning array of feelings in his heart, he smiled and shook his head disbelievingly. "Stay close, okay?"

"You got it."

At least he was smiling.

Together we walked up to the gate and waited for them to buzz us in. The archaic looking set up was just a facade. This place was a fortress of security. Every corner had a pair of guards stationed and I saw those salt circles with piles of arranged stones again.

"What do the non-Sensitives think about this?"

"A low level of compulsion is used on them; they don't see the stones, or the Watchers."

I glanced across at the paired men and women who stood around, dressed head to toe in black combat gear.

"They're the guardians of our people, usually evolved in Sight or Sound, they're incredibly gifted at detecting danger," he smiled.

"Are they always in pairs?"

"There is usually one of each in the pair." He led me toward the gate. "Trackers are usually the only other Sensitives who work in pairs."

"Like my dad."

"Yes, but they're usually reserved for the military. We don't have need for a combination like that here."

"Is that why he was in the army?"

"Yes."

I didn't think I'd ever get used to learning all these new things.

The gate opened, and two Watchers let us in. The man in the pair nodded at Illarion while the woman gave us both a friendly smile.

I nodded as we walked past together. I looked back noticing how swiftly the pair moved back to their post by the gate. I swept my eyes across the yard marveling at how the school kids running past them were completely oblivious to their presence.

"So, do the kids have mixed class then?" I returned my focus on the set up of the school.

He nodded as we approached a group of girls no older than twelve, who were giggling and whispering amongst themselves as they walked past Illarion.

If they weren't swooning over the love of my life, it would have actually been funny.

"Jealous?" he teased.

"Hardly. You were saying?"

"Yes, there are some mixed classes with the Sensitives, but the Sensitives have an allocated set of classes they have to attend throughout their years here which the others cannot attend."

When I scowled at a petit redhead who was in her late teens, Illarion laughed, gently placing his hand on the curve of my hip protectively.

"What explanation does the school offer those students?" I shifted the attention back to the conversation.

"Full class."

He pulled the door open for me.

"That makes sense," I mused.

"I'll be back, wait here," he said softly while another group of girls, slightly older this time looked him up and down and practically kissed the ground he walked on.

Jesus. Was everyone going to make my life hard?

I rolled my eyes and moved across the foyer. I made my way to the sofa, far enough away from the foot traffic but close enough to keep an eye on him. He'd made it clear he was uneasy being here, so I made it clear that I wasn't going anywhere without him.

As I got comfortable in the overly fluffy sofa, I snatched a magazine off the table, and I heard him ask for a woman by the name of Eliza Grey. The woman at the desk replied that he needed to wait until class was over. A quick glance at the clock told me that would be in ten minutes

A few more girls walked past the front desk and I heard each one of them talk about Illarion. Christ, this was going to be a long day.

"Look at his ass though," one girl almost squealed while another clutched at her heart and dramatically fanned herself with a book.

"The Agency seriously does hire the hottest people, which means we, will be in for sure," another said.

Good lord.

But they were right, on both accounts. Had to give them that.

While my attention was focused on those girls, I hadn't noticed the little girl who appeared in front of me.

"Are you a spy?" she asked abruptly getting the attention of the other girls near Illarion.

"What?"

"A spy, for The Agency?" she repeated stepping closer. "You know, espionage and all that."

Was she even old enough to know what that word meant?

"Why do you ask that?"

She smiled stuffing her hands in the pockets of her red and white dress. "Well, you're wearing a suit, like the guy you came in with, he's a spy too. Right?"

"Maybe we're just detectives." I shrugged playing into her observation.

"No, I don't think so. Plus, you're wearing the shield."

Right. I looked down remembering the heavy steel badge stuck to my shirt, I now noticed was peeking out from the blazer I'd worn to hide it.

In the background, I heard the other girls sniggering and my previous years of training made me super paranoid as it were but being back inside the walls of a high school instantly had me backing up against the wall, claws out.

I hated bullies like that. I tried to ignore them and so did the little girl in front of me.

"You're evolved in more than one sense, aren't you?" she asked quietly.

"What makes you think that?"

The other girls tuned in to our conversation at that point, though thankfully they kept their distance.

Perks of being the Divine Sensitive, was that I had to hear and sense almost every thought of every person around me. Someday, I hoped to be able to control that.

My mind seemed to pick up whenever something was pertaining to me and tuned in to it. Damn super sensing. Sometimes I didn't want to hear how much someone was hating on me.

"I'm evolved in Sight," she explained. "So I see auras."

"Oh?"

"Most people's auras, depending on their Sense are a certain color."

"What color is mine?" I asked curiously.

"It changes."

Her eyes took on an unnatural hue, caught somewhere between gold and amber.

My heart skipped.

From what I knew from Aurel and the little I'd read up about this, I knew that wasn't a normal thing. I could hear the other girls" thoughts churning as clearly as I could hear this little girl speaking in front of me.

My head began to spin and I clutched the edge of the sofa to steady myself.

"What do you mean? How can an aura change?"

"You would normally have one color and never more than one, and never really as hazy as yours."

When I remained stricken by silence she continued. "There's something else though, like something is attached to your aura, it's like there's someone else's too. I've never seen that before."

I swallowed hard, Aurel he'd been freaking out every time he looked at me. But maybe it was the connection with me and Illarion. Maybe that's what it presented as.

"What is it?"

"I don't know, it's like a soul that's dying." She moved closer, narrowing her eyes. "Or not meant to exist. I don't know exactly, but it's weak."

My stomach twisted, I *was* sick. Oh God. I was dying, that's what this was. I wasn't meant to exist, was I?

Everyone kept saying I was destined to die. Guess the universe was confused by my existence too so it gifted me with this weird ass aura that didn't make any sense.

"How do you know this?" I asked.

"I read a lot. Maybe this will help you. I'm Faith, by the way." She handed me a small book, *Auras and their Colors*.

And like something inside me snapped, I heard the girls talk amongst each other again, only this time my guard had me all but getting my ass up there and telling them to shut the hell up.

"Faith is going on about all the prophetic shit again."

"Why is she even talking to her?"

"What happened to her face?"

"Do you reckon they're dating?"

"No, no way, he's so hot, he wouldn't have sex with her."

"Do you think she's the Divine Sensitive?"

My rage intensified, and I knew it was wrong, so, so wrong, but I couldn't help it. I balled my fists at my side, ignored the pounding mother of a headache and looked up at them.

Focusing on all four of them at once I spoke. *"One day, if I see you outside of these walls and you lay eyes on me or Agent Lazarev in a way I don't approve of, we will have words, and make no mistake, they won't be as civil as this."*

They collectively gasped and looked at me with stunned expressions. Their mouths gaped jerking back. Guess they had their answer.

"If those girls ever give you trouble, just call okay, my partner and I will be more than happy to help." I looked at Faith with a small smile.

She took the business card I handed her, and I got up, clutching my little book.

"Acacia. They call you Ace though, right?"

"Yeah."

"Just remember, Ace…" she began, suddenly seeming much wiser than her years. "When you have no choice but to give up, don't, we're right there with you, until the end."

My breath caught, I swung my eyes back to her but before I could ask what she meant and how she knew so much, she was gone, skipping away and a dizzy spell nearly wiped me out. I threw my hand out, using the wall beside me to hold myself up.

A strong arm appeared behind me and steadied me. His expression was dark as his eyes darted around and then fell back on me.

"Are you okay?" Illarion asked.

"I'm not feeling so hot, something is wrong."

"Come on."

He looked around again, sensing my discomfort and when his eyes fell on the four girls, he got it. Luckily for them, they kept their distance because the anger coursing through Illarion right now, wasn't something anyone wanted to trifle with.

The instant they saw the look on his face, they stopped, and any smartass remarks died with their silence.

I couldn't tell between the pain in my head and the blinding headache, what Illarion was thinking, but he wasn't happy.

He led me down through the foyer and outside into the cold away from the place that caused him anxiety and gave me a freaking migraine. Once we were clear of the building, he placed his hand on my lower back and walked right beside me, our bodies always touching.

"I felt what you did, to them," he said softly. "It was like lighting going off."

"I know it was petty, and wrong."

"If it makes you feel better, I wanted to throw the whole senior boys swimming team out of the second story window."

I looked up at him incredulously.

"They were talking about your ass," he clarified shaking his head.

We stopped just short of the car and we both burst out laughing. "Oh God, we're pathetic."

"Yes, we are."

A few, short moments later his expression grew grim again. His eyes lowered until they were completely focused on me. He cupped my face in his hand and softly ran his thumb across my cheek.

My breath caught. "Did we get what we need?"

He nodded.

"Memorizing my face in case I don't make it?" I asked, meaning it as a joke, which he obviously didn't get because the next second, he had leaned down and kissed me so hard I almost stumbled backwards into the car.

Suddenly I felt all the eyes of the girls on us who at some point had followed us outside into the courtyard.

All their jealousy and fear of me coursed through my veins…the anger of their words pulsed through me, and if I didn't have Illarion here, the Darkness would have continued to bubble inside me, threatening to erupt.

So, I focused on him, on his touch and his lips on mine. I knotted my fingers through his hair and deepened the kiss, remembering how much was at stake and how much we both had to lose. I knew how this ended. And the truth was that no matter what he got here today, I knew what I needed to do. This was my choice. And the way things were going, it could very well end up being my last one.

Once we broke free he looked down into my eyes.

"Don't say things like that."

"It was just a joke, Ila."

"It's not funny. Losing you is…it terrifies me."

"I'm sorry." I reached up and closed my hand over his cheek.

He pressed a kiss to my forehead. "You're evolving."

"You can feel it?"

"I can feel everything inside you."

"Well, in that case, I think you should feel that we need to go now." I tugged at his hips, grazing my finger delicately over his belt.

His eyes shot down to the very small space between us and a low, hungry breath escaped his lips.

He got it.

Wasting no time to get back in the truck, we sped off down the highway.

♥

Three long hours later we pulled up to a cabin. He took my hand and led me through the door shutting it with his foot.

I started saying something but stopped mid thought when he cut me off with a determined, hungry expression.

He closed the gap, pushing us backwards into the door ensuring that there was absolutely no space between us.

Without a second to reciprocate, he'd wrapped his fingers around my wrist and drew my arm up where he held it in place. My breath escaped in a little, short gasp as he silenced me with an eager kiss.

Breaking free, I shoved him back, my body dangerously alive with heat and fire. His hands worked quickly pulling my jacket and tank top off which was my cue to push him back and pull off his vest and shirt, thank God, he left the jacket in his car.

As all our clothes came off he stopped only once to get a condom and once more to pick me up and press my back into the wall. As his body found mine, I cried out as I felt every inch of him and his soul as it melded with mine. He held me up with one arm while the other was splayed against the door beside my head.

Whenever we had made love in the past it was slow, gentle, every emotion was conveyed through unspoken words. This time it was passionate, eager and completely opposite to the slow, patient caresses we'd shared before. A frantic edge consumed us as everything intensified.

We were both wild; hunger, raw and unbridled raged through us.

As his lips explored mine, a moment of panic set in. Why did this feel like goodbye?

My thoughts were chased away as another, hungry kiss consumed me. I couldn't tell where his mind and feelings began and where mine ended, we were completely connected on so many levels.

At some point, we'd moved to the bed and his eyes met mine, and the raw, hungry emotions looking back at me made my heart race. He was so completely mine there were no doubts in either of our minds anymore. There was no fighting it.

My breathing sped up and matched his and, as a breathless cry left my lips, we both fell over the edge and collapsed into the sheets, still tangled in each other's arms.

"I will never tire of this," I breathed, closing my eyes against his chest.

"Neither will I." His fingers gently traced the faint lines on my arms and then he stopped. "And I will make sure that we have a life-time of this to look forward to."

There was no doubt in his mind this time, he knew that there was a slim chance of both of us walking out of this, but he was determined that he was going to be the one to lay down his life.

Suddenly I was curious to know what he had found out. What had suddenly given him such confidence and strength?

I knew there was no other way, more than one person confirmed it.

Arguments and questions boiled inside me, but instead I smiled up at him. "I know."

"I have to go and meet with Michael."

"Right now?"

"He's only got a small window to meet with me before Damon catches wind."

"I wish you could stay here with me."

"I want nothing more."

I found his lips and kissed again before he got up and left me lying in the bed watching him get dressed in the clothes we had so carelessly discarded only a few hours ago.

I made no attempt to hide my pleasure of seeing his body as he moved about the cabin, collecting his things, preparing himself for his meeting.

He smoothed his dark hair into a ponytail and picked up the case containing the tablet.

"Try to get some sleep."

"It's still light, it's only seven." I glanced at the sky.

"It is, but you're exhausted, I can see it on your face."

"Will this ever get better?"

"In time, yes," he said softly. "That headache that you had, it's going to get worse. You need to sleep it off."

"I don't want to sleep without you."

"You're safe here, don't worry."

There would be no persuading him otherwise. He pressed another kiss to my forehead before leaving me.

He was right, yet again. Only minutes after he left, I felt my eyes grow heavy. The headache was something fierce. I felt the pain building and burning behind my eyes. damn it. This was not going to be fun.

I pulled the covers over myself, slowly letting sleep claim me.

CHAPTER TWENTY-FIVE

ACE

The sun crept through the half-shut blinds warming my face. I opened my eyes and looked around the cabin.

I didn't have a chance to look at anything here yesterday because I was preoccupied looking at *him*.

He came in, sometime in the night careful not to wake me, but his presence always alerted me. We briefly spoke before he wrapped me up in his arms and we both fell asleep again. Now that he was gone, I realized he must have gotten up way before me because the first thing I noticed getting out of the bed was the breakfast and coffee he left on the table for me. Freshly squeezed juice, fruits and bagels.

I pulled my tank top and underwear on and moved across the room running my fingers along the furniture. His energy ran through everything I touched.

But he was nowhere to be found. My heart grew heavy as I spotted the folded up note on the coffee table.

Moya zvezdochka,
I hope you can forgive me for this. I know I said we were doing this to-gether, but the more I looked into this, the more I realized what I already knew. The woman I spoke with, Eliza, she was an informant a long time ago. Her intel is never wrong. She confirmed what I already knew.

Damon needs you to willingly hand yourself over to him for the transfer to work. We also know that the transfer isn't possible for a Divine Sensitive which means that if he has you, he'll keep you alive and he'll torture you until he works out how to use you. I can't let that happen.

Without you, he's nothing. If he's dead. You'll be safe. I know what I must do.

I know you've been told about the prophecy. You know I don't believe in any of it but I don't believe in chance either. I can't let you go to your death based on some Celestial writings. Please understand.

One day soon, I know you'll become the most powerful Sensitive that has ever lived, and when that day comes, you will be the one to end the suffering our people face.

I love you, Ace. I only wish I had told you in person.

Always yours,
Illarion Lazarev.

Hot tears stung my eyes and I found myself leaning heavily on the chair to hold myself steady.

How the hell could he leave me?

I threw the plate of food off the table and shoved the chair out of the way.

This wasn't the way it was meant to go.

Damon would kill him before he even managed to get a shot at him.

I focused my mind on them, though I didn't expect him to have been so careless. Just like I thought, they were both blocked off completely, so I went back to the trusty method of contacting people. The telephone. He would have anticipated I'd get through to Aurel eventually, he was just buying time.

I rushed to the side table where I'd left my phone and pulled it out, dialing Aurel.

Two rings later, Aurel answered. "You two bored yet?"

"He left me. I don't know where the hell I am!"

"Slow down, what happened?"

I sucked in a deep breath and forced myself to hold it together, I couldn't break down on the phone to his best friend. "I'm in his cabin in the middle of nowhere. I don't have a car. I don't have anything." I paused. "He's going after Damon."

The line went silent for a minute before I heard the sound of a door thudding, followed by a car engine roaring to life. "I know where you are, I'll be there soon."

I ended the call and threw the phone in the bag he made me pack last night. Rage flowed through me, as I sat on the bed. How could he leave me and after lecturing me for taking off?

Shaking my head, I got up and found Faith's book, there had to be something in here, something I could use.

I flicked through the pages describing how different emotions meant different colors and stopped abruptly, sitting up straight when I came upon the page mentioning rumored auras of past Divine Sensitives.

There was no single color associated with Divine Sensitives and the haziness showed the evolution level of the individual. Once a Divine Sensitive reached their absolute peak their aura would be a solid color indicating all the color fields combined and completed. However, a few rare occurrences showed that a Divine Sensitive would cross over, and their aura would blacken, indicating that they were teetering on the edge. Neither good nor evil.

I swallowed hard thinking back to all the times I lost my temper for no reason other than it felt good to be mad.

Was I losing it? Was I teetering on the edge of insanity? Would Damon make me crack and go dark side?

My heart hammered in my chest causing my breath to falter.

Almost three hours, and several re-reads later, I heard Aurel's car pull up in the driveway. I closed the book and shoved it in the bag.

The car door slammed shut and I walked outside.

"Are you alright?"

"Yeah," I muttered. "Pissed, but fine."

He pulled my bag from me, furiously walking back to the car. "Come on."

"Guess that's why he got me to pack an overnight bag," I said, nodding to the change of clothes I was now in, a comfortable pair of yoga pants and a pink sweater.

"What happened, I thought you two were going to find answers?" he asked, speeding off down the road.

"We came here after the school. He said he found some information—he was going to speak to Michael about it last night—this morning I find a note telling me he doesn't want me involved because there's no way to help me."

"Is it true?"

I kept my eyes firmly planted on the road ahead.

"Damn it," he hit the steering wheel, then he quietly expelled a breath.

"Who is Eliza Gray?"

A muscle in his forearm tensed at the name.

"Aurel?" I pushed.

"She gave the order that screwed Illarion's parents."

"Well shit."

Sensing my next question, he turned his face to me. "She's never wrong, Ace. She's incredibly powerful, maybe even the most attuned Sight Sensitive, ever."

"She saw how it ended and she still gave the order?"

"It was them, or six hundred people." He said softly.

People weren't a quantifiable, expendable commodity. What the fuck? I couldn't wrap my head around it, I couldn't accept that. We were basically heading down the same path and he was taking it. Blindly.

"She's wrong."

"Ace, she's powerful."

"Damn it, I'm powerful too. She doesn't know everything; she doesn't know what I know."

"Then tell me!"

"There's nothing that can change the outcome!" I looked at him, "All of this, everything he's doing is for nothing."

"What are you talking about?"

"The outcome is set, it's a prophecy, and nothing can change it."

"I don't even know what that means."

"It means that I have to die, willingly, for Damon to get what he wants, for the prophecy to come true, for me to be able to end this. Like for some reason I *need* to go through this, to be able to face what comes next."

"What comes next is death, there's no next after you're dead." His voice rose two octaves.

"Not for me."

He sighed, rubbing his temple. "Illarion said that the transfer wouldn't work with you so why the hell would you give yourself up willingly?"

"Damon is going to use Illarion against me. He planned all along to get Illarion there, so he had a way to leverage me."

"You're shitting me."

"No, and now I have no choice. Damon will torture Illarion and kill him unless I go. Which is why you're going to take me there now."

"You cannot be serious?" Aurel barked.

My dreams were all showing me what my life was leading up to. Everything we had been doing and trying to avoid, had inadvertently led us to this conclusion.

Fucking Oedipus.

"There's no scenario in which I walk out of this. It's me or him."

"No," he said simply shaking his head. "I can't take you there then."

"You have to, he's walking into a trap and he is going to die."

"You're going to die if you walk in there."

"That's the God damn point, Aurel! Illarion won't survive this."

"It doesn't matter, you are all that matters. You've always been the only one who matters," he shouted over me, pulling over to the side of the road. "I have to keep you safe, you're the key!"

"That's bullshit, and you know it!" I yelled, my voice breaking. "My life is not worth more than his."

"Ace, I understand—"

"No, you do not understand, I can't let him die for me, I can't do this, not…not again."

His eyes softened and all that pain I'd been harboring suddenly seemed so unbearable.

"Ace, I know what you went through with Alex. I know how much it hurts, but this," he rubbed the back of his neck. "It's not gonna happen, I'm not letting you go."

He was right, it did hurt, God it hurt like hell. But I wasn't going to make the same mistake twice, then I was helpless, now, I could fight, and I'd be damned if I let him fall for me. I wasn't going to lose him, not like I lost Alex.

"Don't make me take the car from you," I warned getting out, ready to take the car by force if I had to.

"Back off, Ace," his voice was so low I barely heard him. "I care about Illarion too, but this is not happening."

411

Both of us were now outside of the car, ignoring the blistering cold, staring each other down.

"Oh, so because you care you're letting him die for me, is that it?"

"Low blow, Ace."

"Calling it how I see it," I hissed.

He let out a sarcastic laugh and stepped closer to me making me step backwards until my back was pressed against the car.

"He is doing this for you, and you want to throw your life away?"

"He is going to die for nothing!"

"He is dying for you!" he shouted back.

"I'll die anyway, whether he goes there or not."

He stopped. His face grew grim, but he didn't say a word, I guess he worked it out too.

"Every dream I've had has been leading up to this. One way or another, I'm going to end up there to die. He's not preventing anything."

Aurel opened, and then closed his mouth.

"The prophecy stated that I must face Damon. No matter what happens, I will be the ultimate tool for the endgame. The *next* everyone keeps talking about. Don't you understand? I need to die for that to happen. It's the only way I can stop Damon."

"Ace…"

What could he say? That he was sorry? That it was too bad I was about to have my life cut short just before my twenty-eighth birthday? Yeah, sorry kid, you've had a hell of a run, but that's it. Thank you and goodbye?

At least I had a reason, something to fight for. Just like dad said, there was poetry in death when you were dying for someone you love.

Aurel stepped back and turned from me, thrusting his hands through his hair. He paced in front of me, muttering something in

Romanian I didn't understand. Then, he turned around and stepped into my space, bringing his hand to my cheek.

"Fuck the prophecy," his was voice was barely a whisper. "I can't let you die."

"I'll miss you," I whispered, reaching up to brush my fingers across his cheek. "Thank you, for everything, Aurel. I mean it. Thank you so much."

He closed his eyes leaning into my touch.

There would be no convincing him. I knew that, I felt it. I stepped back and made my decision.

I locked into his mind and focused.

"Leave me your car, start walking down the highway and hail the next car, you'll be safe."

When I looked at him again, he nodded handing me his keys. Before getting in the car, I took one last glance at him in the rear-view mirror and sped off down the road.

CHAPTER TWENTY-SIX

ACE

I drove in silence, on my own for what would probably be my last mission. The thought was a sobering one as I took the entrance to the highway and began my long, six-hour drive to save the man I loved and hopefully the world.

I checked in with Aurel as many times as I could and he was pissed. I couldn't say I blamed him. There was nothing worse than using your weapons against your friends.

The last time I checked in on him, he had managed to get a car and was heading back to his house, I was careful not to leave any signs or hints as to where I was going and where Illarion would soon be. As far as I knew, he didn't know about the importance of the warehouse. He only knew it was Damon's.

I sped up weaving in and out of slower moving cars making sure to stay within the speed limit, the last thing I needed now was to get pulled over.

My body ached and my head was worse—much like it had been during our visit to St Augustine's. This was not a good time to stop, but if I crashed my car because I couldn't hold it together...well that would be shit.

Taking the next exit, I pulled into a rest stop. I ordered a large coffee and sat on the hood focusing on my breathing and keeping myself calm, that, and wiping the never-ending stream of blood pouring from my nose. *Real nice Ace.* I cringed retrieving a fresh tissue from my pocket.

These headaches were getting more intense. This is what Illarion meant, that it would hit me and that it would be difficult. But he promised he'd be there to help me. I couldn't help the sadness that washed over me. I felt so alone. He wasn't here, and he would never be here again.

Taking a sip of coffee, I looked on as people continued their normal lives, they had no idea how much was going on.

"Agent Hart," I heard a voice behind me.

I turned and spotted a tall, blond man with a wide smile.

I slid off the hood. "Assuming you're here for me."

"Indeed," he said, stepping closer. "I have something you'd be interested in."

He reached into his pocket and retrieved an envelope handing it to me.

His choice of words left me uneasy; I ripped it open and pulled a single photograph out.

The blood drained from my face, my heart jumping into my throat.

"He's alive, but Mr. Cale wanted to ensure that there were no misunderstandings. You know, in case Mr. Lazarev didn't show up first."

Fuck.

I looked up from the photo of Troy, his black and blue face was contorted in pain while he flinched from the bright flash of the camera light. He was meant to be safe. The Agency was meant to protect him. I scoffed—like we could trust anyone there.

"He knows I'm coming," I muttered, scrunching the tissue up and stuffing it in my pocket.

"Indeed, my dear, insurance, that's all."

He held his arm out motioning for me to walk with him to his car.

What the hell. I was going to die anyway, might as well save the fuel for Aurel.

I locked up the car and followed the man to his black sedan. He opened the door for me and cable tied my wrists together before closing the door. Great, now I was going to bleed all over my sweater too. Perfect.

"We don't have to talk, right?" I asked, looking out the window.

He laughed. "It would make the drive less boring."

"Boring would be nice for a change."

With that, he locked the doors, and we were driving down the highway again.

The fight inside me shriveled and died. Tears stung my eyes, and I was painfully aware of how dry my mouth was. Trying to swallow through the cotton was about as useful as trying to break free from these restraints. I settled for wetting my lips as I tasted my own tears falling down my cheeks.

The last time I would see Illarion would be before I died. I would never be able to hold him again or make love with him again. I would never be able to feel his hands touch me the way only he knew how.

And Troy, oh God, Troy.

He was in this mess because of me. He would have lived his life, met a beautiful girl who appreciated the love he gave her, instead he was beaten and tortured to get to me. A woman who didn't even care for him the way he deserved.

My stomach was in knots, I had no choice but to follow through. This was my destiny. This was always the plan. I could have gotten Illarion out. But I couldn't get them both out. He was counting on that.

"Nearly there, my dear," the driver spoke with the usual upbeat tone. "Don't die on me."

"Still got some life in me."

He chuckled and continued humming to whatever was playing on the radio.

We pulled into a driveway which was not the warehouse I'd been seeing in my dreams, throwing me off completely.

"What are we doing here?" I asked, recognizing Damon's mansion.

"Mr. Cale would like to see you and give you some more appropriate attire before we get down to business."

My heart sped up.

He got out of the car and walked around opening my door. Grabbing my wrists, he dragged me out.

I stumbled for the first few steps while my head settled, and the dizziness went away. I glanced down and groaned, my sweater was ruined.

"After you." He nudged me forward through the front door.

Damon greeted us with a wide smile which immediately sent chills over my skin.

"Sister. You look well."

Rolling my eyes, I turned my head away from his all too familiar green eyes. In person, his presence tormented me even more than it did in my dreams.

"What am I doing here, Cale?"

"I'm glad you asked." He stepped around the guy holding me, like I was in any condition to make a run for it. "I'm also glad you came willingly."

"It was an easier choice out of the two."

He took my hands in his and cut the cable ties. "One choice being, you let Illarion come to me, and you lay low for the rest of your life, hoping that you can live out your days without the guilt eating at you."

"Laying low isn't really my thing."

"I can tell." He brushed my cheek, placing a tissue in my hand. I quickly dabbed the blood around my nose. "Illarion will be disappointed that he came here to die for nothing."

"You won't kill him." I looked up, confidence booming inside me. This moron didn't know anything. "You have me, and you need me to be willing, right?"

"You are a ballsy woman, Ace."

"Not ballsy, tired," I corrected. "I'm tired of this shit and I want it over. Let them go and you get your happy ending."

"Now you know I can't do that. You think Lazarev won't come after me once you're dead?"

"Not my problem, you should have thought about that before introducing us."

"That's where you're wrong," He smiled and clicked his fingers. The man behind me grabbed me by my shoulders and roughly pushed me to follow Damon through the house and up the stairs.

"You see," he continued casually. "You as you were, would have been completely useless to me, I needed you complete, and fully evolved, and now, thanks to Lazarev. You are almost there."

Almost?

He used us. I swallowed the bile forming in my throat. He'd counted on this from the beginning.

"There's a change of clothes for you on the bed." He pointed to the room and motioned for the man to push me inside, locking me in. "Clean yourself up; you've got ten minutes," he shouted through the door.

Great. I looked at the bed and rolled my eyes, the outfit was a barely existent piece of material which I'm sure someone called a dress, and a pair of black heels I would have expected a runway model to wear.

At least I was going to look amazing when I died. That was something, right?

Slowly I made my way to the adjoining bathroom and wiped my face of the dried blood in the basin, I changed out of my yoga pants and sweater and slowly pulled on the dress. I had to hand it to him, the man had taste, the dress was stunning and on me it showed off all the right curves.

Once I put on the heels, I walked across the room coming to stand in front of a mirror. Beside it there was a clothes rack with gowns still tagged and wrapped in plastic. I carefully opened one, it was dark green, long with black lace around the bodice, in size four, my size. I looked at another, same size again. Something shifted inside me.

Why did he even have this room set up? I peeled my eyes away and looked back at my reflection.

"Any last thoughts?" I asked myself. When I found nothing relevant to say, I shook my hair out of the elastic letting it fall over my shoulders and walked over to the door and banged on it. "I'm ready."

The door was opened, and Damon stood back.

"You look incredible." He grinned brushing my hair off my shoulders making me feel incredibly bare and sick.

As if that wasn't enough, he lowered his face to mine, testing every last nerve.

"I'm going to enjoy watching you suffer."

"You're twisted." I turned my face, making sure he knew I was speaking directly to him and unafraid.

If I wasn't risking Illarion's life I would have beaten the shit out of him right here. But I couldn't let him have all the fun. I braced myself, gritting my teeth as I launched my forehead into his face.

A loud thump brought a smile to my lips as he yelped, jerking back.

I almost laughed out loud, but it was short-lived as he slapped me across the face.

So worth it.

Once the stinging subsided, I looked back up at him. He smirked as he rubbed his face. I didn't break anything, but he'd have a nice, huge bruise right in the middle of his forehead.

"You are feisty," he mused, as he walked around and caressed my shoulder, eyeing me up and down.

"Just like you, big brother." I grinned through the blood. "And just like you, I'm willing to do whatever it takes to end this."

He laughed, and to anyone else, it would have looked so far from a situation in which anyone should have been grinning or laughing.

"So, this is it? You and me, the Taker and the Giver, together again."

His eyes narrowed, like he wasn't sure what I was talking about. Then he trailed his fingers down the bare skin of back and across my hips before running them up my stomach and over the top part of my breasts. And whatever thought previously occupied my mind was chased away when he stepped closer.

I held in the breath and looked away from him.

"In another life, you would have made me so happy."

"In another life, you wouldn't have been born," I snapped.

Why my mother chose to go through with the pregnancy would always elude me. But, the choice had been hers and for whatever reason, she'd made it.

He laughed and clicked his fingers, in two seconds flat, the guard he'd brought up earlier was beside me, pushing me to walk.

"Now, like I was saying." He continued walking us through his house. "Illarion will need to be out of the picture when you and I are done."

"You need me willing, and I will not be willing if you don't assure me that he will be safe."

He remained quiet for a few moments as we walked outside and into the waiting sedan.

This time he personally tied my hands and my stomach twisted in a knot feeling his enjoyment in the task.

Once I was secured he looked down at me. "Why do you think I have insurance? It'll be your choice."

And just like that, all the pieces kind of fell into place. Of course. Troy. Troy was his insurance. He was going to make me choose.

He and his guard dog got in the car and we began our drive to the warehouse. Neither man addressed me as we drove leaving me to my own thoughts.

Those thoughts consisted mostly of all the past choices I'd made, all the decisions that somehow led me to this very moment. Had Alex known where we would have ended, even when he first told me he loved me? Did Illarion know? My heart told me yes.

He knew being with me was dangerous, and I pushed him anyway, I pleaded for him to open up to me, this was my fault. His death, or Troy's would be my fault.

The car came to a slow stop and my heart raced again. This was it. This is where I would die.

Facing the music was suddenly terrifying. I swallowed hard and blinked back the tears.

Would Illarion already be here? Was Troy alright?

I closed my eyes and waited for Damon's henchman to open the door and drag me out.

"Ready to make history?" he asked with a smile, stepping aside as a new guard took my hands and walked carefully with me as though he cared about my wellbeing.

My throat dried up.

Something about the way this man carried himself made me uneasy. I couldn't get a read on him. That wasn't normal. Something about him was so off. And his eyes, they were familiar. I'd seen them before; I just couldn't place it. Every time I thought I was about to grasp it, the memory faded as though it was snatched from me.

A few shaky sighs escaped, and I peeled my eyes from his, not before a flicker of curiosity flashed behind them, coupled with a sinister grin that chilled my blood.

"Getting nervous?" Damon cooed. "Don't you wish you'd picked option one?"

"Fuck you."

My exposed skin instantly broke out in goosebumps. The terror was real, as real as the warehouse looking me right in the face, the same warehouse I'd seen dozens of times in my dreams.

We walked in through the gates and around to the right, the old cars covered in sheets were exactly where I'd seen them in my dreams. Up above us was railing, large industrial lighting and I sensed that there were guards, ready to step in should I change my mind.

And as we walked through a large, dusty tarp sectioning this part of the warehouse from the next, my heart stopped. I knew I would see him. But still, I wasn't prepared.

In the middle of the warehouse floor, Illarion sat in a wooden chair with his arms bound, Troy right beside him. A thick strip of duct tape silenced them both.

They both looked up. Fear shooting through both men as their eyes landed on me.

Black and blue bruises covered Troy's face and my stomach lurched. He was barely conscious, and his left eye was swollen completely shut, small trickles of blood mixed with rivers of tears.

As my eyes traveled to Illarion's, I inhaled sharply as they pierced through me, agony marred his usually composed face and I forced myself to look away.

His right cheek was split, his lip bleeding beneath the duct tape and from the way he sucked in ragged gasps, I knew his ribs were broken.

Anger sent my pulse skyrocketing.

Damon wrapped his arm around my waist guiding me to my own wooden chair. Illarion yelled into the tape as he thrashed against his restraints. Damon looked at him with something akin to amusement. I looked away, I couldn't face him.

He laughed snapping off the cable ties once more, this time he bound each of my hands to either side of the chair.

"Don't worry, Lazarev, we'll get to you in a minute."

CHAPTER TWENTY-SEVEN

ACE

I tugged at my bound wrists trying to work out exactly how much shit I was in. My assessment brought me to the same, shitty conclusion. I wasn't walking away from this. I let out a controlled breath and locked eyes with Illarion.

He was so blindly angry. I'd never seen such Darkness in his eyes and the aura surrounding him pulsed black and red, threatening to erupt at any moment.

Was he angry that I was here? *I* was angry that Damon had made me dress like stripper Barbie.

Damon cleared his throat and gestured to me.

"Ace is here to make a choice. I'm here to help her make that choice. I can't say this is what I'd planned, but it worked out better."

Troy's attention shot between me and Illarion.

"Now, I'm not one for romance and sentiment, but I do respect what some people have between one another." Damon said.

I swallowed and looked straight ahead finding Illarion's eyes again.

Damon was still blocking him from me. Unfortunately, I could still feel everything going on inside him. And it wasn't good.

I looked over at Troy and forced his eyes to mine. They welled up and I could swear that if his heart beat any faster it would explode.

My guilt gnawed at me. Yes, Ace, this is your fault. He's here because of you.

Coaxing Troy's eyes to mine, I felt his fear and I held on to it. *"Just stay calm, do whatever Damon asks of you. Everything will be okay, I promise you."*

His eyes widened at my instructions and the way I was able to communicate with him, but he nodded.

Okay, good. One problem solved. Now the next. I forced my focus back to Damon who was now grinning, and the man who stood a few feet away. I couldn't get into either of their heads. What the hell was happening?

"Who shall I start with?" Damon asked.

"Are you going to talk me into submission?" I muttered.

Damon laughed. His voice was deep, but it fell flat. There was no humor in that soul.

"Well your submission isn't the problem, is it? We already know who you choose, this, well this is for fun."

I looked at him slowly, my breath stalling.

Damon stepped around to my left and came to kneel beside me. He traced a line along the inside of my wrist stopping just above the scars from his last attack on me, in my dream.

"How do you think you'll go now? In person?"

A deep, sickening breath left his lips. He enjoyed this. *Sick fuck.* Thankfully, my fast-healing freak gene healed me up.

Illarion screamed against the tape again. If only I could say something to him, to make him understand that this was going to be okay. Somehow.

"Reckon you've got it in you to stop me? You didn't then, but maybe now…" He looked across at Illarion and then turned his attention to Troy. "Well now you have motivation."

Troy whimpered under his gaze.

"You're like a pathetic, lost puppy. Holding onto her like your last meal."

Troy obviously couldn't reply, but the look of shock on his face was more than enough ammunition for Damon to continue his sick, twisted game. He looked at me with wide eyes, pleading.

"Every time you fucked her, you hoped she'd see something worth holding onto. But you're nothing, Johnson. Look at you, boring, average, *human*." He paused for a moment. "You can't compete with that man over there, you know she probably imagined fucking him when she was in bed with you."

Troy looked like he was going to be sick.

"Stop," I snapped. My stomach twisted in knots.

Damon smiled at me and then turned his gaze back on Troy.

"Stop?" Damon looked at me. "Why? Because you know I speak the truth. Though, you could have tried harder, Johnson."

Troy shook his head, tears springing to his eyes.

"Maybe it's because on some level, you didn't think she was good enough. Maybe that's why you didn't try harder?"

"Shut up!" I snapped.

"Is it because she's got these nasty scars? Terrible dreams that wake you after a nice night in?"

"Damon, stop."

Damon remained on his knee and slowly, traced his fingers along the skin on my back. "Maybe it was these scars that solidified it for you?"

I thrashed against his touch and Damon laughed, holding Troy's attention.

"Did you know that she was strung up and tortured, for days. I'm not mistaken, am I? The torture ranged from whippings, stabbings, electrocution...shall I go on?"

"Please stop."

Damon ignored me. "The medics patched her up, while she was awake and lucid." He walked his fingers across each, raw mark on my back. "They didn't want to waste anesthetic on her," he added as an afterthought.

My body shook beneath his touch, and Illarion's heart was thundering in his chest as rage filled him. Troy sat completely still; his face paled several shades.

"Every time you fucked her from behind and looked down at these marks, did you think about how ugly they were?"

Troy was about to pass out.

"Damon...shut up."

"No. He needs to hear this, maybe one day he'll be less of a superficial jerkoff. You are my little sister after all."

"You're a sadistic pig and you have no right to judge anyone." I looked across at Troy. "None of this is true, Troy, none of it. I know you never thought any of those things."

Damon ignored me and knelt on my other side. "Now, these marks are from a solo recon mission that went wrong and could have ended much worse for our dear Ace."

He brushed the long line across my left cheek and the accompanying marks along my neck and top of my breast, where Larry had split my cheek open when he backhanded me through his apartment. They'd mostly cleared up but there was the slight shimmer of a scar left behind.

"You remember this, Lazarev?" He turned his attention to Illarion.

And I had to hand it to him, I have never felt anyone so angry as Illarion was right now, but he remained focused, eyes narrowed and so still I barely saw his chest rise and fall with rapid breaths.

He was trying to break Damon's hold on his mind and my God, he was strong.

"Ace went rogue, she was trying to get information about my operation," he said to Troy, then turned his eyes to Illarion. "To think what she was ready to endure, to save you."

427

My mind went back to Larry's apartment and more than just memories of the fear flooded me. Damon was pushing actual fear into me, and into Illarion. I countered it as much as I could, trying to stop it hitting Illarion, but his compulsion was strong.

My body trembled and I was painfully aware of the tears that streamed from my eyes.

Illarion was in agony. His body shook as tremors rocked him.

"Remember how you saw her," with each word, I felt the waves of energy he was directing at Illarion. He was forcing the images and feelings back into his mind. "Remember how she looked when she was at the mercy of those two men. They would have raped her over and over again. They would have tortured her battered, broken body."

The waves continued and Illarion screamed into the duct tape. His arms shook, tears streamed down his face, fast and furious. It was the worst kind of torture. I would have taken whips over this any day.

"Stop it!" I screamed back.

I pulled my arms as hard as my body would allow, ignoring the pain from the restraints. But Damon ignored me. He continued to push the fear into Illarion.

"You almost didn't make it, did you, Lazarev? All your training, all your skills and you almost failed her!"

Beside Illarion, Troy sat completely still, completely stunned. He was no longer whimpering or shaking. He was completely broken.

"But he did," I whispered, finding what little strength I had. "He did make it."

It did little to appease the painful memories Damon was pushing into Illarion's head. Then, he stopped.

The wave dissipated and the agony in Illarion's face was replaced by relief. His body trembled in its wake, as he slumped forward against his restraints, but the tears continued to fall silently. You couldn't unsee that, or un-feel it. I let out a shaky breath and tried to connect with him again. Still nothing.

My eyes flicked up and landed on Damon's henchman. His eyes were focused on me, the whole time it seemed. Ice settled in my veins.

"So, you see, Mr. Johnson," Damon said getting to his feet. "All the scars you made her feel ugly about are a testament to how strong she is. Why would she let someone weak and judgmental like you live? Because you're a civilian? Because it's the right thing to do?"

I didn't have to look at him to see how afraid he was.

"Why would she let you live, when Illarion loves everything about her. Why would she choose what's right, over love?" He turned his eyes to me. "Isn't that right, sister?"

Illarion tensed. I felt him across the room.

"Illarion loves you—practically to the point of obsession. Do you know how often Illarion thought about you, Ace? Do you know how hard he tried to keep away from you?" He looked to me, playing with a strand of my hair.

Oh. God no. Please don't bring anything up. I couldn't bare another public airing of my soul.

"He began watching you under my orders more than ten years ago, and he was constantly visiting your mind."

I shook my head.

"Didn't you ever question why you dreamt about him—a man you didn't even know?"

"Shut up."

"He wanted you from the day he saw you. Ace, I made the perfect match, and all I had to do was bide my time."

"Shut up or get to the point."

Damon chuckled. "Fair enough. I guess the point I'm trying to make is that even though he knew somewhere deep down inside that pure heart of his, that pushing you to the point of evolving would be dangerous, he didn't stop…"

I squeezed my eyes shut. I knew this, I knew the hours of mental torture Illarion had gone through, trying to make himself forget and ignore the feelings that ran through him. The inner battle he waged everyday while trying to keep me safe.

"So whose fault is this really?"

"You're the only one here to blame," I shot back.

Damon was playing on Illarion's guilt, and it was working. Across the floor, I saw fresh tears slip out of Illarion's eyes. He was breaking.

"You are a bastard," I cried. "I will kill you."

"Cliché," he mused. "But understandable."

Damon wrapped his long fingers around my throat and forced my face up, he wanted me to look at them…to see everything and to *feel* everything. And right now, I felt nothing but Illarion's fury.

Pulling out a knife, Damon gently pressed it under my chin.

Damon continued talking, "He knew making love to you was the final piece, but he was selfish. He just wanted you so damn much that he threw caution to the wind. He did what he wanted to do from the first moment he saw you."

I fought back the urge to scream again.

"Did he tell you that Westen was chosen over him? To watch you over there."

Fresh tears filled my eyes as my gaze darted over to him.

"No, he didn't. Did he?" He chuckled. "Well, it was quite a battle of egos, let me tell you, Ace. Both men were stricken with the prospect. But ultimately, Westen got the job in the end because he was a better, stronger man. Didn't mean anything in the end, did it? He still died for you."

Illarion shook across the room—rotating between tears and dark and dangerous looks.

"Now." He squeezed my arm. "Enough of that, what we're really here to talk about is, you and these two men."

Illarion's eyes stayed focused on mine they were serious, dangerous.

I swallowed back the building fear, I was a goddamned prophesied Divine Sensitive, and I was powerless. I could feel the Darkness creeping up on me. That's what he wanted, and if I let it out then it would be game over.

Damon's henchman was watching this unfold with an amused expression. I couldn't shake the feeling of uneasiness inside my heart. Something was wrong with this picture, with *him*.

I closed my eyes forcing my mind into the dark pit I usually stayed away from. I focused everything on keeping it at bay. If I was going to end this, and make sure Illarion was out. I had no other choice.

"What I want to know is; who will you choose Ace?" Damon turned his attention back to me. "Will you choose what's right, or what your heart wants?"

His voice was close, but my mind was far from the warehouse.

The Darkness coursed through me. It bubbled in the pit of my stomach, slowly it reached like a vice around my heart, then it coursed through my legs and into my toes, it pulsed through my arms and fingers.

"Who do you choose, Ace?" I heard him ask again. He sounded pissed.

When I failed to reply he swiftly moved across the room so fast that my head spun. He pressed the blade to my throat and Illarion's heart sped up. My eyes flew open. Troy was squirming in his seat, his heart was about to jet out of his rib cage.

"Ah. There she is." He grinned looking at me.

My eyes burned and my heart slowed down, a shallow breath formed. I felt the Darkness pounding inside, pleading for release but I couldn't let it out.

Damon smirked at Illarion and then brought his attention back to me. "Do you see her eyes, Lazarev? You did this. You brought about her change."

My eyes flashed across the room. Troy's eyes were so wide I would have found it comical had I not been strapped to a chair in this shit storm. Illarion's eyes shot back to me.

"Did you think this is what your precious Ace would become when you were tasked to Operation Lullaby?"

Before I could register what was happening, he pressed the point of the blade against my skin letting it stop just above my heart, with one, painful strike he forced the blade into my chest, all the way to the hilt.

Illarion's muffled cries were drowned out by my own breathless scream. The blackness inside me grew. *Keep it together, do not let it out.*

Damon pulled the blade out and with a sickly grin. Before my mind even registered the pain, he stabbed the blade into me again.

Black and white bursts flashed across my vision as another scream was ripped from my throat.

"Look at her Lazarev!"

Through all the blinding agony my body was fighting against and all the pain which burst through every shred of my being, I still felt him. And that was more than I could hope for. The Darkness flooded me. I was unraveling.

Damon's face was close to mine and his breath hot on my cheek. He yanked my head back by my hair, still holding onto the blade lodged in my chest.

"I won't kill you, sister, I know enough about torturing the human body to ensure you don't bleed out, but I can make you beg for death. So, just release it, let out the Darkness."

I refused. He twisted the blade and I screamed.

"Just release it and I will stop all of this." He breathed against my neck.

Damon twisted the blade again and a wet, bloody cry left my lips.

"Your blatant disregard for yourself is astounding."

The anger radiated from within me. It was there, just under the surface. It was deadly and powerful, almost stronger than I was. I clenched my jaw, clutching the ends of the chair. No. I couldn't let it out. I couldn't do what I did at Larry's apartment. I couldn't let that Darkness out again.

I felt the blood splutter out of my mouth, as a cough shuddered through my body.

"Just release it, and this will all be over."

I was running on empty, I didn't know how long I could do this.

Illarion was seething, the turbulent energy lacerated the air around us. I could feel *my* Darkness inside him.

"Ace!"

He was breaking Damon's hold. My rage was powering his strength. I squeezed my eyes shut, trying to think around the pain.

Damon twisted the blade yet again. And when I opened my mouth all that came out was a quiet, painful whimper.

"Had enough yet?" Damon's face was inches from mine. "Are you ready to release it?"

"Fuck. You," I spat up at Damon, and just as I hoped, his reaction was more, uncontrollable rage.

He ripped the blade from my chest and tossed it behind him. Before my mind could register the pain, a solid, well-planted fist met my stomach, cracking a rib. He was losing his temper and Illarion was breaking free.

Damon was as fucked up as I was. His sanity was teetering on the edge and much like my own aura I noticed that his was dark, almost black, but slowly it was losing its substance. He was losing his control.

He landed blow after blow to my stomach cracking my ribs, one after the other. And there, through all that torment, a pain I couldn't quite place, exploded inside me, and my heart stopped.

My eyes shot up and found Illarion's. He felt it too, whatever just happened, he felt it and he was terrified.

As another fist connected with my stomach, I tried my best to grin through the pain. "Does this get you off?"

He responded with another right hook to my face, splitting my cheek open.

Blood pooled in my mouth, and it was getting harder and harder to focus on Illarion. He had to be close to breaking through. I could feel the blackness inside him; it was spreading like a virus, infecting everything it touched.

My eyes drifted shut.

"Keep your eyes open, keep them on me!" Illarion pleaded.

I wanted to.

"Open your eyes, Ace!"

I forced my head up and locked eyes with him again, that was all he needed. He was drawing from my energy to fight Damon's hold.

I smirked up at Damon.

Game on.

My blatant disregard for myself, as he put it, was enough to push him over the edge. His rage-fueled outburst broke his concentration on Illarion and without warning; the warehouse was plunged into darkness. And all while this was going on, Damon's creepy henchman remained still, silently watching never once lending a hand.

Before I could give his lack of action any more thought, a loud explosion followed by several stun grenades cracked through the warehouse.

Shattered glass rained down upon us as Aurel and Josh, along with more than a dozen other agents dropped through the ceiling attacking the men who were hiding in the shadows.

They came down on black ropes with guns held high, night vision goggles guiding them.

Illarion broke free from his restraints and was immediately jumped by two of Damon's guards, he fought them as impressively as he'd fought the guys back at the cabin.

He landed blow after blow on one of them while defending himself against the other. He did an impressive tornado kick and sent the guard flying backwards breaking his fall on an upturned chair. The first guard came back after recovering from the kick and he was heading straight for me, Illarion intercepted him and with one quick motion, he snapped his neck.

Aurel cut Troy free from his restraints and dragged him back and away from the action.

His eyes flicked to Illarion and then to me, his jaw hardened but he drew his gaze away.

I focused on keeping my vision clear, which was difficult now. I was losing a lot of blood and as each moment passed, I was getting closer to passing out. My insides ached and the pain in my stomach kept drawing my attention. Something was very wrong.

Illarion dropped to his knees beside me, he cut the restraints off and pulled me out of the seat.

"We have to move, you're losing a lot of blood," he spoke, pressing his hand to my chest.

I draped my arm over his neck. "What took you so long?"

"Oh, you know, I was tied up."

I groaned though a quick smile played on my lips.

As we moved, his grip on me tightened. Each step we took was difficult, to say the least. He was shaking with rage while trying to keep me on my feet, and I was barely holding it together having lost far too much blood.

I felt the Darkness, it was still there, but it was simmering. I managed to keep a lid on it. For now.

Up ahead I spotted Aurel with Troy. A group of soldiers were covering them—I didn't recognize any of them.

As though reading my question Illarion turned to me. "Michael sent us everyone who wasn't already on a job."

When we rounded the corner, and cleared the gunfire, I squeezed his arm grabbing my stomach as a violent ripple of cramps floored me.

"Oh God, Ila, I need to stop for a minute…please."

He didn't hesitate, he moved quickly, swapping our positions and helping me down against a wall.

"Let me see," he spoke quietly ignoring the swearing coming from Aurel beside us.

His eyes narrowed as a muscle in his neck popped. He tossed Illarion a small pouch, which he opened and let the contents scatter on the ground between us.

"God, it hurts." A shaky sob left my mouth before I could stop it. "Ila, Christ, it hurts so much."

Illarion's eyes flicked down, across my body and all the blood that covered me. His jaw worked like he was grinding his molars. He was doing a great job keeping calm for me, hiding the rage that he wanted to let out.

"Where?"

My hands hovered over my stomach, but it wasn't isolated just there, the pain flared through my entire body. Everything was on fire.

Then when both our gazes fell to my legs, I felt the utter disbelief of pain and sorrow floor me. There was blood between my legs, along the inside of my thighs, that wasn't caused by anything Damon had just done.

There was so much blood, I couldn't tell where it all came from. His trembling hands hovered over my body unsure where to press.

He shook his head. He didn't want to think about what had crossed my mind but how could we not? I'd been nauseous, I'd felt like something wasn't right...the way Aurel looked at me, the way Faith said there was something else inside me, another aura...

I drew my knees to my chest and leaned my head back against the wall. I needed to steady my breathing.

Illarion crouched in front of me, his hand cupping my cheek, "I need to stop the bleeding in your chest, okay? We'll figure everything else out later."

I nodded biting down on my lip getting ready to feel the burn.

"It's going to hurt," he said apologetically.

No matter how much I thought I'd prepared myself, I was still nearly bowled over when Illarion pressed down on the two stab wounds in my chest. White exploded across my vision and before my scream could erupt from my throat, he leaned in and stifled my scream with his free hand.

"I'm sorry," he breathed bringing his forehead to mine. "They're still surrounding us." He pulled back running his thumb along my bottom lip before wiping away my tears. "I'm nearly done."

His mind was racing. His head swam from thoughts of what Damon had done, to how we would get out of here now and the blood between my legs.

"What if, Ila, what if I was—"

"We need to get out of here, lyubov, we need to focus on this right now."

"Ila..."

His eyes flicked down to mine, he nodded knowingly but didn't say anything else as he worked.

I fisted a handful of his shirt in my hand.

He retrieved a makeshift gauze from Aurel's kit and pressed it back to my chest. His steely gaze met mine and he forced a warm, calming sensation to spread through me.

I was surprised at the amount of force it took to overpower the dark, but like with everything, Illarion was strong. I focused everything on feeling him instead of feeling the wetness seeping down my chest from the wound. I knew it was too deep to be stopped by a few band aids and by the rattling inside my lungs as each breath burned, I knew it was bad.

"Memorizing my face?" he asked softly, with a hint of a smile.

I almost choked on a laugh before another painful, jolt ripped through my abdomen.

"Ace?" His eyes widened as he helped me stay upright, his brows knotting as he looked over me.

"I'm okay."

He cupped my cheek in one of his hands. "You're walking away from this."

"Whatever you say."

"You're walking away from this with me," he said, firmer this time. "We're going to sail the world, we're going to eat too much pasta, drink too much wine, regret it when we feel sick but we're going to do it all together."

Nodding, I looked up at him with a smile. God that all sounded so nice. Aurel helped Troy to us before he disappeared down the ledge and broke back into the fight.

I glanced at Troy and a pang of guilt shot through me, he was in shock. His good eye was wide open and occasionally he would shake his head. Slowly, reluctantly he moved closer to me.

"We need to move now, you going to be okay to do that?" I asked him.

He nodded, squeezing my hand back. "I'm sorry, Ace, so sorry for everything."

"You've nothing to be sorry for."

Aurel appeared beside Troy, a fresh cut was bleeding from his face and when he wiped it with his gloved hand, he tossed over a small black pouch similar to the one he gave Illarion.

Since I wasn't planning on playing doctor any time soon, I was happy to see that this pouch had Spock in it and a few earpieces. A weak smile formed on my lips.

Aurel smiled.

"Is that my favorite toy?"

"You left it in my car."

"Right." I laughed, unpacking it.

"Thanks for saving my gas." He winked.

Groaning, I laughed again.

I pressed the earpiece into place and handed one to each of the boys.

His crystal blue eyes met mine and he smirked. "It's good to see you punk."

"Likewise."

"You good?" he asked, looking me over.

I nodded, loading a set of arrows. "As good as ever."

"Alright then, let's go." He motioned for us to follow. "Let's get the fuck out of here."

I looked back at Illarion, he had his game face on.

We fell into formation, Illarion covering Troy and me while Aurel covered Illarion. Slowly we made our way to the end of the warehouse where overhead railing hung low. Illarion had to help me up since each movement was a bitch. My chest ached something fierce and my head was splitting.

That same, agonizing pain in my stomach and my heart ripped through me again. I clutched my stomach as the cramps hit me hard and fast.

Once we made it up, we stopped, waiting for the next set of instructions.

He moved me to the wall, stopping me in place. "Tell me how I can help."

I breathed through the pain, "Nothing, there's nothing you can do."

The Darkness between us shifted.

I could make out the concern entwined in his knotted brows, but I shook my head. "We need to worry about getting Troy out."

He didn't like that, but he didn't argue. My logic was sound, and he knew it. Get the civilian out. That was always the most important rule of any mission. He cursed under his breath and waved Aurel on to go ahead of us, swapping formations.

"What's the plan?" I asked through the link.

He pointed to the agent on the far end of the overhead railing we were on. "He's going to break cover and draw the firing that way and we are going to get out through the south side. Josh cleared the exit."

I smiled across the warehouse at Josh.

Before we made a move after Aurel and Josh, Illarion stopped me placing a hand on the small of my back. He brushed the hair from my cheek and planted a kiss on my forehead.

Moments like those made me giddy inside, they were the little moments Illarion let his mask slip and I saw the warm, caring man. The professionalism was replaced by concern, and more importantly, love.

Silently we followed, keeping as low as possible.

Illarion turned his body to me. *"There are other Sensitives here, working for him. We need to try and block ourselves off as much as possible, do you think you can?"*

I nodded looking up ahead. Most Sensitives were only able to properly shield themselves and if they were good, one other and since Illarion just used so much of his power, he was exhausted. It was up to me. *"I've got it."*

"Let's move. That's our way out."

My eyes widened as he pointed up toward the second level of railing. That was going to be a challenge. I sucked in a shaky breath and continued behind them.

Aurel went first, followed by Troy and me and finally Illarion.

We reached the end of the floor and made our way up, staying as silent as possible. I fought every expletive on the tip of my tongue as the pain shot through my body. Each nerve was on fire. My busted ribs were slicing and dicing my insides and my holey chest was bleeding all over me.

I had to push through. *We were so close.* I had to make sure Illarion and Troy were safe. Aurel would be able to take care of everyone else.

The last step came into view and my celebration was cut short when I sensed Damon. He knew where we were, and he was waiting. For what?

My heart sunk. This was a trap, a fucking trap.

I wanted to slam my fist through the grate. Instead, I slowed my breathing and I focused one last time, ensuring Illarion didn't suspect anything.

My walls were strong, but my strength was depleting quicker than I was ready to admit and I couldn't fail now.

I came here for a reason. I knew I wasn't going to be walking away from this so why did I even allow myself to think otherwise? Why did I allow myself that tiny, false sense of hope?

A blanket covered the broken window at the end of the landing, covering the jagged shards of glass still lodged inside the sill. I motioned for them to continue, ensuring Illarion was the last to leave. I wanted to kiss him. God, I wanted to kiss him one last time. I sucked in a deep, wheezy breath and let it out as soon as Illarion was out.

He turned around and held his hands out to help me over window.

Our eyes met and there was a moment when I saw the stark terror in his dark eyes. He knew and he would never forgive me.

I closed my eyes, taking a breath and I forced him back.

As they cleared the railing and made it outside into the cold, wintery night, the blackness surrounding me suddenly seemed so clear.

CHAPTER TWENTY-EIGHT

ACE

There was no time to get antsy now. I balled my fists and walked straight toward him. There was no doubt in my mind that he was sent to make sure I did what I said I'd do. He was powerful enough to have them shrouded from every other Sensitive around, but I wasn't every other Sensitive. I was strong, and I'd be damned if I let him outdo me.

I laughed at that point. I actually laughed. He knew this would have been the outcome one way or another. *Son of a bitch.*

As soon as he spotted me he launched into a full offensive, trained like me, we fought on the platform throwing hits at each other until he caught me in a vulnerable stance and he threw me backwards. My feet slipped and for a moment my mind went blank. That moment was all it took, and I felt myself falling but by the grace of whichever being was watching my ass, I managed to grab hold of the tiniest exposed bit of railing, stopping myself from crashing to my death.

It didn't take long for him to reach me, he stomped on my fingers forcing me to let go. I tried to reach up with my other arm but the pain was too much. I couldn't reach over my shoulder and I was sent careering down toward the hard surface below. As soon as my butt hit the floor, I scrambled to my feet knowing that all too soon I would be in a whole world of pain.

And here I was. In that world and the pain was real. The wind was knocked out of me and I was sure any progress the gauzes made in stopping me from bleeding to death was just undone. My chest was wet and warm, and my vision was getting hazier.

A fist and then another connected with my face and then an ugly leather shoe connected with my stomach. I stammered backwards grabbing my middle.

Ah. There he was. Damon's henchman with the ugly shoes. He had finally decided to join in the party.

I spat out a ball of saliva mixed with blood, successfully hitting his shoes. Damn that would be a hard stain to get out.

An amused smirk crossed his features. He launched into another offensive, clearly indicating that this was now his fight. The other moron was gone and I didn't have time to look for him now.

I focused on Ugly Shoes and threw my hand up stopping another kick to my stomach. I effectively blocked his kick but his other foot made contact with my shin.

Dropping to my knees, I dodged another attempt at my face. I clipped his right foot as he attempted to launch another kick, as I did, he dropped to his knees. Through the pain, I grit my teeth and got up. I couldn't do much with my arms but my legs were still strong. I spun on the spot and my foot met his already raised arm. He pulled me down by my leg, and I rolled out of his way and blocked another kick.

Something about this situation was sobering and oddly comforting. I knew I was doing the right thing for the right cause and most importantly for the right *person*.

I got to my feet and stepped backwards. Then, I clenched my fists and blocked the right hook coming right at my face.

Before I could make a move to retaliate, he caught my hand in his and roughly pulled me toward him. I ignored the screaming in my bones as he picked me up against him like I was nothing more than a sack of potatoes.

Terror seized my heart. I readied myself and threw my head back connecting with his face.

He dropped me with a grunt and I scrambled out of his way.

Swallowing back the bile, I quietened my mind. I was here for *him*. I was doing this for Illarion.

The best thing I'd gotten out of all this was the ability to develop my evolved Senses. I knew now who I was, whom I had been all along. There was a quiet comfort in that.

Being able to connect through my mind into his was a massive advantage when it came to situations like this. We could always stay in touch, even in the worst situations. I could always feel him, and I knew that no matter where I was, he felt me too.

It was a low, constant hum, deep inside my soul, sometimes it was weak, but it was always there, *he* was always there.

I knew before I opened my eyes, before I felt the first and then the second hit to my stomach, I was right where Damon wanted me. I was on my knees at his mercy.

Ugly Shoes stepped back and Damon stepped toward me. At least I landed a good one on his face, his nose was broken and blood came out in thick, steady streams. Instead of anger, his face reflected a sickly smirk.

"Ace, what are you doing?" Illarion's voice broke through, he'd managed to break through a layer of my shield.

His voice was full of panic and confusion. Stark horror flowed from him, filling the whole atmosphere. It was suffocating.

He couldn't be in my head. Not now.

"I'm sorry," I said honestly, forcing back the tears. I knew they were an automatic response to what had happened to my body.

My lungs rattled with each shaky breath and God knew how weak I was. I was lucky that I had regained the ability to control his senses at all, because right now his mind was under my control.

"They're going to kill you, get out of there now!" he pleaded.

"I can't do that."

"They're going to kill you!"

"I'm sorry."

I blocked him from our connection and forced myself back to the present. I needed to be here, completely here if I had any chance of ending this.

Ugly Shoes smirked again as Damon stepped up.

Great. Another kick met my face and this time it threw me backwards slamming my head into the concrete below. I heard and felt the crack. That sudden movement was enough to throw me off, and I realized in that moment that my hold on Illarion was broken. Shit.

I felt his relief flood through me and then my panic set in.

No, I felt him running, faster than I'd ever seen any man move before. He ran through the dark, through the cold, calling on everything within him to get to me on time.

My heart broke.

Ugly Shoes stepped closer to me and dragged me back up to my knees. From the corner of my eye, I saw Damon approach me with that same, smug look I came to know.

"Well, well, well," he said in a half-amused tone. "Have you had enough fun? Are you ready to give me what I want now?"

"How do I know you won't kill them?" I hissed, imagining how savage I looked; blood in my hair, sweat on my face, I was missing a few teeth. I didn't want to think about that now. God, I didn't want to know what was broken and what was about to be broken.

Everything hurt. My whole body was shattered.

"You don't," he said softly, reaching down to move the sweaty strands of hair away from my face. "But right now, you should be worrying about yourself."

I winced.

Ugly Shoes stood a few feet away, arms folded neatly across his chest. Something about the look in his eyes chilled me to my core. He seemed…impressed.

Damon spoke and my attention went back to him. "All you have to do it call on it, call on the Darkness and this will be over."

My head screamed as the pressure building within me. The Darkness roared inside, expanding, filling my veins, pulsing under my skin.

"No." I whispered.

I couldn't let it out.

He shrugged and with a smirk he took a step closer with his hand outstretched. Just as he was about to reach for my face Ugly Shoes was sent flying across the floor where he landed in a heap.

My eyes shot up, following Damon's gaze, horror ran through me. The man I did all of this to protect, was here. Illarion had taken Ugly Shoes out.

Damon turned to Illarion with an amused smirk. Undeterred, he gestured with his hand for the fight to begin.

No, this couldn't be happening.

From the corner of my eye, I saw Ugly Shoes get to his feet, he cast me a quick glance and then took off. He left. He left his boss. What the hell?

I didn't have time to think about that now. I turned back to the two men fighting.

"Get out!" I screamed at Illarion, struggling against the pain. I tried to move, to help, to do anything but be rendered immobile on the floor like some helpless victim.

They fought hard, landing unforgiving blows on one another drawing on all the training both men had.

He fought like a warrior, each meaningful blow hit the target right where it needed to, I saw the moves we trained in, I saw the blocks and the counter strikes.

Somehow, I managed to shake the impeding concussion, fight through the bleeding and get to my feet.

Damon had managed to knock Illarion down and my heart fell through my stomach. Damon wasn't just good at hand-to-hand combat, he had incredible gifts and he was strong. I felt the compulsion he was using on Illarion. He was making him suffer, pushing phantom pain and fear into his mind.

"You cannot beat me!" he shouted.

Slowly, with steely determination he turned his head slightly so that our eyes met.

I understood before I even had time to register what was happening. He was going to kill him. He was going to kill him right in front of me.

Illarion was on the ground, still trying to regain his bearings. Damon's compulsion was destroying him. He was convulsing as pain rocked his body, agonizing screams filled the air.

Deep inside, threatening to erupt to the surface I felt it. The Darkness. It was fierce, and dangerous. It roared and bucked in the pit of my belly and the strength I lacked before was just a ghost of a memory. It sensed the danger Illarion was in and it raged to life.

As I locked eyes with Damon. His grin grew wide. He knew.

"Good, call on it, call on the Darkness!"

I closed my eyes and forced everything to slow down. When I opened them, everything went quiet. I didn't hear Illarion shouting. I didn't hear Damon's taunting words. I only heard the blood rushing inside my head.

Spock was a few feet away; a split second, a split second to end all this. I moved so quickly he didn't know what happened.

Damon chanced a move, a stupid move. He raised his gun and pointed it at Illarion.

I moved faster than ever before and threw myself between them.

That was the trigger; the rage I had been holding in. It erupted and my vision went black. A force of electricity sparked around me, building and rearing rippling out like an explosion.

Damon's eyes widened as I locked onto him. There was energy shifting between us, and he was losing. He was fighting but I was stronger, better. His face contorted in pain and then his heart stopped, and a flash of realization that he'd failed, swept across his features.

As he went for the shot, I raised Spock, dropped all my defenses and fired.

So did he.

Illarion's cry resonated through the vast warehouse drowned out only by the beautiful sound of a twelve-gauge bullet leaving its casing.

A burning, piercing sensation hit my chest and then pain. A pain so consuming, it prevented me from thinking and speaking. I tried to breathe but only a warm, wet cough escaped my lips.

As I fell, I closed my eyes and then strong arms caught me.

When my eyes fluttered open, Damon was on his side, mouth and eyes open and unmoving. I released a shaky, wet breath and looked up. Illarion's mouth was moving but I couldn't hear his words. So many voices flooded my mind as they moved around me.

His arms wrapped around my body as it shook from the adrenaline that had kicked in to support the blood loss.

The grey edges around my vision grew heavier and darker and Illarion appeared to move in slow motion. The rage inside me was gone. I'd succeeded. He was safe. *He would walk away.* And this had ended with Damon lying in a heap, with an arrow between his eyes. Just like I'd said it would. I smiled.

Another voice crept into my head, a voice I hadn't ever heard before, a soft almost melodic tone that was smooth on my ears.

"We were right there with you, until the end. You can let go now."

Illarion's eyes locked onto mine, drawing my attention to him, his hands capturing my face. "Ace, don't let go, stay with me, Ace…stay with me!"

But the voice drew me in and beckoned to follow.

"Let go."

Slowly darkness crept across my vision. Time slowed as I saw Josh, Aurel and Troy running toward us. They circled Illarion and me, as he cradled me against his body.

They were holding their heads, crying and shouting but I couldn't hear anything at all. The gunfire was a distant memory now, the pain was a story I'd once told, and Illarion…Illarion was a fairy tale I hoped people would someday know.

Deep inside, I felt the hum weakening; it was slowly fading, slowly slipping away. Darkness surrounded us, and through his eyes I watched as it surrounded me and flooded my body. My soul was breaking, tearing and ripping apart. Every essence that made me whole was dying.

Above me, Illarion cried. He was yelling for me, clutching my body against his.

His hand pressed down on the wounds in my chest. Praying and begging me to stay with him.

Pushing away the last remnants of pain, I closed my eyes and reached into his mind, one last time. *"I wish I told you in person too."*

EPILOGUE

First came the sound, then the feeling and finally after what seemed like hours in the eerie darkness, came the light.

My eyes adjusted and swept the room. I wasn't in the warehouse any longer, and I wasn't alone. But it wasn't Illarion's presence I sensed by my side. It was someone I didn't recognize.

I craned my neck to study the Celestial symbols that were etched across the ceiling and crept down onto the walls. The second thing which became apparent was that I couldn't feel my powers. They simmered beneath the surface but just out of reach. Lastly, I couldn't feel Illarion.

The pain which had consumed me was little more than a painful throbbing now and the agony which coursed through me as I sucked in my last breath was just a memory.

"You're awake."

My eyes darted around the dimly lit room in search of the voice.

A man stood off to my left, hidden by the shadows.

"Where am I?" I whispered into the dark. My throat was dry and sore.

"There's water to your right."

I turned to my side, and sure enough there was a bottle there.

"What do you want?"

"That's not really what's on your mind, now is it?" the voice spoke again.

A shudder of unease washed over me. I couldn't help the coldness that spread through my insides.

"Come on, Acacia, what's on your mind?"

Letting out a breathless whisper, I looked down at my body. Bandages covered more than half of my torso and a pain, deep in my stomach drew my attention.

"Ah," he spoke again. "I can see the words right there on the tip of your tongue."

My breath came out in a whimper.

The pain, it was real, nothing like the throbbing in my chest or the concussion. This was different, unlike anything I'd ever felt.

"Say it," he spoke, his voice nearing, coming closer as a kaleidoscope of emotions raged through me.

And like a dark ominous presence whispering inside my head, the sadness gripped me. I pressed my hands to my abdomen and held in the soul crushing sob that ripped through me.

"I know who you are," I breathed, afraid to look up.

He laughed, his footsteps neared until they stopped right in front of me.

As I looked up, my eyes focused, I saw him, I saw his face and those eyes, the eyes which looked at me as snow fell across my body, the eyes which watched in fascination as Damon turned me into a living punching bag. They were illuminated by the flickering light cast only by a single bulb above us free now for me to see without the blanket of his powerful compulsion.

God, I had been so wrong, *we* had been so wrong.

I looked down at his shoes, and then back up at his face. "*You're* the Taker."

ACKNOWLEDGEMENTS

December 2015…that's when Ace first popped into my head and began to consume every waking moment of my thoughts. Not long after, her story flourished and became an entire book—my first book, in fact. Ace holds a special place in my writing because she is the one who taught me that I was stronger than I thought and far more capable than I believed

Like the journey I embarked on, Ace and Illarion's narrative is one of resilience and passion that has seen challenges, tears and bittersweet endings (I wasn't ready to say goodbye). The absolute rollercoaster this series has taken me on has been exhilarating and to be able to return to this world has brought me so much indescribable joy and pride!

The team at Vulpine Press must be mentioned and thanked because long after I said goodbye to Ace and her world, they took this fun little series on and allowed me to bring it back to life with my vision, a new direction and new story and every writer knows how much of an honor that is!

To my wonderful editor, Lisa, you cheered me on, backed Ace and reminded me why I loved this universe as much as I did. I've fallen in love all over again and now a new generation of readers will too.

To the readers who have supported me from day one, I'm so glad you're here after all these years and I hope you'll continue to come back.

So here we are, to the original Ace and Ila fans; we're back—bigger and better than ever with so many more adventures to go on and to the new ones, you're in for a ride; strap in, grab your Twizzlers and let's go!

Based in Melbourne, Violeta M Bagia is an accomplished author with a passion for delving into challenging and thought-provoking topics. With a Master of Arts degree under her belt, Bagia brings a depth of understanding to her writing that enriches every narrative.

Whether crafting tales of futuristic worlds or weaving intricate narratives of love and human connection, Bagia is a storyteller with a passion for exploring human emotion.

If you're ready to explore narratives that push and challenge you, pick up a copy of Bagia's latest books, which are available now.

Instagram: @violeta.m.bagia_writer
Facebook: Write Point Coaching
Website: www.writepointcoaching.com